Previous novels

by Lisa Buie-Collard

Evangeline's Miracle

THE SEVENTH MAN

Lisa Buie-Collard

D'Oc Publishing

D'Oc Publishing, LLC
PO Box 564
Lake Park, GA 31636

This book is a work of fiction.

ISBN 10: 0983647844
ISBN 13: 9780983647843

First Edition 2014
Cover Design: Natalie Spasic at OfficeManager4u.com and N.R. Designs
Back Cover photo of author: Steve Heddon

ISBN for soft cover: 978-0-9836478-4-3

ISBN for E book: 978-0-9836478-5-0 Kindle/Mobi version

Library of Congress Control Number: 2014952988
D'Oc Publishing, LLC, Lake Park, GA

Dedicated to actors
Sean Bean
and
John Hannah
for their inspiration

ACKNOWLEDGEMENTS

This novel was originally inspired by an article I read on CCTV cameras and the millions in use throughout the United Kingdom, and two actors, Sean Bean and John Hannah. When I started it they were young enough to have played their respective parts in "my" novel/movie. This has been a very long road, one of the hardest yet for me to travel in my writing. Each novel/story takes whatever time it needs to come into being but this one, out of all my novels, took ages to grow up. I hope you, my reader, find it worthy, entertaining, and informative. Thank you for choosing to read it.

I thank profusely, with bowed head and on bended knee, Detective Sergeant Robin Carr of the London Metropolitan Police Service (recently retired) for his wealth of information and advice, including his work with the HOLMES system. Any discrepancy that might be found in my version of the investigation sits squarely upon my shoulders and not his, writer's license and all that. I seriously wouldn't have this particular novel if not for his invaluable advice and insight into his former world.

I thank the London Metropolitan Police Service for answering my questions, and doing what they do day in and day out to make London a safer city to live in and visit.

I would like to thank Linda Ellis of The Editing Place for her ability to shape my words into a better read.

Natalie Spasic of N.R. Designs and OfficeManager4u.com, produced a cover I could truly live with as well as giving me a logo of my own. I thank her for her persistence and patience in trying to give me what I envisioned.

I thank my beta readers who helped improve this story with their ideas and willingness to tell me what didn't work.

A huge appreciative hug each to Philip King, my step-brother in law, Sarah Clarke, my niece, and to Suzanne Wight Ion, my cousin for letting me use their names.

A special acknowledgment must go to John Paterson, my favorite Scotsman, who gave useful tips on language, and interesting and sometimes funny, information on being from Elgin.

As always I thank my parents, my children, my sister and my far-reaching family and friends for cheering me on and telling me not to give up. I thank my writing group who is always there for me, my blogging community, and my special "goal partners" who listen to me groan, kick me when I need it, and with insight and levity keep me laughing and mostly sane.

Without the support of my husband Geoffrey, I could never have written this novel. He is my rock, the solid earth upon which I stand. I'm not exaggerating when I say I will love him till the day I die.

Definition of 'Wraith':

1. An apparition of a person seen shortly before or shortly after his or her death.

2. Any specter: ghost.

3. Used in similes and metaphors to describe a pale, thin, or insubstantial person or thing

4. A wisp or faint trace of something

1

The tall man stood so still most passersby wouldn't notice him. He watched the entrance to the Royal Bank of Scotland from a slight alcove in a block of flats down the street, waiting for the exact moment. His hands were gloved. His knife lay buried deep within a trash bin where it awaited retrieval because he couldn't take it with him into the bank. He had a small plastic bag, a roll of tape, and a key stashed in various pockets of his Burberry coat. He had his hat set to shield his face from surveillance cameras; he wore the glasses to aggravate the police even more. He needed nothing else. Not now, not so close to the end.

He checked his watch. Seven minutes to go. He stepped out onto a sidewalk covered in slush. Concentrating, he eased through the London winter-morning crowd, crossed the street, and entered the bank. The heist was set for ten thirty a.m. His informant on the Internet had said six men would do the job. In the lobby, the tall man passed through the weapons detector as if he worked there. He'd done this very exercise every day for the last week so no one would remember him as a suspicious character when the police asked. Blending into the crowd by the lifts, he didn't have long to wait. Spot on ten thirty, he looked up to see all six bank robbers enter the building. Firing off a few shots, two robbers took immediate control of the security checkpoint. Screams ricocheted off the stark walls as the rest of the robbers shouldered through the thick glass doors leading into the bank proper and spread out. Taking advantage of the chaos, the tall man slid through the closing lift doors as the leader yelled instructions and the patrons scurried from the lobby into the bank to lay flat on the black marble floor.

He exited the lift at the third floor. Taking two stairs at a time, he climbed from the third floor to the fifth. First came the secretary. She looked up as he strode right to her desk. As she started to ask how she could help him, he lunged forward, grabbed her, and gave her no time to fight. Taping her mouth before she could scream, he then bound her arms behind her and taped her feet together. He bundled her into a closet behind her desk. Only after closing the closet door did he turn toward the door of the office where he knew he would find his prey. Now came the part he hadn't practiced. But he didn't pause, didn't acknowledge the rush of hot adrenaline as it pumped into his body, strengthening his intent. The door opened with a whisper. As silent as a shadow, he slipped in and shut it behind him. The copied key he pulled from his pocket slid smooth and straight into the well-oiled lock and turned without a sound, sealing him in with his victim.

A dignified, well-built man in his midthirties glanced up from behind the desk on the intruder's left. The man looked perturbed at the unexpected interruption but not unduly alarmed.

"What are you doing in here? How the devil did you get in? This is a private office—"

"Mr. Richard McLean? You are McLean, are you not?"

"Well, yes, but my secretary—"

"Is indisposed. Do you know how much time has passed since we last saw each other?" Not waiting for an answer, the tall intruder glanced at the folders and loose papers smeared over the desk, found what he searched for, and picked up a letter opener.

"Look here, I'm calling security." With his left hand McLean reached for the phone, but before he could touch it the intruder stepped forward, grabbed the outstretched hand, and slammed it on the desk.

"Don't you recognize me, McLean?" One deft thrust and he stabbed the dull-pointed letter opener downward, pinning McLean's hand to the desk. As McLean howled in surprised agony, a smile teased the intruder's mouth.

Looming, almost ghostlike, he circled the desk. Snatching the tape from his pocket he quickly wrapped it round McLean's head before McLean could stop him. With his mouth covered, McLean was silent, and then a snuffling charged the air as he drew a raw, panicked breath through his nose. McLean's good hand clawed at the tape covering his mouth, but the intruder yanked the letter opener from the hand pinned to the desk and leaned in close, halting any movement.

The scent of McLean's agony—tangy and thick, like the blood rivulets flowing over his wounded hand—lay heavy in the air.

"I would recognize you no matter how many years had passed," the tall intruder said. "I would recognize you in hell. Please believe me when I say I won't ask you twice to undress."

Under McLean's chin, the blunt and bloody point of the letter opener reinforced the sinister command. McLean complied as fast as his damaged hand allowed. Blood stained everything he touched, and the intruder moved back enough to keep his distance yet still present a threat. When McLean sat completely naked in his chair, the tall man taped McLean's bared arms to it. He wasn't concerned about McLean's legs.

"You should feel lucky, McLean. Not only did I castrate the others, I buried four of you—*alive.*" His lip lifted with a hint of a sneer as he sat on the edge of the desk and leaned in again, to get personal, to get right in McLean's face. "As you have never cared about anything, I'm sure you didn't know they were dead. I've heard it's a nasty way to go, bleeding to death while buried alive. I can't bury you here, though, in your glorious workplace, and I can't castrate you or the police will have revenge as a solid clue, and I'm not done yet. How does it feel, to know what I'm going to do? That you have no way to stop me?" He waited only to see stark terror burning in McLean's eyes. "I know exactly what it feels like, thanks to you and Ryan," he said. "I saved the two of you for the last."

The tall intruder with death in his eyes had to wait less than one precious second to see comprehension dawn in McLean's. "Now you recognize me," he said. "I'm sure you aren't any happier to see me than I am to see you, but this will, after all, be a short visit." The intruder grabbed McLean's shirt from the desk and stepped behind his naked prey. He wrapped the shirt over the handle of the letter opener, and closed his fist around it. He bent slightly over his victim and said, "Go burn in hell, you son of a bitch." In a single swift thrust, he drove the letter opener precisely between McLean's ribs and into his heart. Slowly but proficiently, the intruder wrenched it back and forth, causing McLean's body to lurch and jump with each jerk of the knife.

The shirt soaked up the pumping blood like a thirsty sponge, keeping the blood spatter to a minimum. The tall man finally released the weapon and turned the chair so his victim faced him. He watched McLean's dying eyes register surprise. Then, at the last, there burned in them a shining anger. The tall intruder stared at McLean's chest as it rose and fell, until it fell for the last time and stayed still. He left the murder weapon lodged in the gory wound as if it were a dare. Which, in a way, it was. Now that only one of his victims, the most important one, remained, he wanted Richard McLean's death to make the news. Maybe Ryan would hear of it and start to sweat. In fact, he had an idea . . .

He left McLean's shirt hanging from the handle of the letter opener, checked his own coat for spatter or anything which might give the police a lead on him. Unlocking the door, he pulled it shut and locked it behind him as he exited. Glancing over to the closet where the secretary remained imprisoned, he heard a loud thumping. She was bravely trying to attract attention to her predicament. He turned toward the stairwell and checked his watch. Three minutes, thirty seconds. It had taken too little time to kill McLean. *Hours too short for the likes of the bastard*, he thought. Though he had done the deed himself, his victim's demise had not diminished the tall man's drive for revenge. Still, he must be satisfied with the surety that only one more remained to be removed from the earth he himself trod upon so lightly.

The tall man reached the stairway door and bolted down to the first floor, ignoring the lift this time. Though he could have avoided the trouble the secretary and her description of him might cause, her life was not his to take this day. He'd thought it through and reasoned he should have ample time to get out and away from the building before the police arrived, if his informant had given him dependable information. Using an informant was always risky, but so far nothing had happened out of the ordinary. He didn't worry about surprises. They were inevitable. After the police descended upon the bank like locusts, it could possibly take another twenty minutes or so for them to find her and listen to her description of him, which would be clear only in that he wore a hat, coat, and glasses. The police wouldn't have much to go on and he wasn't concerned.

He made the ground floor lobby and was out the front door, was actually on the sidewalk, when a stir erupted behind him. Two men carrying fat sports bags dashed past him. How original, he thought, as the robbers took off in opposite directions.

With his gloved hands tucked in the pockets of his Burberry coat, the tall man who had just committed murder turned to his right and walked away from the bank, blending into the bustle of the London sidewalks. He passed the first, the second, and then the third set of surveillance cameras before he stopped beside a particular trash bin. Casting a casual glance about the area, he pulled his knife from deep within the bin and slid it back into its sheath, holstered under his arm. He moved on. In the next block he took off his Burberry, turned it inside out, and tried to put it back on when a sudden whipping wind attempted to steal it, and his hat, from him. The wind didn't succeed. The killer kept both and never missed a step. He turned a corner, and then another.

Never slowing the tempo of his stride, he peeled off his gloves, stuffed them in the plastic bag he'd brought, and shoved it back into his pocket. He continued straight on until, halfway down the fourth block, a second gust of wind won the match and stole the hat right off his head. Cursing, he turned carefully to see if he could find it while keeping his face from the cameras. But the number of people on the icy sidewalks made it impossible to look for the hat without calling attention to himself. He'd have to leave it. No one in his right mind would abandon a good hat in this weather, and he knew that move alone would tell whoever monitored the cameras more than he wanted them to know, but it was better than showing his face or giving more people the chance to describe him. If they found his hat they might find some DNA, but since his DNA belonged to what the military service proclaimed was a dead man, he didn't worry over much about it. As long as they didn't see his face, he was safe. He turned his collar up, lowered his head, and kept walking.

2

The phone rang. Halting the click of his fingers across the keyboard, Detective Sergeant Alban Thain reached for the receiver before it could ring twice. "Thain."

Detective Chief Inspector North almost took out Thain's eardrum when he bellowed, "Thain, who else is with you at West End Central?"

"Patterson, sir. We're catching up on paper—"

"The two of you get over to the Royal Bank of Scotland right now."

"Sir, the Flying Squad for the robbery is already on—"

"There's been a murder, Thain, in the same damn bank. Bell will meet you there."

"We're on our way, sir." His jacket lay over the back of his chair. He reached for it, hung up without a goodbye, and shouted, "Clive, come on. There's been a murder at the Royal Bank of Scotland." Veering around the corner from his desk into the hall, he almost collided with Detective Sergeant Clive Patterson, who skimmed down the hall pulling on his own jacket.

"The bank that's just been robbed?"

"The very same."

"North assigned it to us?"

They took the stairs two at a time down to the ground floor. "Us and Rae Bell."

"Sometimes catching up on paperwork is worthwhile," Clive remarked.

"Sometimes, like now," Thain agreed, since that's what they'd been working on all morning.

An hour or so later, as he stood to one side of the office turned crime scene, Thain didn't wince when familiar, yet irrational, discomfort rippled across the thick, two-inch scar on his abdomen. He kept his eyes on the lab sergeant, Ralph Harris, while he finished going over the naked and mutilated body of Mr. Richard McLean, onetime banker and now murder victim. The victim was a mess, and Thain knew what the mortal wound must have felt like. The room closed in on him, he felt like it had dampers in the walls muting the sounds of the crinkly plastic, the soft shuffling of shoes covered with protectors, and the clicks of cameras going off. A low murmuring of voices, relaying a constant stream of information as it was discovered, helped to calm him, bring him back to the here and now. Watching the science team do its job allowed his mind to busy itself contemplating and calculating what he'd gleaned since he'd arrived. Work always provided a useful distraction from the past.

Patterson and Thain had been assigned the initial investigation into the murder as soon as DCI North heard that the bank heist was not the only crime committed that morning in the Royal Bank of Scotland. Clive landed the job of calming the frantic secretary found trussed up in a closet, while Thain talked with the lab sergeant in charge of the crime scene. Detective Sergeant Rae Bell conferred downstairs with the Flying Squad, the detectives working the heist.

By the time the science team packed up to leave, Thain's thoughts had begun to find some order. A few rogue lines of theory signaled in the back of his mind, but so far, he ignored them. He didn't need to pay those lines of inquiry any attention right now, much less tell Clive or Rae Bell about them. As he always did, he would work in his own way until he was certain that what he half suspected could *not* be the truth. If the rogue theories proved positive, then this was a doomed investigation from the start. Not that anyone would believe him. But disbelief hadn't stopped him in the five years since he'd joined the London Metropolitan Police Service. After his service in Scotland and Interpol, the LMPS had finally honed his attitude from brash—and frankly naïve—to invisible, at least most of the time.

Glancing a last time around the room, he not only made mental notes but jotted on his cell phone the pertinent features of the murder.

"The mess on the desk should have provided some clues, but as yet, I've found no noticeable forensic evidence of the executor, not even usable shoe impressions on any of the rugs," Ralph said, noticing Thain's perusal of the room and desk. "I'll know more, of course, once the lab tests are done."

Thain nodded. "The murder appears to have been done with deliberate intent to cause extreme pain for the victim."

"This wasn't a random hack job, in my opinion. Seen enough to take an educated guess."

"I should think so . . ." The weapon was a letter opener with RM on the handle, which evidently had been taken from the desk. The killer had left it in the wound. That the murder weapon belonged here spiked one of those signals Thain didn't want to think about. So did the fact it had been left in the wound. And the single witness they knew of still breathed. He had reason not to like that, too. Not that he wanted her dead . . . He looked up from his notes as Clive approached the doorway, careful to stay out of the actual crime scene. Thain asked, "The witness?"

Clive glanced at his notes. "After I calmed her down a bit, I sent her over to West End Central to give a statement. She's the victim's secretary and her name is Melissa McConnell. She's pretty shaken but seems certain of what she saw, which gives us almost nothing to start with."

Clive Patterson was a year or two younger than Thain, red haired, and near Thain's height of six feet. Clive never wore footwear that wasn't American cowboy boots. He also tended to be precise in his work and had surprised Thain a year ago, when he'd first started in the LMPS, with his easy, yet adept, manner. Clive didn't play petty office politics, which was a relief because politics was the one thing about being a police detective Thain actually hated. "What *did* she give us?" he asked.

"The man wore a Burberry coat, a hat, and glasses. He looked right at her, she says, before he grabbed her, taped her up, and stuck her in the closet. Said he looked about six feet tall."

Touching his smart phone, Thain closed his notes app. "I've already ordered CCTV footage for the surrounding area. We'll start with that as soon as we get a viewing room set up."

"Good. With her description we should be able to pick him out pretty quick."

"Sarcasm, Clive?" Thain almost smiled. "A color on the Burberry? The eyes?"

"Burberry, dark but no color. No color on the eyes behind the glasses. Rae Bell is still downstairs. She's talked with the Flying Squad and is interviewing the security guards now. The guy had to pass through security before he'd make it in here. Maybe they'll remember more about him than the secretary did."

Thain nodded, absently running his thumb across the smooth surface of his phone, which he used like a worry bead. It helped him think. "Wonder why he didn't kill her?" Thain turned his attention back to the corpse now being readied for removal. The initialed letter opener still sat in the bloody chest. Thain swallowed and quickly shifted his gaze to the victim's clothes lying in a crumpled pile at the man's bare feet, minus the white, blood-soaked shirt still caught on the handle of the weapon. Richard McLean hadn't died a quick or painless death, but there was nothing else here to tell them more. They would have to wait for the forensics report to see if the killer left something behind, something invisible to the naked eye. Before Patterson left, Thain said, "Clive, I'm heading back to West End to put my notes on the computer. Meet you there?"

"I'll be right behind you as soon as I find Rae Bell."

Thain said, "If you hear before I do, let me know when and where the chief wants to hold the first meeting?"

Clive winked. "Of course. Glad he's the one handling the press. There's a swarm of them out front already." He disappeared down the hall, tapping his notebook against his knuckles, a habit he'd picked up from some cop show on TV. Thain found it amusing. Sometimes he wished things in real life actually went the way they did on TV shows. On a TV show, they'd have a decent shot at catching this murderer.

3

Celia Wight pushed open Liberty's heavy wooden door with her shoulder, and the chilly winter air hit her rosy, warm cheeks. She faltered, wanting nothing more than to slip back into the heated store and wait for the crowds to thin. Her already tepid Christmas cheer had dampened severely at the overcast day when she'd left the hotel early, before her book signing, to do some mandatory holiday shopping. But she'd forced herself to face up to the challenge anyway, and her efforts had proven successful. Her gloved hands were now weighted with bags of presents for Eva, her dearest and best friend, and Philip, her literary agent. Eva and Philip King had come to England so that when her book tour concluded they could celebrate Christmas together, adding some friendly color to stony-gray London. None of them had expected their Christmas to be white. Though Eva and Philip were British, they lived in the States as did she: Atlanta, Georgia, where most days, even in winter, the sun shone hot and bright.

Inhaling the morning city-tainted air, Celia hesitated. The narrow London sidewalk outside Liberty's was packed with shoppers like her, and she wasn't quite ready to push among them to make her way toward Oxford Circus tube station. She was tired and more than ready for some tea at the hotel, but she was due at the bookstore at eleven and to have lunch with Eva and Philip afterward. She eked her way toward Oxford Street, though she couldn't see more than a few feet in front of her.

Celia didn't like crowds, but at least no one really saw her amongst an anonymous mass of moving persons. She did like that.

But today she was more nervous than usual. *Because of the book signings,* she thought. They always made her a bit jumpy. In Atlanta she was accustomed to the way the city moved. She knew Atlanta, and if she didn't feel completely safe, at least it was familiar. London was huge and she loved to visit, but she didn't know it well enough to feel safe in it. Atlanta seemed to have more space. Here, the strangers mulling around her, pushing, pulling, laughing, and griping, jangled her nerves. When police sirens started to wail farther down the street, coming closer, the noise added to the chaos and her discomfort. The racket echoed, and she couldn't decide which direction the sirens were coming from. She twisted, trying to see what was happening, but was blocked on all sides. She felt trapped by the crowd, propelled by the tide of humanity. At least she was going in the right direction.

Until somebody bumped into her from behind. But her bags tangled against her legs and she couldn't move any faster. Before she could react, someone grabbed her sleeve, spun her around, and put an arm about her shoulders, shoving her face into the middle of his chest before she could see him clearly.

Celia reacted instantly, pushed back against him with her elbows, protest on her lips. But before one word escaped, before her heartbeat aligned with her already escalating panic, the stranger shoved his other hand beneath the back of her coat. A thin, inflexible point pricked her ribs. A knife. "Please, God no—" Then, inside her head panic exploded and she started to scream.

The man reacted, pulled her closer, his head next to hers, his breath hot against her ear as he said, "Be quiet. I can, and will, puncture your heart if you make one sound."

The knife pressed harder, silenced her, reinforced his threat. She started to hyperventilate. Police sirens beat the air. She heard patrol cars screeching on overworked brakes, congesting the traffic all along the constricted Great Marlborough Street. She shot a glance to the side when she heard cops yelling and the rhythm of running feet on pavement. The police plunged through the crowds, rummaging like rabid shoppers looking for a good deal. "Bloody hell," the stranger cursed and tightened his grip on her, blocking out any thought she had except one.

Life or death was all her head could deal with as he pushed her back through the crowd, away from Oxford Street and her tube station. In the alcove sheltering the great wooden doors to the Liberty store she'd just left, he stepped around one of the dark-gray lion statues to the side and backed up against the brown sign proclaiming "Liberty." Enclosed by the foot traffic entering and exiting the store, he turned her to face him and lowered his head next to hers. Even knowing the danger, she couldn't stop struggling against him. When he gripped her tighter, she surprised herself and bit his ear, clamped down, and metallic warmth surged onto her lips and tongue. She jerked back, trying to spit his blood out of her mouth, but he grunted and twisted the knife against her, the point cutting through her turtleneck sweater. Blood for blood. She tasted his in her mouth, on her tongue, felt a queasy slickness on her teeth. He wiped his ear with a movement so fast she barely remarked it before she inhaled to scream. His gloved hand smeared the red stain from her mouth as he pulled her face to his. His lips, which weren't soft or warm but harsh and cold as the winter air, covered her own. She squirmed beneath the tense pressure, but he held her fast. She couldn't breathe. She willed herself away, eyes shut against the reality of him. She strived for escape; her body twisted in the wicked man's steely grip. Her survival instinct cut through her fear as thoroughly as the knife cut through her sweater to puncture the skin of her back. Her mind still whispered, *fight!* She fought him again, but his vice-like grip tightened and the knife sliced deeper. Her skin started to sting.

Like a rejected lover, the stranger held her too fast, too close for her to see him clearly. The pressure of his brutal lips lessened for a breath, returned, softened, and pressed into the warmth of a kiss, a real kiss. Then he broke contact with a sudden jerk of his head, as if she had burned him. When she dared open her eyes, his own flashed ominous and angry through his rimmed glasses before he pushed her head against his chest so she couldn't see his face.

"What have you done?" The words escaped through his teeth, clipped and accusing, but not disguising his British accent.

"Me?"

The stranger remained silent. She felt his head moving as if his eyes were sweeping over the area. He seemed to be weighing his chances of—what, escape? "They'll come back," he said.

Celia hadn't noticed that the sirens now echoed farther down the street. The police cars had vanished.

"They're looking for you," she said. For an instant she wondered what he'd done, but the thin plastic handles of her forgotten, and now leaden, shopping bags cut into her gloved fingers. How could she still be holding them? They started to slip.

"Don't drop your bags."

Surprised, still in shock, she fought to get a better grip. "I, I—"

"Walk with me. Now," he said, pulling her with him.

Celia's heart flip-flopped, pounding against the rhythm of her stumbling feet. His knife still touched her skin. Sweat beaded at the base of her spine as her instinct once again stole the reins from her fear. Another scream rose in her throat, harmonizing with the wavering wail of retreating sirens.

"Not a sound." His demand cut her as surely as his blade had. She choked. Her feet stumbled on the sidewalk. The pressure of the knife-point had eased slightly, but it remained firm on her back, the stinging raw now as he steered her around the corner and into a pedestrian street. She looked up at him.

"Don't."

Celia snapped her gaze back to the crowds flowing around them, the few café patrons daring the winter weather dotting outside tables. But she'd caught a glimpse of clean-shaven cheeks and short dark-blond hair.

"Wait." Celia pulled back, squeezed her eyes closed. "You don't need me anymore."

"Don't argue."

She baulked. "No! I won't look—"

He pressed his point, literally. "Don't make me use this."

Desperate now, she told a partial lie. "People will worry—"

"I don't care." He didn't stop. He didn't let her go.

Farther down the way, sleet started to fall. She stopped dead in the middle of the pedestrian way while people popped open their umbrellas or ran for shelter.

"But why—" She kept her eyes closed.

"Don't ask. Open. Your. Eyes."

This was a dream—a really, really bad one. The dream turned into a full-fledged nightmare as the stranger propelled her under a sign arched over the pedestrian way proclaiming "Welcome to Carnaby Street."

After that, no thought Celia had was straight. Instead, her thoughts ran crooked and bent like the streets he led her down. Searching for landmarks she recognized, she tried to clear her mind, tried to push aside the shock and fear hindering any chance she had at rational thought. But no matter how hard she concentrated, she couldn't forget the ever-present blade wedged against her back.

4

The lift hummed down to the main floor, and Thain skirted around the tape that closed off the entrance to the bank and the reporters crowded like flies around his boss, Chief North. Glad he didn't have to deal with the press, he walked fast toward the West End Central police station a few blocks away. Starting up the steps at the entrance, he quickly pulled back as a couple, a man and woman, came out of nowhere from the left and almost knocked him over. If he hadn't been paying attention he would have ended up on his backside and halfway down the steps. The man had his arm around the woman, his head down near hers, neither one aware of their surroundings.

"Excuse me?" Thain said. Some people . . .

The man, tall and slight of build, looked up, his expression troubled. "So sorry. Please, are you a policeman?"

Hesitating, Thain answered, "Yes. Detective Sergeant Alban Thain." He didn't pull his credentials, as they were at the station and the man didn't ask for them. "Is there a problem?" His impatience to get to the computer clipped his words a fair bit past politeness.

"Yes, Detective, there is a problem." The man reached out and shook Thain's hand in a tight grip. "Maybe you can help us. I'm Philip King." Philip King stood at least six feet two or three, and though thin, he wasn't bony. He had short, well-groomed blond hair and penetrating green eyes, eyes now shadowed with concern. He wore a clean-cut black suit and looked on the upwards side of wealthy. Being only six feet, with dark hair and even darker brown eyes, and not so wealthy, Thain had to ignore his juvenile envy of the man's looks. Philip King motioned toward the redheaded woman by his side. She had alabaster skin and was small of stature, refined, almost regal, and smartly dressed in brown boots and a mid-calf blue wool skirt with matching jacket.

"This is my wife, Eva," he said.

Thain nodded a greeting, thinking that though she was attractive, she wasn't his type—as if he had a type.

"We need to file a report for a missing person," Mr. King resumed as the three of them continued up the steps. Thain held the door open for them.

"I'm sure the front desk can direct you to that unit," Thain said, but his words were lost as a wave of sound engulfed them. The desk was completely hidden behind a teeming mass of people crammed into the space in front of it. Of course. The Royal Bank of Scotland stood just around the virtual corner. Hundred-to-one odds bet these assumed "witnesses" to the heist had all seen something important. It was Christmas, after all, and far too many people were out holiday shopping.

Thain sighed. "I can take you up to the Missing Persons Unit. Someone should be able to help you there. Please, follow me?" So much for getting right to work while all the evidence was fresh in his mind. Knowing the station as if it were a second home—which for him it was—he led the Kings to the lift, got out on the second floor, and guided them through the door and into the Missing Persons Unit office. It was empty. Thain called out, "Sergeant Clarke? Is anyone here?"

Sergeant Sarah Clarke came out from somewhere behind the front desk, her blond hair looking slightly weary and her manner harried. "DS Thain. What can I do for you?"

Nodding to the Kings, he said, "This is Mr. and Mrs. King. They'd like to report a missing person."

"Now? We've all been called downstairs to take statements."

"And I'm supposed to be readying my report for Chief North before the first meeting on this double crime."

Her face a blank, Clarke looked past him to the couple standing behind him. "Do you have a photo and all the pertinent information, Mr. and Mrs. ah . . .?"

"King. Mr. and Mrs. King," Thain filled in.

"Yes, of course." Mrs. King answered. "We brought everything we could think of that you might need." She pulled an eight-by-ten black-and-white photograph from an envelope in her bag and handed it to Thain, who glanced at it as he handed it to the sergeant. But his hand stopped as if of its own volition and he stared at the face looking back at him from the photograph. Haunted. This woman looked haunted. Her eyes . . . he'd seen eyes the likes of these before.

"Oh, it's you again, lad."

"Aye, sir, again."

"Agatha hasn't changed her mind."

"I just need to see her, know she's . . ."

"I know, Alban, and you're a good lad to keep tryin', but she won't see you."

"But, sir, can I see her? She doesn't have to know I'm here, but I'd like, if you would allow me, to at least see her?"

"I'm not sure, lad. Maybe just for a wee minute. Can't say you haven't done right by her."

The door was ajar a fraction, and he peeked in. Agatha sat on a bed, her face an unfamiliar mask until he saw her eyes. Cringing inside, he asked, "Is she, physically, I mean, is there any permanent damage?"

"Physically a bit. Time will tell. It's her mind . . ."

"Aye. I thought if she'd see me, it might help?"

"Not to her way of thinkin'. At least for the now. Best leave it there, Alban. Best to let her come to you."

"If she ever will."

"Aye. If ever. Go on home now. There's naught for you here anymore."

Thain forced himself to look away from the photo. He had to. The unwanted memory was bad enough, but somewhere inside of him, something moved. Something started to melt, and he had to stop it.

"Right, then," he murmured, and almost shoved the photo at the sergeant, who didn't seem to have noticed his hesitation. He glanced at the Kings and said, "I'm off, then. Sergeant Clarke will take care of you."

"Detective Thain?"

"Yes, Mr. King?"

"Thank you for your help."

Thain's smile was more a grimace. "No need to thank me for doing my job."

5

Celia had visited London several times and knew how to find the stores for her book signings, how to get to the Tate and British museums, how to play tourist and see the Tower or Buckingham Palace. But she had no idea where the madman took her now. They turned corner after corner onto street after street and he didn't use the underground or a bus once. This was a London she had never seen.

Finally, her abductor halted before what looked like a small apartment complex that had once been someone's home. Not too fancy, it sat discreetly in the middle of a block. It looked normal and well kept. The door opened and a couple, smartly dressed for the evening, descended the steps. Celia's abductor leaned his head down next to hers again. "I will kill them if you make me. Lose the frown. Smile."

Her mouth felt brittle when she made the attempt, until he reached up with his thumb and smoothed the frown between her eyebrows. For the first time she looked him full in the face. He gave her a small smile and tilted the universe with unforeseen charm. It didn't last. He put his arm around her, outside her coat. He had to be a psychopath. And she'd seen his entire face.

Celia tripped on purpose as the couple passed, her bags spilling over the sidewalk. The woman exclaimed and the man stopped, ready to offer assistance. But her abductor knelt beside her and picked up the fallen contents, helped her to her feet.

"She's all right. Thanks," he said to them as his grip on her tightened again. He didn't allow her to look back as they crossed the street. He said, "Not clever." Celia wanted to scream as the couple left.

Once inside, he guided her toward the stairwell. He kept his arm around her as they ascended the small spiraling staircase, the knife still at her back. Celia's heart slammed in quick harsh thuds against her chest as he kept them moving in a constant climb. She decided to try and escape from him as soon as they reached whatever floor he was headed for. She would scream her head off. No sooner had the thought blossomed than he tugged her closer, his arm tightening around her. Could he read her mind?

"In flats such as these they don't take well to loud theatrics in the corridors. Besides, the rooms here are soundproofed."

Celia blinked back tears of frustration, of fear, of helplessness. *No,* she said to herself. *I won't cry.* How had this happened so fast?

He stopped on the fifth floor, guiding her to number 504. Celia's legs trembled as he inserted the key and opened the door. Once she crossed that threshold, her life would be over.

He put the knife away.

Celia threw her bags at him and screeched as she ran down the hall. She made it halfway to the stairs before he caught her. His hand, firm over her mouth, silenced her. He dragged her back down the hall and into the small apartment before slamming the door closed with his foot. He whipped her around to face him, his frigid blue eyes daring her to scream again. His glasses only seemed to intensify his threat. She gulped air.

"A-are y-you going t-to k-kill me?" She hated that she stuttered.

He didn't move.

Afraid to take her eyes off him, afraid of what he could do now that he had her alone, her mind wailed, w*hy, why, why?*

"Not yet," he said.

Oh God, oh God. This can't be happening.

To one side, by the small alcove of a kitchen, stood a round wooden table encircled by carved wooden chairs. The apartment was small but well appointed. The main room held a couch and a coffee table next to a door that she assumed led to a bedroom. He pushed her the short distance to the table and forced her to sit. With her heart in her throat, she didn't take her eyes off of him.

"Stay here," he said.

He didn't have the knife in his hand. He could only hurt her if he had the knife.

"No!" She leapt up and shoved him, trying for the door. She reached the doorknob but his arm slewed around her waist and pulled her back before she could gain a grip on it. She started screaming again, thrashing with all her might. She threw her head back into his face behind her, but he avoided the thrust. He did little but grunt when her heel or elbow contacted his shin or arm. He slammed her down on the couch and held her there with his full body. She tried screaming but could gain no breath beneath his weight. He rose up to sit on her. His knees dug into her arms, his weight on her abdomen.

"If you continue, I'll knock you senseless."

"Why don't you, then," she screamed, wishing back her words even as she said them. She had no idea what bug of self-destruction bit her, but anger welled within her again, righteous anger, dangerous anger, could-get-her-killed-right-now anger. It overwhelmed her fear, blocked it out for one sweet instant. There were some things worse than death.

"I would prefer you to behave. I don't want to hurt you."

"Then let me go!" She tried pushing her body up with her legs to dislodge him.

He ignored her. Her mind leapt from one horror to another, one stupid question to another. Like, if he were a killer wouldn't she already be dead? *Stop asking yourself stupid questions if you don't want to know the answers.* He pulled her up from the couch. Once again he pushed her into a wooden chair. This time he gave her no time to fight. He took a roll of tape from his coat pocket and began to tape her to the chair.

"No!" She started to jump up. "No, I won't let you!"

He slapped a piece of thick tape over her mouth, pinned her arms with no effort, and taped her hands at an awkward angle behind the chair. She jerked her arms to make it harder for him. She kicked and struggled to no avail. She couldn't stop tears this time, no more than she could stop the beating of her heart.

"Don't start."

Her muffled voice sounded smaller than a whisper. Tears flowed, and her breath choked up as her nose began to run.

"If you don't stop you'll suffocate."

She sniffed, trying to swallow, trying to stop but failing. Panic rose like bile in her throat. She moaned and jerked herself back and forth in the chair. It started to fall to one side.

He grabbed it, steadied it, then leaned down and brought those blue icebergs close enough to her face for frostbite.

Celia stared wide-eyed at him. She couldn't read anything in the chilling harshness of his eyes. He didn't look away from her. She tried to force her panic down, but her throat constricted, hampering her efforts at control. "Stop now," he said. "Get used to listening to me and all will be well. Breathe. Slowly." Gulping, she tried to even out her breath. He stood back, pulled off his coat, and opened the door. Shooting a fleeting glance in both directions, he grabbed her bags, shut the door again, and set them on the floor by the wall next to her.

Fighting for air, she remembered this drowning, suffocating fear. She'd been here before, and ever since that experience she'd made sure her closest encounters with villains stayed in the books she wrote, and the villains were always historical figures, warriors or Romans. This man was clearly neither one, but she'd stood so close to him that she'd noticed the slight indentation of a long, thin scar below his left eyebrow. Besides those eyes, it was the only remarkable feature in an unremarkable face. Did he have more scars? Was that one only a small indication of the violence in the man, and of her fate?

She shivered again, her chest tight with dread. She had reason to fear, had reason to imagine the worst. He put his coat back on. He glanced at her and said, "I'll be back with something to eat." She stared after him as he opened the door and left, taking her useless questions with him. Food? That was the last thing on earth she wanted. Celia focused on her breath, on not crying. She dared to close her eyes for a second, but opened them after one shuddering breath. When the man and his knife came back, she wanted to see them coming.

6

In spite of what some assumed, the LMPS didn't have an unlimited number of cars for their DSs. Thain's strides were long and determined as he walked from the tube station to the Hendon, less than an hour and fifteen minutes after he'd left the Kings at the Missing Person's Unit. He'd spent a precious half hour arranging his notes for the meeting he now headed for, and he hoped he wasn't late. Irritated by his reaction to the photograph of the missing woman, he tried the entire journey to forget it and the memory it had invoked, to put his work first as he always did. It was harder to do than it should have been.

Approaching the Hendon, he barely glanced up at the complex of buildings that comprised, officially, the Peel Centre. A new name and rebuild in 1974 hadn't stopped any of the graduating police officers from calling the college by its age-old moniker, the Hendon. Whether out of respect or sentimentality, it didn't seem to matter. The Hendon it was. The Hendon it would continue to be, so that's how he thought of it as well. The shortest building stood five or so stories and the tallest was at least eighteen. Strewn about outside were fake streets and old cars for staging accidents and such. A driving school, gym, and parade square also made up part of the grounds. Greeting visitors out front stood a statue of Sir Robert Peel, the man who had established the first London police force in 1829. Inside the various buildings were classrooms, a mock courtroom, and a huge call center. Though mainly a training school, it also housed a separate area for murder squad operations.

Detective Chief Inspector Stuart North had called for the first murder squad meeting to be at four that afternoon at the Hendon, and it was now three fifty. He'd assembled a load of twenty-nine warm bodies in a room set aside especially for the murder squad. Luckily, Thain arrived as the chief began. The tall, lean, and intense man whom they all obeyed didn't try to play it cool. Agitation honed the sharp edge of his voice, and his commands cut the tension in the room like a blade.

"A murder and a heist on the same day in the same building are bad enough, but the murdered man was, of course, a prominent official of the Royal Bank of Scotland. You know the pressure we are already under. I want a direction on this immediately. The superintendent won't have us dragging our feet on the murder, and neither will I. It's our heads will roll if we don't catch this guy—and quick—so listen carefully. First, this squad will report directly to Detective Inspectors Jeremy Hawthorne and Paul Carter or me. The HOLMES team will be DSs Thain, Greene, Martin . . ." He paused and asked, "How many do you need, Thain?"

He knew the chief asked him because he'd been the one to answer the phone and the first to arrive on the crime scene with Clive, but being appointed to the HOLMES team took the cake, outweighed everything else for him. Working with the HOLMES program was like putting a puzzle together on a computer, and Thain loved puzzles. HOLMES, which stood for "Home Office Large Major Enquiry System," was the state-of-the-art system now used all over the UK for investigations, especially murder investigations. Someone must have really wanted the system's acronym to be a nod to Sherlock, to come up with a name like that. "Five at the start, sir."

"Right. O'Toole and Smyth as well. Thain, you allocate each position. Get an Incident Room set up on the terminals here, and don't forget to mark down these next assignments and make actions for them. I know that you, Bell, and Patterson were point on this murder, but I want you either on the CCTV footage or on HOLMES the majority of the time. Bell and Patterson, you two will be the legs on this for now."

"Yes, sir," Rae and Clive said together.

Thain asked, "Could I ask a question, sir?"

The chief said, "Go ahead."

"Could Constable Abney be the eyes with me on the CCTV film for this case? He has the best in the department."

"Done." The chief glanced at Police Constable St. John Abney. "St. John," he said, pronouncing his name correctly as *Sinjin*, "you heard the man; put those eagle eyes of yours to work for us."

Thain smiled. Often, those who'd only read St. John's name called him "Saint John," but he certainly was no saint. In fact, though he was a bit of a nerd, those who knew him found the pronunciation "*Sinjin*" to be much more apt.

"Yes, sir." St. John glanced at Thain with a smile on his face. He always preferred reviewing the CCTV to street work, and they all knew his capability.

DCI North continued, "As I said earlier, everyone reports to me or DIs Hawthorne and Carter." North's voice hitched up another notch. "Thain, Patterson, and Bell, as you were first on site, what do you have so far? Thain, you investigated the actual murder scene?"

"There isn't much information yet, sir. To begin with, we've ordered the CCTV footage from each side of the bank and the surrounding area ten blocks out. We have a general description of the murder suspect. The lab sergeant predicts not much evidence found. Patterson is doing the victim's background check. That's about it for the moment."

"Bell, you talked with the Flying Squad at the scene. What do you have?

"We know there were seven thieves—"

"Pardon me, Bell, but how do we know that?" Thain hadn't intended to interrupt, but he had to say something, even if sticking his neck out this early in the game invited derision from the others.

"Six men downstairs, one upstairs. It's simple maths," Rae answered.

Turning toward North he said, "Sir, I don't think we should assume anything. Especially that the murder suspect is one of the thieves."

"Why?" Chief North asked.

"It doesn't add up. The office was locked with no signs of forced entry. Why was the victim, Richard McLean, targeted amongst all the other people in all the other offices on his floor by thieves that were busy downstairs robbing the bank?"

"Maybe the suspect was the leader and used the heist as a diversion from the murder?" said Rae.

He had to admit she had a point, a flawed one but still a point.

Chief North said, "Answer your own question, Thain. That's your job."

This case was Chief North's problem to fix, and Thain knew what he'd say next. "We're all on overtime until the murder is solved, so get to work. Bell, Thain, and Patterson, stay on top, and the rest of you lot, make sure you do whatever it takes to get the information we need into HOLMES." Heads nodded and the group dispersed or formed into clumps around the DIs to get what orders they could so early in the investigation.

Alban Thain eased his way toward Bell and Patterson, unconvinced that one of the bank robbers had committed the murder. But he knew he didn't have anything solid to give to North. For all he knew, Rae's theory could be right. When some of his fellow officers filed past, muttering about the investigation, he frowned. Evidently he was prone to do that more often than smiling, especially when Paul Carter came up to him and leaned in just too close for comfort. The DI had a problem respecting anyone's physical space.

"Hey, Thain, are you going to chase your ghost, or whatever you call him, again on this one? The Wraith is it?" the street-cocky Detective Inspector said, his pretty-boy face mockingly serious. Others paused in passing. Carter and Thain had a long history of confrontation. "Maybe this time you'll catch him. Boo!" Carter grinned.

"Try that on someone who cares, Carter."

"Like you don't? Scottish superstition and overblown ego, that's all you've got to offer."

When Carter walked away, Thain chastised his inner idiot for bothering to respond, but he couldn't stop himself. "If I did think it was the Wraith, why would I tell *you* about it?"

Carter turned, theatrical in the gesture, eyes glancing around to make sure everyone watched. "Because, *D. S.* Thain, you report directly to me," he said with an almost maniacal grin.

Thain shot back, as belligerently as possible, "Of course, *sir*. No disrespect, *sir*."

Carter pointed his finger at him. "One more, Thain. One more snide remark and I'll have you off this case."

Thain somehow managed to hold his tongue as Carter left. Standing there like the half-wit he knew he was, he tried not to think of the team watching. Why couldn't he ignore the idiot? Ever since the verbal takedown Carter had given him five years ago, every stupid conflict seemed to notch up the tension between them. Carter had just made DI, was handsome, was evidently a ladies' man, and loved to throw his weight around whenever he could. Talk about an overblown ego. He'd make a perfect politician one day. He'd taken Thain down publicly soon after Thain had first arrived at the LMPS and, during a murder inquiry, made the mistake of introducing his theory of the Wraith. Ever since, Carter had made it a point to rub the proverbial scar with sandpaper whenever the opportunity presented itself, like today, because still, five years later, though Thain had never again voiced his theory, he also had yet to prove that theory correct. The Wraith had become a standing joke and him along with it.

"Thain, over here," Rae Bell called and waved him over. Recollecting where he should be, he made his way over to her.

"Don't take any notice of him, Thain. You know Carter doesn't use the brains he has." She dismissed Carter with a shooing motion of her small, dark, and talented hand. Rae leaned toward him. "How he ever made it to DI is a mystery we'd all like to solve. He's, well, slimy."

"I thought ladies loved him."

"Not this one, and thank you for calling me a lady." Rae, small and lithe yet stronger than she looked, had the ebony-black hair typical to Indian women, which she habitually wore in a chignon or a long plait down her back. She was smart, diligent, and attractive, and she also happened to be a trained police artist. Rarely did anyone call Rae by just her last name like they did everyone else. Possibly because Rae

Bell's full name was more enjoyable to say, in a work environment where there was little fun to be had. She was also the one person, besides Clive Patterson, who seemed to relate to Thain as more than a joke. He'd asked her once how her family name could be "Bell" when she wasn't married and her parents came from Mumbai, India. She'd smiled when she answered.

"I chose it myself. I honor the traditions of my family and faith—those that I believe have worth—but I don't choose to be *only* my father's daughter." Maybe because of her heritage, and because he was a Scot among the English, their differences gave them some sort of bond. He winced at the thought. Bond? She was only being her polite little self. She didn't believe in his theory about the Wraith any more than anyone else.

Rae smiled at him as if she knew what he'd been thinking. "Get rid of that frown before it becomes permanent," she said, and called Clive Patterson over. The three of them worked on a preliminary plan of action, and once they had it, went to get a DI's approval so they could get started. "This looks good for now," Hawthorne began. He was Thain's height, weighed a bit more, and had light blond hair. He also didn't talk unless necessary, like during investigations, and even then was reserved, the exact opposite of Carter.

"You two," Carter said, walking up and pointing to Bell and Patterson, "make sure DS Thain stays on—"

"Carter," Hawthorne cut him off. "We're in the middle of review."

Surprised, and thankful for Hawthorne's interruption, Thain glanced at Rae. Carter gaped at Hawthorne, who ignored him until he demanded to see the proposed plan of action. "Thain, get with your HOLMES team while I bring Carter up to date," Hawthorne said.

"Yes, sir." Thain ignored Carter's glare and left to gather the HOLMES team together. "All right, any preferences on positions?" he asked the crew.

"Allocate actions?" Greene said first.

"I'll index. Someone has to do it," Martin said.

Smyth volunteered, "You know I'm the best typist, Thain."

Thain nodded. "Guess you'll read statements, O'Toole. You all right with that?"

O'Toole grinned. "Love to read. No problem."

"Great. After I open the Incident Room, Greene will allocate a call for witnesses to the murder and heist—though, going by what I saw earlier at West End, that might be redundant. For once the press is helping us with our job."

"Right."

"Martin, once you've started the index, would you help Patterson find out about the victim's background? We need that information entered as soon as possible."

"No problem," Martin said as he took his seat.

Thain sat down at one of the five terminals set up for HOLMES in the murder room and began what was called "initiating the incident." This entailed opening a new file, or "Incident Room," and assigning user positions for Greene, Martin, Smyth, and O'Toole, so they could log in.

Next he entered all the names of those on the murder squad, the most important being those who would do the legwork, the enquiry teams. Half an hour later, everyone had entered what they knew and there was nothing left to input. Thain took a moment to sit there, and after making sure no one watched, allowed his mouth to stretch into a big, rare, and blissful smile. Here he was at the Hendon, on the murder squad, with access to HOLMES. It didn't happen often enough—the access, anyway. In his own little universe, he considered the HOLMES program his private TARDIS, which in Doctor Who's universe stood for "Time and Relative Dimension in Space." Of course, he was no Doctor Who, but he did his best to investigate and solve mysteries right here on earth, as the good Doctor did, here and elsewhere in the universe. He'd thought of HOLMES as his TARDIS ever since he became intimately connected when he trained on it.

With HOLMES and the Criminal Intelligence Data Base, the CIDB, at his fingertips, he'd spent the last ten years amassing pertinent information about assassinations and the assassins that carried them out. He'd asked to be trained by Interpol when his very first assignment, guarding a public official during a speech, had gone horribly wrong. Compressing his lips, he purposely remembered the warm blood spatter cooling in patches on his face when the official he'd stood next to had been shot. He'd felt the same shame every officer on duty that day had felt at having failed to protect their primary. Who was he kidding? His quest to study assassins had become much more than that. It had become a full-blown obsession. But his training, and those ten years, had not only given him expert experience in tracking assassins, it had also revealed a man who didn't seem to exist. At least that was his theory about the man he called the Wraith.

A private file, on a USB drive he carried everywhere, held all the information he'd uncovered over the years. He'd started the file back in Scotland before he came to the LMPS and after Interpol had "kicked" him out. It held all the minutiae, anything that might eventually be of use in proving the Wraith's existence. No one knew he had this information and he didn't share it. From Interpol to the LMPS, the lesson had been hard learned to keep quiet about the Wraith, and as he did in all his other investigations, he meant to keep his silence no matter what happened during this one.

Realizing the team had finished with setting up and initiating the first actions, he scooted his chair away from the desk and stood. "Guess that's it for now. Martin, you and Smyth mind taking first watch?" They shook their heads. "Good. Monitor the information when the calls start coming in to the call center. Figure out our duty schedule and text me with it. Make sure we're all on for equal time."

"Got it. Where are you going, Thain?" O'Toole asked.

"To view the CCTV footage that's come in. St. John sent me a text. He has the first batch." Thain left the team busy arguing over the schedule. He heard a phone ring behind him as he headed out. Couldn't be calls coming in already. It was too soon, he hoped, until he remembered the crowd at the West End police station. Thank goodness the first of the CCTV footage had been sent to a viewing room in the Hendon Training College. He'd be viewing that footage in a few minutes.

Though he would never admit it in public, he thought that, for once, Carter was right about something. Ever since he'd seen the crime scene, he'd had "Wraith signals" going off all over his brain. Though he didn't look at every murder through assassin-tinted glasses, this particular case had familiar aspects to it, things he'd seen before in his research. Yes, he saw discrepancies in this case, and not minor ones. Still . . . he tucked away a private smile as he thought again of HOLMES.

7

Celia had no idea how much time passed before her kidnapper returned and ripped off the tape that bound her.

"Go to the toilet."

She rubbed her sore wrists and cringed at the stiffness in her neck, but did as he ordered. She'd do anything to get away from him, even if it was only illusion instead of fact.

As she washed her face, Celia avoided the mirror. She didn't have to see her face to know that haunting, deep, and abiding terror had returned to dwell in her light-blue eyes. The corners of her mouth tightened. Her unruly mouth—the one that had bitten that man, tasted his blood, and endured his lips. That had almost, at the end when those lips turned warm and soft, maybe wanted his touch to be a true kiss? *Kiss! No*, she thought, *no way.*

Celia shook her head to hold on to what sanity she had left. There had to be a way out of here. Away from him. Surely Eva and Philip would have reported her missing when she hadn't shown for lunch, but would the police file a report when she hadn't been gone the required forty- eight hours? Did they wait forty-eight hours in England? Philip had probably already contacted Ian McPherson, the other agent he had set her up with here in England, because there was a party tonight that they were to have attended together. She had another book signing tomorrow.

Celia's heart plummeted. Who knew where she'd be by then? Tears stung her eyelids. *No.* She turned on the cold water and splashed her face. Between the numbing cold and her wretched sobs she could barely breathe, but she splashed her face again and again until a small semblance of control returned. It took a moment to find it; she knew she could easily lose it again, but for now her control was back. Eva and Philip *would* have gone to the police when she'd missed their lunch date. She *would* think positively about her chances. She had to.

Celia took one glance in the mirror to prove she could. Her small oval face had turned pink and puffy. She covered it with a towel, shuddered as she sucked in deep breaths.

"Have you finished?"

She started. The man's voice, though on the other side of the door, sounded right next to her. *Breathe, just breathe,* she thought, as one of her favorite heroines had told herself in one of her favorite films. Celia desperately wanted the fairy tale back, wanted to hide in it, as was her habit. The crushing reality of the man this near started her down that slippery slope again. "No," she whispered, "No." Gritting her teeth, she curled her hands into fists. She would not give in to panic.

The strong, hot smell of the food he'd bought permeated the small apartment and made her sick. He ate in silence on the sofa in front of the TV he didn't turn on. At the table, Celia sat staring at the locked door with no hope. The odor of the fried fish caused her throat to spasm, and her rebellious stomach finally won. She flew to the bathroom and threw up while he stood in the doorway watching her.

He made her sit down at the table again, but she still couldn't eat. Her life, as she knew it, had ended earlier that afternoon. She saw no clock in the room, but what did time matter anymore? She had run out of it. Celia pushed her food container away. He made no comment when he picked it up, shoved it back in the bag, and wiped the table clean.

He put her coat on her and forced her into a leather reclining chair. He made sure she lay down on her side before he tied her hands behind her back and her ankles to the elevated leg rest at the bottom of the recliner. Even if she managed to scoot down to the edge of the seat, she couldn't turn around to untie her legs.

"These walls are soundproof."

"I heard you the first time. Why are you doing this? What use can I be to you? Why won't you let me go?"

He hesitated a moment, and said, "You have seen my face."

"Lots of people saw your face today."

Celia chilled as he stared at her. He seemed completely sure of what he did in a way she never had been.

"Sleep," he said, "while you can." He clicked off the light on his way to the bedroom. He didn't close the door.

While you can echoed in her brain, chased away any thought of sleep. Celia noticed a small gap in the curtains and stared out at the few city lights she could see. The moon surprised her when it appeared. *How bizarre. Life still moves on out there. I must be dead already, and in hell.* She'd taken a trip to hell before, and sworn never to go there again. But this was almost worse: the waiting, the not knowing when he would strike.

She wanted to think of nothing but Eva and Philip, of her safe and popular books. They were the only reasons her life had any value. Sobs welled within her, telling her not to go there. It was too painful to try to think of the things she loved in the dark certainty of doom.

8

He didn't lie on the bed to sleep. In the gloom of the tiny bedroom, he sat, as he always did, in the armchair in the corner with no light on. The bare blade of his knife lay across his thigh; his fingers entwined across his abdomen. His brain wouldn't let go, wouldn't stop thinking of the mistake he'd made and what it might cost him. In front of the store window he had touched her, skin to skin. He hated to make physical contact with anyone but had decided in an instant which course to take. He'd thought it the lesser of two evils. How wrong he'd been. His leg started to bounce, his heel pumping, and the knife started to slide. He grabbed it, planted the offending heel on the floor, and kept it there. He repositioned the blade on his thigh. He had never lost control like that. He'd never misjudged himself, his reaction, like that, either.

In his head, the memory of what he'd done kept repeating, like an old scratched LP that skipped. He'd grasped her face, pulled her to him, and moved his hand to allow his mouth to meet hers. He hadn't been gentle with her; he had felt her flinch as his mouth touched hers. He remembered the feel of her as she squirmed against him. He took a deep breath and made an effort to relax, to rid his memory of her perfume. Was it perfume or her natural fragrance? Either way, the light floral aroma still penetrated his nose, as it had on the street. Her scent had crept inside him, had flowed deep into his mind, along with the underlying acrid aroma of her fear. And then conflicting colors of black, pale-yellow, and deep-red shadows had flashed across his vision. A sudden throbbing had stung his eyes as if in warning, as if he'd had a seizure, but he hadn't. Though he'd never had one before, he would know it if he had a seizure, wouldn't he?

He shut his eyes now, for an instant, as he'd done at the scene on the sidewalk. When the cops moved away he'd been locked into the woman, her breath, the foreign taste of her lips; the forgotten touch of a woman's softness. The dreamlike desire to kiss her with complete abandon had overtaken him. The memory of her lips haunted him, and the flicker came again in chaotic colors with a sickening throb in his head, and he found he couldn't breathe, just like outside the store. He remembered his difficulty in trying to breathe, and that it had taken all of his strength and training to stop kissing the woman. But he hadn't been strong enough to leave her. No, instead he'd taken her with him and committed his first real mistake in fifteen years.

9

Thain took the stairs down to the ground floor. Bell and Patterson had agreed that he'd start in on helping review the CCTV footage, as per the chief's orders, but they knew to call him if anything came up that he needed to be aware of. His phone vibrated. Already? He pulled it out, saw Rae's name. "Rae," he said.

"Thain, the Flying Squad rang. They've apprehended all but two of the robbers from the heist."

"Two, with or without the seventh man?"

"With."

So, if I'm right, they have all but one robber, he thought. "Can you call Martin or Smyth and let them know? They're on HOLMES duty right now. And, Rae, thanks."

"I've already told them. I'm up here helping with the sudden rush of phone calls."

"Bloody hell, that was fast."

"You're still leaving?"

"I'm supposed to be viewing the CCTV footage."

"Can't that wait? The phones are going ballistic. We're calling the rest of the team in to help."

"Rae, the films," he began, striding for the door.

"Let St. John view the footage alone for now. Thain, we need manpower here. The crazies have come out in full force this afternoon. Besides, you're the one who said St. John was so good. And if that still doesn't convince you, Hawthorne said no exceptions."

"Right," he replied with reluctance. "I'm on my way." He hung up and rang St. John Abney. "Won't make it over yet, Abney. Proceed without me and I'll be there when I can break away from the phones."

"No rush, sir. Better you than me. Thanks, by the way, for asking for me on this one."

"No thanks necessary. We need the best. And call me Thain, please."

Back in the murder room, he had no time to think about anything but taking phone statements. Twenty of the twenty-nine-person murder squad answered the calls, and it took an hour before the flow began to ease. At least it wasn't boring work. Even if eighty percent of the leads proved false, the stories were all different. Some of the tales people came up with floored him. "I saw a man running from the bank with a bloody knife in his hand," or "One of the robbers is my son. Can you please tell him to call home?" or "The man knocked me down when I tried to stop him." Five-Minute Stars. That's what they called the ones who phoned in just for the attention it got them.

He grabbed his cell phone when it vibrated, thankful for the interruption. "Thain," he said.

"Thain, that missing person couple is here again," said Sergeant Sarah Clarke back at the MPU at West End Central.

"And what does that have to do with me?"

"They want me to make sure you get a copy of the photo of their missing friend."

Damn. He didn't want to see that photo again. "You told them I'm not on your team, right?"

"Of course."

"I'm at the Hendon on phone duty. Please explain for me."

"They won't give up. They want you to have a copy."

He rolled his eyes and sighed. "Tell them you'll give me one later."

"Hold on." He heard her muted voice as she covered the receiver and relayed his message. "They said they want to talk to you."

"What? Right now, on the phone?"

"Yes."

He hesitated. What could it hurt? Doing his police officer's duty and all that. "Put Mr. King on, please, Sergeant."

"Detective Thain?"

"Yes. How can I help you, Mr. King?"

"Isn't there something we can do, answer questions or anything?"

"I'm sure Sergeant Clarke has explained how the process works," he said, trying not to sound rude or impatient, but wanting to finish with the phones so he could get over to St. John. He didn't have time to hold anyone's hand right now. "Please, allow her to do her job. I'm sure she told you that you'll be informed as soon as something is discovered."

"Has he found anything yet?" Mrs. King asked from somewhere in the background.

Thain checked his watch. "Less than three hours have passed, Mr. King, since you and your wife gave your report. I'm sure you were told this afternoon this would take some time, and that I'm not working on your case. Please, I'm sure Sergeant Clarke can ring you tomorrow and let you know if there is anything new to report, all right?" He spoke shortly and to the point, impatient to get back to his real work.

"I guess that will have to do, Detective. But we would like you to have a copy of the photograph as well, just in case."

"Why, Mr. King? I can't do anything more than the MPU is already doing. They're trained professionals."

"So are you." Mr. King paused and Thain sensed his hesitation. "Perhaps because in spite of the fact we should have gone to the American Embassy first, you were willing to, to help us."

"Pardon? What does the American Embassy have to do with your missing person?" Thain almost bit his tongue. Curiosity always got the better of him.

"Oh right. I'd forgotten you'd already left us by then. Detective, our missing friend, Celia Wight, is an American."

"I see."

"Detective Thain. I know it sounds foolish, and I really can't explain why, but I, my wife and I, we would feel better knowing you had a copy as well, if you don't mind."

Now he felt guilty, and rightly so. What did it matter? If it made the Kings feel better, why should he deny them what comfort they could find in this situation? "Of course I don't mind, Mr. King. We all do what we can to help, I'm sure."

An hour later a delivery arrived with a large envelope. On the phone with yet another supposed witness, he raised his brow and motioned to the young constable to leave it on the desk beside his computer. After he finished the call and hung up, glad for a respite, he picked up the envelope, but paused. Celia Wight was American. That was a twist he hadn't foreseen. He peeled back the flap to pull the photo out, and then decided against it. He didn't want to see those eyes again, no matter how much they called to him. He didn't want to feel what those eyes had done to him with that first fleeting look, much less remember. He stuffed the envelope into the drawer of his desk and reached, yet again, to answer the ringing phone.

Later, he rang Sergeant Clarke. "Sergeant."

"I prefer Clarke."

"Clarke, what did you think of the Kings? The couple with the missing American friend?"

"They seem nice. Worried, but nice. She's a writer, the missing American I mean."

"Why do you think they wanted me to have a copy of the photograph?"

"I don't know. I told them as well, you aren't on the Missing Persons Unit, but they insisted. You must have impressed them."

Was that sarcasm he heard? "Are you laughing at me, Clarke?"

"In this line of work, one always needs a sense of humor, Detective. I've been told you don't have much of one. Thought I'd see if that was only a rumor." Clarke chuckled at the other end of the line.

"No, I guess not. And if I'm to call you Clarke, please call me Thain."

Clarke laughed outright then. Thain couldn't help it, but his mouth twitched. "I know you've something better to do than bother me, Clarke. Anything else I should know about the Kings or their missing writer?"

"Evidently she's popular over here. Writes fiction novels. I've contacted the American Embassy, which they should have done first, and requested her history."

"Sounds like you have everything well in hand."

"Too much practice."

"Yes. I guess we all get a lot of that."

He rang off, agitated for a reason he couldn't fathom, and actually felt thankful when his phone jangled again. Celia Wight. The work made it easier to forget the look in her eyes, and the not-so-subtle twist it caused inside of him.

Around seven thirty p.m. DI Hawthorne finally let him loose. Thain had done what he could, for now, with the phones and thought no more about them. Stretching, he strode over to the other building to view the footage Abney probably now knew by heart. Though it wasn't always necessary to view the footage himself, Thain preferred to whenever possible on the cases he worked. Plus, on this one, the chief wanted him to. It was no accident that he'd requested St. John to be the main reviewer. St. John's sharp eyes were legendary. Wasn't much he'd miss, if there was anything to find. Everyone who'd ever worked with him knew his ability. Thain turned a corner, his steps echoing down the long corridor. Just because an American had gone missing didn't mean the chief would condone any slacking on finding the murder suspect. Thain blinked. Why would he even think of her right now? She wasn't his problem.

Entering the lift, Thain pressed the button for the correct floor. As the doors closed he looked up at the ceiling, out of habit, and without permission, his thoughts darted back, as if eager, to the startling eyes in the photograph. Her loneliness haunted him. He grimaced. Idiot. What right did he have to think in emotional terms of a woman he didn't even know? His stomach tightened enough to pull on his scar.

Closing his eyes, he shook his head as if in denial. No good dwelling on a past that couldn't be changed, or eyes that reminded him of that fact.

Wrenching his thoughts from her melancholy face, he left the lift and took corridors toward his destination. It was safer to think about, to study once again, the evidence collected from the crime scene, and Rae's information that all but two of the bank robbers had been apprehended.

The report stated seven robbers were involved, but of course he disagreed and had seen nothing yet to change his mind, much less speak it. The investigation was still too young to jump to conclusions. He'd left himself open to ridicule earlier when he'd mistakenly voiced his private theory that there had been six. Would he never learn? He remained sure that the seventh man wasn't a thief, that he was a murderer. But he didn't allow any thoughts to continue past that point, yet.

Each investigation required finding an available room for viewing CCTV footage, and so was never constantly located in the same one. However, most investigations usually ended up on the same floor and he found the assigned room without difficulty. St. John sat glued to his terminal. "Anything interesting?" Thain asked as he pulled a chair over and made himself at home next to St. John.

"Perhaps, sir," he said.

"Thain. Call me Thain."

"Yes, sir, Thain."

He noticed Abney's slight smile. "Do you want to rewind, then?"

"Already done, *Thain*. I asked them to ring me when you started over here."

Thain turned his eyes to the monitor screen. Within a sixty-second period on the film, six men dressed in dark suits entered the bank. Each face plainly visible. They'd made no effort to hide their identities until they were actually in the bank proper, not just the building itself. He made a note of that. They hadn't taken into account the CCTV cameras. Amazing. St. John went over the first footage again, while Thain took notes for the HOLMES report. The next camera followed the tall suspect described to the police by the teary-eyed secretary. According to her, the man who had tied her up and locked her away had worn a dark Burberry coat, glasses, and a brimmed hat. The man the camera now followed on the screen matched her description as he left the bank and headed up the street to the left of the building.

They lost him when the man turned the corner and moved out of range of the camera. "Do you have footage of him going into the bank?"

"Yes. But didn't think you'd need to see that."

"Well he certainly didn't go in with the others. How far in advance was he?"

"About seven to ten minutes?"

"Show me."

St. John made a few key strokes and brought up what Thain asked for.

"Seven minutes exactly. Now get the footage farther up the street."

St. John punched in the command. "Here it is." They let the footage run, watching every frame until St. John slowed it at one point. "There, isn't that the same person?" He pointed to the man on the screen. "It is," he said, answering his own question.

"The coat's different, but the walk isn't, and neither is the hat," Thain said. "Must have a reversible Burberry, and he changed it when no cameras caught him doing so. Our suspect knows where the cameras are."

"Every one of them, it seems, on this route and at the bank," St. John said.

"That means careful planning. If this man knew the locations of all the cameras, and the thieves didn't care about them, that fact right there sets him apart."

"He still could be—"

"He isn't dressed like them either. But that isn't the proof I need."

"What do you need proof of?" St. John asked, glancing at Thain.

"What I just said. That this man isn't one of the bank robbers."

St. John keyed in a new code and started the next film in the sequence. They searched the sidewalks for the man in the reversed Burberry and brimmed hat. He had to be there, but where?

10

Celia opened her eyes because she smelled him. No soap, no cologne, nothing artificial. He smelled human—light, clean human, almost no scent at all. She would never forget his scent even if he gave her time to. He went over the entire apartment, wiped down every surface they might have touched, before saying, "We must go."

Celia struggled to sit up. "Where? What time is it?"

He bent down, untied her legs, and pulled her out of the recliner. He untied her hands. "Go and get washed."

It was useless to repeat her question. It seemed he only answered when he felt like it. At least he hadn't tried to touch her, yet.

Celia finished in the bathroom as best she could without a toothbrush, and rounded the corner at the same time he did. Spotting the knife sheath beneath his open coat, she pulled back as if stung. She glanced from the knife to his face, wanted to ask why they had to leave in the middle of the night, but one look from his sharp eyes stopped her. She'd never seen a clearer display of determination. He made her stand in the shower stall with her arms folded in front of her while he cleaned the bathroom.

How could she convince him to let her go? Surely, if he'd meant to kill her he would have already. She wouldn't think about what else he might have in mind. Maybe he wanted to take her somewhere else to do the deed.

"Someone's bound to recognize me . . . eventually. If you let me go, I promise I won't tell anyone—"

"I didn't take you for a liar."

"You don't know me to take me for anything."

"You could tell them enough to make my life difficult."

"Like you've made mine?"

The danger in his eyes seemed to crouch, as if some wild cat trapped inside him shone through his eyes, sleek and fit, ready to spring forth into action. An animal like that didn't belong in a city. He motioned for her to leave the bathroom. He stood by, watching as she pulled on her gloves. He headed for the door as she turned toward her bags, the ones holding her purse and the gifts she'd bought for Eva and Philip. His rough grip on her coat sleeve stopped her.

"What are you doing?" he said.

"I'm getting my bags."

He nodded.

After he'd checked to make sure no one was about, they walked down the carpeted stairs. On the second floor, Celia pretended to fall again, to stop him, to make him let her go, but he jerked her up from the landing. His eyes said it first, then his mouth: "Don't do that again."

She didn't know why his eyes always spoke volumes, so much more than his actual words. He avoided the front door this time, and instead took the hall leading to the back of the house, which landed them in a dark backyard. No lights shone there.

Celia tried once more. "Let me go. Please, I don't even know your name."

"You know something much more important."

Tempting fate, she said, "Then why haven't you killed me? I'm nothing but a liability to you."

He opened a gate in the fence and they stepped into the wet street. The puddles reflected the streetlights and made it easy to avoid them. He didn't speak to her until later, when he turned into a murky alley and halted in front of a group of rubbish bins.

"Put your bags in the bins."

"No! Please—"

Those eyes turned on her for an instant, silencing her, and through her jumbled mind passed the insane thought that she'd never again write a hero with blue eyes.

"One of those in the middle," he said. Pressed to his side, she took the lid off a bin and pushed her bags inside. Before she could argue, he dragged her away and into the street. Celia took a sad look at her last link with her old life, her old reality.

"I still don't understand what good I can be to you?"

"They won't try to kill me as long as you're alive."

"How do you know they know you have me?"

"Cameras. There are hundreds of thousands of them in London."

"So they know I've been kidnapped?"

"By now they are sure to."

"But they don't know I'm still alive?"

"No. They will when they find your bags."

"But why would you want them to know?"

He stopped and turned to look at her. He pursed his lips as if what he had to tell her came hard to him. "I made a mistake. I have to fix it."

"Taking me?"

"No."

"What mistake then?"

"Enough." He put his arm around her and made her do the same to him before they disappeared into the night.

Through the misty darkness a city light would wink every so often, as they moved in a steadfast, businesslike way. Sometimes they passed other souls huddled into dirty coats, and Celia would catch a glimpse of a world-weary face under a ragged cap. She shrunk inside, a little, at the toll a harsh life had taken upon such spirits. She'd spent half her life alone, but had to admit that though she knew intimately the depth of their solitude, she still, even now, held hope of escape close in her heart. For some of these people, hope was a forgotten dream.

Her abductor deigned to take the tube, once. He continued to run them in what seemed like circles until dawn, and she saw no reason in his actions. Why wasn't he trying to leave the city? Surely, with the sun rising, someone would spot her with him. Surely, then, the police would catch them. At a little all-night store, with her by his side, he bought small bottles of ammonia and bleach, more thick tape, paper napkins, disposable cups, a small bottle of shampoo, and two thin bath towels.

The rising sun silhouetted the buildings in the mists as they climbed a short flight of steps to a large, old mansion evidently converted to flats. He inserted a key in the front door lock and entered, checking the doors on each side as they walked down the dim cavern of a hall leading deep into the house. He kept her in front of him until they reached a set of descending stairs. At his silent urging, Celia took tentative steps down into a gloomy basement. He guided her through shadows to a nondescript door, which he opened with a key.

Her new home was a cold, lightless one-room flat with a tiny opaque window near the ceiling on one wall, barred of course. It fit her mood: stark white walls with the type of dark wooden bed and dull green tables and chairs that could be found at any cheap furniture store. It smelled dank and musty. There was nothing to indicate who lived there because no one did. And though the first apartment had been much nicer, Celia realized it felt just as cold, just as empty and unloved.

Once the stranger had put the things he'd bought on the table and turned on the radiator, he pushed Celia toward a chair.

"No, not again!" She skittered away. "Please."

He caught her in the corner near the door, but she strained against him, made him work to pin her to the side of the small refrigerator behind her.

"Don't tie me up again."

"Do you want to eat?"

"I'll scream." She squirmed in his grip.

He tightened his hold on her. "No, you won't."

With his face inches from hers, she succumbed again to the cold of his steely eyes. Their chill coursed through her like a physical thing, freezing her will, freezing her bruised sense of survival. The emptiness of her stomach chose that bitter moment to take its toll.

"Why didn't we buy food while we were walking?"

He didn't answer. Celia sagged against the fridge. He pushed her over to the chair and shoved her down. She slumped like a limp rag doll while he pulled her right arm over the low back of the chair and her left under it. With the tape from the bag, he wrapped her wrists together and taped her ankles to the front legs of the chair. It was an awkward position, causing her to lean to one side. If she fell over, not only might she hurt herself but there would be nowhere to go.

He tore one last piece of tape from the roll. She shook her head. "Please, no, I swear I won't—"

He seized her head, held it still, and taped her mouth shut. She tried not to weep because then her nose would be blocked and she wouldn't be able to breathe. She blinked rapidly and kept the tears back by thinking that if he talked of food, he meant to keep her alive. There was always hope if she was alive, wasn't there? But hope for what? He left her alone, bound and gagged, with the silent hanging light for company.

After he'd gone, Celia strained to hear anything, hoping there would be someone in the hall, someone outside by the window. There was nothing to hear but the normal creaks and groans of an old building. No soundproofing here. Who needed soundproofing in a basement? She kept blinking. She couldn't afford to cry.

Eva and Philip deemed hers a sad and lonely definition of a life, but it had been hers, safe and uncomplicated. Accustomed to seclusion after her parents' deaths, sometimes she even enjoyed it, but not now, not like this. She hated this eerie stillness, broken only by the sound of her own tortured breath.

She couldn't shake the thought, running circles in her head, that this was what she got for writing books and making the world aware of her existence.

11

Random song lyrics about time played in his head while Thain sat through the next set of films with mind-numbing attention. It was late, but he viewed with a slow yet careful precision. That's how St. John did it. That's why he'd requested the PC. Darkness had fallen outside long ago and their brought-in dinner sat like a greasy lump in his stomach. They both saw the man at the same time, but St. John recognized him and pointed first.

"This looks like the same guy. Thain, what do you think?"

Thain leaned in closer.

St. John continued, "It looks like you were right about him changing his coat. See what I see?"

"Possibly. He doesn't have a hat on," Thain said.

"But look at his walk."

"Yes. I see what you—what's he doing?"

They watched the man thread his way through a dense crowd in front of a department store. He slipped up to what looked like a young woman hemmed in by the crowd. She looked harried and a bit confused as the mass of people propelled her along.

"Can't be our man if he's with that woman," St. John said.

"Is she with him?" Thain took a deep breath and held it. *It couldn't be* . . . "Where's this footage from, St. John?"

"Liberty, front entrance."

Liberty. Liberty was a few blocks west of the bank and close enough to be more than noteworthy. "I think I need that photograph."

"What photograph?"

"Mm. A photograph of a missing writer."

"What does she have to do with the films?" St. John looked truly puzzled, of course. Thain explained about the Kings and their missing person.

"Well, what did you do with the photograph?" he asked.

"I put it in a desk drawer in the murder squad room." Thain jumped to his feet. "I'll see if I can get Rae to bring it to us, if she's still there."

"Where else would she go? Chief said we're all on until this is finished."

"Out following a lead? I don't know." He pulled his cell out of his jacket pocket and called Rae Bell. She answered on the first ring. "Rae, are you still here at the Hendon?"

"Hello to you too."

He could almost hear her frowning, and he certainly heard a chair squeak. "Sorry, can you do a favor for me?"

"Depends on what kind of favor?"

"I need a photograph that Sergeant Clarke from MPU sent to me earlier today. I left it in the desk drawer where I answered phones in the murder room."

"Now?"

"Now, please?" Thain squinted, hoping she'd say yes.

"That's better. I guess I could use some exercise."

"You are absolutely mint."

"Of course."

A drawer opened. He heard some paper shuffling as she found and opened the envelope.

"Who is this?" she said.

"A missing person. An American writer."

"Got something on her?"

"Are you walking as you talk?"

"Stupid question. Answer mine."

"I might, and it might have to do with our murder."

"I'm hurrying now."

"Thank you, Rae."

He started to hang up, but she said, "What's the rush?"

Thain remembered to be nice to the one person who was unfailingly nice to him. "You'll walk faster, maybe even run, if you aren't talking on your phone?"

"Right. Signing off," and she was gone. Her curiosity would give her wings.

He forced his mind to clarify, to calm down, to think of one problem at a time as they waited for Rae. He no longer considered his wild hypothesis of the Wraith being involved as a valid line of inquiry. Their suspect couldn't be the Wraith. The Wraith would never kidnap anyone. Still, Thain couldn't afford to be wrong. He'd have to check all possibilities. If the murderer wasn't the Wraith, then Celia Wight was probably dead. Because while the man he'd studied never killed innocent people, most assassins were notorious for it. This was one of the many things that set his assassin apart in the field of dealing death. But was Celia Wight as innocent as the Kings believed? A sudden vision of her eyes unsettled him.

Concentrate, Alban.

Ten minutes later Rae burst through the door. For such a small person she could stir the air in a room like a storm. "Hello, St. John," she said. "All right, Thain, what's this about?"

"The photo?" He reached out and took the envelope she offered to him. Easing back into his seat, he propped the black-and-white up by St. John's screen. He'd purposely avoided thinking about it until he'd seen the footage outside of Liberty. He'd been relieved to be rid of it when he'd tucked it in the desk drawer in the squad room, relieved because he'd been nice to the Kings and done what they'd asked. Accepting the photo had meant he could try to forget it, to forget her. Now, gazing at the photo again, the woman in the black-and-white dominated the room as fully as Rae did, and she wasn't even in it. He could seriously lose his logical, impersonal interpretation of life within the very personal distress peering out from behind her eyes. Celia Wight's eyes. The eyes of a woman he had never heard of before today.

St. John picked up the photo. "This the missing American, is it?"

"Hmm." Thain glanced at St. John to see his reaction to her. He didn't like it when St. John also gawked.

"She's beautiful, but she looks so sad," Rae said. "She's a writer?"

"Yes." He tapped St. John on the shoulder. St. John blinked as if he'd just woken up. He knew exactly how St. John felt. "Come on. Let's get back to Liberty. Run the film from the beginning. Tell me what you see."

St. John fast-forwarded through yesterday's early morning images of Liberty storefront, cold and hard in the steady light of a snow-cloudy day. Celia Wight's eyes drew his back to stare at the photo beside the monitor. He couldn't tell their color, but they were lighter than brown, perhaps blue or green. They seemed like beacons of loneliness signaling to him. As if a siren's entreaty from the sea, her eyes reached out, touched him so thoroughly again that he shut his own against their plea. *Agatha* . . . When his lids flickered open he avoided her gaze even as he made the effort to memorize her carefully neutral face. Even so posed a black-and-white photograph couldn't mask her consciousness that life had thrown one too many bricks through her windows. Agatha had worn this same look after . . .

In his work he'd seen such effects too often, but not one had ever impinged upon him the way Celia Wight's did. It was as if this woman had read his soul, discovered a match with hers, and cried for him to rescue her from her killing loneliness. A loneliness he knew too well.

He jerked his attention back to the video. "Slow down, St. John, you're going too fast," he said.

St. John slowed the footage until the clock on the film showed right after nine thirty a.m. then let it run normally.

Rae leaned in. "Is she in the footage?"

"You tell me," Thain replied.

The three of them concentrated on the crowd, trying to spot the woman with haunted eyes. Shoppers milled about, ever changing, never still, in and out of the store. Time clicked off on the clock and he narrowed his focus, alert to every movement, every nuance of shadow on the film.

He stopped himself from pointing at Celia Wight as she came out of Liberty around ten forty-five, pushing the door open with her elbow because her hands were loaded with shopping bags. She stood amongst the throng as if uncertain for a moment, and then hesitantly edged her way through the thick crowd. Heads turned in the direction the bank would be in, as if hearing a commotion down the street. Caught up in the mass of people, she too turned to look toward the evident sound.

"She's definitely your American," St. John said. "And there's our man." St. John pointed to the now familiar figure wearing a Burberry coat slipping through the dense crowd. St. John zoomed in on the face, but again the man kept it down and away from the cameras. Celia Wight didn't, though. She was clear to see. "I wish we could get a good shot of his face," St. John said.

I've been saying that for ten years about my guy, Thain thought, but said, "He knows the locations of all the cameras."

"The other thieves didn't care," St. John said.

"Celia Wight doesn't care about the cameras either. Look how clearly we can see her face," Rae said as if she'd read Thain's thoughts. "She doesn't seem to have any idea of being caught on camera."

Amongst the mix of people coming and going from the store, while others strained to see what was happening further down the street, the man angled toward Celia Wight, actually bumped right into her. He put his arm around her and herded her in the opposite direction of the crowd, and of the bank. Celia looked as if she'd started to protest, but the man urged her along, his arm around her, his head bent to hers in an intimate fashion.

When the police arrived and started checking through the gathering of humanity in front of the store, the man ducked into the entrance alcove, put his back against the storefront sign, and pulled Celia to him in one motion, unpretentious, unhurried, as if he did it every day, again taking trouble to make sure his face was never fully exposed. In the alcove it was hard to see them, obscured as they were, by the shadow of the overhang and the people still entering and exiting the store. He leaned in close to her, head to head, and then jerked back with a small, sharp movement, as if he'd been bitten.

"What's he doing now?" St. John leaned in closer, as did Rae and Thain.

In the dimness of the alcove, the man in the Burberry coat kissed Celia Wight.

"Whoa, look at that. Looks like she knows him all right. Maybe she's in on it with him," St. John said. "That would make it eight on the heist then."

Shaking his head, Thain couldn't understand the wrench in his psyche the kiss gave him. It was too badly lit and far away for them to get any real detail, but he would have sworn from her eyes, from the photograph, that she wouldn't actually kiss a man in public, no matter who he was. Her body language didn't say she wanted to be near him, much less kiss him. And if he still entertained the thought of this man being the Wraith, well, the Wraith for sure would never kiss in public. The Wraith never did anything in public except kill, and even then no one was ever aware of it when he did.

The man in the Burberry seemed unaware of the police officers combing the crowded sidewalk, and yet he abruptly stopped kissing Celia Wight as soon as they disappeared. He talked to her for an instant and then pulled her down the street in the opposite direction from the Royal Bank of Scotland. She stumbled, but the man righted her immediately. Thain cursed when the couple rounded the corner and the camera lost them.

"We need that lot of film round the other side of the store. We need to see which direction they went." He wanted to say that he was sure she hadn't wanted to go with him, but he didn't, not yet.

"She kissed him. Does that mean we have three to find instead of two?" St. John stared at the monitor.

Thain looked at Rae. "What do you think? Do you think she knows him? Is she in on it with him?"

Rae studied the halted image on the screen. "Could you replay from where she leaves the store, St. John?"

"Sure." St. John reversed the film and played it again. Rae paid exclusive attention to the screen, and Thain watched her. He wouldn't say what he thought until he saw and heard her responses to his questions.

St. John watched the footage, as she did. He asked, "What're you thinking, Thain? You don't sound convinced, even with the kiss."

Thain wasn't ready to volunteer what he thought. He wanted to hear what Rae would say.

She straightened and looked at him. "When she comes out of the store, she doesn't look like she's waiting for someone else. She isn't looking for anyone. It seems as if she's completely alone and unhappy about it."

Shoving both hands in his trouser pockets, Thain looked back at the frozen image on the screen as Rae continued. "I think she looks surprised when he comes up and turns her around, as if she's frightened. She reminds me of a puppy that's been kicked instead of hugged. And to me it looks as if she's arching *away* from him before he kisses her. If you want to be kissed you lean *into* it."

St. John pushed away from the edge of his desk and leaned back in his chair, his hands behind his head. "You saw all that from that distance? You should be in here helping me."

Thain asked him, "Do you really think it looked like the two of them could be together?"

"Well, you can't deny the kiss." St. John looked at Thain. "Are you going to tell the DIs?"

"Of course, but I want to check something first," he said. He didn't bother contradicting St. John about the kiss or how "together" the two might look. Why should he? He had no proof of anything.

"In the meantime," he continued, "we need to get someone out there looking for the missing hat, somewhere between the bank and Liberty." Thain called Clive Patterson and told him what they had found so far. Next he called Greene. "Can you put in a call to action to find a missing hat? Yes, we'll send over the footage. The description should be in the secretary's statement. Can you take care of it? Right. Good. Thanks."

"Feel like staying, Rae?" He asked as he sat down and St. John set up another film.

"Yes, I think I do. This is more interesting than I thought it would be."

As more footage spilled across the monitor, Thain glared at it. In spite of the seeming evidence, his brain wouldn't let go of the Wraith. Maybe he really had studied the Wraith too long. Questions kept circling, like buzzards over carrion: If the man on the video was the Wraith, why had he made such a blatant mistake? And if he wasn't the Wraith, how could Thain convince the chief that the man on the video wasn't a bank robber? Did he believe the man on the video could be the Wraith? Well, maybe he couldn't prove who the man on the video was, but it might be possible to prove he wasn't one of the bank robbers. Thain was good at finding proof, normally. That skill had saved him—and what reputation he still had—from Carter in a big way. Not to mention his former position in Scotland and at Interpol. They'd let him go, but not because of his performance. No, they'd objected to his obsession, and here he was thinking again about a man who everyone said didn't exist.

"I've ordered what footage we can get north of the store," St. John said.

"And east, and between the bank and the store?" Rae asked.

"Doing it now."

"Right. We need to look for the change of coat and anyone losing a hat," Thain said, making a note on his phone.

St. John said, "Yes, and between the bank and Liberty, that's not too far a distance to cover. But there're a number of different streets he could have taken."

"I know, St. John, I know."

Half an hour later, when St. John said "They've disappeared," the three admitted defeat. No film from any entrance to the store showed anything more of Celia Wight or the man in the Burberry coat. The detectives had reached a dead end until more footage came in from farther out.

"Should you go and tell the DIs now?" St. John steepled his fingers in front of his face, his elbows resting on the chair arms as he leaned back.

Thain shook his head and glanced at the constable and then at Rae. "First, let's see if we can at least get what direction he chose. It will give us something more than a puzzle to offer to the DIs or the chief. I'll go and have this entered on HOLMES." He stood up and stretched, ready for some tea. "Send the film over to the HOLMES team, right?"

"Already done," St. John said.

Thain picked up his jacket and shrugged it on, straightening the collar. "I'll see you later. Let me know as soon as more footage comes in, will you?"

St. John responded, "Of course."

"Rae, you staying?"

"Yes." She took his chair, which was closer to St. John's screen. Heading out the door, Thain took two steps down the hall and inhaled a sharp deep breath as his brain swam up and out of foggy fatigue and into the depths of Celia Wight's eyes. He needed to find out more about her; if she turned out to be an accomplice, this case would play out on a completely different scale, an international one. And if she wasn't and the murder suspect was the Wraith, which he still hesitated to believe or deny, then the Wraith had made his first mistake ever.

But if he wasn't the Wraith . . . A straight shot of fear bolted through his chest at the thought. If the suspect wasn't the Wraith, Celia Wight in all probability was dead by now. Thain stood stone still in the hall, surprised, blanketed by a thick sense of loss, then anger at himself. He buttoned his jacket and continued down the corridor, knowing that if Rae could see him she'd tell him to stop scowling. But he now had a reason, beyond his own ego, to hope that the man in the video turned out to be the Wraith. Out loud, he said to no one there, "If it is you, my man, you've made a big mistake. And maybe, just maybe, this time I'll catch you."

12

A soft bump on the door announced her kidnapper's return and put a sharp end to Celia's bout of self-pity. He set down the bags in his hands and tore the tape from her mouth. Then he freed her hands and legs. With numb fingers Celia struggled to cover her lips so as not to cry out from the stinging burn left in place of the tape. When she rose from the seat, her legs wouldn't work; they'd lost circulation from sitting too long. He caught her as she fell.

"Don't touch me!" The words stuck to her dry tongue, parched from the lack of movement. Her arms didn't work either as she strived to push him away.

Ignoring her feeble attempts, he picked her up and carried her into the bathroom. He sat her down on the toilet and peeled off her coat before shutting the door behind him. He hadn't said one word. The quiet sounds of him taking food out of bags and setting it on the table made her stomach growl. She cursed it for siding with him. She peed, and knew it was the only good thing that had happened since her abduction. She washed her trembling hands and pale, blotchy face. A nice stinging red rectangle surrounded her mouth.

Celia opened the door and wobbled out on unsteady feet, rubbing her arms. She was cold, and her arms and legs still tingled with pin-pricks of recirculation. But an enticing scent of hot roasted chicken wafted from a takeout box and her discomfort took a backseat. Her abductor chose to eat on the bed, holding his takeout container in front of him as he had before. Celia wondered what he had against eating with her. Then she wondered why she wondered at all about anything to do with him.

She sat at the table under the one light hanging from the ceiling and devoured everything. She hadn't eaten last night, and she'd had but toast and tea before she went shopping the day before, and that she'd thrown up.

Celia froze. What time was it? She glanced at the opaque window. Light still shone outside. Had only one day, one night passed so far? Maybe not even a full twenty-four hours, if it was before noon. Still, she felt as if a lifetime had come and gone. As if the life she carefully nurtured were already buried so deep even her memories were hard to come by. She bit her lip. She wouldn't have any memories if she didn't escape. As if reading her mind again, as he had on the stairs, the stranger looked at her, his narrowed eyes evaporating her thoughts.

Celia stood up and threw her container in the trash. She knew he watched her, probably waiting to see if she made a dash for the door. As if that would do any good. At the tiny sink in the tiny wall that served for a kitchen, she kept her back to him as she searched for something to drink from, found a plastic cup, and drank water so fast she almost choked on it, thirsty as if she'd been in a desert for a year. Water. It was a small enough diversion, but she clung to it. She dreamed of a shower or bath, didn't care which. She wanted to be clean.

"Go take a shower. Lock the door if it makes you feel better."

Celia turned around to face him. "No. I won't take a shower. I won't make it easy for you." It shook her that he'd guessed her thoughts yet again. What was he, an evil sorcerer?

"What if I promised I won't touch you?" His eyes seemed to mock her.

"I don't believe you. Why else did you kidnap me?"

He stood and moved right in front of her. She backed up until she hit the small kitchen counter, but he followed her, his back to the single source of light and his eyes in shadow. "This is the second day you haven't bathed. Neither have I. Do you want to start reeking?"

"No."

"Take a shower. I won't touch you." He turned from her so fast she blinked. He moved silently over to one of the bags he'd brought in. When he came back, he held out some clothing to her. "Take these."

She rifled through the pile. They were brand-new, and for a woman.

She didn't say anything, but kept him in sight as she moved past him and into the bathroom. She locked the door behind her though she couldn't be in any more danger than she was already.

Behind the opaque shower curtain, warm water cascaded over her body and soothed her, but she didn't relax. Celia ran the hot water as long as she dared. She washed her hair twice. Using the shampoo as soap, she lathered up quickly. Her fingers slipped over the new puncture wound on her back. She couldn't see it, but it stung under the hot water. It felt fairly superficial, and she guessed about half an inch long; a cut that size would heal with minimal scarring. Her back would be smooth and normal in no time, if she lived long enough—if that was all he did to her. Why had he bought her new clothes? Finished, she shut the water off and pulled the curtain back.

The two thin towels he'd bought rested on the edge of the sink. She wanted to use both of them but didn't want to give the man any excuse to come out naked and air-dry in front of her, as a prelude. Shuddering, Celia used only one.

Once dry, she pulled on the clothes he'd bought for her. She almost smiled with relief when she found a maroon turtleneck. She only ever wore turtlenecks—with or without sleeves.

Celia flopped down on the lid of the toilet and put her hand over her mouth as she began to laugh at herself, riding the edge of hysteria. She was worried about a shirt.

Collecting herself, she stood up and brushed her teeth with the brand-new brush and paste she found by the sink. She rinsed, and thought again about why he'd bought new clothes for her. Of course. She'd last been seen in her old ones. Evidently he didn't go for complicated disguises, only constant change. At least the new clothes indicated she would live for another day. Grudging the fact that he'd gotten her sizes right, she ignored it as she opened the door and braved the next step with him.

He'd cleaned up the food, thrown away containers and cups, and wiped the table spotless. He motioned for her to sit, and he taped her to the chair. She didn't fight this time. She was too tired.

When he came out of the bathroom, later, he wore nothing but the towel she'd left him. His upper body glistened with humidity. She stared at him, neck to feet, at his trim, muscled shape. Not for him to have the bulging muscles of a bodybuilder. He looked sleek, like the forest animal he made her think of with those eyes. She expected him to crouch or slink, like a jungle cat. The slick beauty of his body shocked her for more reasons than she could admit. Even the myriad scars crisscrossing his torso and arms did not detract from it.

She looked up. That's when she realized he was staring back at her. And his eyes weren't angry this time. They were hungry.

13

Thain, feeling no more refreshed than when he'd gone back to his flat around three a.m. to get a cup of real coffee, a shower, and a quick change of clothes, came through the front door of West End Central. He'd called Clive in transit to tell him he was on his way to the Missing Persons Unit, then St. John to see if anything new had come in on the CCTV footage they'd requested.

"I'll head over after I check in here with the MPU, and finish an interview with Philip King I've set up as well," he told the constable after hearing that new footage had, indeed, arrived.

He headed up to the next floor to talk to MPU about the clip St. John had sent them last night showing Celia Wight and the suspect. After Sergeant Clarke confirmed MPU had received the film, Thain asked her if anything of importance had surfaced during the background check the MPU routinely applied for, or if anything had come in from the US embassy.

"Looks like her parents were with the American embassy." Sarah Clarke said. "Celia Wight's profile reads, well . . . here, take a look yourself." The Sergeant looked uncomfortable. "You can sit at the desk just there if you want to. I'll be over here."

He should have paid more attention to Clarke's discomfort. He took a seat at the desk she offered and began to read the report. Celia Wight, date of birth, age twenty-six, address in the US—Atlanta, Georgia—phone, schooling, university graduate. Then it mentioned her parents, Edmond and Suzanne Wight. Suzanne Wight had served as a US ambassador from the mid 1990s until she and her husband died in a car accident in South Africa thirteen years ago. Celia was thirteen at the time.

He always endeavored to prepare himself for the unexpected. As a detective, one always tried to keep an open mind. But the tragic story in the folder shook him. No way could he have predicted what Celia Wight had lived through. Not only had she lost her parents at a young age, but she'd had another, even more profound blow to deal with—alone—three years after her parents' deaths. At the age of sixteen Celia Wight had been raped, at knifepoint. She carried not only emotional scars but evidently multiple physical scars as well. He closed his eyes and thought of hers—how they spoke to him, how he heard what they said—and now he knew why. Unconsciously rubbing the scar on his abdomen, he made himself finish the file. Within the tragedy of her life, he searched for a link between her and the man who had walked away with her. He couldn't find one.

"Do you mind if I do some research myself?" he asked Sergeant Clarke, sitting on the other side of the room. He stood and handed the file back to her.

"You found the footage and kept us in the loop, so go ahead. Just remember to continue the way you've started. We need all the help we can get. Would be nice if we could crack this before the Kidnapping Squad steps in." Clarke winked at him but didn't smile.

"They do think this could be a kidnapping, then?"

"Yes, but haven't officially announced yet."

"Right. They will soon, though, now they have the film."

"Yes."

"Have you received any ransom calls?"

"None. We have phones set up, but nothing has come in."

"I'll see what else I can find on the death of her parents. Maybe there is something else there that ties her to the murder suspect."

"We're on that as well but, as I said, we won't turn down help."

"About that, I've called Philip King in to ask him some more personal questions about Celia Wight. The background I just read will help, but there is more. Would you like to be in on the interview?"

"Yes, of course."

"Right, then, come on. He should be arriving shortly."

14

He knew it was wrong, but once he saw the woman's cheeks flush with indignation, he couldn't take his eyes off of her. Her look was a muddle of embarrassment, fear, and defiance. Her eyes glimmered, damning him for catching her staring at him. He admired her defiance in the face of the hopelessness she must feel. She was brave. Bravery could get her killed.

The woman, with unconscious appeal, bit her lower lip. The movement triggered him back to his senses. He grabbed the bag off the table and retreated to the bathroom to dress. He didn't know why he shut the door, but he did. He pulled out a pair of jeans, some underwear, socks, and a crewneck shirt, all brand-new, still tagged. He heard the woman sniff in the other room. Ignoring the sound, he ripped off the clothing tags, buttoned his jeans, and pulled the crewneck over his head and shoulders. He jerked the sleeves halfway up his arms and buckled on his light yet snug leather knife sheath. Then he bent down and picked up from the bathroom floor every minute bit of plastic or paper from the tags.

He never kept anything in the lodgings he used so infrequently, never left anything behind that could point to him, even if no one knew he existed. No fingerprints or toe prints would be found; acid, carefully applied a long time ago, had left the pads of his fingers and toes smooth and therefore untraceable. His short hair also left less evidence. He made a habit of paying attention to details.

He pulled his socks on, returned to the main room, threw the clothing tags into the bag of trash, and crossed the short distance to the chair where the woman sat. When he released her, she didn't say a word. She stood rubbing her wrists and mouth, as far away from him as she could get in the small flat. Her wary gaze followed him like radar. He moved over to his coat and emptied the pockets, the contents of which included the British passport he carried for this mission.

"What's your name?" the woman asked.

He glanced at her. Her short, dark, damp hair was a mess, but her face was less red than before. "Here." He threw the passport on the table and went to the kitchen area. He sensed rather than saw her move over to the table. He knew without looking that she'd picked up the passport, was sure she would open it.

"This isn't your real name, is it?"

"Of course not." He fumbled with the cold-water knob in the sink.

"So what do I call you?"

He turned around then. She cowered under his glare. "Do you think you'll be alive long enough for me to need a name?" Her body shook visibly now. "Call me that one." He nodded at the passport in her hands.

"But it isn't real."

"Neither am I."

"You're too real to me!" She threw the passport at him and ran to the door, hurled herself against it screaming for help, pulling at the handle, scratching and pounding. He crossed the small room and yanked her back from the door, his hand clamped over her mouth before she could draw another breath.

She thrashed, kicked, and scratched anything she could touch. He held her as she edged off the cliff of panic and fell right into hysteria. She bit at his hand, but he moved it. She scratched his forearms with her nails, and drew blood. That was not good. None of his blood could be left anywhere, certainly not under her nails. Her action cleared his mind. This he could do something about. He picked her up and carried her to the tiny kitchen, grabbing napkins and tape on the way. He gagged her, which wasn't easy as she fought like a madwoman. But she froze when he turned on the hot water in the sink and held her hands under the spray, working them with soap, scraping under her thankfully short nails with his own. She moaned, keening as her fingers turned red under the blistering water.

He didn't feel the heat. The longer he held her there the stiffer her body grew and she started to hyperventilate. "Breathe, now," he said. "Slowly." She tried, but couldn't control it. He shut the water off and dried her hands, which would be tender but not permanently affected. He pulled out the small bottle of ammonia he'd bought and doused her hands with it, making sure it went under her nails. After washing her hands again, he carried her over and laid her on the bed. As he peeled the tape off her mouth, her eyes accused him, stark and frightened. Then she curled up, grabbing a pillow he had never touched and hugging it like a shield. She didn't cry. She stared at him, sucking in breath as if she'd run a marathon.

He spent five seconds making sure he hadn't bled on anything, and then cleaned his arm before lowering his sleeve to cover the superficial scratches. She still stared. He strode across the room and grabbed her up off the bed.

"No no no!" she cried.

He shook her squirming body. "Stop staring at me."

She ceased all movement. Then she slapped his face so hard it stung. "You bastard," she screamed. "Help, somebody help me!"

He couldn't afford for her to make that much noise or draw more blood. He threw her back onto the bed and pinned her there with his own body, one hand over her mouth, one holding her right arm in a tight grip. Her face crumpled in pain until he saw her left arm trapped beneath them and lifted her.

With both her hands now trapped over her head, her face was inches from his. Her eyes shone a bolder shade of blue than his, her dark lashes thick, and her skin glowed rosy white, where it wasn't red from fighting him.

"Don't scream again."

Slowly, she raised her eyes to his, and he lifted his hand from her mouth and brought her arms down, still entrapped, but now by her sides.

She sucked in air as if she'd been suffocated, her body heaving with effort beneath him.

"I—can't—breathe."

He eased up a little at the fear in her eyes. "Slow down. Slowly, breathe slowly."

"I—I can't."

"Yes you can. Slowly, there. That's better."

Once her breathing slowed, she started to whimper. "Why, why are you doing this?"

"I'm not going to answer that question again."

"You could be gone by now. Why are you still here?"

"Why did you kiss me?"

"You kissed me. I didn't kiss you."

"You returned it."

"You had a knife at my back."

"Yet you bit me."

Her breathing slowed. "You aren't angry now," she said.

"No."

"Your eyes are warmer when you aren't angry."

Their gaze held. He could feel her breath on his lips.

She didn't make a sound when silent tears began to fall, obliterating the inner conflict he'd recognized in her face. "Stop," she said, her voice rising. "Stop, stop."

He let her loose and leapt off the bed as if she'd burned him. She curled into a small trembling ball. He stood staring at her. Unnecessarily rough, he grabbed her up from the bed and bound her to the chair by the table. She didn't resist. He couldn't look at her, couldn't watch her cry anymore. He didn't slam the door as he left. He just got the hell out of there.

15

Downstairs Thain and Clarke found Philip King already waiting. Thain had called him last night and asked him to come in to answer more questions, and to inform him that they'd actually "found" his missing writer. He hadn't as yet told King about her "possible" kidnapping.

"Mr. King, I'm glad you could come in early. I'm sure you remember Sergeant Clarke," he said. After the initial greeting, he continued, "We need to talk with you. We have a few more questions."

Philip King's response carried the fatigue that constant worry produced. "I was surprised when you called. I expected it to be Sergeant Clarke. Thank you. Ask anything. I'll do whatever I can to help."

Thain had never known what smug felt like and wondered if he ever would when he took in King's rumpled appearance. How many hours had passed since he and his wife had come in to report Celia Wight as missing? Not even a full twenty-four? On King's face it looked like a lifetime.

Amid the taut silence in the lift, Thain asked, "Do you have any other clients, Mr. King?" King's tired eyes told him he had little patience with small talk.

"Yes, of course. I also have a secretary and a partner."

"Would you like some coffee, a cup of tea?" Thain offered in recompense for his less than sympathetic effort to ease the other man's worry.

"Tea. Please."

"Of course. Sorry I can't guarantee it will be any good."

Thain and Clarke waited to start the questions until they were installed in an interrogation room with a table between them, holding insulated cups of tepid, milked-down tea. "I don't take milk with my coffee, but I do with my tea. Is that strange, do you think?" He looked at King, whose expression told Thain he'd surprised him with such a meaningless question.

"I don't really know. Never thought about it."

"Do you? Prefer milk in your coffee?"

"Yes, and my tea."

Thain took a deep, quiet breath as his thumb smoothed over his cell phone screen in his lap. He didn't like interrogations. Wasn't good with people the way Rae or Clive were and wanted Sarah Clarke to do the questioning. Especially when the questions they needed to ask were not going to be easy for Philip King to hear, much less answer. He didn't want to ask them. But Clarke had already said she'd rather listen while he did the asking. He didn't have a choice. "How is your wife?"

"As well as can be expected. It's why I've come alone. She's a bit stressed. She and Celia are the best of friends."

"I understand. We need some more personal information about Celia Wight."

Philip King leaned on the table with his arms outstretched, holding his tea as if it were a prop. He glanced from the foam cup in his hands to Thain and then to Clarke. "Have you found her?"

Thain said, "Yes, and no. Please, have you received any ransom calls?"

"We were right, weren't we? Something *is* wrong. She's been kidnapped?"

"Mr. King, have you received any ransom calls? Would anyone think she was well off?"

"No one has called us about a ransom. She's comfortable, but not excessively rich. Her parents died when she was thirteen, I believe, and they left her their life insurance policies, among other investments. I don't know who would know such things about her. Now please answer me. Has she been kidnapped?"

Thain hesitated, unsure of whether or not to tell him what Rae and St. John had theorized. Clarke kept her face neutral but nodded for him to keep prodding.

"We aren't sure. Usually, by now, if this were a kidnapping for ransom, someone would have received a call. MPU has checked with the Kidnapping Squad, and neither of them has received any calls. Nor has the US Embassy." Thain paused. "What more can you tell me, personally about Celia Wight?"

"Whatever I can, but we gave all of her pertinent information to the sergeant yesterday," King said.

"Yes, of course. What I'm looking for is something more personal, like her character; is she outgoing, is she shy, that kind of thing."

"She is excessively shy. Not outgoing in any way. She lives alone, keeps to herself. She doesn't have any family and, as far as we know, has only us whom she counts as friends."

Thain thought he knew why their friend kept to herself so intently, wanted to ask King if he knew of her past. But that was his curiosity again, and he left it unheeded. With this turn of events, King would have mentioned it if he knew.

"What if I told you we have evidence of her meeting a man, actually kissing him in public, and walking away with him?"

"I'd say your eyes deceived you. What evidence? Who is the man?"

"Still think you know her?"

"Who is the man?" King looked at him in total disbelief before anger took over. "It's one of your CCTV films, isn't it? You've found her on one of your films."

"And by the looks of the film, Celia Wight has more to her than you, or your wife, know." Thain couldn't help the disgust with himself he now tasted, for being so brutal. But he had to be because, irrationally, he felt exactly as King did, and that would not do. He'd never lost professional distance on an investigation before. He didn't know how to deal with his emotional involvement in this one. He was turning into someone he recognized all too well, and that bothered him. No, if he were honest, it frightened him. He'd lost himself once before. He didn't want to do it again.

Philip King shook his head, clearly unable to believe what he considered impossible. "No. You've arrived at the wrong conclusion. That photo you have? Her publisher had it taken to put on the cover of her novels. She refused to have it put on the books. She guards her privacy very carefully."

"What about the kiss?"

"I want to see your evidence. Show me the film."

Thain did.

King watched and his confusion returned, creasing his forehead, but his eyes stated his conviction. "I know her, Detective Thain. She didn't kiss that man. It seems obvious to me he forced himself on her."

"Or perhaps it's a setup? Maybe she knew this man before and arranged to meet him there. Do you recognize him?"

King shook his head. "How could anyone recognize him? You can't see him. We've known her for three years, and it isn't in her to let someone this physically close. She didn't do this willingly. It's too unlike her."

"How many times has Celia Wight visited the UK since you've known her?"

"As I said, Detective, we've known her for three years, but I know she's come over at least three times in the last five years. Research for her books."

"Research would be perfect cover."

King's face flushed with an anger Thain hadn't seen before. He'd pushed him too far.

"Cover for what? You should be trying to find her kidnapper, that man," he said, pointing at the monitor, "not making insinuating comments."

"I'm only doing my job—"

"What do you expect me to say? You're accusing an innocent woman, of, of I don't even know what you think she would need cover for! Kissing is certainly no offence. What is going on, Detective?" King glared at Clarke. "Sergeant?"

Thain said, "She seems to have kissed him."

King sighed, as if wondering if Thain were worth the trouble. "No, she didn't, and no, she couldn't have known him before. Why won't you answer my question?"

"How can you be so sure?"

"I told you, she doesn't let people near her easily."

"She let that man get close."

"She didn't 'let' him do any such thing! Aren't you a detective? You would see that for yourself if you'd 'detect.' She had no choice. She wouldn't let a stranger get anywhere near her if she could help it. It's taken her publisher and me six months to talk her into this book tour, which is why she's here. Being in that crowd must have been difficult for her, very difficult." King looked at the table, away from Thain and Clarke. Quietly he said, "She went to the Liberty because she wanted to buy gifts for us, for Eva." Thain acknowledged the guilt in King's tone and hated to continue, but he had to be completely sure.

"How can you be certain she didn't know him? Do you know all of her acquaintances?"

Philip crumpled the empty cup in his hand. Messy bits of Styrofoam fell to the floor as he threw it on the table. None of them paid any attention to the clutter. "As a matter of fact we do, fairly well, know everyone she knows. She's introverted in a near-obsessive fashion. She's much too wary of the world."

"You look unsure."

Philip glared at him and leaned in. "The way you ask your questions would make anyone unsure of their own name. And no, I'm not unsure. I would stake my life on it."

"Is there any possibility she could have planned this disappearance?"

King threw his hands up and leaned back in the chair as if resigned to the ignominy of lesser mortals. "Bugger it. You really don't get it, do you? I thought—" He leaned across the table again, with his keen eyes fixed on Thain, angry again. "She isn't like that. She's a writer. She needed to earn a living. She chose a profession where she could work, eat, and breathe alone. She doesn't want to be around people, especially people she doesn't know. She's a very insecure person."

"Have you ever asked her why she's so insecure? That in itself could be—"

"Yes of course we asked her. Well, Eva did. Celia's parents died when she was thirteen. She was at boarding school and stayed there until she graduated. We think there is something more, something that happened at school, but she won't talk about anything else with us. She's been alone since she was thirteen, Detective."

"So you're saying it's impossible for her to have planned this."

"Yes. Impossible. She's too . . . fragile."

"There is no man in her life?"

"I've told you. No. She's a private person."

Thain stood, as did Clarke. Confronted with the evident proof of the film before him, Philip King still believed what he said. "Thank you for your help, Mr. King," Thain said.

Philip King stood as well. "It would be easier if you would answer my question. It would be easier to help if you didn't try and make her out to be something she isn't and could never be."

"We'll find out soon enough, Mr. King."

King's anger evaporated, leaving the direction of his dour thoughts clear. "What does that mean?"

Thain preferred his anger. "It means we're doing our best to find her, Mr. King. That's all. Go home. Let us do our job."

"Your job *should not* be persecuting her. By God, the man could kill her, he could have already—"

"Mr. King, please calm down. At least, because of the film, we know you and Mrs. King were correct about her being missing—"

"Then you should listen to me *now*," King said, his finger jabbing the table between them. "I know her. You don't."

Now it was Thain's turn to speak quietly. He said, "Mr. King, now we know for certain that Celia Wight has been taken, we need to find out whether or not it was against her will. This is a necessary part of the investigation. The best thing you can do for her right now is to go back to your hotel, sir, and get some rest."

King shoved his hands in his pockets, tilted his head, and said, "From the start of all this, my wife and I sensed something different about you, Detective. Of all the policemen we've met, you had an underlying consideration that helped us feel like you cared. You're on the wrong path and you know it. Don't let 'just doing your job' ruin the man you are."

King left with resentment rouging his thin cheeks. His words, his look, made Thain feel like a heel. Here, again, was proof that he really wasn't good at dealing with people. Computers and facts were his forte, not emotions, which got in the way and skewed one's view of the facts, and certainly not melancholy eyes that wouldn't leave him alone. The problem was, he believed Philip King, and the man knew it. King had chided him for his stubborn insistence on pursuing a misleading line of inquiry. But Thain had to push King to be sure of his opinion of Celia Wight, even if he didn't agree with St. John and the conspiracy theory. All avenues had to be checked. His scar pricked again, reminding him of the memory that had accosted him the first time he'd seen that black-and-white photo.

"Thain, are you all right?"

Sergeant Clarke's voice silenced the reminiscence, killed the old pain and brought him back to himself, himself as he was now, not the battered young man he'd been before becoming a police officer. "What? Oh, yes. I'm fine. Just thinking about what Mr. King had to say. Celia Wight hasn't told the Kings about what happened to her."

"No, that's evident. So that's in keeping with what we've learned about her character."

"Aye, she doesn't trust even them with such personal information."

"When you get the notes from the interview written up, send them over, will you?"

"Sure. Of course. Thanks for coming."

Clarke winked at him again. He guessed it was just one of her mannerisms. "Thanks for asking me."

Alone, Thain left West End, troubled, though loath to admit it, that the memory of that last conversation with Agatha's father had shocked him clear through. The man had been more than understanding yet had never again let Thain see her after that last time. Agatha.

He picked up his head, and his pace, and shook his shoulders. He wouldn't indulge in self-pity, not when he might actually be able to help Celia Wight. "Forget the past, Alban. Focus on the now." An urgency to talk to his team took over. Movement. He needed movement, and not only in his body. He needed it in the case as well. Heading for Oxford Circus tube station, he phoned Patterson to tell him he was on the way. He took the Central Line east to Tottenham Court Road. He'd told Clarke he would read up on the death of Celia Wight's parents. He hadn't told her that he would also put his time-tested research skills to work on it, would look into every detail to try and see if their deaths had indeed been accidental. If they had not, he would try and find out which assassin—ambassadors weren't usually killed by accident—had done the deed and why.

16

Silence invaded the room like a shadow at sunset, except it was full-on day. Celia slumped in the chair where the stranger had left her, convinced nothing would save her now. How could she have felt the desire to kiss him? He'd been too close, closer than anyone since . . . He hadn't held his knife to her back this time. He obviously didn't need a weapon to be dangerous. He was himself dangerous enough.

Between her fear, her scalded hands—aching and bound behind her—and the constant sting of the raw skin around her mouth, Celia couldn't pull her thoughts together to form any coherency. *Oh,* she thought, *he didn't gag me.* She screamed for help, screamed again and again until her throat grew hoarse. Her head sagged with weariness. No one could hear her. She closed her eyes. The effort to keep them open compounded her defeat, and his victory.

"Celia, darling, don't worry, don't worry." Her mother's voice called to her.

"Mom, where are you?"

"I'm here, love, where I always am . . ."

"Mom!" The croaking scream woke her. "Mom! Where are you? Ah, no." Celia yanked against her bindings and wished herself back in the dream, even though the echo of her mother's voice in her heart hurt worse than she remembered. It had been so very long since . . . Years had passed before she managed to banish her parents' voices to the dim recesses of her being. Why had her mother's escaped now?

Stop it, Celia. She must think of something else, such as, why had her kidnapper gone? She didn't care why he'd gone. She grasped at any thought to escape the broadening ache her mother's voice had created in her chest, the tight, suffocating one. She was glad to be alone, even if tied up. At least she didn't have to think about the kidnapper when he wasn't in her face. Yet once she drove out her mother's memory, that was all she did, waiting for any tiny sound at the door. She couldn't stop neurotically counting how many times she jumped at odd noises. It frayed her nerves one tense fiber at a time.

Soon she wished for a clock to tick—anything to stop the dead silence. Hours crawled by, she thought, and she squirmed around toward the window to see if the sun had gone down. She couldn't turn that far without falling over, so she carefully scooted the chair back and craned her neck. The window was darker than before. Dusk was falling on her second day with a madman. She thought apprehensively of her mother, of her unfamiliar presence in the dream. Even after all this time it still wounded her to hear that voice. Celia closed her eyes, feeling like a coward because, for all her efforts to push her parents' memories away, tucked deep into a closet in her apartment back home were all of their family videos. She hadn't thrown even one of them away.

17

At Tottenham Court Road tube station Thain made the switch to the Northern Line and stood, holding on to the metal bar, amongst the crowd on the train. During the ride a hazardous thought broke through the others, one he'd systematically ignored until now. But Philip King's words played over in his head, and he realized that since he'd read Celia Wight's harrowing file, he wanted to find out what had happened to the man—the monster—who had raped and mutilated her.

A woman across from him raised her eyebrows in surprise, forcing him to hold in check the intense rage that he obviously wasn't concealing. He shot a tense-lipped smile at the woman, but an honest smile, a real one, wouldn't come. He looked away, forced himself to breathe, and closed his eyes for a moment. He couldn't afford to let emotions like rage or pity, or guilt, out of the dark and private place where he kept them. Once upon a time he'd allowed them full reign, and they had come too close to destroying him. As it was, he still didn't talk to his brother. Still hadn't seen his parents since he'd moved to London. He couldn't afford to indulge. He couldn't afford the risk. Couldn't afford to think about his brother, and yet . . . just out of hospital he and his brother had argued, and that argument had put a stamp on his decision.

"You don't know what you want right now, Alban."

"And you do, Ellis? You don't know anything about it."

"There you're wrong. I'm a cop meself, remember?"

"It's what I want."

"It won't change how she feels about you."

"*Eh, what's going on in here? What's the shoutin' for?*"

"*Nothin' Dad.*"

"*Alban wants to go to police academy,*" Ellis said.

"*Ellis! Damn you—*"

"*Oh, aye, two coppers in the family to worry about. Your mother will love that. What about university, Alban?*"

"*Dad, I want to go to the academy . . .*"

Alban swore he'd never forgive Ellis for telling his father in that way. Maybe that's why . . . What was wrong with him? *Get your thoughts back on safer ground, Thain. Forget Agatha. Forget Ellis. Concentrate on this case. The case of the Seventh Man.* Thain took a deep breath and ignored the lady glaring at him.

Thain needed to access the private file he kept on the USB drive in his pocket, which contained every shred of information he'd ever gathered on the Wraith, down to the most obscure tidbit, and the conclusions he came up with using the Criminal Intelligence Data Base, the CIDB. He saved his conclusions on the USB drive, never to the CIDB main database. Though on the CIDB he could search any details pertaining to the murder of Richard McLean that might uncover a match and no one would be the wiser, he still wouldn't save his conclusions anywhere but on the drive. He didn't want to leave any "footprints" to be followed. HOLMES would work much faster at a problem such as this, but he didn't dare input his "Wraith" information into HOLMES. Too many questions he wouldn't be able to avoid might be asked if he did. He couldn't use HOLMES only for searches, which he could on the CIDB.

At Euston Station he took the Edgware Branch of the Northern Line to Colindale Station. There he made quick work of the walk to the Hendon. It had taken little more than half an hour for the journey, but it felt like a lifetime.

He needed to talk to Patterson and Rae before they informed the DIs or Chief North of what they'd discovered so far. When he found them, he told them about the interview with Philip King, but not what he'd found in Celia Wight's file. He knew he should, but wasn't ready to talk about it yet. Then the three of them spent an hour going over the film. They rehashed the arguments and possibilities the film presented. Meanwhile Greene reported that he'd issued the call to action to find the missing hat, and Smyth confirmed that he'd entered the pertinent film into HOLMES.

"I think we've enough to let the DIs know what we've found, and they can decide if we need to inform the chief yet," Clive said as they paused the film and took a break.

"Right," Thain agreed.

"You want to ring Carter or Hawthorne?" Rae asked.

"How about Carter?" Detective Inspector Paul Carter said as he came through the door. He sauntered over and they all stood up in unison, as if presenting a united front.

"Yes, sir," Bell said, glancing at Thain, as if to tell him to keep calm and let her do the talking. "We've a first report, sir."

"Let's see it, then." Carter held out his hand and Rae Bell put the folder in it.

"It's all in there. If you have any questions, we'll be happy to answer them as best we can, sir."

"Come on, Bell, what's with all the 'sirs'?" His look over Rae's small body couldn't have been more insulting, and Thain, watching her tamp down her anger, almost went off on him. It wasn't hard for him to get riled when Carter opened his mouth any day of the week, but today, especially, Thain had even less restraint. His emotions seemed to be oozing out from under the mental door he usually had locked up nice and tight.

"Just doing my job," Rae answered, sitting back down at the table.

"Why don't you explain this report to me over coffee downstairs?"

Thain couldn't stop himself. "She has better things to do. You do know, I suppose, how to read a report, *sir*? *We* are here to answer any questions you might have, when you're ready." He clipped the sentence as if he'd locked it with handcuffs. Then he, too, sat down, as if daring Carter to say something. Mistake, because he did.

"Stand at attention, *D.S.* Thain."

Thain slowly moved to his feet.

"What is your problem, *D.S.* Thain? Since when do you ride safety over Bell?"

"Since she's on my team, sir."

"Oh? Does she need protection from her commanding officer?"

"With the look you gave her, apparently, sir." He kept rubbing that 'sir' in.

Carter sputtered. "I've reason enough to kick you off this team right now."

"And that reason would be what . . . sir?"

"Insubordination, talking back to a higher-ranking officer, to start."

Thain would have enjoyed this interchange if it had taken place anywhere or anytime but here and now, in front of his team, again. It seemed like Carter always picked a time with the most people around to try and humiliate him. His bad humor wasn't helping and neither was the timeline hanging over their heads. Caution flew to the wind anyway. "I'm sorry, sir, if I pissed you off."

"That's it," Carter roared, throwing down the report on the table in a dramatic gesture. He raised his fist and took a step toward Thain. The door opened and Detective Chief Inspector North stepped into the room.

"What the hell is going on here? Who is the idiot bellowing?"

Carter's fist fell to his side. But both of his hands remained clinched. Then he pointed at Thain, "This, this Detective *Sergeant* insulted me. I want him off the team. He has no respect for his betters."

"I have perfect respect for my *superiors*, sir. You're not my 'better.'"

"See? See how he—"

"Tell you what I see, *D.I.* Carter."

Whenever North started a sentence in that quiet tone, unique to him, they all knew to look out, and Carter instantly brought himself up short. He stood at attention as if waiting for the proverbial axe to fall.

"I see bickering children when, I assume, there's work to be done. I see a room full of people acting as if we don't have a killer to catch. I see one of my DIs acting as if he's still in primary school. Now get out of my sight, all of you. Don't bother me unless you have something new to report on this investigation. Am I clear?" He didn't have to yell. All he had to do was use that tone and they all obeyed without objection, usually. Except this time.

Maybe if Thain said it now, they'd be able to bypass Carter's annoying interference. He cleared his throat. "Sir, we do have something to report."

North had turned to leave. Now he stopped and looked back at Thain with a glare. He waited. So did Thain. So did the whole room, which held at least half the team.

"Well, Detective?"

Thain began to breathe again. "It's a missing person, sir."

"Oh?"

"An American woman."

North frowned. "All we need now is a missing American. What about her?"

"I think we've found her last known whereabouts."

"Why you? Shouldn't the MPU or US Embassy be taking care of that? And what does this have to do with our investigation?"

"Yes, sir, the MPU is on the case and the US Embassy has been contacted about it. I've also heard it will soon be turned over to the Kidnapping Squad."

"Then why bother me with this information?"

"We thought you'd be interested to see where she was last seen and who she was with. Could you watch some footage, sir? We can show you easier than trying to explain."

"Again, I don't see what this has to do with—"

Thain dared to interrupt. "It pertains to the murder?"

The chief's eyes, which were glued to him now, narrowed. "And why didn't you say so?"

"Sorry, sir."

"Show me this footage."

"First, you should see this. It's a photo of the missing woman, Celia Wight."

Chief North took time to look at the photo. They all waited. "All right. I've seen the missing woman." North sat in front of the monitor they'd used earlier. Rae, Carter, and Thain all stood back while Clive started the film.

A little over five minutes later, the chief stood up and frowned. "You're sure this is the same man from the bank?"

"Yes, sir," Clive said. "The Royal Bank is just south and west from this store. I'm guessing he realized our boys were on his trail."

"It's obvious the woman is the same as in the photo here."

Thain glanced at Clive and Rae. "There's a theory that Celia Wight could be in on the heist."

"Of course she's in on it. Look at the evidence," Carter stated.

Thain grimaced, but ignored him. "The Kidnapping Squad has looked at the clip and evidently *they* have concluded that this *is* a kidnapping, but it's not official yet, sir." He glared at Carter. "When it is, the case goes to them and the MPU is out. We also made a copy of her background file. Her mother was an American ambassador. She and her husband died thirteen years ago in a car accident."

Rae threw her two pence in: "Sir, maybe Celia Wight thought the murder victim at the bank had something to do with the death of her parents and hired this guy to take him out."

"Then I guess we don't have to worry about whether she's alive or not. He won't hurt her if she's hired him."

Thain said, "But her parents were both American and died in South Africa. The bank victim is English. I think we should seriously consider that the kidnapper, murder suspect, used her for a shield, sir."

"Either way, Thain, the murder at the *bank* is our *first* responsibility. Let the MPU or KS worry about the American's fate."

"But, sir, they're together," Thain insisted.

The chief's tone took a dive again. "They *were* together. You don't know that he didn't do exactly what you said and then dropped her as soon as he was safe." He looked around the room at the team members assembled there. "In case I need to reiterate to everyone, your top priority is to find our *man*, yesterday."

No one said a word as the chief left. Thain glanced at Rae and Clive, who both stood with their arms crossed.

"Now what?" Clive asked.

Carter pointed a finger. "Took you down didn't he, Thain. Only what you deserved, interrupting him like that."

"If you say so, *sir.*"

Rae lightly touched his shoulder as if aware of the silent tension permeating his body. "Wonder where we go from here?" she said. "Hope the chief doesn't hand the case over to Kidnapping and cut us out."

Her light touch jolted through him and diverted his eyes from Carter's retreating figure. Looking at Rae, he felt thankful, though he couldn't say it, for her well-timed distraction. He'd been ready to take up where he and Carter had left off. "He would never do that. It happened in our district. We'll stay on top of this because of the murder and heist." At least he hoped that were so. He didn't want to lose his first chance at cracking the case, or proving his theory, because of protocol. At least that's what he told himself. The truth was fast becoming something else.

"Want to go over this bit again?" Clive asked as he took a seat in front of the monitor.

"I guess." Thain sat, stuck his elbows on the desk, and tapped his fingers together. He stared at the screen, wondering if Celia Wight had more guts than the Kings gave her credit for. As far as anyone knew, she was still alive. If she were a wimp or a simpering fool, they would have found her body by now because no kidnapper would let someone like that drag them down, no matter what the original excuse for her kidnapping might have been. She was their key, even if the chief didn't see it that way.

"Clive, Rae, I understand what the chief wants, and we're working the murder, but maybe we should try and concentrate a bit more on the Celia Wight angle of it?"

"The chief said—" Clive started.

"I heard what the chief said, Clive. We'll work both angles. We find her, we find him—and vice versa. The sooner we find them, the better our chances are of finding her alive. If he took her for cover, that need is over. He'll not want the trouble of holding on to her when she can be recognized. If she's innocent"—he hesitated—"Celia can't have much longer to live."

"Celia?" Rae said, her look full of questions, and misgiving. "Celia *Wight*, Thain. Don't get too involved in this case. You know the odds of the investigation having a happy ending."

He glared at her but didn't bother to respond. He didn't bother because Rae was right. He didn't think of Celia Wight as just a case. Once he'd seen her eyes, all thoughts of her being "a case for the MPU or KS" disappeared. Again he stared at her photo beside the monitor. At least the long-ago rapist hadn't touched her face. He wondered if she felt grateful for that. Silently he admitted he wanted to save Celia Wight from the Wraith—*bloody hell, the murder suspect,* he corrected— but also that an unfamiliar need had pervaded his usually rational mind: a need to put some laughter back in those melancholy eyes. He tried not to think about the fact that he'd never had the chance to do that for Agatha. He sat up. Then stood.

"Where're you going?" Rae asked as he grabbed his coat and threw it on.

"Over to the viewing room. See if St. John has found anything new."

"He would have called."

"I know. But I'm going anyway. Is that all right, Detective Sergeant Bell?"

When she raised her eyebrows, he had the grace to look ashamed. "Sorry, Rae. I can't watch that footage again right now."

"Accepted. Call us."

He agreed and left.

18

Celia hadn't a clue how much time passed before a scratching at the door banished her lethargy. Her every sense heightened as the door opened. She tried to scream, but all she managed was a dry croak. If he noticed her effort, he didn't acknowledge it but entered without a sound, a lumpy package in his hand. He didn't look at her right away. When he did, he seemed calmer, if such a description could be applied to him in any way. He was still alert but not as tense, she thought, thankful he hadn't heard her pitiful noise.

He took off his coat and put it on top of hers on a chair by the door. He removed the tape without touching her. Celia stood up and attempted to move her stiff, cold limbs. Her hands remained tender but not painful enough that she couldn't rub circulation back into her legs and arms. Thirst parched her mouth and her throat felt raw. She weaved her way to the sink, poured a cup of water, and drank. "Are we leaving?" she asked as she threw the paper cup away. Her voice sounded rough and she saw that he questioned it.

But all he said was, "Yes."

"Do you ever stay anywhere more than twenty-four hours?"

"I don't make a habit of it."

At least he was answering her questions. "Where are we going?"

"Go to the toilet."

She did as he told her without fuss because she had to go anyway.

As Celia came out of the bathroom, the stranger pulled a new coat out of the package and put it on her; a stocking cap followed. He wrapped a warm scarf round the lower half of her face and checked over the apartment without saying a word. He cleaned the bathroom and kitchen with ammonia and wiped down every surface they might have touched.

"Aren't you going to vacuum?"

He ignored her risky sarcasm. Finally he seemed satisfied; he turned the water off and took everything with him—the trash, towels, dirty clothing, previous coats, and the pillow she'd cried upon—as he ushered her out the door. When they passed what she realized was the boiler room, he pushed her inside. With the small door to the ancient burner open, the heat warmed her face while he threw the clothes, cushion, everything into the flames. No one would know they had ever been there unless someone went over the place looking for hair that might give away their DNA. But why would anyone do that here? No one knew to look for a place like this.

The night air stung her eyes with its brisk cold touch. More snow covered the sidewalks, and the air woke her up, refreshed what little of her face remained uncovered, and relieved her hands, which were still too raw for gloves. She walked with him side by side, his arm around her, hers reluctantly around him, where he'd placed it. Celia lost track of time. Her only clue was that, although it was dark, some businesses had lights on and were open and busy.

He turned into a small shop selling tobacco, newspapers, and magazines. He picked up a newspaper, checked something on the cover, paid, and moved them on their way again. This time they took the underground to a small hole-in-the-wall pub several stops away. They sat in the back where he could watch anyone and everything, surveying the lay of the land. Celia recalled her image of him as a slinky jungle cat. She almost expected him to sniff the air.

Her stomach felt bottomless, and she ate a large bowl of hot, creamy potato soup and a baguette with butter. Perfect. She even had a cup of tea, but shouldn't have. It was the tea that got to her. How often had she taken a simple cup of tea for granted? She glanced at her kidnapper and quickly wiped her eyes, her wet cheeks. No crying in public, no drawing attention. Americans might cry in public places, but not the British.

19

In the viewing room, St. John looked as if he hadn't moved but for his change of clothing. Thain said, "Good afternoon, St. John."

"That it is. Have you talked with the chief?"

"Yes, brought him up to date."

St. John flashed a glance his way. "We have new film. I've studied some of it."

"So you said, but you haven't called, so . . ." Thain sat down.

"Where's Rae Bell?" St. John asked without looking up from the monitor.

"With Clive, working on the Celia Wight side of the story."

St. John nodded.

"We have to find out which direction the man went. Have you found anything?" Thain said.

St. John shook his head. "Like you said, I would have called."

Thain's phone blipped an incoming text. The message was from Rae. *Call me if you can. It's about Celia Wight.* He instantly obeyed.

"Tell me the details?" he asked nicely.

"Celia Wight's bags have been found in an alley near Adie Road," she started.

"Hold on, Rae, I'm putting you on speaker so St. John can hear." He pushed the speaker button and set the phone on the desk, telling St. John what she'd said so far. "Okay, you're on."

"Someone got to the contents first, but as luck would have it, they either left or dropped her American ID, a driver's license. Forensics have already gone over the bags and found some strands of hair, which are in process now. We should know soon, hopefully, if the hairs are hers or belong to someone else."

"Even if they are his, that won't tell you who *he* is unless he's in the system." St. John shrugged. Thain marveled that St. John's eyes never left the film he continued to review.

"Or they could belong to whoever made it to the bags before we did," he said.

St. John's gaze faltered from the screen and he turned his brown eyes on Thain before he asked Rae, "Did they, um, find any signs . . . any other type of DNA samples?"

"No. Nothing to suggest whether or not she's dead or . . ." Rae didn't finish.

St. John's restless fingers playing on his keyboard spoke to Thain's own thoughts on what Rae didn't finish saying. "So, she could still be alive," St. John said.

"Why else would he leave the bags to be found?" Thain stood up. He tried not to grimace, sure Rae would actually hear him if he did. He paced around the room, one hand on his hip, the other rubbing his forehead. "Rae, is Clive there with you?"

"Yes, he's been listening in."

"Good. Here are some thoughts. So far, this is a guessing game. If our murder suspect *is* a bank robber, and he took Celia Wight to shield himself, she could still be alive *if* she didn't see his face, and *if* he isn't the killing kind. The robbers didn't hurt anyone seriously in the bank, right, Rae?"

"Correct. Some bruises and one fracture, but the robbers stayed pretty hands-off in the bank lobby. Thain, if they kissed—"

"Wait a minute. Let me finish. The alternative is that this guy is just a nut-job psycho-killer, leaving no possibility she could still be alive, and it's only a matter of time before we find her body. However, leaving her bags to be found doesn't fit that profile. He would have left her body along with the bags. And you said no blood was found at the scene, correct, Rae?"

"Correct. None. I'm thinking that's a good thing."

Thain's thoughts ran down the new path the killer now presented to them. He couldn't help but fall back to what he knew, which was that the Wraith was a fastidious man. This brought him to a new piece of the puzzle. He stopped pacing and pointed at St. John. "Think about it. Why did he leave her shopping bags and driver's license somewhere they were likely to be found? It means he knows *we* know he has her." He rubbed his forehead again as if somehow it would make his brain work better. "Which makes sense if he wants us to know she's still alive. It's his way of warning us to be careful."

"What you're saying is, this might be our first actual contact with Celia Wight's kidnapper, that he's sending us a message,"

"Telling us that he holds her life in his hands," Clive chimed in over the speakerphone.

St. John said, "Celia Wight no longer has identification, which makes it harder for him to leave the country with her."

Rae perked up. "She would still have a passport if she's in on it. Or he'd know how to fake one," she said.

"Or know someone who does," Clive added. Thain wondered if Clive or Rae were trying to play devil's advocate when they accused Celia Wight outright of conspiracy to murder. He walked a little away from St. John, reached into his pocket, and pulled out his cell phone. He dialed the MPU while Rae and Clive continued to expound upon their theory, upon how the two of them had it planned, which ran opposite from Thain's thoughts on the matter. When Sergeant Clarke answered he asked quietly, "Did the Kings have Celia Wight's passport with them when they reported her missing?" He nodded, thanked her and put the phone back in his pocket.

When he rejoined St. John, St. John asked, "Who did you call, Thain?"

"I called the MPU. They have Celia Wight's passport."

Rae's and Clive's voices on the phone irrupted, but St. John said, "A lack of ID does make it harder for him. We've every conceivable entry and exit to this country under surveillance, and as of this report she hasn't been seen trying to leave with or without a man."

Thain shook his head. "And that's where the theory of her being in on it falls down threefold. She's a face, especially since we've now put her photo all over the media. If she'd planned to run off with him, why did she go shopping? And, last, why wasn't *she* trying to avoid the cameras as he did, even in front of Liberty? No, I think it's clear she served a purpose, to get him away from the police."

"Then where is she? Why haven't we found her body? Thain, you know we have to look at all the options. We can't close the door on her culpability," Clive said.

"Simply because it's the only other option we know to think of? It doesn't fit."

St. John shrugged. "So, back to the videos?"

"What else do we have? So, yes, back to the footage," he said. "Thanks Rae, Clive. We'll need to report this conversation to the DIs. Could one of you do that?"

"I will," Clive volunteered. "Don't need to witness another Carter-Thain show," he finished, and they rang off.

"Have you found anything yet, St. John?"

"You've been here the whole time, Thain."

He paced again, something niggling his brain. He stopped right next to St. John's chair. "St. John, where did they find Celia Wight's bags?"

"Near Adie Road. Wasn't that what Rae said?"

"I'll call to confirm." He punched in Rae Bell's number. "Rae, yes, listen. Where did they find Celia's bags, again? Yes, I know Celia *Wight*. The street name?" He wrote it down. "Thanks, Rae. I'll call you as soon as I know something."

"What's up, Thain?" St. John asked.

"Order the CCTV footage from all around that area. We have a known location now. Also, think about it. We now have a direction. We don't need to slog through all this around the store and bank anymore."

"Except to find the hat, or what happened to it, at least."

"True, so we stay on that limited area. But maybe he holed up in or around an flat or bedsit and left some evidence. Are there any in that area? We need to look for a mistake, any mistake the man might have made that will tell us where he's heading." He punched in Rae's number again.

"I think we should also make a map, sir."

"What did I say about that?"

"Sorry. Thain, we should get a map and follow his known movements. Maybe he'll work in a pattern we can see,"

"Which might help us figure out where he'll be before he gets there! Brilliant, Police Constable Abney. Brilliant."

20

Celia had no time to recover her composure before they left the pub and moved on again. She still had no idea where he planned on taking them but hoped they would stay in London. At least in London she might be found before she died, or at least before she putrefied, if he killed her. She didn't ask herself why she still lived anymore, why he hadn't hurt her; she was only grateful that it was so.

Snow tumbled around them as he set a brisk pace. After her tears in the pub, Celia found her mind calm in a manner that unsettled her. Why wasn't she a terrified basket case by now? She should be a blubbering idiot, as any normal person would be in this situation, as she had been earlier. But she wasn't anymore, and a part of her guessed why. Simple survival. She wanted to live. For the first time in years, she saw her life as good and worth living. She wished she had a way of letting Eva and Philip know she still breathed.

"Is there some way I can let my friends know I'm still alive?" she asked.

"No need. The police will tell them about your bags."

Well, that was that.

"What do you plan to do with me?"

Silence, his usual answer.

"Okay, *Ryan.* If that's the way you want it."

He stopped; a tight grimace turned his eyes icy and hard again, hard as the sidewalk beneath their feet. "What did you call me?"

"Ryan. I've decided that since I need to call you *something,* I'll call you Ryan. I've always hated that name."

He seemed to struggle with something, but the impression lasted a mere second before he continued walking, in complete control of his emotions again. Nothing made a dent in him or bothered him except to make him angry. She knew how to do that. If she hadn't cared about staying alive, she'd have already tried running, or the making-a-scene-in-public ploy, but the knife rested ever present against her back, and she believed him when he said he wouldn't miss her vital organs, or that he would kill someone else. It was one thing to do battle with him in private, another in public. Strange, how when they were alone she felt somehow protected from the knife, yet in public she didn't doubt his willingness to use it.

As the morning sun topped the buildings and her feet truly began to hurt, they stopped at a café. He sent her to the restroom while he ordered breakfast to take out. Celia searched for a back way, checked the windows, halls, everything. The tiny window in the toilet was barred, the back door reachable only in his line of vision. She could find nothing to write with. When she thought of walking out of the toilets with the scarf off and her face bared, she knew she wouldn't do it because if she did, she or some other innocent would have no chance for last words.

He hadn't said it out loud, but Celia knew he could escape much more easily without her. So why did he keep her alive and with him? There had to be more to this than evading the police. If she could get him to talk, maybe she could figure out why he wanted her alive. It obviously wasn't for a ransom. What could be so special about her? Impossible questions with impossible answers locked somewhere in his mind, as unreachable as a Swiss bank vault.

He gathered up their order and they left. It had all felt so ordinary; no strange looks from the waiter or cook or any of the few customers in the café. He knew his way around well. He stopped at a small post office, bought a large mailing envelope, and sent off the newspaper he'd bought, though he hadn't even read it. Once they left the post office, he guided her along another ten blocks or so until he reached a small alleyway, dank and unloved.

"You do like the dark and dreary, don't you," she had to comment.

"No one asks too many questions in a place like this."

"Of course not, or you'd kill them."

His glance was sharp, but he didn't deny it.

The basement flat was a bit larger than the previous one, with a separate bedroom but no windows that hadn't been boarded up. The world could die outside and no one inside would be the wiser. "You definitely like your privacy." She took off her coat, cap, and scarf and rubbed her arms to warm up, but realized the air was toasty.

"Is this where you came yesterday? You turned the heat on and got it ready for today?"

"It was colder inside than out."

"Thanks."

He didn't look at her. "For what?"

"For thinking ahead."

They ate their breakfast in silence, Celia at the table, he on the sofa, but this time she watched him while she ate. She'd never met anyone like him. What an understatement. Now that she felt a small amount of assurance he wasn't going to hurt or kill her, at least not right away, her fear had diminished enough for her brain to function, and she was curious about him. Ever since she'd started writing, she'd been able to withdraw from the world—which frightened her—and feed her natural curiosity safely within her research. But here, she was alone with this stranger, and he was a mystery she couldn't solve on her own. She had no Internet to ask questions of, no books to consult on the subject of him.

When he'd finished eating, Celia dared to go over and take his containers from him. She washed the dishes and a corner of her mouth rose up a bit when she realized she'd made him angry again. She began to understand that he took whatever emotions he might have felt and turned them into anger. She decided he must be socially challenged and wondered what kind of criminal he was.

Once she finished in the kitchen, which was large enough to have its own separate area, she turned around. "What kind of criminal are you? Do you rob banks? Or are you some kind of foreign spy? No, not a bank robber or a spy; they use guns."

He sat on the edge of the sofa without a hint of relaxation in his body. Celia walked over and turned on the TV. Before she could move to the far end of the sofa from him, her face splashed all over the screen, then pound signs. But that was all she saw before he jumped up and slammed the off button. "Can't I watch something, at least see what they're saying about me?"

"No."

"Why not? You aren't a great one for conversation, and I'm tired of hearing silence."

"Silence can be good for you."

"By the hour, not by the day."

"Why do you hate the name you called me?"

She stared at him, surprised that he'd actually asked her a question. She couldn't tell him, not in a hundred years. Not ever. Instead she gave him a half-truth. "In tenth grade there was a bully in my class named Ryan, and he wouldn't leave me alone. My parents went to the principal about it, and I was teased for ratting and needing mommy and daddy's help. I hated tenth grade." She didn't tell him that her parents had already been dead for three years by then, or what the bully had really done. "Ryan" seemed to believe her, but she couldn't be sure about anything with him.

"How old were you?"

"Sixteen. Fifteen and sixteen are the usual ages for tenth grade in the States. I don't know what your tenth grade would be here." Silence. She didn't ask any more questions, because she feared he'd ask her ones she couldn't answer. She stood up and headed for the bathroom beyond the bedroom. "I'm going to take a shower."

"I'll guard the door."

Celia turned. "Humor?"

The warm water flowed over her and cleansed more than her body. For the first time in over forty-eight hours, her stiff muscles loosened. She let her arms hang at her sides, but she didn't close her eyes.

When she came out she felt warm and sleepy. She didn't even mind the cold in his eyes because for some reason it didn't feel so intense tonight. He passed her and went into the bathroom, shutting the door behind him. Celia stood there in the doorway between the bedroom and the living area looking at the door to freedom, wondering why he hadn't confined her while he took his shower.

Celia shivered. Maybe he was testing her. He could be standing right behind the door waiting for her to bolt. Then he would run out and trap her again. Then he would tie her up again. Maybe he was testing her fear. Maybe he was trying to feed it so she'd eventually stop thinking of escape. Maybe he really was a psycho and would play this cat-and-mouse game until he drove *her* nuts as well.

Celia had never thought of herself as brave, knew in fact that she wasn't. But she still took a tentative step toward the outside door, then another and another. Her eyes never left the bedroom doorway. She stuck her hand out, touched the doorknob. She turned it and pushed. Nothing happened. She pulled. She tried again to open the door and it didn't budge, didn't rattle in the frame when she shook the knob and beat on the door. The door was a literal steel trap.

She laughed out loud until she realized she sounded hysterical again. She backed up and fell on the sofa, despairing of ever being free. The door was deadbolt locked, and of course she had no key. She didn't bother to search for it. He would have it in there with him. He hadn't needed to tie her up because he knew that she couldn't get out. Knew there were no windows to signal through. The silence crept into the core of her and stole the rest of her flagging strength. The thick walls blocked all outside noise. She could hear nothing but her own breathing, the shower, and the slight ping and hiss of the radiator. He knew it was safe to leave her untied. She should have known as well.

21

Thain was in a mood for sure, and it wasn't a good one. They had found a map and set the three marking pins of the murder suspect's known locations: Adie Road, the bank, and the store. Since the footage from Adie Road had yet to come in, they'd spent the last two hours, according to the clock on the computer, studying the newer surveillance footage from between the bank and the store where Celia had been abducted. They'd expanded their viewing area by ten streets, but St. John had yet to find results worth mentioning. Thain sighed in frustration. "This is taking entirely too long."

"I can't argue with you there, Thain, but I'm going as fast as I can and still give the attention to detail that this needs. Hats are small. This time of year there are too many people on the streets. Even the DSs out there looking for it haven't turned up anything."

"I know." He stood and glowered at the screen from behind St. John's chair. But St. John didn't need Thain hanging over him, so he paced the room like a prisoner and said, "I just don't understand why he's holding on to her. I can't figure out why he wants Celia Wight alive. If she was only at the wrong place at the wrong time, why is she still breathing? Without her, he could be long gone by now, but he left her bags for us to find, to tell us he still has her."

Thain knew the Wraith would never have kidnapped anyone, much less take on a partner. "I need a change of scene. I'm going over to the murder room. Call me if you find anything, will you? I'll take the map over there in case any more sightings from interviews have popped up that we haven't heard of yet."

"Of course. Sir, I mean, Thain, I've a question."

"Yes?"

"Would you mind asking the chief about having someone else assigned here, to help view the footage? Since time is crucial, I could use another pair of eyes, or four."

"I'll make the call myself."

"Thank you. Much appreciated. I know she's point on this, but I don't suppose . . . ?"

"Can't guarantee anything about Rae, but I'll try." Thain actually winked at him.

St. John actually blushed. "Thanks."

"Call if anything pops up?"

"First thing."

So, St. John likes Rae. Would the lady detective date a lowly constable? Why was Thain even thinking about such things? He quit thinking like a gossip columnist and called the chief, who gave them the okay for another CCTV film viewer. "Sir, could it be DS Bell?"

"Thain, she's point. Get Jenkins on it."

"Yes, sir." When he entered the murder room, he informed PC Patrick Jenkins of his new position on the team and sent him off to help St. John. He'd already texted a message about the change to Hawthorne. He certainly wouldn't call Carter. Greeting the handful of people in the room—Greene, Martin, and O'Toole—he asked Greene to enter Jenkins's new position. Putting the map up on the wall, he explained St. John's and his theory before signing in for access to the Incident Room on HOLMES. He tapped on the keyboard and the IR screen popped up while he rubbed his face, tired and frustrated. This investigation was spread out too far. London was too big a warren. They had no idea where to look. *Get over it*, he told himself and shook off the useless sense of futility. Instead, he plowed into the mass of notes that the team had taken during phone calls and legwork and entered over the past two days.

Later, all he could think of was a break. His red, irritated eyes—not to mention his head—needed a rest. After viewing all the footage with St. John, and after an hour of catching up on HOLMES, a break sounded like a dream. But he hesitated. Celia Wight couldn't take a break. He wasn't the one alone with a madman. She didn't know of the twenty-nine—or more—people on the job, round the clock, trying to find her because she had been kidnapped by the man they were searching for. She didn't know that he'd pushed the angle of her abduction more than the murder with each new bit of information they'd gained. Hell, she didn't know he existed. But he didn't stop. Agatha's image, the pure gladness of her laugh echoed in his mind. He'd never had a chance to apologize because she'd refused to see him after . . . *Stop it*, he thought. Don't indulge yourself. The past didn't help, only hindered. He knew that all too well from experience.

The thought that Celia Wight was running out of time depressed him. Then again, maybe she wasn't the one running out of time. Maybe they were. The suspect could leave London whenever he chose to, judging by their lack of progress. Thain decided to change tactics for a moment. Because they didn't know where the kidnapping/murder suspect had gone, the search had been declared citywide, and searching the entire city would be a near impossible feat. The map of the sightings stayed pinned to the wall, but with only three known areas, no discernible pattern had emerged, and he wasn't sure it ever would.

His brain needed a jump start. He paged down to scan through the calls received and interview statements taken since the murder and kidnapping had occurred. The detectives out doing the legwork had been told to ask in shops, cafés, tube stations, etcetera, for information on anything out of the ordinary involving any man who might resemble their suspect. Their plan entailed throwing the net wide enough to catch more information that they could then slog through. He clicked on the automatic indexing for free-text matching— instructing the computer to scan the reams of notes for certain words—to see if anything popped up. Nothing did, which meant one of two things. Either he'd forgotten to turn on the auto indexing for text-matching when he set up this Incident Room, or there really were no matches, which was unusual. There should have at least been text-matching errors.

He went back through the setup. Had he set the automatic indexing on for free-text-matching? No. He must have gone too fast. He fixed his error and waited a moment for the Incident Room to reorganize, glad he'd caught his mistake himself instead of O'Toole, who'd entered all of the statements.

He clicked again on the indexing, then free-text-matching, and over twenty items showed up. A half hour later, eyes blurring with fatigue, he glanced at the next item in his search and though he saw the match immediately, its implication didn't register at first. He read the complete sequence over again. Fatigue vanished, eyes cleared. He put up the two interviews that contained the matched phrasing side by side on his screen, and read the full accounts. The first statement came from a clerk who worked in a small department store in North Camden. Thain's inner detective smiled. The southernmost edge of Camden was not so far away from the Royal Bank of Scotland.

"A man came in and bought a woman's coat. He didn't talk much and seemed in a bit of a hurry. He paid in cash and didn't want it gift wrapped, though said it was for his wife. Not many people pay with cash anymore in this store."

He blinked. He'd been right. The first match HOLMES identified was *"paid in cash."* His fingers flew, bringing up the second statement: *"Late this afternoon a man bought some clothes for a woman. He wasn't talkative and paid in cash for the clothes."* The detective who'd taken the report asked if the saleswoman remembered the sizes of the clothes, and she said they were size tens, she thought, a small size. *"The man appeared to know what he was looking for."* This interview had taken place in a larger store in North Camden. The two locations being in Camden was HOLMES's second match. Mentally I thanked HOLMES, my trusty TARDIS. In both cases the detectives had asked about CCTV footage. So that could help, once it came in. He tagged an action to prioritize the need for that footage from both stores.

"He paid in cash." Thain couldn't help it. His brain started down familiar channels of investigation. He knew neither he nor anyone else investigating assassinations had ever traced the Wraith by credit cards, checks, or a savings account of any kind. He'd concluded long ago that the man used only cash, which gave him an idea. He dialed Clive's number immediately.

Clive answered on the first ring. "What is it? Found something?"

"Possibly, I don't know. We'll need to do more checking."

"But you called." Clive sounded disappointed.

"Yes, I did. I have an idea, and perhaps we have a tip worth looking into. How soon can you get to the murder room?"

"Ten minutes?"

"Right, I'll ring Rae as well."

On the phone, Rae said she'd be there shortly, as she wasn't far from the Hendon. He texted St. John to let him know he'd put in an order for the film in and around the two stores before he turned back to Greene. Energy pulsed again; Thain felt regenerated. "Listen, Greene, we need a call to action for more officers on interviews. Have them look for any anything being bought or paid for with cash. Food—"

"Restaurants?"

"No, too many people still pay cash in restaurants. Try local grocery shops and big supermarkets. Have them ask about supplies like toothbrushes or shoes or clothes in women's sizes. Anything at all—and check to make sure they were paid for by a lone white male."

"Shouldn't we check with the DIs first, or the chief, before I put out the call?"

"Yes. Yes, but do it all now."

"What did you find?"

"I'll let you know as soon as Patterson and Bell get here."

22

Celia lay on the sofa and stared into the room seeing nothing, feeling nothing, her mind a blank. The shower stopped, the bathroom door opened. She closed her eyes and pretended to sleep.

Though she heard nothing, she sensed it when he came and stood over her, watching her in silence. The longer he stood there, the more nervous she became. She opened her eyes. He was gone.

She turned over and drifted into sleep. But the images that came to her in dreams had no order, no kindness, no reason, only fear, only pain. *A scream rose in her throat and she ached with the effort to subdue it. He wouldn't find her if she didn't scream. But the scream climbed up her throat, threatening to expose her. She couldn't make a noise or the knife would hurt her again. She wouldn't die before the misery of death settled upon her like a vulture and ate her alive.* Celia screamed.

"Wake up. It's a dream." A distant voice cut through the crashing waves of terror.

"Wake up." Hands lay upon her shoulders and she fought them off. The grip felt too tight, too sure. Celia screamed again but woke up fully when a hand covered her mouth, suffocating her for real because she couldn't breathe fast enough to catch up with her slam-dunked senses. She twisted her head away, trying to escape the stranger's hand, as her pulse raced on. He pulled her up against him and held on to her. His hand left her mouth but hovered, ever ready.

"It was but a dream."

Hopeless tears churned inside her, ready to spill. "But you're not."

"No."

Celia didn't ask why not.

"Your dream was about me." He guessed part of the truth.

Celia said, "You scare me."

"You should be scared of me."

She pulled away and looked at him, but he turned his head. The room was dark, but she could see his profile, soft for once in the dim light from the bedroom. "Why should I be? You don't act like you're crazy. If you wanted to, to take advantage of me, you could have done so numerous times by now. You carry a knife and no gun. You hide under the noses of those looking for you. I don't understand." The last came as a whisper. Celia shook her head, confused. She felt as if she'd stumbled into complete darkness with no light to give her hope of escape.

She stared at his silent face. Celia surprised herself when she reached up to brush her fingers through the stranger's hair, but he caught her hand before she could touch him. He glared at her, annoyed, but he didn't let go of her. Tension writhed from his hand to hers like a furious serpent, gleaming, shiny. Wildness climbed inside her, crazy, sparking a flame in her belly that in the end would explode, bringing, she feared, not bliss but death.

Celia freed her hand from his but her heart accelerated. Her blood raced through her veins as if to prevent her, but she touched him anyway. Everything in her said that to touch him would be dangerous, that she should stop before it was too late. But her fingers, though timid, caressed his hair, and this time he didn't stop her, didn't protest, nor did he take his eyes from hers. His hair felt unexpectedly fine and soft under her fingers. Other than her father's, she'd never touched a grown man's hair.

He didn't move at first. Then he raised his hand to her hair, which wasn't much longer than his. His touch was hesitant yet curious, as if he'd never felt another person before. His eyes shifted to watch his moving hand, a gentle tracing of her face, brushing her cheek, the line of her jaw. His eyes followed every move, yet his face remained unreadable. Celia stopped breathing.

He reached for her hand and pulled her to her feet. Dread stalked like a specter as he pulled her into the bedroom. He turned her around and fear spiked through her. "I won't hurt you," he said from behind her. He lifted the edge of her shirt. She closed her eyes and held her breath. His fingers found the cut his knife had made on her back and smoothed gently over it. "I did this to you. I'm sorry." Then he turned her to face him and sat her down on the bed. His hand took hers again and his thumb caressed her palm for a short while. Then he put her hand back in her lap, slowly, as if reluctant to let it go, and a shadow darkened his stern face. "You sleep in here this time."

Kindness? It was the last thing she expected, and the only thing she'd ever wanted. Her abductor left the door open when he returned to the main room. Daring herself, and him, she turned the light off. She heard the sofa creak under his weight, strained for any sound of him stealing back into the room. Without bothering to ask herself why her heart didn't slow to its normal beat, she drifted into blessed sleep.

When she awoke, he had gone, and she was tied to the bed.

23

Eight members of the team—Greene, Bell, Martin, Smyth, O'Toole, Patterson, and DIs Hawthorne and Carter—plus Thain sat in the murder room. Eight in the morning had come too early. Everyone looked haggard, and Thain didn't want to think about the risk he'd decided to take; if he did, he wouldn't be able to convince them. If the footage from inside the two stores had given them a frontal shot of the suspect, Thain wouldn't be in the position he now found himself. But St. John had gotten the films from both stores, sooner than expected, and found nothing more useful than in the films of the bank heist and the store where their suspect had kidnapped Celia Wight. The man had kept his face away from any clear shot. The one thing that had clinched Thain's decision was that the man in both stores had been white, alone, similar in build to their suspect, and he'd bought women's wear of the correct size.

Thain decided he would say as little as possible, enough to plant the seed; but the risk remained all the same. He didn't trust himself not to punch Carter—no matter who was watching—if Carter started ridiculing him on the Wraith issue again. He'd do anything to avoid that. Almost. He had to be extra cautious, because what he knew of the Wraith already tempted him to walk that familiar path and he couldn't allow that desire, that habit, to bust through his locks and chains and publicize to the team just what made these two matches so important.

All eight looked at him, and he remained cautious. *Just plant the seed. You don't have to grow the tree.* He inhaled. His breath came too shallow, too fast. He deepened it, slowed it down. *Here goes nothing.* "I have two questions," he began. "What if this killer uses nothing but cash? And if he does, could that narrow our field?"

"How, exactly?" Hawthorne, in the seat next to him, asked the first question. "I mean, according to you he's already bought her clothes. Why would he buy her more? How do we know he's the one who bought those clothes to begin with?"

"Because of what we *can* see of him on the store videos. There are enough similarities to think he's our man." Thain had to explain this without anyone guessing why his thoughts had started down this path. "We have a description of the women's clothing purchased. St. John has already changed the profile he's looking for on all the incoming CCTV films to match those clothes. I think it's possible the suspect bought a coat for himself as well, but no one would think to notice that in the same way they notice a man buying for a woman. Even if we don't find either of them on film, the suspect won't know that. He might keep changing their clothing in case we're smart enough to guess he would use that angle. But that's not the only point. So far we have a *theory*, if you prefer, about the two shops. There could be more. If you were on the run, staying in the city for whatever reason, would you want to be traceable? No, of course not. More people use credit or cheque cards now, so cash purchases should stand out a bit, especially those involving a lone male buying anything for a woman. Clothes aren't inexpensive. Most people use a card for payment. Even cheques are used far less than, say, ten years ago." The room remained silent. He began to wonder if they'd heard him correctly.

Rae stood and went to the map on the wall. "You think if we canvas stores selling these items—"

"Large stores where he'd be less likely to be noticed," he amended.

"—we can somehow find him? Thain, beg pardon, but there are thousands of stores in London."

"Yes, I know." *Don't blow this, Thain, not when they're at least asking questions.* "But now we have something specific to look for and"—he paused, wanting to cover all his theories but not to alienate anyone who might find those theories too improbable—"we've limited our questions to clothing and the like. I think we should continue to do so, but also to target rented rooms or flats paid for in cash or any other form of payment that can't be traced."

Carter shook his head. "Whatever for?"

"What if he rented a place to stay, where he's holed up, waiting us out? What if he's rented more than one? What if he stays in a different place each night, or . . . You know," he mused, a new thought interrupting his carefully rehearsed speech, "besides the very first films when our suspect kidnaps her, we haven't found *any* films of them together, much less during the day. The confirmed sightings of him alone have been from people's interviews."

Carter looked peeved. "So, that confirms he's already gone. This is a waste of time."

Thain stopped breathing, waiting for Hawthorne to agree with Carter. Hawthorne said, "I think you should at least finish, Thain." He kept his eyes on Thain and ignored Carter.

Thain didn't hesitate. He pointed to a pin on the map. "Look at where he left Celia Wight's bags. And here are the two shops where he purchased women's clothing." He moved his finger over two other pins. "In my opinion this confirms that it's entirely possible that he stays in one area and shops in another. He could be anywhere."

Clive nodded and said, "Bedsits?"

"Especially bedsits. Some of those one-room rentals have their own baths. Perfect cover. Guess I don't need to say to check anything on or near Adie Road."

"Why not hotels, inns, or bed and breakfasts?"

"Too public. He wouldn't risk it. Increases the odds of someone recognizing her."

"Since you, Hawthorne, seem to believe this a valid line of inquiry, I'll call the chief right now," Carter said, and Thain ignored the slight yet couldn't help but think, *Of course you will, and you'll be taking the credit for this, if it works.*

"What put you on to this, Thain?" Hawthorne's question put him back on edge. He reminded himself to maneuver carefully on this terrain.

"Look at this." He went over to the monitor and pulled the chair aside so everyone could gather round and see what he'd seen. "I read this one first." He pointed to the window on the right side of the screen. "See here, this is what I told you about a man buying women's clothing. This is the part that HOLMES caught; he paid cash for them."

Hawthorne moved a little closer. "Yes."

"And here, in this report, a lone white male, same approximate height and coloring, and wearing the same kind of coat, came in and bought a woman's coat. Everything he bought in both stores was for a woman approximately Celia Wight's size. He paid cash for everything."

Clive looked at Thain with wary admiration. "You aren't thinking . . ."

Thain sighed, trying to calm the stress flooding his body and more than thankful Carter was still on the phone with the chief.

"We aren't talking about the Wraith, Clive. Is he all you have on your mind?" Everyone chuckled, thank heaven.

"A lot of people still use cash for those items," Martin commented.

"But not for bed-sitting rooms. I know they do for clothes and such, but on big items, like rents, cash is becoming a thing of the past."

Clive sat back and frowned. "The odds seem pretty overwhelming against the man at both of these stores being our man."

"I know, but the films show that both men were white, about the same height and build, and wearing similar clothing. It wouldn't be the first time, would it, that the odds didn't favor us and we still came through? We're cops, right?"

Rae smiled and said, "If we look at this your way, appears to me we have another reason to think Celia Wight is still alive."

Thain wanted to hug her. Instead he said, "Seems more than likely, don't you think? He must be set on keeping her that way for a while. Why else buy the clothing? Why ditch the bags to tell us he knows we're on his trail?"

"I wish we could do something else, something that's more—I don't know—proactive." O'Toole stood back and chewed an already shortened fingernail. "This is like taking a shot in the dark."

Carter hung up and walked over to them as they stood around the monitor. "The chief approved more interviews and checking on the rents. I explained what we're looking for and what we're up against. He said this sounded like more of a lead than anything else so far."

"Looks like you have your wish, O'Toole," Thain said. "You can help us with all the legwork the chief just authorized."

"It will take some time to get the information on the bedsits and such," Greene said.

Hawthorne took charge. "So we'll concentrate on shops and stores for now." He moved back to his own desk as he continued giving them their orders. "Smyth, call the absent team members and give them their new assignments. We'll do this in two-person teams. Greene, do you have that call to action ready to go?" He glanced at Greene, who was already seated at his terminal.

"Yes, sir."

"Enter these teams and we'll get started."

"Hawthorne, what about—" Carter started.

"You've made the call to the chief, Carter. It's time to list out the teams." Hawthorne read out who would be on which team. Carter glanced at Bell and started to protest when Hawthorne named Thain as her partner, but the others ignored him and started putting on their coats. No one could forget it was still bitter outside with winter's icy touch.

"Thanks, Thain. Love this part of the job," Clive winked at him and zipped his coat up. "Ready to ride, O'Toole?"

"Am I ever. Been stuck in this room too long." The two headed out as Rae joined Thain at the door.

"You and me, looks like."

Thain said, "Glad of it. Are you?"

Did he imagine her slight hesitation? "Rather be with you than Carter. I must thank Hawthorne some day for taking lead on naming the teams. I thought for sure I'd get stuck with Carter if he'd had the say."

"He tried. Did you see his face when Hawthorne took charge?"

They laughed all the way down to the front door and outside. Laughing . . . Thain hadn't done much of that in a long while.

24

Fresh, icy air hit the tall man's face, and he welcomed its bracing effect as he moved into the streets. Midday still sat an hour or so away, but gray snow-pregnant clouds, with their ominous and cold predictions, already dampened the spirits of even the most ridiculously happy Christmas shoppers. He usually preferred early morning, when all seemed new, empty, and untainted, when the quiet allowed him to sneak up on a small sense of satisfaction, the only semblance of contentment he knew.

But today the colorlessness of the sky felt as bleary and frozen as his mood. He still carried the burden of a hostage, and the police shadowed his every move, even if they hadn't found him. He could feel their proximity. Though he knew they didn't have a photo of him, every time he passed a bobby, his back stiffened as he waited for a shout demanding that he halt. He sensed something—no, some*one*—close, too close on his trail. The time had come to get out of London, and with her in tow, time ran against him.

Why had he touched the woman, touched her face, her hair, her hand—soft, lovely and frightened, all things he'd managed to stay away from? He craved her, wanted to taste her, and so he'd left the flat. He had no memory of her taste during that reckless, impromptu, mind-altering kiss. He'd been too preoccupied with his safety, with the discordant drums in his head, the flash of colors he wouldn't acknowledge. He had never been reckless, and yet look what he had done. No excuse was good enough for him to ignore his training. Nervous tension, and confusion, fused inside of him, foreign, alien to all he knew himself to be.

He didn't know her name because he'd avoided knowing it, but he knew her scent. She remained his captive and meant nothing to him but a means to an end. Yet he understood, better than he wanted to, the damage done to him by one stolen kiss. His heart thumped now, as his head had pounded when he'd kissed her. He hadn't paid attention to his heart in years.

Forget the heart. Get your mind back on the goal. Head out of London at once instead of evading the cops for the prescribed five days, as per usual strategy.

Two days had come and gone; now the third had begun and he decided to cut short his time in London. He needed to finish the last part of the obsession that imprisoned him. It must override any other desire, including the one for the woman.

He approached the Internet café he'd chosen and reached for the door. The café looked crowded, which suited him fine. He made his way to the counter and requested time on a computer. There was a wait. He ordered takeaway lunches with coffee and tea. Last night he'd seen, by her brave attempt not to cry, that she liked tea. He paid, and waited until the computer he wanted was free, then he pushed through the crowd, taking the one with a seat turned to view the room, logged on, and handled the business he knew would be waiting: a new job.

He'd finished giving instructions on where to send his fee when he glanced up at a couple coming in the door of the café. His heart rate shot up. Cops. He knew without a second look what, who, they were. He cut short his email and logged off. Just then the clerk waved to him and held up his two orders. For once, time had chosen his side. He stood and made his way to the counter as if he were in no rush, as if his blood pressure hadn't shot up to two hundred over ninety. He stood so close to the end of this final play. He wouldn't get careless, or any more careless than he'd already been by taking the woman in the first place.

He didn't look at the cops, a man and a young Indian woman, as he gathered his order and headed for the door. He had to walk straight past them, close enough to brush the man's coat sleeve. "Sorry," he said, moving on. The cop glanced at him, nodded, but did no more than that as he turned and placed his own order. In a crowded café everyone expected that, because of the close quarters, someone was bound to at least brush against you from time to time. Once the tall man hit the sidewalk he gritted his teeth and kept his feet moving until he turned the first corner. Then he paused and checked behind him to be sure they hadn't followed. Why would they? They had no photo of him. Those two cops had no idea who he was. Angry, he chided himself for his unnecessary reaction. He couldn't abide his irrational behavior, or his heartbeat racing far above a normal pace. Ever since he'd touched the woman, nothing had been normal.

Halfway back to the flat, he forgot the incident as he struggled with acknowledging that a dramatic twist had taken place in his universe. He didn't ask himself what it was, because he didn't want to know. But he no longer denied that the twist had happened. Which is why the woman would die. He could hide her body well enough to give him lead time, and though the thought made him physically sick, he forced the scene into this last act of his play. Before anyone could be the wiser, he would be in York finishing what had started long ago. Honor demanded it. His demons demanded it. The choice was made, but this woman had him considering what might come next.

Right in the middle of the sidewalk, he stopped. *Bloody hell.* He shook his head and continued on, mentally shoving away images of the woman reclining on a beach, her body in the sun with drops of ocean water glistening over her tanned skin.

Upon entering the apartment building he made his customary check before unlocking the door. He set the food and drinks upon the table and moved into the bedroom. The woman lay where he'd left her upon the bed, looking not the least bit sleepy.

"Food and tea? Oh, good. I'm so hungry," she quipped.

He released her in silence, then went back to the table and took off his coat. He sorted the lunches—ham and cheese on baguettes—took one, picked up his cup of coffee, and headed for the sofa.

She followed him and pulled a chair out at the table. "Am I the reason you sit over there, or do you never sit at a table unless you're in a restaurant?"

He didn't look at her, didn't speak, did his best to ignore her questions.

She stayed at the table, eyes on him. He bit into his sandwich but it was like chewing on dry leather. He couldn't swallow. He gulped his coffee without tasting it, stood and tossed his sandwich and cup away. He *would* get rid of her. He *would* stay focused. He *would* keep his ten-step lead ahead of those searching for her, and for him.

Then he made the mistake of looking at her. Those blue eyes scared him. They scared him because in them he saw questions that someone inside of him wanted to answer, but couldn't.

25

After three hours of riding tubes and tromping over the section of London assigned to them, Rae Bell and Thain had managed to rule out five department stores and ten smaller shops, coming up with no results.

"I'm cold and I'm tired. Want to find a good cup of coffee?"

"Do I ever," Rae said. "We passed a small Internet café up the street. Want to go back and try it?"

"Sure. Anything close sounds good. I didn't have breakfast this morning, did you?"

"No. Don't usually. I'm a morning coffee girl."

They moved at a brisk pace, threading around whoever happened to share the sidewalk with them. When they arrived they could see through the windows that the place was brimming. But some tall chairs lining the street-side windows looked empty.

"Packed out, but maybe we can find a seat over there." He pointed and Rae agreed.

Standing in line next to the counter, she said, "So much warmer in here, and the coffee smells divine." She perused the room, rubbing her gloved hands and making small talk. "Look at all these computers in this little place. Ten. Only one open right now—no, two. That guy's order is ready."

The guy picked up his order and squeezed by, apologizing as he brushed Thain's sleeve. Thain took it as a good sign that some people were still polite. They placed their order and took their steaming cups over to two chairs in front of the window. "Thain, can I ask you a personal question?"

"Depends."

"I've worked with you on many homicide cases, and I've never seen you get the least bit stressed or . . . involved, the way you have with this one."

"Is that a question?"

"Depends."

"Right. Well, is that a good or bad thing?" he asked.

"I don't know. You tell me. I'm as concerned about Celia Wight as anyone, but you seem to have more invested than you usually do. Mind if I ask why?"

"I do."

She shook her head and looked at him. "But I'm asking anyway."

"Because you're concerned I don't have enough objectivity?"

"No. I get the impression something about her gets to you, and no, not like that." She paused, staring hard at him. "You aren't thinking you're in love with her are you, Thain?"

He glared at her and didn't say a word.

She glanced down at her steaming mug and said, "No, I guess that would be beyond ridiculous, and though you're eccentric"—he raised his eyebrows at that—"I know you aren't stupid. It's, you have a look on your face when you look at her photo that says you're relating to her in some way."

"Apparently St. John was right about your powers of observation. Does that come with the pencil and paper talent?"

She smiled and stirred her coffee. "In a way, I suppose."

"I don't like to talk about the past."

"Well, I got that. So?"

"So?"

"Do it anyway. Talk. Let me in, a bit. Tell me something I don't know about you."

"Then you'll do the same?"

"If you want. You already know more about me—"

"Than you know about me. I get it."

"The only thing I know about your past is the assassination that made the papers, and that Interpol kicked you out because you were, shall we say, obsessed with the invisible Wraith? They said your obsession was negatively affecting your work."

Thain sipped his coffee, the steam thawing his frozen cheeks. "Well, then. Seems you do know as much about me as I about you."

"Not so. At least you know about my parents, my siblings. You know I'm from Mumbai."

"All right. I'm from Elgin, up near the North Sea. I have two parents, still living, and an elder brother. I wanted to be a policeman, so I went to the Scottish Police College in Kincardine, less than an hour northwest from Edinburgh. After I graduated, and the botched first assignment, I asked to train with Interpol. After that I asked for a transfer to the LMPS and here I am."

"Wow. You really *don't* like to talk about yourself."

"I did warn you." He wanted to but couldn't smile as he said it.

"Have you always been this reticent?"

"Rae—"

"Yes?"

"What do you want to know?"

"What happened to make you have such empathy for Celia Wight?"

He stared at Rae but didn't see her as time shifted and turned him eighteen again . . .

Agatha laughed at his joke and kissed his cheek as they turned the corner of the park, the streetlamp blazing upon them, lighting their steps as easily as the night freshened their faces after the meal they'd just shared at the pub. He pulled her closer, not questioning his good luck.

Out of the dark, the men hit fast, taking him down with one blow. But he leapt back to his feet, fists flailing, roaring as he attacked his attackers. Too many knuckles punched him in the gut, in the face and head, and Agatha's screams died abruptly. Looking for her, he saw a man dragging her off with his hand over her mouth as her tiny fists hit anything they could; her heels kicked, her body whipped and writhed like a captured snake, for what good it did her. He punched again but someone rushed him; a sudden sharp pain pierced his stomach. He fell hard. The pavement hurt his knees as he watched, helpless, while the two men carried Agatha away. His limbs didn't answer his demands to run after her. And then, no sound, as if he were suddenly deaf. His stomach. He looked down. Blood discolored his shirt, its warmth seeped down his abdomen and onto his jeans. One of his hands touched the growing stain, the other reached out toward where he'd last seen Agatha. He yelled, but still heard no sound. Only when his head struck the pavement did he stop yelling.

He'd never told anyone in London about Agatha, about his brother, or why he'd become a police officer. Had never wanted to. But Celia Wight's case—not the bank murder, not the heist—Celia Wight's case preyed upon him as if she crouched in his head, her mouth open in a soundless scream—like Agatha's when she was kidnapped before being brutally raped the night he'd let her down. The night he'd been left with nothing but a scar on his stomach and her complete rejection of him.

"Thirteen years ago my girlfriend was kidnapped and raped. I was with her when she was taken." He didn't know why he said it. He just blurted it out.

Rae sat back and said, "Raped? I'm sorry, Thain. She isn't dead, is she?"

"No." He stared at her, rigid and angry.

"How old were you? You had to be—"

"Eighteen, final year of secondary. She refused to see me, after. I tried but she wouldn't see me. Never has." Now that Rae had breached the dam, he couldn't stop and he wanted her to know what she'd done, that it was her fault she'd opened this door. "I don't *want* to think of her. I don't want to think about what happened that night. But she's why I became a cop. I couldn't help her, but I can help others. I can help Celia Wight. She's had it too rough, Rae. Does it matter that it was a blown tire the chauffeur hadn't been able to adjust for, that the ditch had been filled with water? No. Her parents still left her—Celia—alone. They're still dead, and nothing will ever bring them back. She has no one except the Kings that care if she's found alive or dead."

"Thain, I'm—"

"I know because I checked on her parents' case. You want the details?"

"Thain—"

"Remember when I went to West End Central the other day? I spent two hours at my desk checking on everything in her file and found nothing suspicious. Could be a really good cover up, or just a horrible accident. On the way back to the embassy from a formal event, a tire blew and their driver lost control of the car. It rolled four times down an embankment and landed top side down in two meters of water. Her parents drowned when they couldn't get out of the car. The Wights weren't particularly influential or ambitious people. In fact the only remarkable detail, because of the time period, is that Mrs. Wight was the ambassador, not her husband. I'd meant to, but haven't yet said anything to you, to the team, about these details, but I think it's obvious that they clear Celia of being in league with anyone, much less her kidnapper. Of course, that brings me no closer to guessing why she's important to him."

"Us, Thain. It brings *us* no closer. But I agree. If what you say is true, she's an innocent in all this."

"You have no idea. I went through literally everything I could find on her parents, and her life after, and you know, losing her parents wasn't the end of it—"

"Thain, Alban, you don't—"

"You wanted to know, didn't you?"

"Stop it, Thain, just stop it."

He stared at her, fuming inside. "I warned you."

"All right. I understand. She's had it rough and so have you."

"I haven't, not like she has. Not like Agatha did."

"You're overreacting."

He wanted to leave right then. "You said you wanted to know. Now that I've told you, you chastise me?"

"I didn't know you'd go off like that."

"Have I confirmed your supposition that I'm too close to the case for objectivity?" Without waiting for her answer, he stood and grabbed his empty cup. He took it to the counter and headed out the door. Her hand touched his sleeve before he made it to the corner, and he slowed.

"I'm sorry, Alban. Really. I had no idea."

He halted beside a streetlight and bowed his head. The snow had started again while they were in the café. Rae moved closer, her hand still on his sleeve. It was impossible to feel the warmth of it through her glove and his coat sleeve, but he felt it all the same, pulsing and alive.

"I shouldn't have reacted that way," he said. "I hate this part of the job, Rae. I never let cases get to me. There are too many with sad endings." He looked at her then. "I don't want hers to be one of them."

26

"Have you finished?" Celia's abductor glared at the untouched steaming tea on the table. She shook her head, then picked it up and sipped it. He gathered her empty sandwich wrappings and threw them away.

"You're a neat freak," she commented.

"Get some rest. We'll leave right after dark."

"Are we going to be up all night like the last two?"

He hesitated. "Yes." He sat on the couch and leaned back, crossed his arms, and closed his eyes. He didn't look the slightest bit relaxed. Celia finished her tea and threw away her empty cup. She went into the bedroom and lay on the bed, and though she sensed that he wouldn't come in till the time came for them to leave, she left the light on. A room without windows was too dark to bear.

A strong sense of being watched woke her. She sat up fast and found him standing just inside the doorway. "Is it time?" she asked as she swung her feet to the floor and started to rise.

"No." He didn't move. He didn't say anything more, but his face radiated cold again, dark and glacial, like a snowstorm. He stayed there staring at her for so long, goose bumps broke out all over her body, a premonition, a warning. She stood and faced him. What else could she do? She had no defense, nothing to fight him off with if he'd changed his mind about what he would do to, or with, her. All she had were her guts and her wits.

"Have you changed your mind?" she said.

He frowned and glared at her. "About what?"

"About me. Let me go. Tie me up and leave me somewhere I won't be found until after you're safe. I can try and stall them, if you want."

His face showed no inkling that he'd heard one word she'd said.

"Please. I don't want to die." She didn't dare look away or bow her head as she wanted to. She prayed the lock on their gaze would keep him from rash behavior; she willed him to accept her compromise. Because now she understood that while he'd been gone he had reevaluated her threat to his safety. He had realized what a drag she would be on his ability to travel in a stealthy mode.

"What happened out there to change your mind?"

This question got a reaction. Just a flicker across his forehead.

"Please, I don't want to die," she whispered. Her throat closed on familiar dread. "Please, please let me go."

27

Thain guessed his creased forehead gave away his frustration during the next meeting when Chief North asked for updates from the DIs—which also meant Rae, Clive, and Thain—because the chief wouldn't stand still. He paced in front of them, one hand in his trouser pocket, the other holding his chin as he looked up and asked Thain point blank, "You've had some news, and it's not good?"

"It could be good, in the long run, the very long run. But we all know time is a factor here, and I"—he glanced at Rae and Clive—"*we* think our time's running out, sir. The information on the flats or bedsits and cash payments is taking too long to come in from the rental agencies. And in the shops, more people pay for things with cash than we'd thought, especially at this time of year."

"Before Christmas."

"Yes."

"Have we found anything that could be a lead?"

Rae answered, "Nothing from the stores, but we've found some promises in the rentals we have information on." No one wanted to give the chief false hope, but they didn't want to disappoint him either.

"Show me what you have."

Clive pointed to a small stack of folders on the table in front of him. "This is what we have from the rental agencies, miscellaneous rentals paid for with cash or other forms of payment besides credit or cheque."

Then Thain held up a lean folder. "But these are the interesting ones. We've been able to get access to some of the utility payments as well. They've located four possible properties—so far—that could interest us. The utilities use at these properties is sporadic, and all were paid for, of course, in cash, or they have meters installed. The names are different on each address, but they're all men's names, paid for by post, not in person."

"Good. What are you doing about them?"

"With your approval, we'll send teams out on these."

"Right. You have it. What do we have on the murder victim's past?"

Rae stood. "Richard McLean came from York, sir. We've found the typical: went to school, left home for university, landed a job with the Royal Bank of Scotland and has been there ever since. Married, one child—a boy. Owns a flat in Knightsbridge, in Pont Street. His parents still live in York and have been contacted, of course, as has the wife. The parents and the wife were interviewed yesterday. Nothing to go on there, sir. He's about as plain as unbuttered bread."

"Have someone dig deeper. People aren't murdered in their own offices for no reason."

"Yes, sir." Clive said.

Rae said, "Mr. and Mrs. King phoned in."

"The abductee's British friends from the States?" North actually sat down. That was a first, the chief sitting during a meeting. Usually he leaned on a table or desk.

"Yes. They saw her photo on the news."

"How are they coping?"

"They're terrified she's dead. They want to know if there's anything they can do. They're tired of waiting."

"As are we. Anything else?" The chief gazed around the room and Thain stood.

"Yes, sir." He looked for reassurance from Bell and Patterson and they each gave him a slight nod. *All right,* he thought. *All right. Bell and Patterson won't catch flak for my ideas.* "Chief, may I be blunt?"

The chief glared at him, and then at Rae and Clive, as Thain had expected he might. That's why he'd already gone over this with them and garnered their, well, if not their approval, at least their agreement that he could sink his own ship as long as he didn't take them down with him.

The chief said, "If you must." He glowered, and Thain's nerves popped.

"I'm fairly certain the killer hasn't left the city."

"We've put men on all major exits to the country. No one's seen anything out of the ordinary and they've stopped hundreds of people, so you could be right. I suppose it's possible he's sitting tight until he thinks we aren't looking."

"Sir, if he's still here, why?" Thain said, his glance darting to Rae and Clive again. "There are plenty of other suitable places to hide on this island. A man and a woman traveling together would be nothing to notice especially, even if the woman were identifiable, if he'd left right away, before news of her kidnapping made it out. Perhaps, sir, he's following a pattern, only this time it's harder because he has Celia Wight with him. He must hide in a way he doesn't usually have to."

"Yet we still can't find him."

Thain had kept his hands in his pockets, and he had no luck trying to still his thumb as it rubbed the smooth screen of his cell phone in a nervous rhythm. "Still, I know he's here."

"You *think* he's here. He could've done exactly what you said before and left straight after the murder."

"But we have this man who bought those clothes—" Clive said.

The chief disputed, "He could be anyone. How many days has it been? Three?"

Thain nodded. "Yes, sir. If the buyer is our man, he could've left the city by now, I know. But—"

"Is this cash chase a dead end?"

Looking at the chief, Thain said, "If you ask me—"

"Of course I'm asking you. You're the one talking, Thain."

"Sir." Thain almost stopped there, knowing the chief's tolerance for tangents. *Celia Wight. Think of Celia Wight.* "I know I can sound a bit—well, my ideas are sometimes different from others'."

"Putting it mildly, I'd say."

Thain faltered, but with a concerned look from Rae, continued. "And I'm aware we have but the two linked clues that HOLMES has given us. However, my instinct says our man bought those clothes, sir.

He's still here." Pausing again, he looked at the abyss in front of him and took a leap of faith. "If the man isn't one of the thieves, and if he's a killer smart enough to have *risked* using the heist as cover, we must think about him in a different way. What if this isn't his first murder? What if this man stays in the area after he kills someone and doesn't try to leave? If he has a place to stay, or maybe more than one, he could conceivably hide in plain sight, and we'd never see him because he isn't trying to run."

Chief North stood up again, began to pace again, as if Thain's speculation took some time to digest. "You think that's what he's doing now?"

"Possibly." He dared to add, "Probably." He managed to keep his hand in his pocket, and his thumb finally stilled as he continued laying out his argument as blatantly as if he'd hung his underwear out to dry in the murder room. He had everything to lose, but so did Celia Wight. "If you consider that he hasn't left a trail, that perhaps he never leaves a trail, that he disappears as soon as his job is done, and no one knew he was there to begin with, this course of action might make sense."

"So he's a killer for hire? Bloody hell, Thain. Are you going on about the Wraith again?"

"Sir," he started.

"Do you never let up?"

Thain's hands flew from his pockets as if they could calm the chief down, make the chief listen to his idea if he waved them around enough. "To be honest, sir," he rushed on, "if you'd asked me that question before this case, I might have said yes. But the man I've studied all these years never took a hostage before, never made a mistake, and—"

"I don't want to hear any more about this."

"But—"

The chief peered at him through narrowed eyes. He pointed at Thain. "You are a good if not better than good detective, Thain. Except for this one obsession. Don't change my opinion of you now. I'd hate to lose a good detective, but I won't tolerate anymore of this talk. Understood?"

"But this man knew the location of every CCTV camera on his route! Every. Single. One. Even at the store where he took Celia Wight, which is blocks from the bank."

"That is more like what I want to hear. Something valid to *this*," and he jabbed the air with his finger again, "investigation. This one, Thain. Not cold cases."

Heated, and with frustration coloring every word, Thain pulled himself up. "He knew where the cameras were along the entire route between the bank and the store, and the route he took after he left Liberty with her. We haven't found him on camera since, and yet this man has bought clothing and we don't know what else. He's taken a hostage, and made them both evaporate. He's kept her hidden for three days now."

The room stood still as if everyone held their breath. What would the chief say? What would he do to Thain for his defiant interruption? Thain had the grace, or cowardice, to look at the floor.

"You are pushing my patience, Thain. The press hasn't let up. Neither have the Super and the rest. This once," Chief North said, "I will overlook your manners and your tone. Follow up your 'instinct,' as you say. You've done it before with good results. But you stay on target. I won't condone you going off on a tangent. I will hear no more talk of your ghost, understood?"

Thain nodded in total disbelief, and even a bit of hope. He still had a job. "Yes, sir. Thank you, sir."

"And you two," the chief added, pointing at DIs Hawthorne and Carter, "keep me informed of anything new."

The rest of the meeting didn't take long, and Thain stood by in embarrassed silence until the chief left. He wanted to leave immediately, but knew he had to thank Rae and Clive for their support. He hoped they weren't angry at how the chief had taken his comments. Walking over to Rae and Clive, Thain shrugged on his coat. "I'm sorry."

"Don't be," Rae said.

Clive shook his head. "I thought you were out the door there for a moment. Chief was piping."

Thain took a breath. "So did I."

"I can't believe you kept going, and with that tone. Never seen you get that angry, if Carter isn't nagging you."

"Right. I know. Apology accepted?"

"No need. We got what we wanted, didn't we?" Clive's smile didn't go as far as Thain would have liked in lifting the dire weight that had settled on his chest since his outburst. He didn't want any of the chief's fury to land on Clive or Rae's shoulders. This was his fight, not theirs, and he didn't like the thought of his actions putting their jobs and reputations in jeopardy.

"Didn't we?" Clive repeated, his expression questioning Thain's hesitation.

"So far."

"Yes, so far, and that's all we can ask for right now, correct?"

"Aye. Got it, Clive. I'm listenin'."

"Love it when that Scottish brogue kicks in." Clive smiled and thumped him on the arm.

Thain knew Clive was trying to cheer him up. "Right. Listen, I'd like to go home for a shower and change of clothes. I'll be back in forty-five minutes. That all right?"

Rae sighed. "Sounds like a wonderful idea. Don't forget to eat."

Clive, as tired as the rest of them, gave half a smile. "You could go now as well, if you'd like, Rae. Neither one of you has to come back in straight away. Take a break. I'll take care of HOLMES while you're gone." He picked up the stack of rental files and moved toward the HOLMES stations. Then he turned, his face unusually serious. "Both of you keep your phones close with ringers on high."

The case wasn't just getting to Thain. It was getting to all of them. Maybe that was why, as they headed out, Thain said to Rae, "Want some breakfast?"

Her eyes opened wide in surprise. "At this time of the night?"

"I do it all the time, breakfast for dinner, I mean. Easy protein. I could make us some egg sandwiches?"

"At your place?"

Totally discomfited now, he said, "Bad idea, huh? Don't know what—"

"No, great idea. I can't believe you're inviting me to your place after my prying."

"Ah, that's a good excuse, isn't it? You can make it up to me?"

"Sure. If you say so. Come on, make me a sandwich."

"I have tomatoes too. Warning you, I use butter not margarine."

Rae smiled at him when they hit the sidewalk. "I'm not only a morning coffee girl, I adore butter."

28

The cold crept under his coat as the wind picked up. A storm was brewing. Snow or rain, he couldn't tell. The woman's hands were chapped and her nose gleamed red. The kidnapper knew her lips would be blue but for the scarf. She trembled against him as they rounded the corner onto Methley Street where he'd rented a bedsit for the last six months, the last one they'd use before they left London. The building sat nestled halfway along the block. The assassin didn't slow as they approached from the opposite side of the street, ever careful. As they passed it, two men stepped from his building and stood on the steps conversing for a moment. Cops—in plain clothes, but he could tell they were cops. As he watched, the policemen looked up and spotted him and the woman walking through the spill of light from a streetlamp. There wasn't time to think.

"Keep walking, and run if I tell you to. Don't ask why, just walk." He couldn't afford to leave the woman now. She could give them too much information. He kept their pace as normal as possible until they reached the turn onto Bowden Street. The police had followed them, as he knew they would. At Bowden he turned on the speed. Small though it was, he knew how to use his lead.

The woman kept up with him but her breath shortened. He glanced back. The cops ran, now, after them. He grabbed her hand and sprinted, faster with each stride. He knew she wouldn't last long at the dead-run pace he'd set, but they didn't have far to go. The darkness shielded them from the cops' line of vision and would help once he found what he searched for.

They turned left onto Cleaver Street. There it was. He halted before a tall iron gate with bent unsharpened spikes at the top, pointed toward the street to keep out undesirables. Though it was high and dangerous to climb, he knew of a remedy. He quickly pulled off his coat and threw it up and over to rest on top of the gate.

"I will lift you. Use this bar here in the middle to push off with your feet. Stay on the side and it will be easier to balance using the wall. Pull yourself over the top. My coat will protect you from the spikes. Once you're over, it's an easy climb down the other side."

"For you, maybe. I've never climbed anything like this before."

"If you want to stay on the gate until I get over, do so. But get going."

He hoisted her up before she could respond. She set her feet, and he turned his head hoping the cops weren't close enough to see them yet. As she clumsily pulled herself over the top, he'd already begun his assent. Clinging to the bars of the gate, his feet set on the metal band across the middle, which read "Cornwall Court," he pushed her high enough that she could bend over the top. Once over, she clung to the other side like a monkey. He turned his body toward the street, took hold of the top bent spikes, and curled his legs, then his body, up and over the incline of the spikes, landing on his stomach across the top of them. He slid till his feet hit the ground, then reached up and pulled her down. The woman fell readily against him. He held her close when he dragged her into a shadow as the cops ran by the gate. Too late he realized he'd left his coat on top of it. He listened to the thumping of their feet retreating. Grabbing her by the hand he moved back toward the gate. He could just reach the edge of his coat. He pulled it off. The pounding feet returned. He pushed her before him and melted into the shadow again. The cops stood in front of the gate pulling out cell phones.

Backing away with the woman in front of him, he kept his shoulder to the wall, letting it guide them further into the alleyway that led to the back door of the five-story flat building he planned to use for their escape. He regretted the bright security light over the door, waited to see if the cops cleared off from the gate. Instead one of them began to climb over it. The assassin glared at the light over the door into the building, their escape route; he knew they could be seen from the street, but he couldn't wait for the cops to get over the gate. He pulled her into the light with him, quickly picked the lock, and pushed the door open. He heard one of the cops yelling as they slipped inside. In the hallway, a small click echoed as he shut and locked the door behind them. He stood with his back against a wall. She peered up at him, trying to catch her breath. Her scarf had fallen to her throat during the chase, leaving her face a pale oval in the dim light of the hall.

"Sh," he whispered. "No sound now."

He felt her take a deep breath, perhaps to shout, but she held it when his hand hovered near her mouth. Soon, the police would have this entire area barricaded. He couldn't see much in the darkness, but as he propelled her up the stairs, the sharp odor of new paint said someone kept the building maintained. They had to get to the next floor. On the first landing he paused when the faint whine of sirens sounded. The din came through the window facing the intersection where Kennington Lane and Kennington Road joined and crossed Cleaver Street. He started up again, pulling the woman along, her small cold hand in his.

He had explored this building as one of the many backup plans he'd formulated for the bedsit on Methley Street, where he'd first seen the cops. Backup plans were a must for any of the flats or bedsits he used, whether in London or abroad. But this time was different because of the woman. Their chances of getting away without being seen were minuscule. Alone, no one could stop him. The all-important goal had to be achieved. But killing her went against everything he believed about himself. That's why he still kept her with him, wasn't it? He would figure a way out with her, or it was all for naught.

They climbed four flights before coming to the top of the staircase. As on the other floors, the lighting came from small sconces set between the numbered flat doors. The heavy permeating aroma of last night's roast said at least one of these flats was occupied. The sign attached to the outside of the building had announced that one of these at the top was 'to let,' which meant it would be empty, but he didn't know which one and he didn't want witnesses. He tugged her along with him, his steps silent as a cat's, while he checked the landing window facing Kennington Lane. Through the window he saw a ledge running along and above the roofline with a narrow indented foot space inside. Implanted in the narrow flat surface of the ledge were a number of vertical pipe railings all attached together horizontally, meant for security he supposed, but he wouldn't trust them with his weight. He unlocked the window and pushed to open it. It wouldn't budge. New paint. Turning to the woman, he said, "I don't want to kill anyone. Do you understand?"

"You want me to promise not to scream or run."

"Yes. I have to open this. I need you to stay right beside me."

She looked at the floor, her shoulders slumped. "You can't let me go now, can you?"

"No. Not yet."

"Not yet?" She looked surprised, almost hopeful.

"I don't want to kill anyone."

She hesitated and then said, "I promise."

It took less than two minutes to cut the paint and wrestle the window open. He glanced at the woman. She flicked her gaze away from the window, telling him she wished she were anywhere but there. "You're not a coward. You saved innocent lives," he said.

"What about mine?" she asked in a small voice. He didn't answer.

With her beside him, he leaned out the window to see if what he remembered came next. The roof, covered with wet shingles, slanted up at a steep incline on either side of the window, and he'd seen from the street that in both directions the neighboring roofs were joined, with high cement walls set between each flat and the one next to it. A slice of dawn's gray light brooded on the horizon, melding with the black of night and the dark stain of the heavy clouds sitting directly above them. Daybreak would come too soon, if the storm didn't swallow it. He hoped that if the clouds unburdened themselves it would be of snow and not rain. He glanced at the top of her head.

"You will go first. Stand straight and stay on that thin bit inside the ledge. Don't walk on the ledge. Lean in toward the building and ignore those poor excuses for railing," he said to her. "I'll be right behind you, and don't look down. From up here the landing would be unkind."

"I don't want to go out there."

"I know. But we have no choice. Now, go now."

She scooted out the window, turned to face him, and stretched her feet to find the foot space inside the ledge. He held her arms as she clung to the windowsill until she said, "I found it." Her voice wavered, but she didn't panic.

He guided her to one side, before he twisted out and down, finding the thin space easily.

"There's nothing to hold on to," she said. This time her voice shook, and she reached for one of the railings.

"Don't touch the railing. Lean in toward the building."

"I can't do this!'

"Yes, you can." He moved beside her and shifted until his arm encircled her back. They made it to the next window without having to climb a security wall, but this was a large building and he knew what it would take, on his own, to get to the edge of it. If they had any hope of escaping to the perimeter of the more elaborate search that he knew would be underway any minute, they would have to climb the security walls between the flats. He didn't tell her that yet. She had flattened herself and continued inching along. He tried not to hurry her as they moved across the cold and clammy all-but-vertical roof tiles, on their toes in the slight indent given them. The front of his jeans soon stiffened with damp, and the ground was a long way off. They had to make it to the end of the building. There, he knew a way down to the one-story shops fronting Kennington Lane. No other option existed. Escape was a given.

They hit the first divider. "We have to get over the security wall," he told her.

"I can't!"

"I will push you up." He balanced himself and pulled off his coat.

"No, we can't do this, we'll fall."

He took her chin in hand and stared through the dark at her. "We will do this. There is no other way."

"Leave me. Leave me and I won't say anything."

He must get her to think instead of panic. "I'll not leave you up here alone. I'll get you to safety, but you must do as I tell you." Her nod, no matter how reluctant, was all he wanted. "Take my coat. When you get to the top, bend over it and while on your stomach, swing your feet to the other side. That will bring your head to this side. Stay there. Balance on your stomach. Swing the sleeve of my coat to me and as I come up, you'll go down the other side. Find the roof, then the indent with your feet. All right?"

"No."

"Do it anyway."

She did. It worked more or less perfectly, and when they made it over the second one her movements became more confident.

They passed the fourth divider before he heard the helicopters. He glanced at the clouds overhead. Where was that snow? Hell, he'd be happy for rain. Beggars couldn't be choosers and all that. Staring at her short-cropped head of hair in front of him, and knowing they had at least one more wall, he made a decision. "Let me by. We must make that wall before the 'copters arrive."

She flattened herself as best she could. He stepped around her, holding his breath, not looking toward the ground. Ignoring all the space to his right, he raced to the partition and turned, his hand outstretched to help her.

She stood right where he'd left her, wild-eyed and stiff, as if turned to stone. The 'copters sounded louder, closer. He guessed that in less than a minute, bright searchlights would pin them, like dead moths on a collector's board. He couldn't leave her to tell all, and he couldn't kill her from this distance. He'd counted on her confusion, her trepidation at the height and slant of the roof. The instant he started toward her, she twisted away, trying to head back the way they'd come. Perhaps because of the policemen below, her fear of him seemed greater than her fear of her precarious position. Damn her fear, or was it bravery? He knew what would happen, and it did. In her haste, she teetered off balance, and grabbed for the flimsy pipe rail. It gave instantly, bending under her slight weight, and over she went.

29

Thain and Rae rode the tube back to his place in contemplative silence. His thumb played across his cell phone and gave him focus. In spite of his close call with the chief, his thoughts reached for that elusive assurance he wanted to have about whether or not this murder suspect and the Wraith were the same man. "Rae, if I talk about the . . . the Wraith, will you think me an idiot?"

"If I think that, I'll keep it to myself."

"Right." Thain took a breath and plunged. "I keep asking myself, what do I have, really, that could point to this man being the Wraith? Yes, both men seem intangible. Yes, both men used whatever convenient tool they found at hand. Yes, they both left the murder weapon in the wound. Yes, they both left a witness alive. Yes, they both, apparently, only use cash. But everything else is different." He paused, afraid to look at Rae and see the disbelief and even incredulity he'd seen on other faces when they heard him ramble like this, before he'd quit talking about it. But her look was intent, as if she truly listened to every word he said. If he continued, would he lose one of the two real friends he had in the department?

"Thain, go on," she prompted. "This is stuff I've never heard you say before."

He grimaced. "No wonder there."

"No, guess not."

Now that Thain had started, his mind took off, and he put into words the puzzle he had been ruminating over. "The murdered bank official died an extremely painful death. The wound was purposely messy. Celia Wight was kissed and kidnapped by the suspected killer.

Would an assassin change his methods this drastically? And if he did, why now? Why her? An assassin changing his methods is serious. It bothers me and makes me doubt what I'm seeing. If this man is the Wraith, why would he have made such rash mistakes as to, first, almost get caught, and, second, take a hostage, when he is a master of disappearance and escape?" Rae nodded as the train stopped, and they tossed ideas and theories around as they left the tube station and made their way to his flat.

When he put the key in the front door of the building, it hit him that she was the first person in months he'd invited to his place. She followed him as they climbed the stairs and he opened the door to his second-story abode. His neighborhood was decent: no high crime rate, no mansions either. He didn't care. Anyone entering this flat would know right away how he felt about the one place he called his own. Here he was free to be alone, to be himself, even if he didn't like to admit to himself just how alone he was.

Though the building itself needed a face-lift, not to mention new wiring and some updated plumbing, he'd decorated his small one-bedroom flat with utility, art, comfort, and a slight sentimentality in mind. They took off their coats and hung them on the pegs for that purpose decorating the wall by the door. Rae waited until he moved into the living area before following him in. Nervous without really knowing why, Thain said, "I've spent the last five years investing every spare penny I have in this place." The subtle blend of modern and antique furniture and fixtures created warmth without making the flat feel crowded or bombastic. At least, he thought so. It also helped that it wasn't too far from where he worked. "What do you think?" He wished immediately that he hadn't asked.

His flat was more than a haven to him. It was home. He and he alone had created this eye-of-the-storm peace in the midst of the chaotic work life he led, and he didn't want to hear anyone's judgment of it.

"Those are amazing photographs. Did you take them?" she asked. The walls bore numerous black-and-white prints of Scottish landscapes:

windswept highlands, pastoral lowlands, harsh coastlines, and some off-the-beaten-path scenes of Edinburgh, the work of a Scottish photographer he admired; his little slice of Scotland in the middle of the big London pie.

"No. I just like them."

"And the painting?" She'd moved deeper into the small living area. "Is that your family?" Above the mantle hung a framed painting of his parents, his older brother, Ellis, and himself at a time when life had held happiness and the promise of more. A family portrait. His parents had pounced upon the chance to have it done on a whim, the year before Agatha, the year before he'd finished school and gone on to the police academy. He allowed himself some comfort in knowing his mother would be happy he had it up, and not sitting in the back of a closet somewhere, even though he didn't look at it much, especially his brother. "Aye, it is."

On the fireplace mantle squatted his father's small antique clock, ticking away as it had all of his life, creating a homey, comfortable sound, a sound he would never admit that he craved. He didn't need to rub a cell phone screen when he had that magical and comforting *tock* to listen to. Each time he wound it he sensed his father standing next to him, nodding as if he approved of Thain still using it. His father had insisted he take it, when he left for London, as his mother had that he take the portrait. He was glad now that he hadn't fought either one of them about their wishes.

Rae leaned nearer to the mantle. The clock sat amongst several photos of groups of friends and some rugby trophies from the days when he played, when he actually had a life outside of work. The days before he'd moved to England and made it home, leaving Scotland and painful memories behind.

"You played rugby?"

"Surprised?"

"To understate it. You don't look the team sport kind of guy."

"I'm learning." Thain wondered from time to time if he'd made the right choice in leaving Scotland, but not today. Not with Celia Wight out there counting on him—though she didn't know it—to save her. Today he was as sure as he'd ever been, even if the murder suspect wasn't the Wraith, that he, Thain, was exactly where he should be.

Glancing at Rae he said, "Come on. I'll make you drool." He strode to the small kitchen and made a pot of strong aromatic coffee. From the tidy little fridge he pulled out eggs, a tomato, and bread and butter.

"I can't say I've ever had breakfast for dinner," Rae said, leaning her hip against his mother's small antique wooden table by the window.

"It's definitely not my first time. Doesn't take long to prepare, and we can eat it on the way back to the Hendon if Clive calls." He paused long enough to use the remote to turn on the stereo. As Dougie MacLean's light Scottish brogue and brooding guitar filled the room with soothing music, Thain asked, "That all right?"

"Lovely."

He nodded, stared at Rae a second, and then turned back to the stove and toaster. The music seemed somehow more romantic of a sudden.

Rae sat at the table and stared out at the flats across the way, and then she pushed to her feet. "Give me something to do or I'll fall asleep." Thain handed her the eggs, a bowl, and a fork.

"You can beat these up?"

"Of course. Thanks." Was it him, Thain thought, or did she seem a bit nervous?

Later, while Dougie sang yet another song in the background, they munched on their sandwiches, elbows on the table. They sat in companionable silence, both of them lost in the world outside the window, the street below, the puddle of light at the foot of the lone streetlamp in view. The clock chimed half past ten. Another long day. They'd all started to run together like a watery painting, and tomorrow would come too soon. Thain watched a young couple enter the streetlamp's beam, arm in arm, and the image of a black-and-white photo bearing a face with lonely eyes stole away his momentary tranquility. His thoughts skittered back on track as Dougie's voice relaxed him, the guitar dulling the raw edge of his stress. "What I wouldn't give for a glass of French Bordeaux with these."

"I'd forgo the wine for a shower."

"So take one. It's clean, I promise."

Rae's eyes held his for a long moment. Questions he'd never seen before seemed to spill over. "No worries," he said, and she looked away. He couldn't tell if she were disappointed or relieved.

"Thanks. I think I will."

They tidied up the kitchen, moving around each other carefully, the air between them charged with an energy that he hadn't felt in the five years he'd known her. "That way?" she asked once they were done, pointing toward the obvious bathroom door. He nodded and watched as she leaned forward a bit, swinging her long, heavy braid around to her front. "I'm ready for that shower now." Her small hands freed the strands, and a wash of black silk spread like a cloud over her body, almost covering her entire torso. He cleared his throat. "Aye, towels are here," he said tearing his eyes from that dark cascade. Brushing against her small frame as he stepped before her into the tiny bathroom, the scent of patchouli engulfed him. Passion surged through him, reminding him that it had been too long since the last time he'd felt such a thing. "Be careful, the cold and hot are reversed. Haven't bothered to change them yet."

From behind, she leaned around him, nearer, to inspect the shower knobs. She was so close he felt her body heat against his front. "Thanks for the warning," she said.

He inhaled her familiar patchouli perfume. Never before had it enticed him as it did now, inciting the beat of his pulse. "Rae," he said. He didn't have to reach far to touch her body in the minuscule bathroom.

"Alban," she whispered. He didn't think as he kissed her, her lips soft, hot and inviting under his. He pulled away to stare into her bright, inquiring eyes. Her face creased in a smile but quickly turned woeful as she said, "Please sir, I want some more." He laughed out loud and responded, "What? Ask for more?" He pulled her into his arms. "You'd make a wonderful Oliver." Rae beamed. He didn't wait for a second invitation.

30

He lunged and caught her wrist as she fell. She hung there in the thin cold air, dangling above the police-packed street below, one wrist trapped in his hand. His grip started to slip. The rain started: icy, sleeting, rain. His heart pumped on overtime.

The 'copters wouldn't be able to stay up long in this kind of weather.

"Please," she said, and he yanked her up hard and fast, and then held her safe and tight as she sobbed against the wet roof. Unexpected desire to comfort her overwhelmed him. He refused it. But his hand, his arm didn't listen to him. His hand still throbbed with the tension of her weight, but he reached out, pulled her to him. He peered into her wary face. The sleet started to freeze in her short hair.

"Come on, then," he said. They made it over the last barrier and found the drop-off to a line of buildings a story below where they stood. Beneath them, running parallel, lay a long line of flat roofs covering one-story shops. The 'copters buzzed closer. He wrapped his hand in one sleeve of his coat. "Take the other sleeve and wrap it as I have." After she'd done as he told her to, without warning, he swung her over the edge and bent until he lay flat against the roof shingles. He lowered her as far as he could to the next level. He hadn't given her time to scream. Before she could, he yelled, "Drop now. You're only a few feet above the next roof." Thankful though he was for the rushing rain masking his voice, it still didn't camouflage the heavy thumping of the 'copters' blades cutting through the sleet toward them. They hadn't backed off because of the weather yet. She didn't let go of the coat. She hung against the building kicking her feet. Her eyes pleaded with him, he saw her mouth say "no."

"Let go. I promise the roof is right below you." She peered over her arm and saw he spoke the truth. She let go, and he quickly slid over the side. He kicked off slightly from the building and landed right beside her. He crouched, pulling her with him. Here, they were invisible from the street below but not from the 'copters. They needed to move down to the next level. Like a crab, knees bent, he sidled across the roof until he came to a large pipe running down the face of the building to the flat-roofed shops a story below. He glanced up into the rain, searching for the 'copters, whose searchlights dazzled in the dark. They were close enough he could feel the beat of the blades reverberating in the slick, freezing air.

He pointed and said, "We're climbing down that pipe." He yanked off his shirt, and jammed his arms back into his coat. His fingers were already too cold as he slung one long sleeve of the shirt around and under her arm, tying it securely over her shoulder. He looped the other around his. Through the water pouring down his face like cold sweat, he looked at her and said, "If you slip, you won't fall far. We're attached, all right?" He didn't wait for her nod. "Go now." She climbed over the edging and grabbed on to the large metal pipe. He followed, wishing all the while they weren't so visible, climbing on the side of the building like spiders with no webs. Searchlights cut the night and blazed white trails along the streets, over the rooftops, illuminating the slanting needles of icy rain with scorching clarity. The light allowed him to make out the cops everywhere below, combing recesses, splashing the lesser light from their torches wherever the 'copters' lights couldn't reach. So far, the searchlights hadn't found them. He felt naked and trapped, but didn't slow his pace. He constantly watched for the killing beams of light. He constantly wiped the water from his eyes with the back of his forearm, couldn't afford blurry vision. The woman slipped once but didn't let go. He'd have been proud of her if he'd had time to think that much. When they finally reached the relative safety of the flat roofs, he dropped to a crouch beside her. She handed him her half of his shirt. With his eyes trying to follow the blinking skylights of the helicopters, he tugged the knots out of the shirt and then shrugged his coat off. The soaking shirt stuck to his skin as he yanked it on. She pulled it down in the back for him, held up the coat so he could stick his arms into it. He dragged the collar up close to his wet, bare neck.

If he remembered correctly, and if they could make it to the end of the row, they would find a wall abutting these roofs. He thought they could climb down the joint created by the uneven edges of the buildings. If they could reach that point, it would be near enough the end of the street for escape. Seconds passed as they skittered over the rooftops and the partitions delineating each shop, one after the other, like hurdlers in a race. An abrupt swath of light appeared to their left and he threw himself, and her, into the corner by the slightly raised edge facing the street. Lying flat, panting, his head turned to watch the searchlight's pattern, he didn't move. Under the rain, under the beating of the 'copter blades, he heard her labored breath as she lay underneath his arm. Incessant rain poured over them while they waited for the broad beams to go and dance somewhere else.

Darkness swallowed the searchlights, and he sprinted for the next wall. Right beside him, she kept pace, dodging, ducking, and climbing when he did. Twice more they had to stop and lay flat against one of the partitions or the lip of the street-side edge before they hit the towering brick wall that marked the end of the flat-roofed shops. He peered over the side. Right where the buildings met, he saw the joint he remembered. A drainpipe ran beside a pillar topped with a carving jutting up, decoration for the shop or restaurant below. There was also a cop standing on the sidewalk in front of the pillar, close enough to be touching it.

He could work his way around the tall carving on top of the pillar and lower himself until he could land right on top of the cop, if the cop didn't look up. But she'd have to descend on her own; he wouldn't be able to lower her as he'd done before. If he left his coat for her to drape around the carving, she'd still have about eight feet to fall. Once he'd taken care of the cop, he could help break her fall. But what if she ran instead? What if, after all he'd done to keep her, she escaped and gave the police his description? If he left London immediately it was possible they wouldn't get his description out soon enough to be a bother to him, but . . .

He turned to her. "I have to go first this time. If you don't follow me, the cop down there will die." He jerked his head toward the street and she looked over the edge. Pursing her lips, she nodded, and looked away. He explained what she would have to do. After the next swath of light cut the darkness and found nothing but rain, he slipped around the carved cap of the pillar and lowered himself silently until he hung against the wall right above the policeman, who stood in a hooded slicker blowing warm breath onto cold hands. Wasting no time, he let go, dropping straight onto his target, knocking the cop to his stomach flat on the ground. He straddled the man, grabbed his face, and pulled back, holding the knife against the exposed throat. Staring up through the rain, he watched her maneuver around the carving as he had done and, with the coat wrapped around the neck of the tall carving, swing down and hang in the air next to the wall.

He almost smiled. To the cop, he said, "Today is your lucky day," and then thumped him on the back of the head with the butt of his knife. He stood and braced himself, held out his arms and motioned for her to descend. The woman let go one end of his coat and dropped straight down while holding the other. The coat slid off with her and she landed lightly on her feet as he caught her around the waist.

"Thanks for bringing the coat," he said, shrugging into it.

With the woman stuck to his side, they moved like shades away from the commotion. He focused on getting them out of range before the searchlights returned. The end of the street lay but ten paces away. At the corner he checked that the cop was still prone on the sidewalk. Focusing on the police torchlight beams and helicopter lights, he remained alert, ready to run if one moved toward them. The sleet helped mask their movements even with streetlights glowing. Shouts echoed from where they'd been. He put his arm around the woman, who shivered at his touch, and without a backward glance they disappeared into the rain-drenched grayness of dawn.

31

First a cool dampness on his shoulder, and then a steady silence woke Thain. Bleary-eyed, he glanced at the clock on the mantle. Five o'clock. What? He grabbed his phone. After their shower—shared—they'd both fallen asleep on the couch and evidently slept like the dead for six hours. "Bugger," he said.

His abrupt movement woke Rae. "Is that the real time?" she said, but stood up before he could answer. She'd left her hair unbound, but now began braiding the damp mass while Thain shook himself. "We've got to go." He grabbed an insulated cup, filled it with fresh brew—black, no cream or sugar—and yanked his coat off its peg.

Rae said, "Coffee smells good. Should I pick one up on the way?" She put on her coat while he sputtered.

"Bugger again. Sorry, I'll get another cup."

"Now, that's the Thain I know. Don't worry. I'll pick one up on the way. Better that way. No questions or sly looks. Aw, you're blushing."

Thain's tongue wouldn't work. "I—" He paused and looked at her.

But she didn't look at him when she said, "We'll be fine. Don't worry."

He couldn't tell if she was upset or not. He said, "I didn't think about this part."

"To tell the truth, I didn't either." She looked straight at him. "But I'm not sorry."

"Neither am I, Rae. Neither am I." He put a world of meaning behind his words.

"I don't want—"

"Believe me. I think I know what you don't want, and neither do I. Are we good?"

She nodded. "Better than. Come on. Clive might be crawling the walls by now."

"He would have called." Pounding down the stairs to the street, Thain didn't think about the ache in his forehead, or the overwhelming fatigue that had led to their unanticipated nap. On the contrary. Perhaps the time spent with Rae had been exactly what he'd needed because now, in spite of the headache, he felt great. Eager to see what would happen next, because he wanted—or needed—to believe that something in this case had to break soon. They boarded the tube on the Northern line heading toward Colindale and the Hendon. Finding seats, they both leaned back, and Thain watched Rae close her eyes before he did. He wondered what she really thought of what had happened between them. What she thought of him. His phone rang out in his pocket. It was Clive.

"Where are you?"

Thain glanced at Rae, who sat up to listen, and mouthed, *Clive.* "On our, on my way," Thain said over the noise on the tube.

"Good. Because there's been a development."

32

The train charged along the low-lying blackened tracks, and its rattle blocked out all other sound. Celia swayed back and forth as the train carried its early morning load to multiple destinies. Not one person in the mass of people made eye contact with her, but she'd never been so content among so many before. After the harrowing climb over rooftops and buildings, she felt nothing but relief. She still lived.

Her abductor stood right in front of her, close enough that she couldn't see his face and could almost forget his presence. But she remembered he'd saved her from that horrifying fall. His expression hadn't been one of anger when he pulled her up with what she considered a Herculean effort; it had been nearly tender. What was she thinking? She'd been right on top of the cops yet had not saved herself. Tired, she watched her thoughts tumble over each other like clothes in a dryer. No sense, no logic.

"Here," he said. "This is our stop." She followed him up from the underground station into the street, where daylight was well on its way. The mists had dissipated and the sun sent slight sentinels through the cloud cover to let mortals know of its coming. How poetic. What *was* she thinking?

"Where are we?"

Of course, he didn't answer, but she read the sign on the station: Mile End. They didn't have far to walk through the empty, bleak streets before he guided her to the door of a row house with a sign in the window: "Hotel-Vacancies."

He, with her ahead of him, entered the small, seedy foyer and spoke to the man at the window cut into the wall. After handing over some cash, he was given the key to a room on the "first floor"—which she would have called the second—and she preceded him up the stairs. Her nose wrinkled at the smell of the place. Is that what curry and cabbage smelled like when mixed with human sweat? Lovely. "Do they cook in the rooms? Why do we have to stay here?"

He walked the length of the hall in silence, checking each door. "No one will ask questions. No one will hear anything, either, even if they do."

"Have you been here before?"

"I never stay in places like this."

"We're here because of me?"

He opened the door to their room without answering.

He entered first, and she watched him check over the small dingy room: inside the one armoire, under the bed, out the window that overlooked the street. The room held nothing else but a tiny table and two rickety chairs. The bathroom they'd already found at the far end of the hall.

"And tomorrow?"

"We leave tonight."

"Leave London?"

A nod was her only answer.

She hadn't realized he'd kept the roll of tape.

"Not again," she said. "How can you go out during the day alone? With all those cameras you talked about, someone is bound to see you."

"Without you they don't know who I am."

"Then why am I here?" she asked yet again, before he gagged her.

"My reasons are my own."

She didn't fight as he pushed her onto the bed and tied her hands to the slotted headboard. He wrapped her ankles together. She closed her eyes as she heard the door shut behind him. Alone again, naturally.

Pinned beneath a heavy weight, she screamed and fought as a face leered over her. Next to the sick grin etched into her memory, his hand held a knife. His voice echoed, "I've been watching you, planning this date for months. You keep turning me down. You think you're pretty enough little girl, but I think you need some cosmetic surgery." The knife slashed toward her face. She twisted her head. The blade sliced down the side of her neck instead of her cheek. Again the knife loomed into sight above her. Somewhere her brain registered the warmth flowing down her hairline. Her blood. She might have only minutes left. Scream, fight, fight him off—and she did, but he cut her again, on her raised arms, bared stomach, then— "No no no! Daddy, help! Daddy save me!"

33

The heist/murder/kidnapping team assembled again in the task room the morning of the fourth day. Thain leaned against the wall inside the door, purposely quiet and still, not wanting to be noticed. He glanced over at Rae standing with Clive on the other side of the room. He'd already decided to let them do all the talking this time. When he'd mentioned it, Rae had agreed with him. Last time he'd come too close to the ever-shadowing ridicule. The chief had accused him right out, told him not to mention his "ghost," and even said the Wraith's name.

"Well, finally *I* have something to report to you," the chief started, pacing and obviously angry. "The good news is that, thanks to the tip on rentals, the team saw our perpetrator on Methley Street near Kennington Lane around five a.m. this morning. The bad news is, we lost him again, though we had twenty men and two helicopters blanketing the area. The sleet didn't help. Evidently, the murder suspect took a constable by surprise. The constable's pretty sure the woman was with him because the man held a knife to his throat for a moment, like he was waiting for something, and then told him he was lucky before bashing him over the head. And he *is* a lucky bloke. A lovely bump's all he's nursing."

Thain's pulse quickened. Celia Wight was still alive. For his life, he couldn't keep his mouth shut. "So the Methley flat was his? Did anyone get a good look at him?" Rae and Clive's expressions both said they were ready to throttle him.

"No, he and the woman were on the other side of the street and down a bit, walking toward Bowden. Our team only noticed them because they slowed near a street lamp. A man and woman at such an early hour and near to the flat they were checking, well they thought it worth investigating. He didn't run straight away, but he knew they were police because he ran shortly after the team started to follow him."

Thain wanted to ask *Now do you believe me?* but didn't. It wouldn't do any good, and he didn't want to disappoint Rae and Clive. The team still couldn't prove the identity of the seventh man. But following through on what he knew about the Wraith had brought them closer to finding him, and that fact did make him happy, in a wary sort of way. *We're still too slow,* he thought, trying to keep perspective. *The killer is staying one step ahead of us because he knows we're too slow. Even with a hostage he continues to move faster than we can.*

The chief's voice rose. "The media is already on this. The papers this morning, the news spots all blame us for losing the man, for not rescuing the American writer. She's all over the Internet right now, and so are we. The LMPS is taking a bath here, and we have nothing new to assuage the media feeding frenzy." Still pacing, he said, "I want to know if we've got anything new here." He turned and glared at Thain, then Rae.

Rae didn't even glance at Thain but started right in. She shook her head and said, "Not from lack of looking, sir. St. John and Jenkins have made it about halfway through the newest batch from between the store and the bank, outside the stores in Camden, and Adie Road, where Celia Wight's bags were found. We've put in to get what we can from last night on Kennington Lane, Methley, Bowden, and surrounding, as well."

"Kidnapping team?"

Thain crossed his arms while Clive said, "No, sir. Nothing yet."

The frustration in the stark room oppressed Thain, as if it were his fault nothing else had turned up in the clues department.

"Forensics has searched six flats and five bedsits so far. The teams are still working," Rae continued.

"He'll have left the city by now," Carter said. "We need more men on the exit points, sir. That's where we'll catch him now that he's on the run."

"He's not on the run," Thain murmured in disgust. "Not yet."

The chief stopped pacing and leaned his head to one side. "What's that, DS?"

Thain stared at the chief as if he'd been caught doing something wrong, which he had. The chief's question hung in the air, tense and heavy, and he remembered what primary school felt like. "Nothing, sir."

"Bring it out into the open, Thain. Don't be shy. We all know what you're thinking," Carter chimed in. "Come on, you know you're dying to."

"Carter," Chief North warned.

Thain appreciated the interruption, but didn't want to say out loud that which would bring the derision of his chief down upon his head yet again. Quickly, he needed to think of a reason for saying what he'd said.

"You think he's your damn Wraith," Carter quipped again.

"Carter, if he isn't to talk of that, then neither should you." The chief used his quiet voice.

Thain had pushed it too far last time and now would pay for it. He refused to look at anyone while he waited for inspiration, and for the laughter he expected from his colleagues. That would be a perfect way to finish out an already rotten meeting. *Wraith*: the very name challenged him, taunted him, writhed under his skin.

But the hush in the room stretched. He looked up. Everyone stared at him, waiting. *Laughter be damned.* To find Celia Wight alive meant more than whether or not her kidnapper could be the assassin who'd eluded him so long. He could live with his colleagues' derision—had for years. But Celia couldn't. She didn't have that much time. The longer this went on, the closer she came to her captor's breaking point—whoever he might be. Thain had to talk about the Wraith even if the chief fired him on the spot.

"Well, Detective Thain?" The chief's prompting clinched his decision. He uncrossed his arms and put one hand in his pocket, curving it round his trusty phone, his thumb brushing that flat, smooth screen. He bolstered his nerves with a glance at Rae and Clive, his partners in this. If they stuck by him now and he turned out to be wrong, they'd sink right alongside him. He shifted his gaze to Chief North and didn't look at anyone else.

"Sir, I know you told me not to go off on a tangent—"

"Don't you start," the chief warned, glaring at him.

Thain hesitated. "Don't ask me to explain then, sir, if you don't want to hear the truth."

Chief North didn't move. He stared at Thain, who resigned himself to working on his CV after the meeting. Still, he had to try one last time. "Sir, we're at an impasse. We have nowhere to go, nothing to go on. The media and your superiors are eating us up. We've had four days now and have nothing except suppositions and a few bits of film to go by, notwithstanding what happened last night. I was right about the flats, wasn't I? Won't you at least hear me out?"

Chief North stared at him for a long, quiet moment. No one made a sound. The chief resumed pacing, then nodded, reluctance clear with every movement he made. "Say your piece, then."

"Thank you, sir. Look how this man is playing with us. We can't even catch him in a confined area with a hostage. We don't know what he looks like because he knows the location of every bloody camera in this city. He can't have that information unless he's spent years studying it. St. John and I don't know where half of them are, and we study them all the time." Irritated now, Thain couldn't stand still. He pushed off from the wall. "This man isn't a common bank thief. This man's a serious killer, possibly an assassin. I know you don't believe that *my* assassin exists, but whether or not the kidnapper is the Wraith, he can afford to laugh at us because he knows he's invisible. If he *is* the Wraith, this is the closest anyone has ever got to him, and the only reason that is so is because he has a hostage."

"You've never found proof, Thain, definitive proof."

"Does it matter, sir, in the end? If we use the information I have on the Wraith to help us find her, does it matter if he actually *is* the Wraith or not?"

"You're asking me?" Disbelief tinged the chief's words.

"Yes, sir. I know it sounds insane, but yes. At this point I care more about Celia Wight being found alive than being proved right about the Wraith."

The chief said, "I know you've worked your theory, Thain—"

Thain straightened, his hands restless now, in and out of his trouser pockets. "You want us to find the killer, sir, the murder suspect, no matter who he is. The tip on the rentals has already given us movement. That information came from taking what I've learned from the past and using it with what HOLMES put together for us. If you would listen to my reasons, if you would let me try . . ."

Silence again. Phones rang in the distance, voices could be heard, but no one moved in the bleak over-bright murder room. No one twitched or shuffled a paper. The entire crew waited to see the chief's reaction to Thain's unusually vehement stand. He had a hard time breathing, started to sweat and his armpits turned sticky; he rubbed his clammy hands on his trousers to dry them. He'd never pushed this far before, never dared. But he'd only ever let one victim under his skin before, and that was before he'd become a cop. Right now he couldn't afford to think of Celia Wight, or what she'd done to his equilibrium.

Thain wanted to break the awful, waiting silence. *The Wraith has never made a mistake, until now.* Keeping the shock of sudden hope strictly away from his emotions, an idea surfaced and caused Thain to reconsider his argument. He said, "There are two more points to consider, Chief. If this man is the Wraith, why has he changed his methods? We need to ask this question because it could be our main lead to finding him. If he *is* the Wraith and this is personal for him, that fact alone could explain the discrepancies in the hit, like the messiness and the brutality. If the hit is personal, why is it personal? What does he have to gain, what is his motivation? Who was Richard McLean to him? Could this unknown factor be the reason he kept his hostage; he knew we would be wary of him killing her? But he isn't aware that I know that the Wraith doesn't kill innocents, only his mark—"

"How do you know that?" the chief asked, in spite of himself, it seemed, from the look of surprise on his face.

Thain shook his head. He had to keep going while the chief was off guard. "Sir, I *know*. But he doesn't know that I, that we, understand this about him. If Celia Wight isn't in on this with him—and you've seen that what I've found on her and her parents deaths confirms that—then he's made a mistake. His *first* mistake. We have to take advantage of it." Thain desperately needed Chief North to see reason, to believe him just this once. He dared to look at Clive and Rae, who both bobbed their heads at him ever so slightly, as if to say, *Go on, finish what you started.*

"Unless he's going to kill here, in London again—and we don't have any idea one way or the other about that—he's going to leave the city, and soon. Because we came close this time. We must find him before he leaves, or he may be forced to break another of his rules, and that means Celia Wight, and god knows who else, will die."

Chief North leaned his hip against a table and crossed his arms. Clearly, he needed more convincing. Old habits did die hard, but at least he was listening. "And when would you estimate that he'll try to leave?"

"Within the next forty-eight hours sir, if not twenty-four."

The chief remained motionless, his head bowed in thought. When he looked up, Thain stood perfectly still. "Tell me why you believe this man is your Wraith and not some random murderer, or a different assassin with a similar operating style."

St. John's phone blipped and he glanced at it before he held up his hand. "Sorry to interrupt, sir, but Thain asked to be told as soon as we found anything new?"

"Go ahead, St. John," the chief said.

"Jenkins just texted me. He's found the footage of the lost hat. And, Thain," St. John grinned, looking ghoulish as he did it so rarely, "we might have a partial profile photograph."

34

The stench of the place grated on his nerves, disgusted him, though he'd smelled much worse. Blast it all to hell! The police had come much too close this morning, and to compound that problem, the woman had stirred up things best left unstirred when she'd fallen off that roof, helpless, eyes pleading for him to save her. Once he'd done so, once he'd held her safe in his arms, all he'd wanted to do was kiss her. Bugger it all.

Discipline was everything, but only if one used it. He bowed his head, lifted his collar, and made his way up the littered street toward a greasy-looking store, beyond which stood a fish and chips place. They would do. He needed minimal cleaning supplies and food to hold them over until they left London tonight. They? Could he really take her with him? He badly needed to take back control over the havoc in his mind.

Ten minutes later he returned to the room with two bags under his arms, one from the store, and one from the fish and chips shop. The woman lay where he'd left her, bound and gagged, but she strained and tossed from side to side. Her red face rippled with extended blood vessels, and her body thrashed as if on fire. Her eyes were tightly closed.

He raced over to her. "Another bad dream," he said out loud, and then louder, "Wake up, it's only a dream." He peeled the tape off of her mouth and winced at her deep, guttural cry of despair: "Daddy, save me!"

"Wake up, wake up." He couldn't cut the tape her with her straining against her bonds, so he held her, pulled her head close to his and whispered, "Stop it now. Come back. It's only another dream." He withdrew a bit and her eyes flew open. Terror poured forth and she started to scream again.

He covered her mouth until her eyes focused on him, until she came back to herself. Then he released her and cut the tape on her now limp wrists and ankles. "It was only a dream."

Drawing ragged breaths she said, "A nightmare. Dreams don't hunt you down."

Brutally, he suppressed the inconvenient desire to hold her until her fear disappeared. He had no need to ask why she cried for her father to save her. "I've brought food."

"We leave soon?"

"First, we eat."

Rubbing her mottled cheeks, she asked, "Then can I have a shower?"

"No. Not now."

"But—"

"No."

They spoke not another word as they ate, he standing by the window, she at the small excuse for a table. His heel started to pump against the floor again as it had that first night. He stilled it. When she stood and collected the empty paper wrappings, something in him snapped. "Stop it. Sit down. Don't move. Don't say a word."

She sat. "All right," she said, waiting, as if she knew . . . Good. This time he would follow through. He couldn't afford the vulnerability he'd left himself open to. He must finish what he'd started. Rules were meant to be broken. Wasn't that what everyone said?

Because of her, the police had come too close to tripping him up. He couldn't take her with him, and he couldn't leave her alive, not now, not yet. Getting out of London took priority, as did finishing the job he'd built his life upon. But she knew more about him than anyone did. He couldn't leave her to give that knowledge to the police.

He quit thinking. The edges of his vision darkened, sweat cooled his heated forehead as he concentrated on keeping his mind on the goal—on all that mattered, on finishing his task so he could save another's soul, and save his own. He started toward her. Each step he took hammered at the door he'd closed and bolted against the past. Her eyes widened as he slipped the knife smooth and easy from the sheath under his arm. The sooner he got this over with, the sooner he'd truly put the past to rest. Only this woman and her pleading eyes stood in his way.

35

North reacted before Thain could close his open mouth. "DIs Hawthorne and Carter, St. John, DSs Bell and Patterson"—he hesitated only a second—"and you, Thain, you're all with me. The rest of you wait here till we get back."

Thain followed Chief North and the team as St. John led them over to the viewing room in the next building. He oughtn't dare to hope for a real photograph, but he did.

As they all burst into the room, Jenkins said, "I've paused it right before the loss of the hat, St. John."

"Thanks, Jenkins." St. John dropped into his chair and made sure everyone was situated where they could see the monitor. When he started the footage, Jenkins leaned in from one side and pointed out on the monitor screen what they all hoped would be the first completely solid break, not just a lead.

"Here, this man; watch what happens."

St. John slowed the video. Thain watched their man wearing the hat and reversed Burberry easing with quick, sure steps down a narrow sidewalk next to a building. A sudden gust of wind whipped the hat off the man's head. He turned carefully, trying to find it, but kept his face from the cameras. Evidently he decided that there were too many people around him to search for the hat without calling attention to himself, because he continued on his way. He didn't try to retrieve the hat, didn't look up or throw a backward glance. He kept going until he disappeared off camera.

"You see what I mean, there in the beginning?"

"Oh, yes," Thain answered. "Where is this?"

"Maddox Street, right across from where they've construction going on? That's what took so long with getting the footage."

Chief North said, "Go back to when the hat flies off."

St. John rewound and stopped as the hat flew away.

"Bring it in closer and try to tighten the focus," the chief said, leaning in like everyone else.

St. John enlarged the image of the man's face, but couldn't get it much clearer, and the height of the angle obscured part of the view.

Thain straightened and peered at Rae. Her eyebrow arched. How she could do just the one, he didn't know. "Care to take a closer look, Madame Police Artist?" he asked, a rare smile playing on his lips. Rae Bell's accurate touch for putting witnesses' descriptions of criminals on paper, her reputation as an artist, was the envy of the LMPS. She also happened to be killer with the newest computer software, which allowed her to reconstruct partial images and make them whole. Her face betrayed nothing as they all moved aside and she took a closer look.

"Tell us what you can do with this," Chief North said.

Rae stared at the image. "Do you think he's the Wraith, Thain?" She glanced up at Thain and winked.

"Come on, Rae," he said and stuck his hands in his pockets. He didn't dare glance at the chief when he asked her, "Can you work with it, see if there's a match? Possibly make a composite photo for us, or a reconstruction?"

"A profile, if I get anything at all from this. I'll see what I can do about a composite."

"I've some other excuses for photos I can give you as soon as we're done here, if you think it would help," he said.

"Every little bit—" she started.

"Do it now, Detective Sergeant. Top priority," Chief North ordered.

"Yes, sir." Rae smiled at Thain, giving him the impression she'd known all along he wasn't crazy. Then she put her hand on St. John's shoulder. "Send it over to me, St. John."

"As the lady wishes." St. John gave her a salute. A new energy bubbled in the room.

Thain rubbed his hand over his cheek while staring again at the monitor. Had the murder suspect, even if he wasn't the Wraith, been captured on film they could actually use? He felt hopeful, like perhaps the mist had begun to lift, and it was much too soon to indulge in such nonsensical thoughts. He had to admit, though, that earlier, when he'd wished for a break in the case, they'd gotten one.

"This is the best shot we've had of him," he said.

"No one reacts like that when the wind blows their hat away, especially at this time of year," Clive agreed.

"He knows where every surveillance camera is."

Carter said, "But it doesn't mean he's your Wraith."

"No, it doesn't," Thain said, starting to bristle.

"Tell me now why I should believe in *your* invisible man and not some other, Thain. Go on. Convince me," Chief North said.

The sweats returned. Thain hadn't always followed through on his hunches. There had been times after he'd first come here when he'd let the office ridicule stop him from exploring his intuition. But not this time. This time Celia Wight took precedence. He had no real life outside his desk at the office, outside his lifeline to the criminal world, and that's the way he'd wanted it since the debacle that had begun his very first day as a police officer. Who was he kidding? He'd wanted it this way since Agatha had cut him out of her life and refused to ever see him again.

Now, it seemed like, not only was Celia Wight trying to change that, but Rae was as well. A life outside of his job? He'd chosen a policeman's life because he'd wanted to avenge Agatha. The plus was that he was good, more or less, at solving the puzzles and mysteries presented him in this line of work. But after the assassination of the man he was assigned to protect, he'd added another goal to his primary one, and it had taken over, changed his life dramatically, and sent him from his home and family to London. That pinnacle atop the mountain of mysteries and puzzles was the one achievement he'd never been able to seize. Now there might be photographic proof of identity, which gave him an edge. Now there was Celia Wight driving him down a road he'd never traveled.

"Detective?"

Thain quit ruminating and took the plunge. "The man I've researched always works alone. I know that doesn't match up right now with the Celia Wight kidnapping, but give me a chance to explain. In the last ten years I've studied certain assassination cases that have all had at least three things in common. First, there's never *any* useable evidence left, never *anyone* to tie these murders to. Second, he never uses a gun. He always uses a knife or knifelike object, like this murder, where he, whoever "he" is, used a letter opener belonging to the victim, and, sir, he *always* leaves the murder weapon in the wound. His third trait, the one that I mentioned before, is that he doesn't kill innocents, only his mark. He doesn't kill randomly. He's too tidy to ever have the need, until now. In each case I've studied that I believe to be his, his target dies, but no bystanders, no spouses—"

"Do you know if he's killed any women?"

"Not in any of the cases I've found, but I can't say for sure. Men aren't the only ones who occasionally want someone cleared out of the way. Sir, to me, the method in which Richard McLean was killed reinforces the idea that our suspect isn't one of the thieves. I believe he is a 'seventh man,' not related to the heist."

"Yet, the scene was messy, not clean."

"Which is why, as I said earlier, this must be a personal kill instead of one the suspect was hired to carry out."

"Go on."

Thain's eyes widened. *Go on!* "You want proof. Up until now, when it comes to photographic proof, all I've found is a few grainy films of a man leaving some of the jobs with security cameras in use. Usually the cameras are taken out before the kill, which is why we don't have many examples. If not for those films I'd think my assassin was a *literal* wraith, nothing but a ghost. But all the data I've compiled suggests a flesh and blood killer who murders for hire and is never seen. Not by the people who employ him or others in his field. If my theory is correct, and this time he killed for personal reasons, that action makes him vulnerable. It means he has a score to settle and he's out settling it. If so, it may mean he will react differently than when he's performing a hired hit.

He may kill differently, hence the mess. All the pro jobs I've seen of *my* assassin were done so quickly and discreetly that the victim felt almost nothing. He wasn't brutal. This kill was messy and extremely painful. It has to be personal, sir. And, if it is the same man, he won't be able to change *every* habit. Two things: he left the secretary alive, and, sir, the fact that the letter opener was left in the wound, well, that *is* the Wraith's trademark. Even if he isn't *my* assassin, sir, the data I've collected on him could still prove useful to us."

"I can't risk you being wrong, Thain."

Thain winced. He saw this moment for what it was: the turning point of his entire life. If he failed now, he'd be out of a job or relegated to the figurative basement. If he failed now, the last ten years of his life were a waste. If he failed now, he would never have the chance to know Celia Wight. He wanted to know her. He took a deep breath. "I'm not wrong."

Chief North didn't say anything, at first. "I guess he could have made a conscious decision not to kill the secretary, though she saw him before he tied her up and locked her away."

"Yes, sir."

The chief pushed away from the desk he leaned on and stared at Thain. "What makes you so sure the 'hits' you've studied aren't the work of more than one assassin? What makes your Wraith solid, Thain?"

"Out of the sixty or more cases I've studied, I have on file fifteen all bearing the same identifying features. One is that he's undetectable and has been for at least ten years that I know of. His precise methods don't show up anywhere before that. He doesn't use credit cards or cell phones of any kind; he doesn't own a car or flat that I know of; there's no way to track him because we have no usable photograph."

"All you're telling me convinces me of the opposite, Thain. You're describing a ghost."

"Yes, sir. How many ghosts, how many *wraiths*, do you know that actually exist? How many assassins are there in the world that have never been seen or haven't slipped up even once? Sir, we have an extensive list of amateur and professional hit men. Why? Because they all invariably make mistakes or show off or want the money and notoriety. They want us to know they exist. This man doesn't. Somewhere he learned how to hide, and to do it better than well. It's almost as if he has left nothing but a hole where a man should be. As Sherlock Holmes said, sir, 'Eliminate all other factors, and the one which remains must be the truth.'"

Chief North wasn't frowning. He had his hand to his chin, staring at the floor. He looked deep in thought, and everyone waited to see where he would go, what choice he would make, whether he would laugh at Thain's theory, again, or believe it, for once. Thain found it increasingly hard to breathe.

North glanced at Clive. "Do we have anything more on the victim's past?"

Clive shook his head. "No, sir. Beyond finding out the names of his schools, we don't have anything new. He's still too clean, sir."

"You say he's from York?"

"Yes, sir."

Chief North looked at Thain again, but said, "Bell, Patterson, what do you two think?" His eyes cut away from Thain to them. "Would you take a risk on Thain, and his theory?"

Clive answered without hesitation, "For three reasons, sir."

"Name them."

"One, Thain's a diligent DS, has taken heat ever since he's been here over his belief in the Wraith, and still hasn't given up. Two, he turned out to be right about the cash payments on rentals, and that there was basically no DNA evidence to be found at the murder scene, which he predicted before the lab confirmed it. Sir, he also pointed out that the secretary wasn't killed, though she could point a finger."

"And you, Bell?"

Rae said, "Thain's the one who noticed that the seventh man knew all the CCTV camera locations when the rest of the bank robbers didn't, and, as far as we know, Celia Wight, a potential witness, is still alive."

The chief's face looked fierce. "Because of the severity of this case, the ridiculous time constraints, and because we aren't making anything called headway fast enough, I'm forced to use extreme measures here. This theory of yours, Thain, still sounds too radical for me. I don't like it, but I'm running out of choices." The chief looked him right in the eye, looking frustrated and discouraged. "You might have a photo worth using. I'm giving you two days to find him."

"Sir?"

Carter stammered when he said, "Sir, you, you can't be serious."

Chief North ignored him. "If you don't find this suspect in two days, Thain, you're off and I bring in the big guns."

"Yes, sir. I'll do my best, sir."

Chief North smiled, wryly. "You *and your team* will do your best, Thain. You aren't alone this time."

"If you say so, sir. Of course."

"And you better hope your best is good enough." Chief North turned his attention to St. John's monitor. "Is it too late to find that hat?"

Clive frowned. "Probably."

Thain said, "We've tried before, but now we have a definite location to search."

North paused, then said, "Let me know the results. Good work, everyone, St. John, Jenkins."

St. John dragged his red-rimmed eyes from the screen to the chief. "Thank you, sir."

In the doorway, Chief North looked over his shoulder. "Thain, you and your team report directly to me and only to me from now on. Hawthorne and Carter, are we clear?"

"Sir, of course," Hawthorne said, but Carter barely acknowledged him.

North shook his head and nailed Thain with his sharp eyes. "I can't believe I'm doing this, so don't disappoint me. This is too big."

"Yes, sir." Thain said and frowned. If he hadn't found the Wraith in ten years, it was a sorry state of affairs to think he could find him in two days.

36

Her captor's narrowed eyes shimmered, menacing like the first time Celia had seen him. His breath dragged against the thick air between them as he advanced toward her. After all they'd been through, after saving her life, he'd decided after all she wasn't worth the risk. A whimper caught in her throat as she stood and stumbled away from him, knocking over the flimsy chair, helpless. She had nowhere to go. If she screamed, no one could arrive before the knife did. *Not again!* shrieked in her head, hating him somewhere behind the terror. She'd never truly forgotten her past; the world she'd created for herself was as fictional as her books. "God damn you!"

He didn't react. He approached, one hand loose and ready at his side, the other grasping the thin blade she dreaded, his body taut as a bow strung and ready to fire. Her universe became the knife in his hand, the cold judgment in his glassy eyes, his threatening catlike movements.

"Ryan, don't do this, don't—"

"That's not my name."

"I don't care!" Fear blurred her sight, panic choked her breath. He pinned her to the wall, grabbed the thick tape, and cut the yelp in her throat short as he plastered it over her mouth. She fought, yanking at the sticky strip as he raised the blade toward her throat. She couldn't get the tape off her mouth.

She didn't want to feel the slash of a knife ever again, knew then, as she'd never known anything else, that she'd rather die than relive that torture. She fell to the floor as if death had already struck, loose and sudden, trying to escape his grip on her. He jerked her to her feet again, but her legs remained boneless. The sick promise of agony drove her tenacious need to avoid it.

Celia collapsed again, pulling him along with her, and this time he stumbled and fell on top of her. The knife sliced through her shirt, barely grazing her side. The tape still silenced her; her throat contracted, her mind screamed. She thrashed, hit and kicked him, fighting for her life as she had the last time. The knife moved closer. She almost collapsed, he was so strong. But she didn't. His other hand clamped onto her wrist but she twisted and hit him again. The knife sliced downward, and cut deeply into her forearm.

An abrupt spring of rich red blood, her blood, flowed from her arm, but it happened too fast. She didn't feel anything at first. Then the stinging started. Then the unbearable ache of skinless flesh exposed to the air.

His eyes widened as he held her petrified in his steely grip. He stared at her blood, seemed mesmerized and yet horrified by it. He cried out and wrenched his eyes from the wound. His knife clattered to the floor. Growling, he grabbed his head with both hands, swinging from side to side as if trying to shake something loose. Celia couldn't breathe. Confused, she couldn't tear her gaze from his desolate face, etched with agony.

Looking crazed, he careened to his knees beside her as if she no longer existed, as if he'd forgotten her. Holding her arm, blood pouring through her fingers, she scooted across the floor toward the door, but her movement snapped him out of whatever spell he'd been under. He reached out and grabbed her leg. She tried but couldn't scream through the tape. He pulled her into his arms, and in one fluid motion, lifted her up. Jerking the door open, he carried her into the hall, venting his murderous wrath on the bathroom door when they reached it and found it occupied. He kicked at it, shouting, "Out, get out now." A small, dark man timidly opened the door, yelped as he was yanked from the bathroom and thrown to one side.

With his foot, her kidnapper banged the door shut behind them, set her on her wobbly feet by the sink, and turned on the faucet. She started to black out as he cleansed her wound, but the stinging brought her back. She stiffened as the torment, stark and brutal, flowed over her, as the water flowed over her wound. She wished the water would wash away the agony as it did her blood down the drain. He pulled the tape from her mouth, and between the sudden harsh bite of the tape and the gory sight of her wound, too deep for a bandage, she threw up. Her vomit mingled with her blood. Spitting in the sink, she could barely rinse her mouth. He held her, stroking her hair as if to comfort her. Dizzy, she started to shake.

"You need stitching." His eyes were blank, detached, almost life-less, and that scared her more than his anger or insanity. "I can do it," he said.

"No, you can't. I need a doctor. I need—"

"I can do it. You must stand the pain. It won't be much. You've endured worse."

How did he know what she'd endured? How did he know? She squirmed in his grasp, ready to fight. "Sh . . ." He pushed the hair back from her face and kissed her forehead. Where was he in his mind? Who did he see through those eyes? With his vacant look and his strange resolution to stitch her arm, he wasn't seeing her. "You'll be fine. I promise. I'll take care of you."

Frenzied now, beyond any confusion, Celia lunged away from him. Though her blood coursed from her arm, she fought his hold on her like a demon, hoping to shock him out of the alarming trance he was in.

It worked. She saw him take possession of his face, his eyes, as if he were a lost spirit returned to its body. He returned, and so did his anger.

Once he realized she wouldn't stop fighting him, he picked her up, took her back to the room and taped her to the chair. He gagged her and wrapped her arm as tightly as possible in a towel.

"I'll be back."

Had she fainted again? Black waves gave way to a sharp piercing of her wounded flesh. *I don't want to die* . . . Mindless agony splintered her, consumed her being, as the needle and thread pulled and tugged through her skin, time after time after time, without anesthetic, without relief. At last the world vanished.

Someone shook her. She opened her eyes to find a face, his face, inches from hers. "We have to move," he said.

Celia groaned. "Not yet, please."

"The man in the lavatory, he'll have told someone. We're moving now." He hovered over her. He put his arm under her shoulders and gently lifted her until she sat up. He'd already put her coat on her. She couldn't move. He pulled her legs off the bed and forced her to stand. "Lean on me."

"But you haven't cleaned the room," she mumbled, her thoughts hazy as she glanced around.

"Yes, I have. Don't worry." But Celia thought the horrid little room hadn't changed its appearance. It still looked dingy and stained. In the hall he held her like a lily, guided her down the stairs and onto the sidewalk. He didn't forget to scope the tiny reception area and the streets before they left the hotel.

Outside, Celia squinted against the sharp gray light of late afternoon. She missed the sun. She had no choice but to lean on him as he'd told her to do. She felt weak, from shock she supposed, and her arm throbbed terribly. She wanted to cry but felt drained of emotion. He hurried, and her feet moved as if mechanized.

The light of day had lessened only slightly, as far as she could tell, by the time he found another place that suited him. He helped her to a ground floor room, took her coat off without jarring her arm, and laid her on the creaky bed. "It hurts," she said, groggy. But the throbbing, the constant beat of her blood, rocked her to sleep and she forgot everything.

37

The chief left the viewing room. Everyone but Jenkins, who stayed behind with eyes glued to his monitor, followed in his wake, back to the murder room and the bulk of the team still waiting. No one was in any doubt that Chief North was on a tear. Thain's chest started to burn with the weight of a responsibility he'd only ever dreamed about. Now that it was real, he felt its brutal force with rising panic, remembered his brother's lack of faith in him. He turned sharply at Rae's light touch on his sleeve. He looked askance at her, at Clive and St. John who had grouped around him as they hurried after the chief. "What just happened?"

"You won the lottery, mate." Clive thumped him on the back.

"That or a death sentence on your career," St. John volunteered.

When they arrived, Chief North strode into the middle of the room and bellowed, "Everyone, you'll report directly to Thain, Bell, and Patterson on this case as of now. You're all on their team until I state otherwise. You follow their orders. You do your damned best, if not to prove Thain right in his theory about the Wraith, to at least use his information to bring our killer in."

Solid, audible gasps filled the room and all eyes turned to stare at Thain. He wanted to run, especially when he saw the vicious look on Carter's taut face.

"There will be no snickering for two days," Chief North continued as he took up his usual pacing. "You will all, and I mean *all*"—he glared at Carter—"give Thain the benefit of the doubt, because if he fails, you fail." He turned to Thain again, crossed his arms and stopped pacing. Instead he took up a more familiar stance and leaned against a nearby table. "What's your first move, Detective Sergeant Thain?" He didn't even sound sarcastic.

Seriously, Thain was going to have to change his shirt. The sweats were back and his adrenaline had kicked in as well. "Find the hat; there might be DNA on it. Study the films we still have coming in. Sir, we need more eyes on the CCTV video. There is too much ground to search with only four . . ."

Chief North didn't say anything but "Continue."

So he did. "Rae must get us a photo worth seeing. One we can show to the robbers from the bank to see if they recognize him, and to the secretary and the store clerks for the same reason. The teams already out need to continue checking the leads on the flats and bedsits. Also, we need the map of the man's sightings updated immediately. Sir, we also need a dedicated team to check, in more depth, on Richard McLean's past. If this is a personal hit, we need to know why. There should be something there to find."

"Hawthorne and Carter, you work on Richard McLean. If you have to go up to York to do it, so be it, and report to Bell. I need four volunteers to man the CCTV videos." North held up his hand as some of the team started to answer. "Give your names to Greene before you leave. He'll let me know who volunteered. The rest of you, you heard the man. Get to work." Chief North didn't smile at Thain. His look remained worried and fierce. Thain knew they were all in a tight corner, but especially the chief. Others whispered comments while they dispersed back to their desks, all except four who went up to Greene and gave their names. Greene logged in the changes on HOLMES and gave instructions to head over to St. John directly.

Thain walked over to "his" desk at the HOLMES station and sat down. He rubbed his hands along his thighs, which began to quiver, to wipe away the perspiration. He felt depressed. Why, when at last he could work on catching the Wraith aboveboard? No one could make fun of him for at least two days, and not ever if they caught the man, no matter who he turned out to be. Thain's chances of success in that endeavor had now supposedly increased exponentially, with everyone working toward the same goal. Right. Two days? His head hurt from lack of sleep. He wanted to feel rejuvenated—by the hope that they might have a working photograph soon, and by the chief's faith, shaky though it was, in his theory. But he didn't.

He thought of Celia, her unforgettable eyes, their dark sadness speaking unmistakably to his own. She'd insinuated herself into every aspect of this case and into his thoughts. He wondered what she'd thought when the police had been so close to rescuing her and failed. Why didn't the Wraith kill her or hide her away somewhere if he didn't want her death on his hands? The knowledge she must now possess about him would be too valuable for him to set her free. The police could use it to catch him dead or alive. Thain preferred alive because he still wanted to find out what drove an assassin to live the life he'd chosen, to shun society.

Did the Wraith shun a public life? Thain didn't know enough about him to guess, but he thought it likely. Hell, the Wraith could be a prominent figure leading a double life for all he knew. His ethereal trail crossed every continent, almost every country, but still he remained elusive and unfathomable. Depression, and yes, fear and fatigue stood at the ready to eclipse Thain's hope.

Rae's voice was as soft as her footsteps when she walked up and stood behind him. "Thain, I'm working on the photo. Anything else you want me to do?"

"I can't believe this is happening."

"I know. Congratulations."

"No. Don't."

"Don't what? Congratulate you?"

"Rae, listen. I started something ten years ago that I thought would be done and over with long before this."

She pulled a chair closer and sat beside him. "I know. Well, at least I know of the last five of those years."

"I started with male missing person files in all the western European countries. I mean all of them, even Lithuania. This year I started on the UK and found some hopefuls. But I've found hopefuls in most every country. I've spent so many hours on computers I can't believe my eyes still work, searching, piecing together bits of information from any cases involving suspicious deaths. All to see if I could find a man who is a dedicated killer, a man everyone else says doesn't exist." He hung his head.

"Now . . . today, everyone is supposed to work with me to perhaps find that same man. The first problem has always been that there is no way to tell who the Wraith could be. The second is, what if he's Russian? Or Romanian, or Czech, or Hungarian? What if he's Greek or South American, or Canadian or American? I've studied all types of assassination cases over *ten* years. How else could I have developed my theory of the Wraith? Those efforts have given me an extensive database we can use, but even with a possible photo that might level the odds against me—us—a little, this is an impossible task."

"In other words, don't congratulate you before the deed is accomplished?"

"Right. Don't jinx me, us." He wanted to smile but couldn't. He looked at Rae and said, "At least you've never ridiculed me as the rest have, and I appreciate it. You know this is the end for me. What the chief wants . . ."

"Thain, was it the assassination in Edinburgh that made you start studying assassins? That one on your first day as a copper?"

He almost smiled at her. He supposed after the other night she deserved an answer. "Yes."

She did smile, a full one, happy with his curt response. "Guess it makes sense, in a strange way."

Tired to the bone, the weight of the chief's expectations that he now carried, and in public, made it worse—until Thain thought of the black-and-white photo, always there, imprinted all over his mind, the back, the front, the in-between. Celia. He stood up and grabbed his phone. "I'm going back to West End Central for a bit."

Rae stood and laid her hand on his arm. He glanced down at it. It was the fourth time he'd been touched by her in as many days. This time, however, it felt more intimate because of the night they'd shared in his flat. "You aren't alone any more, Alban. Maybe we'll actually succeed and find her, find him." Her eyes spoke more than her words. He saw her for the true friend she was, that she really meant what she said.

"Thank you, Rae. If Chief North can actually place a little faith in me, why can't other miracles happen as well?"

Thain didn't hurry down the hall toward the stairs as Rae's voice echoed in his head. Her expression had said more to him than her words. She was on his side no matter what. One flight down, and focused on her voice, he didn't register the footsteps he heard behind him, not until someone grabbed the back of his jacket, twisted him about, and shoved him against the wall. "What?"

Carter's face, livid, and inflamed, filled his view. "You think you're such a clever boy, DS. But we all know better. I don't know how you managed to get North to play your little game, but it won't wash with me. No one in their right mind would believe your pissy little theory about an invisible man. If I have to, if you don't bow out now, I'll go over North's head to get you off this case."

"What, afraid I might show up your incompetency? Get your hands off of me." Thain pushed the man, trying to get some distance, but they both lost their footing on the steep steps. Thain reared back against the wall as they started to fall, and threw his arms to each side. Problem was, Carter didn't let go. They both toppled, and then crashed down to the landing ten steps below, rolling the one over the other.

"Thain!" Clive yelled, as he raced down the stairs. "Carter, are you okay?" He reached the landing just as Thain moaned and rolled from his back to his stomach. He made it to his elbows and knees before Clive said, "Stop, Alban. Don't move. Something could be broken."

Thain crawled over and leaned one side of his back against the landing wall. The other side hurt too much to put pressure on. He heard noises at the top of the staircase and knew Clive's shout had been heard. A crowd was forming. He stared at Carter, who Clive was helping to sit up as well. "Neither one of you should be moving," Clive said.

"Clive, Alban! What happened," Rae cried as she ran down the stairs.

"I'm all right," Thain said, tasting blood where he'd bitten his tongue and cheek in the tumble down.

Clive stood up beside Rae, who was now on the landing with them. Carter sat moaning against the wall. Disgust tainted Clive's words as he stared at Carter, "What an idiot."

"Did you see what happened?" Thain asked, hoping against hope.

Clive nodded. Rae said, "What did happen?"

Thain almost collapsed with relief. "You'll admit that, to the chief?" he asked as he wiped his mouth and tried to stand. Clive reached out to steady him.

"Guys, what happened?" Rae insisted, but they didn't respond. She glared at them, and then looked down at Carter before crossing her arms and turning her attention back to their conversation.

"Of course I'll *admit* it. Carter has a vendetta against you, not me."

"He will, if you speak up for me."

"Thain, you and I've been friendly ever since I got here and he hasn't so much as raised an eyebrow at me. Don't make it worse than it is."

"This isn't bad enough? I didn't make him attack and threaten me, Clive."

"Did he threaten you? I couldn't hear what he said, only saw what he did."

"That should be enough, I hope, to keep him off my back, at least until this investigation is over."

"I've never seen an officer, and especially not a DI, attack another officer. That was not a pretty sight."

Carter started trying to move. Clive put out a hand to pull him to his feet. Thain began to say something to him, but Rae interrupted. "Don't say anything, Thain. Wait until this goes to the chief."

Carter, still unsteady on his feet, reeled toward Thain and pulled his fist back. "This isn't over Thain. You won't even have your rank when I get—"

"Sir," Clive said and grabbed the DI by the arm, pulling him up the stairs. "Let's get you back upstairs and see if we can have someone look you over. No telling what might have happened during that spill."

His quick, guarded glance at Thain was a warning to get out and file a report before Carter did.

38

When Celia awoke, she was lying on a bed. Her bandaged arm throbbed with an insistence that her fatigue could no longer silence. Curtains were drawn, but a dull light from the streetlamps threaded through the weave, muting the unfamiliar room to a soft old sepia. She moaned and rolled over, wishing to be anywhere but wherever she was, wishing for painkillers to dull the constant ache in her arm. A sound from beyond the bed froze her in place. She heard his voice, but not in a way she'd ever heard before. He mumbled and spoke in disjointed sentences, short, clipped sometimes, and long strings of words that made no sense. He was talking in his sleep. No, he wasn't just talking. He was begging.

He repeated one word, a name: Rose. Celia peered over the side of the bed and found him huddled in the corner on the floor. His arms visibly trembled, covering his head. He whispered, "Turn off the light. Don't let them see." She jumped as he screamed, "Rose!" The name tore from his throat, savage and painful. He sat straight up, his eyes open but seeing something she couldn't. His agonizing desperation struck her as if it were her own, and she gasped. What could have caused such grief? Who was Rose? Could he really be human after all?

Celia forgot her arm. With her only thought to wake him, to save him from the grip of something she knew too well, she reached out and touched his shoulder. As if shocked by electricity, his eyes flew open and he stared right at her. Through the dim light she saw a sheen of sweat glistening on his brow. His hollow cheeks were wet—with tears? His jaw was set with grim force to hold in whatever he'd almost let out.

"What are you doing here?" His words came rough, as if it were hard for him to speak out loud.

"I've asked you that same question for four days now."

He pulled himself up from the floor, twisting away from her. "Go back to sleep."

"Who is Rose?"

He paused halfway to his feet. Celia felt sure this mysterious Rose person had something to do with why she was there, why he'd flipped—even more than she had—when he'd seen her blood.

"Who is she?" she asked again, softly.

"No one you need to know anything about." He fell to his knees, his back to her, as if he had no strength to rise.

"So she does exist?"

His head hung forward. "It doesn't matter."

"It does to me."

He turned his head slightly. "How could it possibly matter to you?"

"I'd like to understand why I'm here."

Silence. He bowed his head but didn't move. She waited, hoping he'd break the stillness with something worth hearing.

"She was a girl I knew a long time ago."

She waited a bit, then asked, "Do I look like her?"

He raised his head, glanced back at her this time, his look speculative. "No."

"Why didn't you kill me?"

"It's . . . not time."

Celia sat up on the bed to look at him eye to eye, ignoring the throbbing in her arm from the sudden movement. "I don't believe you anymore." She lay back, wondering where her sudden assurance had come from, and if it would last.

Sometime later, her arm woke her again. She turned over and stared through the thick air at the ceiling. It took about five seconds for her to feel his eyes upon her.

Her heart pumped faster. Adrenaline raced through her body, heating her. He sat in a chair by a lone table she hadn't noticed before.

His hands formed a steeple in front of his face. She couldn't see his eyes, lost in the grainy-sepia gloom, but she knew they were aimed at her. He didn't blink, didn't move. She wondered how long he'd been sitting there. She wondered why she wasn't more spooked by the thought.

"Why aren't you afraid?" he asked.

"Why do you think I'm not?"

"If I let you go now, you can tell the police too much about me."

She sat up, wincing at the sting of her arm. "I believed that before, but not anymore. Do you know why you're keeping me alive?"

"Yes."

"Why won't you tell me?"

"It isn't necessary."

"Why won't you tell me about Rose?"

"The past is done. It does no good to discuss it."

"Right. That's why you have nightmares and scream about a girl named Rose."

Silence again.

"Talking about it helps sometimes, I've been told." Like she would know.

"Spoken like a true American."

"It's a fact, a worldwide fact, not an American one." As if she knew this.

"Only in America does one have the luxury of indulging in emotional pity for oneself."

"Well, I haven't ever tried talking like that, but I've heard it can be good to get things out before they damage you beyond redemption."

"Redemption. What a useless word. There isn't such a thing."

"I believe in redemption. At least I think I do."

"You've probably never had to be redeemed."

"You know nothing about me."

He was on the bed before she could blink, looming over her on all fours in the dark. Celia pulled her bandaged arm close to her chest as if it could ward him off. "What . . . stop."

"I want to kiss you."

"Why?"

"You know why."

"Because you kissed me before?"

"No."

He lowered himself toward her, slowly, as if daring Celia to stop him.

39

During the ride to West End Central, the deep rumbling of the train goaded Thain's thoughts to grim and dour predictions about his coming fate. His body, already stiffening from the tumble down the stairs, made him feel old. Thain had never seriously considered that Carter might outright physically attack him. Verbal assaults he knew to expect, but not a physical one, even though Carter sometimes acted as if he might slug him, when they had an audience. That was strange as well. Usually Carter only pounced when there were spectators. This time he'd made sure there wouldn't be any. Pure luck, that Clive had been there. Most people took the lift.

Rae had wanted to come with him to West End Central, but he needed some time to think. He had taken Clive's implied advice and promptly filed his report about Carter's attack, so there was nothing more he could do there. *Forget Carter,* he told himself, even though he knew he wouldn't.

Without the Carter incident to dwell on, and without Rae to distract him, Thain was left with nothing but the impossible task ahead of him to focus on. No one heard him sigh. In two days his whole world would crumble to nothing. He'd be a laughing stock and probably end up in some small seaside town where a crime was someone shafting the bartender his fifty pence tip. Maybe his brother was right after all. Alban still felt the sting of his brother's judgment after the assassination in Edinburgh.

When his brother had shown up at their parents' house afterwards, he'd said, "I'm glad you weren't hit, Alban."

"But the target was, Ellis. We failed. I failed. I was right next to him. I had my head up. I did everything I'd been trained to—" Just in the remembering, his anger pulsed beneath his scar like an offbeat drum, as did his shame.

"It was your first assignment. You're a rookie, Alban. Don't make more of it than it is. Happens to the best of us."

"Right. A rookie. I was good enough they put me next to 'im, didn't they? They must not've thought I was such a rookie as all that, Ellis. You think you know everything." He turned away from his brother, furious at being called incompetent.

"Alban, that's not what I meant—" Ellis's hand reached out, but Alban shrugged him off.

"Leave me be, Ellis. I can make my own way from now on. I know what you really think of me, have thought ever since I told you I wanted to be a cop."

"Ah, Alban. I was worried for you, and Mother and Da. You decided so soon after Agatha's—"

"But you're not always right, Ellis. I'm a good cop, or will be if given a chance. One it's clear you don't want me to take. Just leave me alone."

Happens to the best of us, Ellis had said. Thain scowled at the thought. He wouldn't wallow in his doubts or what could happen to him after this. He would still try. Celia had become his motivator as Agatha had once been, and her presence imbued the rolling tube train as if she sat with him. He wondered what her name meant. Cell phone in hand, he keyed in the search. Celia meant "heaven." He wasn't the least surprised.

If Celia had to keep trying to stay alive, to keep doing whatever it was she was doing, so did he. Yes, he admitted to being possessed by her eyes and passionate about meeting her, but he also remained convinced that she was a piece to this puzzle that didn't fit. Celia Wight had some power over the Wraith. A power the man hadn't counted on when he'd accosted her. Thain was certain Celia Wight was the key, but the key to what?

40

The man's internal clock told him the sun would soon rise and bring the morning with it. He'd slept, spent the night with her, when he'd thought to get out of London. Instead he woke on the bed with a headache and the woman lying next to him, her wounded arm cradled on her stomach, her face peaceful in sleep.

He'd kissed her last night. She'd hesitated at first but then melted like bliss beneath him, reminding him of another young woman who had tasted like sweet nectar. The one he'd found heaven with, and then hell.

He got to his feet, watching the sleeping woman, trying not to wake her, and flinched. His head felt bruised from the vicious pounding he'd experienced last night, from the grotesque chaotic colors—black, red, and the damned pale yellow—that had cramped his stomach and squeezed his head with such unrelenting power that he'd reeled away from her, clutching his head to stop the ache. Only after his lips left hers had the sickness and colors dissipated.

Too aware that he'd hurt her, he was no less aware that he couldn't look into her eyes, because then he'd remember more. He'd fought a long, hard battle to banish dangerous memories now thinly veiled beneath the surface of his thoughts. The only thing he remembered with clarity was that he'd wanted to forget everything in the first place. He was no more capable of handling the horror now than he had been in his youth, no matter how many horrors he'd seen since. Delving too deeply had caused this damage to the woman, he knew, because of the feelings she'd forced him to remember. He'd been a fool to think he could kill her, could control what was happening between them. He couldn't afford this, nor could she.

For fifteen years his life had served one reason, one purpose, and he'd never strayed or been distracted from it in all that time. Nothing had been more important than wreaking systematic havoc and taking retribution on those who deserved it, and yet now, when the last act stood staged and ready to play, he wanted this woman so much he felt physically sick with need of her.

In spite of what he'd done to her—was doing to her—she still saw him as human, not as the enemy or the means of her destruction. Only one other person in his life had seen him that clearly, and she'd been taken from him in a way he could not afford to think of. His parents hadn't known what to believe at the time. He didn't blame them; he had kept an eye on them over the years, though they didn't know he still lived. And he'd put any need of contact with them away. He'd never looked back.

Or so he'd thought until now, until her. He glanced back at the sleeping beauty on the bed. The desire to know her name weighed like shackles upon him with ever-increasing pressure, and yet he knew that to learn it would truly be the beginning of the end of his mission. If he knew her name his brain would be compelled to accept what his heart was trying to trick him into believing.

That he could have a real life. That he could live and breathe the air of a free man. That he could love again.

But it was an illusion, a dream, a reality he would never see—not with her. This woman had a real life, everything he didn't, and he knew better than to hope, after what he'd done, that she could—much less would—give it up for him. Yet that was exactly what his heart kept tempting him with. Knowing him for a handful of days, could she love him? Would she leave her past behind to share a future far from everything each of them had ever known? His heart wanted to believe it. His head called him a fool. He knew his head was right.

Donning his coat, he left to find some painkillers and perhaps something for her to eat. For her, he had made sure they averaged two meals a day. He knew she would be hungry when she awoke, though food was the last thing on his mind. She had needed painkillers last night but seemed comforted by his presence at her side while she slept. Each time she'd moaned or moved and he'd chanced to see her face, creased with unconscious pain, he caressed her forehead or pulled her into his arms and held her until she relaxed again. Though he hadn't slept much, he didn't care. He hadn't been this close to joy in fifteen years. He'd thought kindness lost to him, thought any emotion but anger abandoned long ago.

Stepping out into the still-dark, cold, and hazy morning, he moved carefully over the icy sidewalk crunching under his feet. In a better part of town, not far from here, he knew a place with decent takeout. Over the years he'd cased most of the chain restaurants in London. The employees of chains didn't tend to be overcurious in the name of being friendly.

Warm thoughts of the woman intruded, but he concentrated on the mundane, on what they would do after the meal. Though it would be in broad daylight, they would leave London. He would have to take her with him—had to, he now realized. In spite of his multiple mistakes, he wouldn't be caught in a trap of his own making, and to arrive at his destination early wouldn't hurt the schedule he'd planned with meticulous accuracy. His prey lived according to a clockwork regime, and that wouldn't change until he changed it for him.

Scanning the sidewalks ahead, the side streets, and the buildings, he crossed the street he'd turned onto. The restaurant sat on the far corner already filled with clients for breakfast. Right next to it was a small pharmacy, which would carry painkillers. Perfect. He stepped inside the restaurant and inhaled the scented warmth that surrounded him, which reminded him again of *her* warmth, *her* scent.

For the first time he wondered who would win: himself, or she who was unconsciously giving him back his humanity? Pushing through the early breakfast throng to the counter, he placed his order, paid for it, and stood against the wall at the back of the restaurant, collar up, his eyes on the exits and the people ordering or waiting like him. Did he really want to win? Stupid question. No matter what his heart told him, no matter what idiocy he dreamed up, he had to win. This was the final act of the play, and it had to be a real showstopper. He wouldn't lose.

41

Police officers were nothing if not determined, especially with the caliber of the man they hunted. Now that the chief had given Thain a real—if tenuous—chance, even if the chief didn't outright believe his theory, the disease began to spread to the others of the team.

Crowning glory. That's what he'd thought for years. The Wraith would be his crowning glory. But the Wraith, or whoever, was making him—making all of them—sweat for that glory. Being more than casually acquainted with the Wraith's record, he knew the prize would be far from easy to earn, especially if he was correct. With a hostage, the Wraith's strategy had to be different, but even with that difference—and police officers seeing him with their own eyes—the man hadn't materialized solidly enough to be caught.

Four days had passed since the murder of Richard McLean and kidnapping of Celia Wight. Now they had visual proof she still lived. Not only had the cops checking out the bedsit seen her on the corner with the kidnapper, but thanks to the newest media call for information, a couple from a flat near where Celia's bags were found had come forward to report that they had seen a woman drop her bags on the front steps of their building, a day before the bags had been discovered. They'd seen Celia on the news and put the pieces together when they heard of the bags being found, and where. Though they'd confirmed the woman was Celia, the description the couple had given of the kidnapper was of an ordinary, nondescript man. He'd kept his head low and away from them, so they gave no useful identification of the suspect. And the cop who'd gotten a knot on the top of his head had the impression that Celia's presence was the reason he still breathed. Thain kept coming back to one question as if it sat upon a lazy Susan, forever turning and returning to pester him. Why hadn't the Wraith killed Celia? Because of her innocence?

Back at his desk at West End, Thain was eager to forget everything but the case, and hours passed without his noticing. He worked on remembering, sorting, and looking for something in his files that might have eluded him before. He checked to see what dates he'd entered when he'd thought the Wraith was in London over the last five years. Once back at the Hendon, he would check to see if his dates matched up to any of the flat rentals they knew of, especially the one on Methley Street where he'd actually been seen—and almost caught—with Celia Wight. Thain updated his files with the information from this murder investigation, and lastly checked back through the limp excuses for photographs he'd collected. He would give them to Rae, though they held no more information than they had the last time he looked. He saved everything to his USB drive, took it from the computer, and looked at it lying across his palm. His hand quivered. He grasped the drive, squeezed hard, and his hand stilled. Was he really going to turn over all his hard-earned data to HOLMES and the team just like that? He shook his head and wondered how Rae was getting on. As if on cue, his phone vibrated.

"I've a composite photo for you to look at," Rae said when he answered.

Pushing to his feet, he groaned as his movement reminded him of the bruising he'd taken. Ignoring the aches as best he could, he shoved the precious drive in his pocket and donned his coat. "Are you a mind reader?"

"Not last time I looked."

"I'll head back now, then. You're still at the Hendon?"

"Where else would I be?"

"Point taken. Silly question. Put it down to brain fry. I'll be there shortly. Rae"—he paused—"thanks."

He could almost hear her smile as she spoke. "Come on, then, we're waiting for you."

He put his computer on standby and hurried out.

42

A light shone on her face, pinking her eyelids, and Celia woke up fast. Daylight? He'd let them sleep all night? She felt the lack of his presence at once and grimaced, admitting she didn't like that lack. She shook her head. What was wrong with her? He sliced her arm open and she misses him? Was she succumbing to his negative attention, to all his devotion to keeping her in his power? Did that make her a female who secretly craved domination?

It was too soon after waking to think such thoughts. Groggy, Celia sat up and looked at her arm. No blood had seeped through the bandage, but the wound still throbbed. Where was he? Celia stood up and stared at the door. She had no reason to think it would be anything other than locked. Even if only from the inside. She could try the door, or scream now, and maybe someone would help. But what if he came back in the middle of a rescue? He'd have to kill anyone who saw her. She didn't want anyone's blood on her conscience.

Her arm reminded her of how dangerous he was, how easily her life, or someone else's, could be over. But last night he'd kissed her like she'd never been kissed, as if she were the last woman on the planet and he the last man. She fell back on the bed. He'd taken her somewhere she had never been, which frightened her, because he had to be insane. What did that make her?

Was she turning into one of those kidnap victims who fell in love with her kidnapper? Would she soon think she was the only one who understood him, who could save his lost soul, could help him heal whatever horror lay in his past, and all that?

Celia didn't know how it worked, but she'd heard of what had happened to Patty Hearst, and those other people in Sweden years ago, brainwashing of the most subtle and deep kind. Could he be doing it on purpose? Why? What good would it do him?

If he'd wanted sex he could have already forced that on her, unless he was trying to get her to initiate it so that later she couldn't say he'd raped her. Logical, if he planned on letting her live. But he had come too close to killing her.

The stranger's kisses made a lie of any coherent thought, telling her she was magic for him. When he kissed her, his anger seemed to disappear, and sweet-hot desire took its place as if they were adolescents discovering kissing for the first time. He was brainwashing her. Of course, he was sick. That must be why he always pulled away from her, why he looked tortured after they kissed. He was dragging her into his sickness. He was crazy; he would soon take her life and be done with it. But not before he took her soul first, and made her as crazy as he was. Celia wanted to believe that. What else could she think and still know herself? She must defend against the feelings he roused in her. How? She didn't know how, but she knew she had to.

Evidently he saw it in her face the minute he walked in the door. Maybe he'd expected her doubt, her defensiveness. He said nothing as he set a bag and two insulated cups on the table. He removed his coat, took a bottle of pain relievers from his pocket, and handed them to her. While he set the food out, Celia watched him as if watching a film, detached yet fixed. No matter the excuse, she realized, she hadn't tried the door. And he hadn't looked surprised to find her still here.

Once the table was laid, he motioned to her. She thought he would take his food, as was his habit, somewhere else. But he didn't this time. He pulled her chair out for her, and sat right across from her, his arms on the table on either side of his food. He glanced at her once or twice but wouldn't keep eye contact. Then he looked at her and his eyes didn't stray.

"Aren't you hungry?" He glanced at the food and steaming cup of tea in front of her.

She nodded, comforted, in some unrealistic way, she was sure. "Yes. Yes, I'm hungry."

So they ate at the table together. Afterwards Celia started to clear up, but he placed his hand on her good arm, gently but with firm intent. "Your arm isn't up to that yet."

He took the food wrappings from her and finished cleaning up.

Celia sat at the table and stared at him. As if in an alternate reality, she thought they could be but a normal couple during their morning routine. A shiver ran up her spine, shaking her as if someone had walked over her grave. What a strange saying that was. How did you know where your future grave was? You didn't, but that didn't mean it wasn't somewhere, being walked on while it waited for you to come and fill it. *Stop it,* she told herself. "Do we leave today?"

He didn't turn around or stop cleaning. "Yes."

"Today, not tonight?"

"Today."

She sighed. "When do we stop running? I mean . . . I know it's a stupid question. You probably never stop running. But the police are on to your apartments now, aren't they?"

"Only one."

"That's enough though, isn't it?"

"Yes."

Celia waited until he turned around. "Why won't you tell me what this is all about?"

At first he didn't move. Then he did. He wiped clean the entire room with his usual fastidiousness, using massive amounts of ammonia and bleach as if to erase the stench of the place as well. Her nose wrinkled as she tried not to breathe in the acrid, harsh chemical stench permeating the small room.

If they left London, the chance of being rescued would become grotesquely smaller, practically nonexistent. She had to be found before it was too late. Celia stood. "I want to know what you're going to do with me. You're insane to keep me like this and make me—"

He halted and glared at her so intensely she took a step back. "Make you what?" he said. When she didn't answer, he threw the wet rag on the floor and advanced on her. "Make . . . you . . . what?"

Anger, and a dangerous question too, lurked behind his menace. Celia backed away, but the wall brought her up short.

"Nothing. No . . . Yes, you make me kiss you."

He moved closer. "You kiss me back."

"I have to. It would hurt otherwise."

"I thought you said you weren't a liar." Only a breath separated them now.

Celia didn't want to look at him. "I'm not. I—"

"You like to be kissed."

"No, I don't!"

"Yes, you do." As if to prove it, he kissed her again. God help her, she kissed him back, again.

He pulled a millimeter away; but stayed close enough his ragged breath warmed her skin. "By me," he said.

"You confuse me. You're doing it on purpose."

"You're no more confused than I am."

Celia began to cry now. His body heat radiated onto hers like the sun, and she felt trapped by it, seduced by its warmth. His hand tilted her face up.

She started to pull away. "I don't understand. You don't make any sense."

He stopped her. "What does make sense right now is touching you."

Celia moaned. She was losing this battle. She pushed against his chest, "Leave me alone. Tell me what you want from me and stop playing games."

"Kiss me."

Seductive, warm, insistent, he put his arms round her and held her, body to body. His lips caressed hers until she could no longer think, much less fight.

When he finally released her, she found her arms around his neck. She pulled them away as if burned and clasped them round her torso as if to protect herself from him somehow, or maybe to keep herself in. Weeping still, she whispered, "What do you want from me?" She slowly slid down the wall and collapsed on the floor, huddling, afraid for the first time that he would answer.

He had broken through her defense, insinuated his essence into her very being. Soon she would be beyond help. Did she want help? She didn't know this person she'd become. Everything in her screamed to escape, to never let this man touch her again. Everything in her wanted to stay and heed the call of his tremendous need, which somehow echoed in her. But his need also recalled her past, a past she'd spent the better part of her life trying to forget. She didn't want to face it in the light of day ever again.

He made her want too much. All these years her writing had kept the demons at bay, had allowed her to live outside herself—in words, on a page—and to keep secrets locked up and unreachable.

This haunted man made her want to unlock her heart and feel it beating next to his. She wanted to discover the part of him she knew she would understand, the part of him that understood her. Celia wanted to stay with this stranger, maybe forever. He had won, but she refused to meet his eyes.

Celia didn't hear his belabored breath, didn't see the doom in his tortured face as he backed away and himself crumpled to the floor.

43

Forty-five minutes after Thain left the West End station, Rae handed a photograph to him in the murder squad room at the Hendon. Looking at it, his aches and frustration took a seat, at least temporarily.

The photo contained a blurred profile shot—not the best in the world, but he felt a twinge of hope. "Will you look at that, lass?" He tore his gaze away from it to look at Rae. "If this murder suspect is the Wraith, I've waited too long to see his face. If it isn't him, well, at least we know he's our suspect ."

"It's not a great shot."

"We need all the help we can get, Rae. You just gave me, us, hope."

"And a reason to not think of the extreme two-day deadline we have to find this blurry-but-deadly killer?"

"The photo leaves a lot to be guessed, sure. But we don't have anything better. The jaw line looks strong, the cheeks defined, but not overly. The eyes still aren't clear, and his whole package isn't near enough out of the ordinary, but—" Puzzled, he frowned. Something about the face niggled his brain, gave him a little message that meant trouble.

"Thain, there's something—" Rae started, but he interrupted, totally absorbed by the photo of the killer. Even knowing it was a far-fetched possibility that this image was the face of the Wraith, it fascinated him anyway.

"Would you call this man handsome?" he asked, wanting a female's point of view.

"Maybe in a roughish sort of way. It's a very masculine profile. Thain—"

"Could we use this to make up the other side, to get an idea of him from the front?"

"Thain. I need you to listen a minute."

She had his attention then. "All right."

"I—oh, never mind. You'll think I'm crazy."

She frowned and he chided her, "Hope that frown doesn't stick." She'd said that to him so many times, he couldn't help himself. On her face a frown was rare.

"You're proof they don't," she shot back.

"Okay, so about the photo?"

"Already tried. Here's the result."

Rae handed him another photo. He thought it amazing. "How close?"

"I'd say pretty close."

"Put it through the passport—"

"Already done."

"And?"

"I found more than one possible match."

He stood up. "What do you mean?"

"When I put this frontal view composite photo through the passport database, I found at least fifteen photos that matched or almost matched. All of them have different names."

"Are they all the same nationality?"

"No. All of them are different. Four of them could be promising."

"I'll need the whole list."

Rae handed him a folder. "I thought you would."

He opened it and found photos and information about each passport.

Rae said, "I'll tell Clive to get over here." He nodded while glancing through the folder. When she'd finished texting Clive, Thain looked up and managed a grin, a real one.

"You're a gem. Where were you in my past life?"

"Ha. Overworked and underpaid, I'm sure."

"Spoken like a true workaholic."

"You should know."

"All right, so . . ." He flipped through the images in front of him again and saw she was right. The men all favored her composite photograph, some more than others, and he thought at least three of them were truly different men. But Rae was right. Four remained, four which were strikingly similar. Was he really looking at the face of the Wraith for the first time? Or at least the suspect? Why had the blurry face—and these four passport photos—triggered something in his brain? *Let it go and it will come,* he thought.

"Do you think it's him?" Rae leaned in to look at the photos in the folder. "What's wrong? Now you're frowning."

He pulled his coat off and dumped it on a chair before spreading out the images from the folder on the table. "I don't know . . . Rae, this composite is good enough, along with the four passport photos, to show the store clerks that were interviewed, and the robbers, and the secretary. Won't hurt to use the blurry profile shot as well. We need to run all of the photos through HOLMES to see if we find any matches on the surveillance footage."

"You want me to call that in to the HOLMES team or talk to the chief first?" Rae asked as she turned to go.

"Right. The chief first."

"Thain," Rae said, and then halted as if hesitant to continue.

"Aye, Rae?" Her brow furrowed and she glanced down, and then said, "Any word on Carter?"

"What do you mean?"

"Like, is he still on the team?"

It was his turn to frown. "The chief said he'd let me know at the next meeting." She nodded as Clive walked in the door.

"What have we found?" He too, slid off his coat, and he strode over to join them. He looked at the photos spread on the table. "Okay, spill it."

"I will. Rae," he said as she prepared to leave, "Thanks."

She nodded. The corner of his lips raised enough that she smiled back at him. Thain said, "And perhaps you should try missing persons first, then the chief?"

"Here, or the continent?"

"Start here. Our suspect knows London too well. And also York, since that's where our victim was from."

"I'm on it, oh, and, I'll need your USB drive." He pulled it from his pocket, locked eyes with her, and hesitated.

She held out her hand. "I won't lose it. I promise," she said.

"Right. I know." He gave it to her. It took effort, and it was only to Rae he realized, that he could give it over.

She smiled. "You'll have it back before you miss it, if after this is all over, you still need it."

"Right. I know." She left as he turned to Clive and said, "Look at what our master artist has come up with." He and Clive went over it all again. He kept his impatience in check, his hope in the background. Too many times in the past he'd thought he'd closed in on his target, only to lose the phantom Wraith in the mists of the man's transparency.

But the excitement emanating from Clive spurred his, and he couldn't restrain his own inner questions. Could this be the second major break? Could they be on the verge of actual success? *Stop it.* This time might be different, but he wasn't going to get excited yet. *Wait, Thain,* he told himself. *Wait until you have the real man in front of you before you clap yourself on the back. Until then, he's still a Wraith, a wisp in the wind. Until then, you have nothing, and Celia Wight could still die.*

44

He staggered back when the woman slid down the wall as if her legs had no bones. The misery in her voice, on her tearstained face still soft with passion—a passion he'd encouraged—twisted him inside, made his throbbing brain worse, the flash of colors more chaotic. He crushed his hands against his eyes and slumped to his knees.

No! He pushed aside his own discomfort. *I only want to see her smile.* He knew the danger, but he was bloody tired of asking himself what the bloody hell he was doing, or why his bloody head exploded with sickening colors, pounding like an offbeat drum every time he kissed her. He blinked as the intensity lessened. He glanced at her sitting in a small heap at the base of the wall. "What's your name?"

She looked up, clearly confused. "Why do you want to know now, after all this time?"

"I could've looked in your wallet back at the first flat. I could've watched the news, seen a paper. I didn't want to know, until now," he said. It wasn't the whole truth, but he would never tell her that.

She didn't move. She stayed against the wall as if she expected him to hurt her again. "Why shouldn't we remain nameless to each other?"

Her words tasted bitter to him. He hadn't meant to cut her. No, he'd meant to kill her. But her blood, her anguish, had forced a recollection, and he now recognized the image that played out in relentlessly pounding, head-hurting, chaotic colors each time he kissed her. He'd thought he'd erased it. What an egotistical fool he was to believe he could ever be rid of it before his job was done.

He stood, turned from the woman slumped against the wall, and like a robot finished cleaning the stupid little room. He put two pills in her hand and made her take the painkillers. He put on his coat, pulled her to her feet, and helped her into her coat. He wrapped the scarf around her lovely face and pulled her woolen cap down far enough to cover her ears. He took care to avoid hurting her bandaged arm. On the way out he gathered their belongings and the trash to throw away somewhere.

"I have to use the bathroom."

He stood outside the door while she did so, and then they left the building behind, as they had all the others.

The woman moved automatically, as if she no longer had conscious thought. Her eyes were vague and hooded, her step listless beside him as they ventured into the slushy gray world of a downtrodden part of the city. It had not snowed since their spectacular escape, and sooty dirt lay stark against the leftovers, unwelcoming, old.

She didn't talk or react, didn't ask him any questions. He ignored a sinking feeling in his gut and put his mind to the task ahead. She would stay with him until they reached his destination. Walking out of London would be best, hitching a ride with some well-wishing individual. He didn't trust the woman's strength to stand up to the hitchhiking so soon after being wounded and taking painkillers, but ever-present cameras made traveling by train or bus more risky than hitching a ride. He could possibly use the multiple taxi strategy he'd developed long ago, and be gone before the police started tracing his trail, but the taxi companies would already have been notified, and their drivers would be watching for a pair such as them.

Stealing a car was too blatant even in a city where hundreds were stolen every day. Renting one was out of the question, and he didn't own one. He had enough cash to purchase one, but it would take time, and a salesman would remember him. A car could be followed, traced by its whereabouts and movements. That left his first option. It wasn't the safest, but it was the least traceable solution.

They would walk and hope for a ride with a driver who hadn't paid much attention to the news about a missing woman and her kidnapper. He knew where to go to find such drivers—north, toward the small airport at Luton.

Travelers and tourists usually listened in a vague way to news reports, even after disasters like America's Eleventh of September. A holiday was just that. A time to leave the real world behind and play, relax, or race around trying to see as much as possible in an absurdly short period of time.

They took the underground to the farthest point north and walked until, right before dusk, they reached the M1 motorway where it crossed the M25, the motorway encircling London. At a Little Chef restaurant and petrol station they stopped for dinner, but she looked feverish and wouldn't eat. He hoped her wound wasn't infected. Blast that dirt hole of a hotel. He'd done his best to cleanse his utensils with bleach, but only time would tell.

Luckily, he found an elderly Welsh couple filled with Christmas cheer, heading north to Leicester to visit family for the holidays, and who offered to take them that far.

Crossing the parking lot to the couple's car, he bent close to the woman. "They mustn't discover that you're American . . ." The look on her face, the tears ready to spill, said she'd brave it out because though she might no longer believe he'd kill her, she still believed he'd kill them.

He helped her into the car and sat beside her in the back seat. When they asked, he told the couple she suffered from a sore throat and didn't feel like talking.

Not once in fifteen years had he cared what anyone thought of him. He knew what he'd become and why. He had no friends. He had no contact with anyone outside of his business needs, and those contacts he kept minimal. He preferred it that way. But she didn't like what he was doing, though she kissed him with a hunger that matched his own. Her opinion should mean nothing to him, but it did.

And what was in a name? Why had he asked her for it? Why should it matter? He'd cared for a name once, cherished the name because he'd cherished its owner. But that name was gone, over and done with as was the name his parents had given him thirty-two years ago. His parents. For the first time in years, he wondered how they managed. Once, when he'd first taken up this work, he'd dared to peer into their windows as he made the second of many drops. They'd looked well enough. It had hurt to see their faces with no smiles upon them. Hurt not to go in and put the smiles back, talk with them, hear their voices. So he'd never done it again. They'd gone on and lived their lives without him. He doubted if they thought of him anymore.

These thoughts came because of the woman beside him. Her now-familiar, slightly floral scent teased his nose and he took a deep breath. She looked up at him and he returned her searching gaze, the one that always asked why. He couldn't tell her what he wanted from her, because every time he thought of it, he knew she was a mistake that would cost him more than the fantastic price he'd already paid.

He turned away from her and looked out the window at the darkening countryside flying by while the little car raced farther and farther from London, closer and closer to his meeting with destiny. He tensed when she rested her gaze upon him, no doubt wondering about his thoughts and what he wanted from her. He didn't have to hear her words to know her questions.

She thought he was in charge. She didn't know how close to a lie that was.

45

"Here, look at this, Thain." St. John said, interrupting Thain's manic perusal of the murder suspect's photos. St. John had called him over to the viewing room where, while he waited for St. John to get to the footage, Thain tried to glean more from the profile and composite photos.

"Look right here." St. John pointed at the screen. "The woman's covered from head to toe, and he doesn't let go of her the whole time the camera has him in its sights. Though the light isn't good, I think she's still wearing her original coat, not the one the clerk described."

Tired beyond thought, Thain couldn't believe in fortune, even if, for once, it seemed the gods favored them over the Wraith. He knew better than to trust the gods. "Where was this taken?"

"Adie Road, near where we found Celia Wight's bags. Isn't far from the Hammersmith tube station."

"When?"

"Four nights ago."

"And there are more like this, you say? All at night?"

"Yes, and from five different locations. We've found three films with them wearing the first coats, the ones that they wore the day of the murder, and two others where they're wearing different coats. In those other films, her coat does seem to match the one the clerk said was bought with cash. I called Greene and he checked the description on HOLMES. The man is wearing a new coat as well. In every film, the woman is always completely covered. He keeps his head averted from the cameras and sometimes wears glasses. Looks like you were right on two counts, Thain. He bought himself a new coat and it does seem like he doesn't stay put anywhere, but keeps moving. In a city like London, who'd guess at his identity? Who'd think to look for him on the streets, and at night?"

"Especially since we've had no photograph of him."

"Yes, and we've yet to match any of these films with the composite or profile photos, because we can't see his face clearly enough. How can he know where *all* of the cameras are?" St. John said, shaking his head as if it were impossible. "You know how you commented earlier that we didn't have any footage of them during the day? Were you already thinking about them moving at night?"

Thain didn't look at St. John when he said, "Yes. Which raises a question, doesn't it: where is he during the day?"

St. John's forehead wrinkled. "At another of those flats or bedsits we've only found one of?"

Thain heard someone clear his throat and turned to see the chief standing at the door watching them. "How long have you been there, sir?"

"Long enough to see you've found them."

"Perhaps. We have no positive identification."

"But *you* think it's him."

Thain nodded, committing once again to the inevitable. Why not? What more did he have to lose? "Yes, St. John and I both do."

North joined them and stared at the footage on St. John's screen. Thain perched a leg on the edge of a desk behind St. John's and picked up the original blurry profile photograph.

This was the face of the murder suspect, perhaps even the Wraith. But he wished it were a more decisive photo so that matching it would be easier. Even though they had four passport photos that closely resembled each other, they had nothing but the frontal composite photograph to compare them to. In a television or cinematic film, cops could always hone in on photos and sharpen them up to a point of clarity, but he knew that, so far, technology still had its limits. They were lucky to have this much.

"What're you looking at Thain?" North asked, breaking in on his bad mood. He handed the chief both photographs.

"This is the profile and this, the frontal composite view Rae Bell made for us."

Thain sat back as the chief perused the photos, his mind still restless, uneasy. Every time he saw the profile it irritated him. "Can I see the profile view again, sir?" he asked, reaching for the photo.

Chief North handed it back to him. "It's not very clear."

"No. But it's the best we have for the moment, and it's more than we've had before." Thain stared at the photo, trying to see what it was that irritated him.

The chief leaned forward. "Do you recognize him, Thain?"

He held it out a bit farther, his forehead hurting with the concentration. "No, sir, I don't. I wish I did. Still there's something . . ."

"But I do, sir."

The chief and Thain turned around to find Rae had come in while they were preoccupied with the photos. She stood with a file in her hand behind St. John. She swallowed and said, "Remember when we checked the shops, Thain? We stopped at the Coffee Cup on Hampstead High Street?"

"Yes, of course. That's what's been bothering me. You mean the guy who brushed my sleeve on his way out? Once again, Rae Bell, you are mint." He dialed Clive's number. "Clive, get the crews checking flats and bedsits to concentrate in the residential areas anywhere near Hampstead High Street, and put a call in for video from that area. I'll call Greene and get him to allocate the actions."

"What have you found, Thain?" Clive hollered through the phone.

"Rae thinks she's seen him, Clive. She recognized him from a café we were in."

"I'm on it." Clive hung up and Thain looked at Rae and the chief. That's when it hit him. Celia . . .

"We were so close." He ached with remorse.

"To him, but not to her," Rae said.

"If we'd known . . ."

"How could we?"

The chief said, "Thain. At least now we're tracking him."

"Tracking a Wraith. With all due respect, sir, I've tracked him for years without result."

"*If* this man is the Wraith. And remember, Thain, you hunted on your own, not with a team behind you. Don't forget *this*." North picked up the composite photo and shook it at him. "This *is* our killer."

Thain took a deep breath and stared at the chief, awash with sudden conviction. "As I said earlier, sir, we should show it to the robbers. If they don't recognize him, that answers the question about the number of thieves. We should also show it to the shop clerks and the secretary. If they can confirm he is the man who bought the clothing, if the secretary recognizes him, then we have to put the photo on the wire."

North turned to Rae. "Are you that sure, Bell?"

She hesitated. "I'm sure." She looked at Thain. "I'm sure, Thain. This is the same man."

"Thain, it's your call." The chief didn't look happy.

He knew she was right, but if he went with Rae's conviction and was wrong, if this turned into a wild goose chase, they would lose precious time and give the Wraith, the killer, whoever he bloody was, a greater lead—not to mention Thain's own loss of credibility, so hard fought for, so easily lost. But if his instinct was right and someone recognized the suspect from this photograph, they would narrow the man's lead by a wider margin than any of them had dared dream. "If the shop clerks and the secretary agree with Rae, I don't see it's much of a risk, sir. When he finds out we have a photo of him, well, we're still groping in the dark and he knows it."

46

The couple driving Celia to her doom chattered with an endless capacity, completely unaware of her resignation. They had no inkling of the distress they caused with their carefree, friendly attitudes. She couldn't react, shied away from any thought. The painkillers, on top of the trauma to her arm, had induced a stupor of defeat that held her in its thick, remorseless grasp. Yet it didn't help dispel the thoughts that incessantly plagued her.

Were they so different, she and he? Something had happened to him in his past, scarring him beyond any surgeon's help, as her own past had scarred her. He'd chosen to hide inside himself, as she had. His body bore scars like hers; she'd seen them. She was glad he didn't know about hers, only the ones he'd given her. How many more would she endure before this was over? How much longer could she go on and stay sane? Was she still sane? Was she still the person she had been?

The little car's heater worked too well. Celia couldn't get comfortable, couldn't sit still until he looked at her, angry all over. The will to survive remained inside her somewhere. She could feel it sometimes. But the rest of her she didn't know anymore. She didn't know the person who'd begun to crave this strange man's touch. His need emanated from his every pore and she responded to it. Why? What was wrong with her that she wanted to see him smile for once, that she wanted to know his name, wanted to destroy the torment driving him down this path of doom? Celia needed to find out what had scarred him so deeply. If she understood him better, then she might begin to understand herself.

She saw a road sign for Leicester. Celia had traveled the M1 before, during a research trip a lifetime ago. She'd been in the driver's seat then, not a kidnapped passenger. The elderly couple let them off in front of a restaurant on the outskirts of Leicester, not in the city proper.

Farther along the motorway, he led them to another petrol station and bought Celia a bottle of water. She drank it sip by sip without tasting it, automatically; it was something to keep her hands occupied. Her arm throbbed; her head felt uncomfortably hot. Her feet burned with cold, but felt numb as bricks by the time he found another ride.

They headed north toward Nottingham. He didn't talk to her, had barely glanced at her since they'd left London. Their second ride left them near enough to spend the rest of the night in Nottingham. They took a taxi to a small inn not far from the motorway, quaint and quiet except for the pub, which was full of people, warmth, and cheer. As they walked toward the desk, Celia saw some merrymakers playing darts, while others enjoyed a 'spot o' dinner' and a pint. She was suddenly thirsty and very hungry. She wanted more than anything to walk into that pub and laugh with the worst of them. She pulled his coat sleeve.

"Can we eat dinner in there tonight?" She dragged her hungry gaze from the warm promise of the pub and looked up at him.

His eyes stayed as cold as her feet. He shook his head and looked toward the pub. She could see indecision. Maybe he wanted to go as well. "Come on. I promise I won't try anything."

He looked at her and her heart plummeted.

"They can still see your face."

He paid for their room and signed the register with whatever fake name he had come up with. Celia blinked back tears as they bypassed the pub and mounted the stairs.

From the look on his face she understood that the room wasn't as secure as he would have liked. He spent a good ten minutes going over every inch of it. He pulled the chest of drawers over in front of the door, as the door handle sat too high to wedge a chair under. Then he put the chest back.

"Why didn't you leave it there?" she asked.

He didn't answer. He opened the window of the second-story room and looked out, checking beneath the window, looking to either side and across from it, where she could see nothing but the blank wall of the building next to the inn. She knew him well enough now to guess that he calculated the distance to the ground, taking everything in like a computer and filing it away. He checked the hallway, and took her with him as he checked each guest room door. Finally he appeared satisfied.

"Are we going to eat anytime soon?"

"You'll want to bathe first?"

"Well, yes. But—"

"You bathe while I order dinner."

"We can eat in the room here?"

"Yes."

He looked away from her. Celia was beyond tired of being a prisoner. She said, "I like lager." It's all she could manage.

She retreated to the bathroom and found they didn't have a shower, as such. Instead she found a bathtub with a spray adapter that connected to the faucet. She shivered with anticipation of the warmth soon to seep through her chilled body. She ran the bath and took off her clothes. She unwrapped her bandaged arm with care and saw that though the cut remained red and a little puffy, no more bleeding had taken place. She found a surprising treat of bath salts and shook some into the steaming water. Slowly she slipped one foot in, then the other, grimacing against the burn of hot on cold, of returning circulation. She lowered her aching body into the thawing comfort of the water.

She took time to bathe her arm but not submerge it. She knew too well how to care for wounds of this nature. Her toes tingled now, no longer painful, and her skin itched and turned pink. Once she'd submerged her body, she used the spray adapter to wet and wash her hair one-handed. She wiped her face. Then, slowly, she glanced at her body, allowed herself to look at the four mean, ugly scars deforming her stomach, chest, and upper arms. She didn't need to see the fifth one on her neck. She hated their disfigurement of her once beautiful body, hated these repulsive souvenirs of her useless fight against butchery . . . and rape.

There, she'd actually allowed herself to think the word.

The small room held no sound but an occasional drip of water into her bath. She closed her eyes against her tears and concentrated on how clean her damaged body now was, focused on the warm water lapping, tickling, against her legs, her breasts, and her neck every time she made the slightest move. She ignored the horror of the past and thought of nothing but the silence in the room, the water, and the heat enveloping her. Her mind lapsed into a sleepy lethargic haven. Yet, slowly, insidiously, a longing rose within her.

Celia couldn't ignore the want, the craving. In spite of her scars, for the first time since that horrible day long ago, she reached out, set her fingers restlessly, but with intent, on her stomach, caressed the skin there. She let her hand wander to her thighs, touching her body the way she thought she was supposed to be touched by a man who loved her—not that one ever had. She imagined her kidnapper touching her like this and her back arched, she gasped with foreign, deliriously painful desire. Safe in the tub, alone in her fantasy, a fantasy she'd never been capable of having before, she disappeared. She wasn't the person she'd been since the attack thirteen years ago. She had become someone else, someone she'd denied ever since her parents' deaths.

Was life like that for him, too? Did he deny who he had been? Celia knew he did. She wanted, right then, to really and truly forget everything. She wanted him to come through that door and find her like this. She wanted him to touch her, to want her so much he would forget who he was and remember who he, too, had been before.

Before what? The question lingered in the light and dark of him.

When he knocked on the door her eyes flew open and she sat up too fast, splashing water everywhere, all over the floor. Oblivious, her chest ached with what she had dared to think, to feel, and she struggled to draw in air as if she'd run a mile. He hadn't even been in the room and she'd acted like, like . . . she'd had thoughts . . . feelings.

Celia grabbed a towel and stood to dry herself. Her skin, pinky-red with heat, felt too sensitive. He would see what she'd done in her face, flushed and damp. He would know.

"Dinner has arrived."

"I'll, I'll be right out."

"No hurry."

Yes, there was. She dressed as quickly as possible. She wouldn't give her body another chance to betray her. She couldn't, because this man could hurt her more deeply than the other—and not with his knife. If she gave him a chance, he'd inflict such devastating destruction that recovery would be impossible: her heart was not that strong.

47

Staring at the bleak and restless sky from the window of the murder room at the Hendon, Thain thought of the sense of accomplishment he should feel after watching the first BBC newscast last night and seeing the profile and frontal rendering, the composite photograph of the face of the man who he hoped, for Celia's sake, was the Wraith. He'd tried for so long not to see the Wraith in every unsolved murder that now, when he could use his obsession, use the research that had made him the joke of the department to stop a suspect who may be the elusive Wraith, he didn't know what to feel. At least the information he'd collected now finally served a purpose, even if the suspect wasn't who Thain thought he could be.

Out of habit, he had tried not to think of the murder suspect and the Wraith as the same person. The reversal of that took up too much space in his head and he, they, still had no proof either way. Still, he had watched the newscast and seen what he'd waited ten years to see: the face he hoped was the Wraith's plastered on every screen in the nation and continent, even if the photos weren't good enough to guarantee that the man would be found. He refused to think about what it meant if the man they chased wasn't the Wraith. All he wanted now was for Celia Wight to still be alive, and the best chance of that was if the Wraith had indeed kidnapped her.

Perhaps now the suspect would have to lay low, which was a drawback. But could he lay low with Celia Wight? He'd done just that so far. Thain hoped the man wouldn't have easy access anymore to his favorite haunts, if he had any, or his invisible bank account. He prayed the Wraith hadn't changed his rules so drastically that he was driven to kill Celia. That one thought kept him chilled, and yet on fire. *I might slow you down with these photos, but I know I haven't stopped you. Not yet. Celia Wight must be the key to accomplishing that.*

Give me time, Celia. Stay alive long enough for me to find you.

48

When she walked out of the bathroom, her short hair damp and spiky, he sensed a shift in her emotions. Her delicate pretty face shone red as if in full blush and she wouldn't look him in the eye.

When she finally did, her back straightened as if to tell him to go to hell. He would be the last to tell her he was already there. He frowned. Her eyes flicked over him; she looked wary, as if fighting to keep up her defiant facade.

He walked over to her—slowly, so she would understand he meant no harm. He took her gently by the arm and led her to the bed. He began to wrap her wound with the bandages he'd obtained from the innkeeper. "You must keep it covered for it to heal properly." He saw that she watched his every move. The more he touched her, felt her nearness to him, the more he wanted to run; the more he wanted to stay.

He wanted her, knowing she would be the end of him. And as the battle within him raged, the less sure he became of who or what he was. For the first time in fifteen years, his path stretched out before him as if to prove he had a future beyond his final act of justice. The endless sun on faraway beaches would mean something if he didn't have to walk them alone. He'd banished these thoughts from his mind before, but they returned with maddening frequency now, and he felt the ground shift beneath his feet like quicksand. He didn't know where to step.

She looked at him as he paused, and he met her gaze. He didn't move but sat beside her holding her arm in his hand. Its warmth seeped into his skin as if it wasn't just heat but her essence invading him. He quickly finished wrapping her wound and pulled her sleeve to cover the bandage. He turned from her, but her hand caught his arm. He didn't look back. He couldn't, not with the insane thoughts running through his disobedient mind.

"Who was Rose?" She asked the question softly, as if she knew the misery herself, as if she had felt it and endured it. Maybe she had; how did he know? He knew nothing about her or her life before. He didn't want to.

"Dinner will cool if we don't eat now."

"I'm not hungry."

He grabbed her and stood her up fast. His sudden fury stood on the edge of his reason and he wanted to scare her, to scare himself back to sanity. "Third time you've lied. Do not ask questions that don't concern you."

Defiance. She wasn't scared. In fact she seemed triumphant in some way he didn't understand.

"I have yet to lie," she said. "How can I think of food when you won't tell me why you've kidnapped me? You haven't killed me, though I think you meant to when you cut me, but something stopped you. I think Rose stopped you, and I want to know why."

He wanted to make her shut up. He didn't want to hear that name again. But he couldn't release the fierce and unforgiving grip in which he held her. She didn't flinch when he squeezed harder, his desire to shake her right out of his life threatening them both. She seemed to recognize it, as if she fought the same inner strife.

"Why do you have to know?" He had no warning; the words came out with no conscious thought, passing his lips as easily as her caution passed into compassion right before his eyes.

"Because the thought of her causes you such suffering." She bowed her head, as if somehow ashamed of what she would say next. "I . . . I have known the agony that I heard in your voice the night you talked in your sleep. I know how you live with it."

"They are but dreams," he said.

"Nightmares."

"I don't remember them."

"I do. You're making me remember, too."

She reached up and peeled his hands from her shoulders, and he let her. She moved closer to him until their clothing touched. "Why haven't you taken me?" Her voice whispered against his chest but echoed in his ears, caused his blood to leap. He kept his arms by his sides but his hands fisted on their own. His arms began to shake. Directly behind her lay the bed. It would be so easy . . .

49

Thain's eyes felt gritty, like he had sand in them, and he knew without looking that they were red. He'd forgotten what not being tired felt like. Over the last twenty-four hours, he'd caught some sporadic sleep, an hour here and there, but each time he drifted he started to dream of her lonely eyes. Once he imagined he heard her laugh, as if he'd caught her by surprise and the laughter had burst from her. The joy in her eyes mirrored her laughter, and then Agatha's face, unseeing, staring into space, replaced the joy, and he'd woken with a start. Sleep didn't come easily to him after that. He lived, breathed, and felt nothing but coffee, and it wasn't good coffee. He would have preferred an espresso—or eight—but that would have to wait. After today, they had one day left.

"Thain, you have some visitors."

Rae startled him, and he turned around rubbing the two-day sandpaper on his jaw. "You're still here?" he said.

"Takes one to know one."

"Visitors? It isn't the Kings, is it?"

"No. You'll want to see this couple."

"Can't you see them for me? Joking," he said when she started to protest. "Where did you put them?"

"In the first interrogation room."

His eyebrows rose. "You think this is serious, then? Not another prank or more publicity seekers?"

Rae said, "Hawthorne thought they were valid. He's the one who brought them to us, from York."

"York . . ." He mused as he followed her downstairs. "Did he come with them? I thought he and Carter were working on the Richard McLean side of this."

"He did and he is. Carter has just got back. I think the chief delayed his return as long as he could. But he needs all able bodies and can't afford to suspend Carter until this is over. Carter has orders to stay away from you."

"Lot of good that will do."

"Stop frowning. Hawthorne's the one who decided you needed to hear their story. By the way," she said, stopping before they entered the room, "You look a bit rumpled. Straighten your tie at least?"

His hand went to his tie, hanging loosely in front of his shirt. He looked down, then back up, embarrassed. "Right." He pulled the knot closer to his neck and tucked his shirt down. "Better?"

Rae smiled. "Not much, but it will do."

When they entered the interrogation room, he saw a man and woman he guessed to be in their late fifties or early sixties sitting at the table, looking as if weary was all their faces ever wore. Rae made the introductions: "Mr. and Mrs. Malcolm Elliott, this is Detective Sergeant Alban Thain."

Astonished at her unusual formality, Thain glanced at Rae. She actually winked at him. Rae never winked at anyone. He pulled the chair out and sat opposite Mr. and Mrs. Elliott at the table. Rae took a seat beside him, her thigh brushing his for an instant. Not daring to acknowledge his surprise, or pleasure, he focused on the couple across from him. They looked unsure of themselves, ill at ease about being there, which was normal. No one liked visiting these rooms, much less talking to a police detective.

"Mr. and Mrs. Elliott," he said, his thoughts back on task, "thank you for coming in. What can we do for you?"

Mr. Elliott took his wife's hand and spoke first. "As we told the other man in York, we saw the newscast last night. We saw the photograph of the man you think kidnapped that poor American woman."

Thain nodded, hoping to encourage them. "Yes?"

"Well, it wasn't a very good photograph, you see, so we're not sure. But we think the man you're looking for might be our son."

Thain went cold all over. After so many false leads in the last twelve hours, he held himself very still. Rae and Hawthorne wouldn't have bothered him with this if they hadn't decided it was more than important. "Will you tell me why you think the man in the photograph is your son, Mr. Elliott?"

"Our son disappeared fifteen years ago after, after something terrible happened where we live."

"And you live in York, sir?"

"Yes, in York."

York lay to the north. The victim, Richard McLean, came from York, originally. No wonder Hawthorne thought he should see the Elliotts. Thain didn't want to hope. "Please continue," he said, trying to project calm and compassion, not the tension tying knots in his stomach, aggravating his scar.

"He, our boy, was accused of murdering a girl, and we—" Mr. Elliott faltered and bowed his head.

Mrs. Elliott squeezed his hand. "Go on, dear. It's too late to change anything now," she said, her sadness so familiar to her that she wore it without heed. But her words seemed to give her husband strength to continue.

"We, we knew when he came home that night something very bad had happened. We'd gone to bed, as it was late and we hadn't waited up for him, but we heard him right enough, in the bath, sobbing and carrying on, but we could tell he was trying not to make too much noise. So we tried the door, but he'd locked it. He wouldn't let us in, would he? Wouldn't tell us what was wrong. He said he was all right, said he'd drunk a bit too much, didn't feel too good. But we knew our son. He didn't drink too much, ever, even at seventeen. So we waited, and when he finally came out, you should have seen what he looked like."

Mrs. Elliott wiped a tear from her face and looked anywhere but at Thain and Rae as her husband continued. "His face was bruised and beaten. We could tell he was trying to hide that he could barely walk. Then he broke down and told us what'd happened with—with Rose, the girl we found out the next day had been murdered, sure enough. He said she'd—she'd been ravaged and murdered by some boys from their school. That they'd beaten him when he fought them and tried to save her.

"We, we couldn't believe something like that could've happened but . . ." Mr. Elliott hesitated as he wiped dampness from his eyes. "But the police came early the next day and told us the girl's family accused our boy of killing her, and said that their girl and our boy had been seeing each other without their consent. We went to his room but he'd gone. We've not seen him since."

"Mr. Elliott, what—"

"Don't you see? He left because he thought we'd turn him over. He thought we believed he could commit such a crime. Why else would he have left?"

"And without a good-bye," Mrs. Elliott said, tears flowing uninhibited down her careworn cheeks as if following familiar tracks.

The Elliotts' guilt and lonely suffering dug in deep, burrowing into Thain's psyche. Today of all days, their anguish made his own that much starker. Was this grief what his parents were going through since he'd gone? Trying to ignore useless emotions from his past, and questions he had no time for, he concentrated as best he could on Mr. and Mrs. Elliott. "I understand you're anxious to know what has become of your son, but why, after all this time, do you think this man could be him?"

Mrs. Elliott let go of her husband's hand. She reached into her purse and pulled out an old black-and-white photograph. "The one we saw on the telly last night wasn't very good, as we said, but it looked close enough to us to be our boy. He's, he's so grown-up now." She dabbed her eyes after she gave the photo to Thain, and took her husband's hand again as if it were a lifeline for both of them. "This was taken shortly before he left. It's from his last year in school. One of his friends took it. We thought maybe he was dead, since we hadn't heard anything all these years. But now we wonder if he could really be alive?"

Thain knew better than to trust the eyes of loving, regret-filled parents who had lost their only son, who possibly only saw something they wished to see. But the minute he saw the image Mrs. Elliott handed over, he knew they hadn't made up the likeness in their own minds. The photo in his hand, a profile shot, showed a smiling youth whose resemblance to Rae's rendition was remarkable, even unmistakable. The image burned into his brain, hot, clear and totally focused. The young man's smile shook him when he thought of who it might be. How could this smiling adolescent be a cold-blooded killer? But many killers were handsome and charming on the outside. He handed the photo to Rae. "Rae, look at this."

She took a deep breath. When their eyes met, hers said it all.

"We need to make a copy of this right away."

She nodded. "I'll go."

Thain saw her glance at the couple across the table.

"Please have someone come in to take their statement as well, would you?" he asked.

"Of course."

He returned his attention to Mr. and Mrs. Elliott. "DS Bell would like to take the photo to make copies, all right?"

"Yes, of course. But—" Mr. Elliott said.

"I promise I'll return it to you before you leave," Rae said.

The distraught parents agreed and Rae disappeared.

Thain leaned forward, put his elbows on the table, and absently thumbed his phone screen. Acutely aware of his shortcomings in dealing with people, he decided to proceed with his questions cautiously. If they were the missing link, he needed to let Mr. and Mrs. Elliott tell their story their way. He had to be absolutely sure of them because he finally felt that he, no, that *they* were on the right track. He didn't want to derail the team's efforts for lack of careful listening or investigation.

"Do you have any details about what happened to the girl?"

"What do you mean?" Mr. Elliott asked.

"Like, did he mention names or, or a number? How many boys?"

"Why, yes. I think he did. He said six, didn't he, dear?" Mr. Elliott looked at his wife. She nodded in agreement. "But he didn't give us any names."

Six boys. Six men at the heist. Wasn't that a cosmic and ironic twist? No way the six would be the same, and he didn't have time to waste on that angle. It didn't matter except, when he thought about it, both sets of six had brought the seventh man down, if the seventh man was one and the same. Thain in no way believed in such a thing as coincidence. He knew that the seventh man in both cases was the one they were looking for, if not the Wraith himself. He stilled his restless mind. Yet another angle presented itself. If what the grief-stricken Mr. and Mrs. Elliott had told him was true, could Richard McLean, the official murdered in the bank, be one of the six boys from that long-ago crime?

An awkward silence invaded the small room, making it feel stuffy and close. Mr. Elliott's voice broke as he bent his head, stifled a sob, and said, "We, we would've stood by him, if only he'd have let us." Mr. Elliott squeezed his wife's hand, still lodged in his.

"Of course," Thain answered. He started to look away from them, as their emotions tugged so strongly on his own, but he didn't, he couldn't. Their misery enthralled him like a spell, held him captive, enveloped as he was in his own suddenly fragile state of heart. The unwise impulse to spill his own morbid regrets threatened to blow his professional policeman's image, rumpled though it was at the moment. He didn't want to scare the hell out of these gentle people whose poignant emotions so closely matched his, who might have innocently handed this case to him on a platter. And he wouldn't desert them, wouldn't give in to his own pity, so he asked the only question he could think of: "Mr. Elliott, what is your son's name?"

Mr. Elliott looked up and a world of love shone with such brightness Thain's eyes stung. "Duncan. Duncan Elliott."

50

She touched him. He felt her hand tremble as she caressed the bare, taut skin of his left arm, trapping him as surely as if she'd put chains on him. He watched as she laid her hand fully on his chest. She looked up at him, and her tears shocked him. Why was she crying?

He didn't think past the question. He put his arms around her and stood there holding her, no words, no sound but her sobs. He had nowhere to hide from the trap she had laid for his soul.

Because for all his years of hiding from it, his soul held the memories he refused to acknowledge. This small, helpless woman had brought his heart forth and made it feel again. He'd thought he'd forgotten how to feel, had hoped that to be true, had believed it to be true until now. Until her.

And again the question raised its lively, ugly head: would he throw his life away for her? Would he give up everything he had become to try and be with her? Shocked to the depths of his consciousness, he suddenly knew the answer. It had been staring at him all along, only he had refused to see it.

He held her closer. He put his head next to hers and drank in the perfume of her, a woman's scent, secret and half-remembered. He wanted to tell her he wanted her. He wanted to take her then and there, but her tears ripped him to shreds. "Don't cry anymore. There is no reason—"

She laughed. She pulled away from him and laughed again, slowly at first, then hysterically. He'd seen her get this way before, and this time the walls of their room were thin. "Don't . . ." He pulled her back into his arms, but she fought him. She struggled, pushed, pounded and kicked him. And she cried great sobs of grief, of fear and desperation. He was determined not to remember those feelings himself, but they found an echo inside him anyway.

"Damn." His lips found her face, feathering kisses all over it, then her mouth, his hands in her hair, on the back of her neck. He pushed her onto the bed, his mouth continuing to explore the world she was, until neither one of them could breathe, until she stopped crying and kissed him back.

He fought the pounding in his head, the tumble of too-bright colors, and traced her damp face with his fingers, desperate to commit to memory the feel of her, the look of her. He never wanted to forget, not this time. Not that forgetting was likely. He'd been a fool to think he could ever erase what had happened to him before, and with whom.

Here lay this woman beneath him, telling him with her body, if not her words, that she wanted him—that she fought not him but her own inner battle. He understood that each of them was alone, yet not. They both fought the inner beings they'd banished long ago, terrified of what it would mean if the persistent inner voices won, if they lost the battle to remain as they had become.

He continued to discover her skin, the soft easiness of her neck, and his fingers stumbled upon a long strip of hard, mottled scar tissue.

"No, don't—" she cried out as his fingers began to follow the seam of it. She pushed his hand away.

She squirmed under him, trying to escape, but he didn't let go. How in the bloody hell had she gotten a scar like that? "Tell me."

"No. I can't—I thought I could—" Her body heaved under his in desperation.

"Someone hurt you?"

"Stop, I can't—oh, God." She moaned and shoved his searching fingers away again, frantic now, panic in her eyes.

"Sh . . . I won't hurt you." His lips caressed hers again, tenderly, then with hopeless passion, wanting her more than ever, no matter his splitting head.

She sobbed, and finally clung to him. He held her tightly, crushing the breath from her. She grasped at him as if afraid to let him go.

Her weeping resounded in his ears, and his head throbbed harder, the thrumming remorseless.

He fought not to hear the other cries, the remembered cries, but soon they drowned out those of the woman in his arms, and memories battered at his fortified gates, as if they realized this woman held the key and could let them loose. He shook himself free of her and crawled off the bed with his head a swamp of pulsating images and sounds he didn't want to see or hear. Not now, not ever. The hateful odor of damp, musty hay invaded his nose, and vomit rose in his throat, stinging, choking him.

He gulped air and struggled to make it to the toilet in time, shaking his head, holding it until the pain started to ebb, which it did once he let loose the contents of his stomach.

He got the message. He must finish what he'd started, what those others had started. Until then, he couldn't touch the innocent, beautiful woman he'd kidnapped. He could not afford to feel. There could be nothing but the emptiness he knew so well.

Otherwise he might not succeed. And he had to succeed. It was the only way to erase the past completely. The only way he might have a chance to be something, instead of the nothingness he had become.

51

When DI Hawthorne entered the interrogation room to escort the Elliotts out of it, Thain thanked them for coming and left. He needed to know the story after Duncan Elliott had run. He couldn't wait to find out if the young man had turned himself into the Wraith and, if he had, how? If he was the Wraith, Thain now knew the *why*.

He barged into the murder room and grabbed a chair, flipped it around, and sat at his station. He yelled at Clive, "Clive, we need information on an old case in York, fifteen years ago. Can you get on it?"

Clive yelled back, "What type of case?"

"Murder, young girl named Rose something."

"And why am I doing this?" Clive asked as his fingers tapped in the question with rapid precision.

"I'm looking for a young man named Duncan Elliott from York, right now."

Thain busied himself with the keyboard entering Duncan Elliott's name.

"Who's Duncan Elliott, and what does he have to do with the assassin?"

"He might be one and the same. Elliott's parents are downstairs right now. They brought in a photo—ah, there we are. Found him."

"I've found the case. Girl's name was Rose Etheridge," Clive hollered.

"Right, got it. Duncan Elliott disappeared after she was raped and murdered," Thain said, filling in details as to why he was looking up the information.

"So he's wanted for killing her?" Carter walked over, as did some of the others. Thain's temperature rose at the close proximity to Carter. Busy background noises gave way to silent expectation as more team members stopped working and listened.

Thain forced his shoulders down and nodded, but Clive answered for him. "Yes. No one knows for sure who did it, but he's the one they looked for." He paused. "Thain, did you know how bad this case was?"

He shook his head and stood so he could see Clive, and distance himself from Carter. "Read some more?"

"This report says the girl's family was convinced he did it. His parents claim he told them six boys attacked him and the girl, and that they were the ones who killed her. But nothing was ever proven one way or the other, because Duncan Elliott disappeared before giving his parents the name of the boys. No one ever knew if the story was true or not, but no one cared once he ran. To her family, that proved his guilt. It's no wonder they wanted a scapegoat. She was literally a bloody mess."

"I wonder—" Thain started.

"Any photos?" Carter interrupted as he slid over to Clive.

Disgusted, Thain said, "Isn't the description enough for you, Carter? Why would you—"

"I just asked," he responded, as if anyone would do the same. "If she was such a mess that means our boy is psychotic."

"If he's guilty."

"He ran!"

"If you *think* about it, so would any seventeen-year-old," Thain said. In his pocket, his hand gripped his phone hard enough to crush it. Why did Carter never fail to bring out the worst in him? Why did he let him? He had no idea if Duncan Elliott was psychotic or not, but he'd seen Mr. and Mrs. Elliott's faces, heard their inconsolable sorrow. Though he had no inclination to let an assassin off the hook, he couldn't allow their son to be condemned, again, without at least trying to find out the truth.

Carter retaliated, "You certainly would have."

That hit Thain where it hurt. His scar pulsed, his body tensed, ready to take Carter down.

"Enough!" Clive shouted, bravely taking them both on. "Get back to the point, all right?"

Thain calmed down, flexed his fingers open, and focused on what he'd started to say before Carter opened his famous mouth. "I wonder what happened to those boys."

"If they existed," Carter insisted.

Thain glared at him, and Clive stood up, taking a defensive stance. "Carter, get over there," he pointed to the other side of the room. "Everyone in here is aware of what you did, and of the chief's orders." Carter glared at Thain, and slowly backed off. But it didn't dispel the tension between the two.

"Why six?" Thain asked, trying to ignore the wretched man. He had more important things to think of right now. "Why would he make that number up? Did he run because it would have been his word against theirs if he were brave enough to name them? Did something else happen we don't know about? Could he have been a part of their gang and something went wrong so he ran, after blaming the others? It happened before the regular use of DNA in investigations, and he was young. Clive, did you find any prior history of violence or criminal activity for Duncan Elliott?"

"I've just finished checking. Didn't find anything. Clean as a whistle."

"If he was telling the truth, he would've been frightened, probably in shock," said Greene, who stood behind Thain.

"Thain, do you think he's the Wraith?" Clive asked.

"*If* the man we're after *is* the Wraith, remember?" Carter said from his corner, and Thain tensed again.

Rae walked in right then, looking like a detective with a shiny new clue. She halted mid-stride and glanced them all over. "What's going on?"

Thain turned his back on Carter and raised his hands. "Nothing. We're discussing the Rose Etheridge murder, and Duncan Elliott's possible connection."

She didn't look as if she believed him, but when he glanced back at Clive, he nodded. She shrugged, but her look said she sensed a concoction brewing. She said, "If that's true, then I have another intriguing fact about York."

"What've you found? Is it better than the murder case?" Carter asked. *Better?* Thain seriously needed to throttle the man.

"I thought about what you'd said Thain, about searching missing persons all these years? I ran the request targeting York and guess what? Over the last ten years, four men, all in Elliott's and McLean's age range, have disappeared. They were all in your database, Thain."

"Only four?" Carter sneered. "Over a ten-year time period? What could that possibly have to do with *our* case?" Evidently, Carter still felt slighted by Rae Bell.

But Thain stared at her because he knew exactly what it had to do with their case. "Do I need to ask if they all went to the same school, and if so, which one?"

Rae's smile made him look at her twice. He'd never seen that particular one before. He could melt under that smile. She put a piece of paper in his hand. "All four went to Duncan Elliott's secondary school."

The paper held copies of photos from an old secondary school year book. Four school photos of young men the same age Duncan Elliott had been at the time of the murder. "Four," he said, musing out loud. "Our murdered man Richard McLean came from York."

"Ah. Clever Thain." Clive's voice smiled as he sat and put his fingers to work on the keyboard. "Oh, yes. Found it. Mr. Richard McLean went to the same school. Maybe our Mr. McLean isn't so squeaky clean after all. Now we might have a real connection."

Thain sucked in a deep breath. "We have more than that, Clive. If we're correct in our theory, the four plus McLean makes five. Who and where is the sixth boy?"

"That, Thain, would be the lucky question of the day."

Thain was awake now, wide awake; couldn't be more awake, which said much after the week they'd all had. And he no longer even registered Carter on his radar. "We need the name of every boy who knew Duncan Elliott in that school. They must be interviewed, and we need to know who that sixth boy is before he disappears as well, if he hasn't already. If he is still alive then perhaps he's still in York. I would bet my life our suspect will head north when he leaves London, which he might have already done. He dialed St. John right away. "St. John, try and find any footage heading north out of London. Yes, north. Try toward Luton. I think our bird has flown."

52

Celia's head felt clearer and her arm didn't hurt so much. She had no more need for the painkillers. She couldn't watch him. She stood waiting for him to finish cleaning the room with a sadness weighing upon her, though she didn't follow the feeling long enough to figure out why. She didn't want to think about it. She ended up watching him anyway.

He took the sheets off the bed—the sheets that only she had slept on—and shook them out the window. He wrapped them in a bundle and set them by the door. His actions seemed rote, like habits formed from years of hiding, of living without a trace. Perhaps it had been easier for him before the widespread use of DNA testing, but obviously he'd adapted. He never let her help him clean.

From the moment he'd stepped from the bathroom the previous night, he'd reverted. It was as if he'd never held her, never found that damned scar and traced it, gently, as if he wanted to make love to her in spite of it. He'd pushed her away and grabbed his head again, as if in pain, the same way he had when he cut her, and when he kissed her afterwards. For the rest of the night he'd stayed in a chair as if afraid to touch her.

Celia had no idea what she'd been thinking. And she shied from the question pressing in on her. Why did she feel desperate to be with him instead of being alone?

She didn't want to think at all as they left the inn and walked toward the motorway. Snowflakes fell with increasing speed and she realized it was really cold. But she wasn't. She was warm, inside and out, even though bitterly cold white flakes fell upon the small bit of her face not covered by the ever-present scarf. He glanced at her as they walked, wondering, Celia felt sure, what she was thinking. He probably knew. For an instant her heart felt ready to stop. If he let her live, this chapter in her life had an ending in which he would leave. He would be gone, this mysterious man, so full of unfulfilled dreams and horrible memories.

In her logical mind she knew they weren't the only ones in the world damaged by the past. She knew they weren't exceptions to any rule. They were the rule.

And yet when she looked at him, at his serious face, now familiar to her, frowning at the day, she knew none of that mattered. He'd stirred up shattering emotions in her she hadn't known existed. She wanted to feel his hunger, wanted to feel the way her own answered it. She wanted to succumb to the temptress in her that needed to be a lover, his lover, if only in her mind, because he touched her as she'd never been touched before.

What was this crazy sensation—love, or need? Desire, or survival instinct? She had no idea. Did it matter? A tempest had caught her up in its howling winds and thrown her to the universe. It didn't feel safe, warm, or fuzzy—no, more like brutal and unforgiving, sensual and scary. She felt alive.

What was she supposed to do now? What would he do next? Being at someone's mercy for days on end was harrowing enough on its own, but now she'd gone and let him into her heart. Kidnapper's syndrome or whatever it was they called it. That's all this was, of course. But she didn't believe it. She needed to prove that she felt more than a syndrome. So she stopped walking. He looked at her with impatience, then wariness.

"Kiss me." She demanded it, for she wanted to know he felt the same mixed-up confusion and helplessness she did. He hesitated, but when his lips touched hers, they didn't leave until she forgot her doubt. When he stopped and pulled away a little, his breath was harsh, as if she'd forced him to climb a mountain.

"Do you love me?" she whispered, her mouth close to his, her breath vaporizing against the skin of his face.

"I can't."

"But you do, or you would have killed me by now."

"You don't know what I am."

"A monster? A spy? A—"

He pulled away from her. "I'm an assassin. People *pay* me to kill other people. You can't love someone who kills for a *living*." It wasn't a denial; it was a dare.

Stunned by his confession and his apparent dismissal of her feelings for him, Celia felt as if her thoughts were still hampered by painkillers. Uncertain and confused at first, she soon realized she was sure of only one thing. He hadn't answered her question. She moved closer to him and he didn't pull away. "Do you love me?" she whispered again and lifted her face to his. "Do you?"

"Yes." No hesitation this time. No silence for an answer. Only one simple word, which fell to the ground with the snowflakes, just as precious, just as unique, just as doomed.

53

"Thain, you should see this," St. John called out.

"Coming." At five in the morning on their last day to accomplish something, yelling across the viewing room was no longer frowned upon. Here, as over in the murder squad room, the diligent souls who weren't off for a few minutes rest were too busy and too tense, not to mention too exhausted, for niceties. Ten people now manned monitors with footage from all of the northern routes out of London. The phone had rung nonstop since they'd announced on the wire that the man they searched for might be heading north. Trying to weed out real leads from imagined or manufactured ones was the same headache it had been since the robbery just days ago, days that felt like years.

Thain stepped over to join St. John where he stood next to Jenkins's monitor, and bent down to get a better look. Thain ignored the raw stinging of his strained eyes. His couldn't be any worse than St. John's or Jenkins's. "What is it?"

"This footage came from a security camera at a café along the M1, northbound, toward Luton. The café is just outside London. Look here." St. John pointed to two figures standing at the side of the road. "We're fairly sure it's them."

"Can you enhance it, Jenkins? It could be regular hitchhikers."

"At this time of year? Regular hitchers usually slack off when it snows."

Thain's pulse quickened. They'd caught three images of couples who they thought could be the kidnapper and Celia. But the pair still remained elusive in London's maze of a city. If these new images were of the Wraith and he'd left London, as Thain thought, all previous footage of him was now irrelevant and they needed fresh footage from along this route. "If this is them, then our chances of nabbing him might have gone up. If they stick to this route, it will be easier to track them than blanketing the whole of London."

Jenkins worked on zooming in and clarifying the footage as St. John said, "In this weather hitchers are rare, especially on that road. You said your man doesn't own a car, as far as you know. It makes sense they would hitch. His chances do seem greater for escape if he's willing to chance a ride in a private car over regular travel. If Celia Wight isn't recognized, he won't have to kill anyone. He doesn't have to worry about being reported the way he would if he took a taxi anywhere, or rented a car, or bought one. Hitching might be risky, but it's still the safest way out, from that point of view. And besides, with her face covered, how would anyone know who Celia Wight is? This is perfect weather for that."

Jenkins said, "That's the closest I can get. What do you think? I think her coat matches the clerk's description."

Thain agreed, "Aye."

St. John tapped his fingers on the desk and said, "There's an airport in Luton."

Thain straightened. "But they aren't going to Luton. Have any other videos come in like this?"

St. John's sigh spoke his fatigue louder than any complaint. "I'll order all footage on that road."

"Past Luton, not before," he qualified. "When was this taken?" he asked Jenkins while St. John put in the call.

"Yesterday afternoon."

Thain crossed his arms and stared at the screen. With young Mr. Elliott's disappearance from York, and his parents' photograph closely resembling the composite photo, Thain felt deep in his gut that York must be Duncan Elliott's destination. And if that were true, he could have taken the A1 though it was a smaller road and the going would be slower. Because it was a smaller road, the chances of being caught on camera would be fewer. Thain stood there thinking. "Why take Celia Wight with him?" he said.

"This is when the innocence question pops up again," St. John said and sat next to Jenkins.

Thain shook his head. "There is no way she's an accomplice. He isn't using her for safe passage out of the country, because he isn't leaving." The words rang as clear as a tuned bell through his mind. "St. John, let us know when you've looked through the new footage you've ordered. I'm fairly certain he'll continue to follow the M1, which would lead him straight up to York. Get in touch with Leicester and Nottingham and see if they can find anything on their CCTVs. I'll let Greene know to enter the action on HOLMES. I'll bet you money HOLMES ends up agreeing with me."

St. John stood up. "I think we should forget footage between here and Nottingham. If that footage was from yesterday, we need film along the M1 from Nottingham until it turns into the A1. That's where they'd have to leave the main road to go toward York."

"St. John, you might look like hell with your eyes red as traffic lights, but your brain is obviously still functioning."

"As is yours. And you don't look any better," he said with a rueful smile. "I'll put in for that footage."

"Right. I'm off to inform the chief. Thanks, St. John. And Jenkins, we should name you Hawkeye. Good work."

"Thank you, sir."

"Thain."

"Thank you, Thain."

54

So much for his determination not to touch her, and even worse, he'd admitted he loved her. He'd almost talked himself into believing this little slice of paradise could be real. Dreamer. Delusional was more like it. She was here with him now, body and spirit, as Rose had once been. When he told her what he was and she hadn't rejected him, he'd believed—for an insanely wonderful instant—that he could protect her from the life he'd lived, love her, keep her with him the way he had wanted to keep Rose.

But now that she knew the truth about him, she would eventually drown in self-loathing for what she allowed herself to feel for him. He knew this because she was an open book to him. A filament, fine but strong, linked them. He felt everything he saw in her eyes, in her face. She was his mirror.

But unlike him, she wasn't good at keeping her emotions at bay, much less hidden. She'd been hurt, and she carried a large scar to prove it. When, how, and by whom had she gotten that scar? He would never ask.

"Where are we going?" she asked as they waited in the cold for another ride.

"North." To the town where his long road had begun, and would soon end.

When they had left the warmth of their room at the inn in Nottingham, he had avoided her eyes. He'd wanted only to think of the way she had looked at him the previous night, the way she had trusted him, wrong though that had been. She'd given her very essence to him, and the woman he'd loved in the past had intruded, violently, as if to say, *look what happened to me when I loved you.* It had been so long since he'd felt anything but anger, he almost hadn't recognized Rose, or the love he'd once felt.

He knew better than to let the woman trust him again and yet he'd admitted he loved her.

And he did, but it felt alien to him, wrong and yet right at the same time. Over the last fifteen years, through practice and discipline, he'd suppressed his emotions so efficiently he eventually felt nothing but anger. Death dealt by his hand came and went as easily as his breath. Until he touched this woman—which had been the first mistake, but was now only one among many.

Pulling his shoulders back and straightening his spine, he closed his heart and set himself to the business of finding a ride. He had to finish with the past. They had to keep moving.

As they approached the motorway, she asked, "Do you have another place to stay where we're going?"

"No."

"Then why—" she began, but stopped speaking.

They found one ride after another past Kirkby in Ashefield, past Sheffield and Leeds to the A64. Another kind motorist took them by Tadcaster and Copmanthorpe straight into York.

In York he felt on solid ground. Even with the surveillance cameras that he knew were everywhere, cities—especially this one—still remained easier to hide in than small towns, where people were more likely to ask questions and remember strangers, or old friends. No one remembered him here. He knew this from experience. Of course, he'd never walked into the police station either.

In this old city he knew so well, his companion came alive. Her eyes lit up when she saw the great wall surrounding the older part of the city, and she sighed. "I've been here before."

He watched her, unwillingly fascinated by the first happiness he'd seen on her face, her unabashed joy at seeing an old fortified wall.

"I walked the entire length of it last time. Three miles. Took me hours," she said. Her face glowed. He'd not seen her like this before.

She turned toward him, and then looked away. Did she love him as well?

He laughed inside, to think he'd considered trying to capture her heart. How could he give her this kind of joy? How could he expect her to live the way he did: on the run, hiding, living as if he didn't exist? If he took her to his fabled beaches of sun, she would never be able to relax or look at the world with the wonder of a child again. If he took her with him she would live in the shadows of his past, of who he was and what he had done.

He knew the enchantment of her character, the generous nature of her being, and dreamed for a moment that he could own it, take it with him and learn to live like a free man again.

But that dream was illusion, as was he. He looked at the woman beside him, at the small hint of a smile returning to her endearing face, and knew he loved her as he had never thought he would love again. For the first time in fifteen years, he felt the passion of wanting to make a woman happy, to love her so much nothing could ever make her cry again. To feel the fulfillment of being loved in return. He wanted to help her heal her wounds and free her spirit from the cage she had put it in. How strange; what a twist of fate that all this would come to him here, of all places and times.

Yet he knew the moment had come to finish what those others had started fifteen years ago. He would do what he must, no matter the cost. As he had done before, he would make himself forget the rest.

55

Thain sat tapping his thumb against his cell phone screen, waiting as the team convened for yet another meeting. He couldn't stop wondering how he could prove that Duncan Elliott and the Wraith were the same man. Or if he needed to. At this point, did it matter? If he told himself the truth, yes, it did. He wanted to know if Duncan Elliott and the Wraith were one and the same. His intuition said they were, and truth be told, after ten years of chasing an elusive ghost of a man, and five years of ridicule, yes, he *needed* to know.

But finding Celia Wight alive mattered more. Now that he knew HOLMES had come to the same conclusion that he had, he'd decided he would volunteer to stay here in London if the chief decided a team should go up to York. If doing so would give DCI North another reason to agree that the trip was necessary, he'd do it. He bit his lip, literally. He'd hate it, but he would stay back if it helped somehow to save her life.

Chief North arrived and the noisy room quieted. He began before he took off his coat. "I've heard some positive rumors running around here." His gruff tone belied the good news of his words. After ditching his coat, the chief stood in his habitual stance, leaning against a desk, his arms crossed. Thain was well aware that the chief's stress was no less evident than theirs, knew that time still wasn't on their side, in fact quite the reverse, for him if not the team. "You've located," the chief started, "at least on film, enough images of our infamous couple that we no longer need doubt who they are or in which direction they're now moving. I've also been informed about an interview with a Mr. and Mrs. Elliot about an old case. This meeting is to make sure we are all working on *this* case. I need relevance and how that interview helps us. DS Patterson, or Bell, I don't care which, bring me up to date."

"Yes, sir," Rae said, standing up straighter. "First, the interview's relevance to this case. After Thain's and Hawthorne's interviews with Mr. and Mrs. Elliott, who are from York, we believe we have a positive match on the photograph we released to the media."

"And?"

Rae's eyes darted to Thain. "Our killer's name is Duncan Elliott."

"Ah, finally, a name," the chief said.

"Second point of relevance, sir. We've found a direct link in Richard McLean's past that might have something to do with his murder. Following Thain's line of reasoning, we believe that Richard McLean might have had something to do with a fifteen-year-old murder in York, sir, one in which our suspect, Duncan Elliott was also involved. We're just not sure of Richard McLean's connection yet."

Chief North looked around the room. He pinned Thain to his seat with such a pointed stare that Thain wondered how he'd gone wrong, when he'd been so sure they'd made progress.

"That old murder, the one with the girl, Rose whatever?"

"Rose Etheridge. Yes, sir."

"What is your line of reasoning on that, Thain?"

"Sir?"

"Stop quivering and tell me what *that* case has to do with this one. And don't repeat what you already mentioned in your report."

Thain's stomach clenched, pinching his scar. He realized he'd probably never get used to seeing the chief's glare or trying to earn his respect. "Revenge, sir. It all comes down to revenge and the six boys. You know about that theory from the report, and according to the deadline you set us, we have a bit less than twelve hours left. My 'line' of reasoning says we should take everyone off the phones and film and put all manpower on a search for the last of those six boys, who we anticipate is still alive. We know the names, of course, of the four who are missing. Out of all the boys that went to his school during Duncan Elliott's last year there, we have to find one name."

Clive grimaced. "Apologize for the cliché, but this case is nothing but needles in haystacks."

"True," Chief North said. "But we have a photo of our murderer and also a possible lead on a connection between the victim and his killer. It's more than we had five days ago. Thain, tell us again why you think the sixth boy, or man, must still be alive." The chief had never come down on him so hard. Thain felt the pressure of passing the chief's test.

"If Duncan Elliott is looking for vengeance—and you've seen the photos of McLean's body—if Elliott told his parents the truth all those years ago, perhaps he's been picking them off one by one over the years. He came to London to kill McLean. Perhaps the last of the six boys is still in York, and for reasons we don't know, he saved this particular one for last."

The chief uncrossed his arms and pushed away from the desk. "As Thain has pointed out, the clock isn't slowing down for any of us." He nodded to Hawthorne, glanced at Carter lurking in the back, and then looked straight at Thain again. "DI Hawthorne, you get with Thain and see what he has in mind. The rest of you get to work on finding names."

56

Yowk bustled and thrived with modern life amongst the history that embellished it with a unique palette of colors. Celia had visited here once before and had always wanted to return, especially to walk again the ancient fortified wall encircling the city, to stand outside and gaze at York Minster, that amazing and beautiful cathedral.

Her captor didn't give her much time to sightsee before he found an inn, the Mason's Arms, picturesque and gracious. Not another out-of-the-way, cramped apartment or dirty hotel room. Celia waited in the small lobby while he checked them in. She stood the farthest from him that she'd ever been—in public—since she'd known him, a whole ten feet or so. He kept his eye on her, but she knew this time it wasn't because he feared her running.

She didn't know what to think or feel as they took the stairs up to their room on the second floor. Caught in the strangeness of his alternate reality, her thoughts remained erratic and illogical; at least, that's what she told herself.

Once again he checked the floor over, making sure he understood the layout before he ordered dinner. She bathed and wished for clean clothes. They moved around each other careful not to touch, and yet acutely aware of their proximity.

They ate in silence. Readied for sleep in silence. Her heart flip-flopped when he prepared a bed for himself on the floor. Kindness again—or was it? Maybe he couldn't stand being so close to her anymore. Maybe the scar he'd stumbled upon truly revolted him, as it did her. Lord knew what he would think if he saw the rest of them. A man having scars, as he did, gave him bragging rights. Not so much for a woman. She lay on the bed and tried not to think of his rejection. Her scars went more than skin deep. A man had put them there. They reminded her constantly of why no man had ever touched her again, until this man. She hadn't purposely sworn off men, not intentionally. Her aversion had fixed in her being so deeply, she hadn't known it was there.

She preferred being alone. Wasn't interested in women either, though she'd heard some women went that route after experiences similar to hers. She had shut up shop, put out the 'closed' sign, and forgotten the pleasures that she, as a teenager, had anticipated before her attacker ruined that ideal.

Shut up, she told herself. Sleep. Forget. Don't think about tomorrow, or the too many yesterdays.

Celia awoke during the night and heard him whispering Rose's name. He thrashed on the floor, the level of his anxiety appearing to rise with each breath. Celia slipped out of bed and knelt beside him. She caressed his forehead, which was damp with perspiration, and called to him. "Ryan, it's only a dream."

"No!" His cry pierced the air and he flung his arms out as if fighting an imaginary foe. She shied away and then shook him. "Wake up. Ryan, wake up."

His eyes flew open and he grabbed her, squeezed her arms. "Why did you call me that? I told you not to call me that."

"I don't know what to call you."

"Anything but that."

"Why not Ryan?"

He cringed as if she'd hit him.

"Who is he? Does he have something to do with Rose?"

He growled, almost roared.

Celia flinched as he pushed her away and forced himself to his feet, his legs visibly quaking. He stumbled to the window and shoved it open, gulping in air like a smothered man rescued. She stood watching him; the grim determination on his face seemed to struggle with what she knew was an aching heart. His scars ran as deep as hers, perhaps deeper.

Celia had never thought of anyone else's scars, never thought of anyone else's pain. But here she found herself acutely aware of his trauma because her own cried in sync with it. She felt at once ashamed and freed.

His nightmares had grown worse. Her fear had lessened. What it meant, she didn't know. She didn't care, either. All she cared about now was healing. Living a lie alone would no longer serve. She had never moved beyond her suffering, her fear, her violation and mutilation. Maybe she never would, but he made her want to. If she could heal herself, maybe there was hope for him as well.

Thinking of his strife made hers less alienating, less a badge of martyrdom than of cowardice. He had lived with his a long time as well. He had never healed. If she could change anything in her past, her ordeal would never have happened, her parents would still be living. But she couldn't change anything, until now. Until him.

Celia didn't think anymore. She moved slowly across the room to stand by him, a whisper away, the evening breeze washing over them both as if to simply say with a hushed breath, *yes*.

He leaned his hands against the windowsill, breathing hard, calming himself with an effort she recognized. She touched his shoulder and he glanced at her. His eyes dark and shadowed, his mouth grim, his short hair disarrayed in a way that calmed her, reminded her he was human and not a monster as the other man had been.

She unbuttoned her jeans and slipped them off. She pulled her arms, one at a time, out of the long sleeves of her turtleneck. She huddled inside herself and then took a deep breath that caught on a sob, and pulled the sweater off. She stood before him in the bright blue shadows of the night, in the chilly winter breeze blowing across her vulnerable skin, in nothing but her panties and bra.

Her sweater fell to the floor. She had never revealed herself, never been so bared to anyone ever. She had never been naked with a man. Even her assailant hadn't fully undressed her. She'd worn a skirt and shirt. Poor armor, as easily torn—or cut—as it was ignored.

She shook as she stared at the man for whom she had exposed herself and all her morbid details. What would he do? What would he think once he saw the terrible blighting scars?

He turned to her but didn't move. He didn't say anything for a long, desperate time. She shut her eyes, wondering if she'd made a mistake. Then he reached up and gently, softly, traced the damage of the long slash on her chest. He took a step closer and touched her arms, rubbing his thumbs over each scar he found on her biceps. He leaned forward and kissed the scar on her neck, knelt and kissed her damaged stomach. He touched every one of her five companions, lightly, with respect. He stood.

"Open your eyes."

She did so, hesitant now that she had laid her half-healed wounds open to him—half-healed because she had never before gone this far.

"Someone did this to you."

She nodded and tears slipped down her cheeks. She wiped them away, determined to continue.

"A man?"

She nodded.

"Did he—"

"Yes." She looked away, unable to stand it if he found that wound uglier than the rest.

"What must you think of me . . . ?" He pulled his hand away, taking his warmth with him.

She took a step back. "What do you think of *me*, now, now that you know?"

He looked at her in disbelief and anger. He was angry again. Oh, so not the reaction she'd hoped for. He growled, his fists clenching sporadically. "I can't believe . . . what men can do."

"But what about me? What do you think of me?"

His anger faded as he looked at her. "I think you are beautiful."

Her hands covered her face as she bowed her head and cried. No words could have been more precious to her. He moved past her and turned on the light by the bed. She glanced up. The soft golden beams displayed her faults even more, and she moved to turn it off. But he caught her and pulled her into his arms. She stood shaking and frightened in his warm embrace as he traced the scar on her chest again.

Then he released her and took off his shirt. Deep and numerous, his scars latticed his body. "They are medals of honor, as are yours. Don't be ashamed of them."

"I fought back, but he won."

"No. You won. You're alive. Don't ever forget that. You won. You are alive."

Fierce, adamant. She saw he truly believed his words. Could it be true? Could it be that she had won by not dying, not giving in to the grief, pain, and remorse that had plagued her until she'd started writing, and hiding?

"Kiss me," she said.

He kissed her, then picked her up and carried her to the bed and fell upon it with her in his arms.

"My name—" she whispered, but he laid his finger over her lips.

"No."

Celia reached up and traced the weathered lines around his mouth, the lines that curved down his cheeks from his nose, and the shadowed slash of scar over his left eye. She wondered fleetingly how he came by so many scars. Beneath the faint, bitter lines lacing his thin face, tragedy lay deep in his spirit. Buried under the shield of a thick, icy anger that had dominated until now lay handsome features she'd not seen before. His had always been a face of stone, cold stone. He didn't say anything to her, yet she smiled, knowing that for now she made him feel something besides anger.

"What makes you smile?" he asked.

"You."

"A reflection."

"Maybe. Why don't you want to know my name now?"

"We have no need of them."

"But—"

"Names belong to another world."

Celia knew that wasn't completely true, wasn't his real reason. Rose was. But Celia let him have his way. She closed her eyes again.

He ran his thumb down the length of her face. "Don't think. Open your eyes. Stay with me."

She opened her eyes and stared into his, the blue of them so deep she wanted to let go and sink into their oblivion.

"Make love to me," she dared to say.

His entire body went still. In her arms he felt taught and wary. He started to pull away from her. "No."

"No? You won't make love to me?"

"I—. Bloody hell." He wouldn't look at her.

"I'm too ugly with, with—"

"No." He looked at her. "You're beautiful."

"What, then?" Desperation took hold of her and wouldn't let go. She thought he wanted to make love with her. She was wrong, obviously really wrong.

"Stop. Don't cry anymore." He pulled her close again.

The warmth of his bare skin stopped the panic rising in her, and she held on to him as if he were her life buoy in a raging sea. Clearly now, she saw that he could save her because she wanted him to.

She pulled back and looked at him. Questions danced in the silent air between them like intermittent fireflies.

"I can't promise I won't cry," she said.

"I don't need promises."

His lips touching hers shook through her like an earthquake. Her skin touching his brought his face to life and she saw the youth in him, she saw in his eyes the light of a true smile, which traveled down his grim face to reach his lips. He kissed her with that smile.

When he touched her scars again, when he unclasped her bra and took it from her, she sobbed. She wanted this, but it was so hard to let go of the fear. She thought of his knife in its sheath on the floor amongst the clothes by the bed, where he had left it. She was with him now, not with his knife. And though she trembled, though she gasped for breath as her fear burned bright in the intense heat of awakening passion, she reached out and touched him. She kissed him and let her tears wash her clean.

And then, somehow in the midst of her hard-won joy, she realized that although she was no longer afraid, he was.

57

Minutes passed as if each one were a tiny grain of sand waiting its turn through the choke hold of an hourglass, an hourglass Duncan Elliott held in his hand. Only a few hours had passed since the last meeting, but DI Hawthorne had called the chief back in once Thain had explained why at least a small team had to return to York. They needed the go-ahead from the chief, which meant they had to explain to him the why of it.

"Sir," Thain started. "We've been able to contact or verify proof of life on all but about twenty of the young men whose names are in the pot. The majority of those we've been able to reach say they either knew Duncan Elliott or knew of him. Clive is trying to determine who, if anyone, within those last twenty might have been closest to the missing men—you know, their best mates back in the day."

"We're still working on proof of life for those last twenty as well, sir."

"And," Rae interrupted, "we do have one conclusion we feel is accurate, and the data coming from HOLMES seems to agree with us."

"And that conclusion is?"

"That the answer to all of our questions is in York."

"Am I correct in assuming that, once again, you have no actual proof of anything?" Chief North wasn't pacing yet, but leaned against the ever-present desk, arms folded, glaring at all of them. The glare was a new habit of his.

"We have supposition, circumstantial, yes," Thain replied, "enough to investigate Duncan Elliott for the Royal Bank murder, but you are correct, sir. We need proof and we have none. Instead, we have hearsay and videos that could be viewed in a number of different ways. What we have won't stand up in court. Everything the team has chased down is immaterial without definite proof, and that will only come from finding the man and/or Celia Wight, alive. That involves finding the sixth boy."

"You want to go to York."

"Yes, sir."

"You, yourself?"

Thain hesitated. "With the team, sir." Here lay the point he had to make, to prove to himself the kind of man he was. "If you prefer, I'll stay here while the team goes. I can tidy up loose ends. The most important thing is finding Celia Wight alive and getting the proof we need to close this case."

The chief smirked, right there in front of everyone. "You don't fool me, Thain. But don't worry. Take the team and go find my killer, and the woman too. Don't come back until you do."

58

Her kidnapper stumbled from the bed and fell to the floor. He crawled to the light and knocked it over, breaking the bulb. "Don't touch the blasted light," he practically growled. Celia stared through the dim glow from the window as he picked himself up and grabbed his clothes.

"I can't do this," he said. His eyes squeezed shut and he shook his head, his hair damp with sudden perspiration.

Celia inched down the bed toward him. "What are you doing?"

He started to say something but stopped. He looked at her and she recognized what she saw, the panic in his fierce eyes, the desperation.

"What's wrong?" she asked.

His eyebrows drew together and his face contorted with effort. He shoved his legs into his jeans.

Celia jumped from the bed, snatched up her turtleneck shirt, and quickly drew it on. "You can't leave." She moved in front of him to block his way to the door.

He put his shirt on, then the knife holster. "I need to get out."

"So do I! I need my life back, and, and I have nothing but you."

He stared at her, livid, tense. "You can't understand—"

"Try me." She put her hands on her hips, not caring if she looked the total fool that she felt.

"Get out of my way." He picked up the knife and stuck it in the holster under his arm.

Celia didn't let a sudden rush of adrenaline stop her. "Tell me who Rose was, and I will."

He stooped to grab his shoes but halted as if she'd hit him. "I've told you before, this has nothing—"

"Yes, it does. You can't expect me not to want to know why you're in such pain."

"I'm not in pain."

"Who's the liar now?"

He straightened, his lips tight, his eyes narrowed. "You don't know what you're doing, what you're talking about."

"But you do. Every time you kiss me, something inside you hurts. Each night I wake up to your terrible cries, to her name on your lips. You have the look of your nightmares on you now."

He faltered and looked away. But she sensed rage building in him. Standing in his way, defenseless, helpless, the old fear of him snaked its way into her chest. She'd seen the jungle cat in him before; now it returned, its back arched and spiky.

She ignored it as best she could. "Why? If you love me, and you said that you do, why won't you tell me?"

"Do you love me?" He threw the words at her like a gauntlet, a dare, and this time she was the one who faltered.

"I, I don't know what I feel."

"Yes, you do, but you can't say it. After what happened to you, after what I've done to you, how can you say you love *me*?" He jabbed himself in the chest.

"Why are you doing this?" She started to cry. He was a hunter and he knew how to strike. It hurt worse than she could've imagined. "I thought—"

He moved so fast she had no time to react. He grabbed her and threw her on the bed, and she scrambled away from him toward the head of it. She pulled the bedcover up over her body, a flimsy defense against his anger, against his knife. What did love mean to a man like this?

He stood towering at the end of the bed like a giant. His face was as grim as she'd ever seen it: his mouth but a line, his brow low. He clenched and unclenched his hands. When he spoke, it was if he forced the words out by sheer will. "You want to know about—" He couldn't say the name.

Celia hesitated, and then said, "Yes."

"She was the first and only woman I ever loved, until you."

"What?" Until her? "No one else?"

"No one."

"Why do you have nightmares about her?"

"I never have, until you."

"Never?"

"Not in too many years to count." He was sweating now, as if telling her this was a great effort.

"Is she dead?"

He looked away. "Fifteen years . . . dead."

"Fifteen years?" He hadn't loved another woman in fifteen years? "But you must have been with other women . . ."

The look in his eyes cut straight to her heart as surely as if he'd used his knife. "Until you, I haven't so much as touched another woman."

"What happened to . . . her? What would make you . . . so—"

"Unreachable? Untouchable? *Loyal?*" He sneered.

She nodded, afraid to speak.

"She was murdered. She was sixteen. I was seventeen."

Celia pulled the bedcover to her mouth as if somehow that would help her hear what he now told her. He paced back and forth like a caged animal, not seeing the room, not seeing her.

"She, she was better than me, bred I mean. Her family was rich. Mine was not poor, but not well off like hers. She knew they wouldn't approve. For a year we met at different places all over town, because we didn't want anyone to know. It was our secret."

"Did someone find out?"

"You could say that." His hands knotted again; his mouth firmed, taut and grim. "We met in an allotment shed one night, near where I lived. No one would be there gardening at night. We'd met there before because of that. This time we'd decided we wanted to, to be the first for each other. It was . . . paradise." He lifted his head up, his eyes shut, and as if lost in a memory, stopped pacing for a moment. He started again. "She talked of marriage. If we waited two years, until she turned eighteen, we wouldn't need her parents' consent.

Afterwards . . . we lay on the hay in the shed. I'd brought a small pocket torch for light. I should have put it out, but I wanted to see her while we," he clenched his fists again, "talked of our future, of the things we would do together—finish university, work, have children.

"There were six of them. Boys we went to school with. I'd never liked them, nor they me. They found us like that. What they were doing on the allotments at that time of night I don't know, unless it they were ruining people's gardens or stealing their vegetables. When I, I stood, they laughed because I'd no clothes on. When they saw she didn't either, they stopped laughing."

Celia's breath came fast now. She knew what he intended to say, and she didn't want to hear it. Her chest tightened with dread. She knew this scene. She didn't want to see it again.

"Too many. I had to stop them. I fought back, but couldn't fight all of them. Four of them wrestled me to the ground right next to her and held me there while they—. Each one of them. She screamed my name, but they covered her mouth. She turned to me . . . her eyes . . ."

He closed his. Celia knew he wanted to stop, to not have to say another word. But he didn't.

"I cried out to her, but they gagged me. I never stopped looking at her. She needed to know I loved her no matter what they did even if I couldn't save her. I watched her cry. I saw her tortured. I watched her give up hope."

He stopped pacing and folded in upon himself. His knees bent until he sat on his haunches, his arms squeezing his shins. Celia left the bed and knelt beside him. "I can still see her face," he whispered, his head on his knees.

Celia didn't touch him. She was afraid to. "After?"

His head turned toward her. "After what?"

"After they left, what did you do?"

"After they'd done with her—no!" He lurched to his feet, grabbed a chair, and threw it against the wall over the bed, breaking the glass in the picture frame hanging there. The shards showered down onto the exact the spot where they had lain together. He didn't stop with the chair. He threw anything he could reach.

At first Celia cowered against the foot of the bed and screamed, "Stop! Stop it!" When he didn't, she leaped up and threw herself at him. He grabbed her and shook her, rattling her teeth, snapping her neck back and forth.

"You did this. You brought all this up again when I'd—"

"When you'd what? Gotten it under control?"

"Control is better than this."

"No, it's not. You can't change the past, but you can change the future."

"I have no future."

"What happened to Rose? What happened to you?"

"You ask too much."

"You ask too little."

He glared at her, but then his eyes softened. "Not from you."

Celia stared right back. "No, not from me."

"At first I thought . . . but now I know how wrong I've been all along."

"About me?"

"About us."

"Don't do this. Don't tell me you don't care for me, because I won't believe you."

He held her there by the shoulders, and the deep warmth of his hands seeped into her skin. His eyes filled with what looked like an all-consuming misery, and it seemed to course over his cheeks instead of the tears he refused to cry. He forced the words out between his teeth: "They took me next. Are you satisfied? After they were done with her, they . . . took . . . *me*."

Heart sick and speechless, Celia didn't recoil, but waited for him to continue. When he let her go and went to finish dressing without saying another word, she dared to ask again, "What happened after that? What happened to Rose? What happened to you?"

He looked through her, clear back to that other time. She knew he saw the nightmare of his helplessness. "I don't remember when they left. Only Rose. Her blood—. I ignored mine, my—. I crawled to her and held her in my arms, but she was already gone. She left me alone. I've been alone ever since."

"But your parents—"

"I used my clothes to try and clean her of the blood. I put her clothes on her as best I could. Somehow I dressed myself. Her blood covered me, but I carried her home and left her in front of their door. I knew they wouldn't believe I hadn't done that to her, not with so much blood on me. There wasn't accurate DNA testing back then. They wouldn't have believed me if I didn't—"

"Didn't tell them what had been done to you."

"I went home. My parents—I couldn't tell my parents, so I left."

Celia knew something of what it must have been like for that seventeen-year-old, and she grieved for the man before her. He put on his coat. She stood facing him with no words. What could she say? She longed to reach out and hold him, to comfort him and take away his suffering. She knew he wouldn't let her. She shivered when he picked up his shoes and put them on.

"Don't leave me now, please?"

He shook his head as if too weary to answer.

"I love you." Her love was the only gift she had.

He stood still, fully dressed now. "Don't. Loving me will hurt you, will only bring you down."

"It's too late—"

"Order something from room service, or get some sleep."

"Aren't you afraid I'll . . . ?"

"No." He opened the door, and cold air from the hall rushed in to steal away his warmth. Celia shivered, wondering if she'd ever be warm again. He glanced back at her, held her eyes with his own. Without another word he left. Celia stared at the door as it closed behind him—shaken, unbound and completely alone.

59

The low drone of voices hummed out of tune with the air conditioning in the plane. Thain glanced around at the team, all busy with their parts of the investigation. He'd dreamed of having a team like this—no, of leading a team like this—and now, because he'd surrendered his hard-won information and helped the team make something of it, they'd formed what the chief seemed to think was a working hypothesis. His dream had become a reality. What would Ellis think if he could see him now?

Rae, sitting next to him, was on the phone; Clive talked with Greene; and Hawthorne was typing on his laptop. Everyone, even Carter, chased what few leads they had to a boy—a man—they all hoped to find alive. Whomever their suspect turned out to be, the Wraith or not, he was still, in Thain's opinion, headed for York with one purpose in mind. If this turned out to be some kind of mix-up— which it could possibly be, going by such an old photo and such a rough one—he would lose everything, his credibility and his job. But Celia Wight would lose much more. She would lose her life. *Where are you, sad lass?*

"Thain?" Rae's soft voice cut through the background noise.

He turned his head to her. "Aye."

"May I ask you another personal question?"

"Brave woman that you are, I guess so. Can't say I'll answer it though. At least, perhaps not now."

Pensive, hesitant even, she asked anyway. "I've been wondering ever since we, um, well, at your flat, how did you come by the scar on your stomach?"

He glanced away, resentment burning his belly, and sat forward as if to get up. But this time, beneath the familiar angst something else kindled, an unexpected desire to let it out, let it all go and free himself from the burden of his shame. Because finally he realized that's what this was, shame, not the anger he'd worn as armor ever since Agatha's refusal of him. He hung his head and tilted toward Rae, peering at her. He still resisted, unwilling to share, much less think of what had transpired after the attack. And yet he knew why she asked, and he didn't want to lose what seemed to be starting between them. He knew in that moment that if he could answer her question, it might truly change his life, and perhaps his future. Did he want that change? He leaned back in his seat, his hands took hold of the armrests, and he drew a long breath. "I, um, well, I told you of Agatha, of what happened to her. I was with her when she was taken."

Once he decided to say even that much, the nightmare that had begun after Agatha's kidnapping and rape rushed in and he couldn't help but squeeze his eyes shut and ride the wave of stinging memory. He'd woken up to sheets drenched with sweat and searing pain refuting his hope that it had been but a dream. His abdomen burned where the surgeon's knife and needle had repaired the nasty wound that had put him in the hospital. "I was stabbed when we were attacked. I fought them, but—"

"Oh Alban. I've done it again haven't I? Stuck my foot right in it. I'm sorry. I didn't—"

"Someone found me or I'd have bled out. When I woke at the hospital, all I could think of was Agatha. They told me that I begged for news of her. I don't remember that, only the pain after the doctors sewed me up. But once I came round for good, I had too much time to think. There was only one thing for me to do. One course for my life to take, and I knew my mother would cry and my brother would call me a fool. But I didn't care."

"Is that when you decided to become a cop?"

"Aye, it is."

"So, is that why you're so fascinated with Celia Wight? Do you think you can save her like you weren't able to save Agatha?"

Thain's fury returned with a kick that surprised him. "What's that supposed to mean?"

"It's all right, I understand." Rae looked down at something she fiddled with in her hands. "I guess it's only human to keep trying when one believes one has failed in something and is given a second chance. But, Thain. Alban." Now she looked right into his face, hers as serious as he'd ever seen it. "Celia Wight isn't Agatha. Saving her won't make Agatha see you again. It won't fix her."

"Bloody hell, Rae!" Thain spit through clinched teeth, not wanting to attract attention to their conversation. "That's not what this is about."

"Are you sure?" Her face said she already knew the answer to that, which forced him to think about his fascination with Celia Wight, if that was a fitting description of his reaction to her. Shaking his head, he refused to deal with this right now, resisted the excruciating thoughts of what he'd lived through after losing Agatha, and then the humiliation of the assassination. His ego had taken a huge hit and his brother hadn't helped by calling him a fool. Ellis, his brother, who'd been his hero until then.

Rae's light touch on his arm shocked him back to her presence, her kind eyes asked him again to trust her. Like a window opened to allow a cool breeze, again his temper gave way to a brighter desire to unburden as she sat beside him waiting, with her infinite patience, for him to speak. "I didn't like who I was after the attack. Celia Wight's eyes remind me of that whenever I look at her photograph. I saw that same look on Agatha's face the one time her father let me see her. I can't get that look out of my head." *Or the emptiness that still lingers,* he thought. *The failure that still haunts me.* "Much later, after I'd discovered the man who doesn't exist, I thought perhaps I'd been marked by the blade just to be able to find this invisible phantom who uses nothing but a knife to kill. Funny how the mind plays tricks."

"Our minds always try to help us deal with the unacceptable, Alban, in any way they can." Her small hand crept into his, squeezed and let go before anyone noticed. "We all have demons. At least you've put yours to good use."

Thain closed his eyes and leaned his head back on the seat. He sighed. "Right. Now if only I could let them go."

"Perhaps once we've found Celia Wight and her kidnapper you will."

He looked at her then, saw her fatigue as clearly as he felt his own. But he smiled, trying to let her know he heard what she didn't say. "Perhaps."

Celia Wight's kidnapper. He closed his eyes again but his mind kept going. Now that he knew something about Duncan Elliott, he thought he understood why the man had taken Celia Wight and kept her with him. Thain would have, also, if given the same chance. But he didn't tell Rae that. Some things didn't need to be confessed.

60

Celia waited for him to come back. Shaking with cold, she took a quick bath to warm up, dressed, and paced the room waiting for his return. She didn't turn on the television. She didn't read. She couldn't eat. She looked out the windows into the black of night but saw nothing because she didn't care what might be out there. All she cared about was the man who wasn't in the silent and empty room with her.

She ended up staring at the door. Could he be waiting right outside of it, testing her? Did he want to see if she'd still run? Celia walked over to it, put her hand on the knob, and turned it. She pulled the door open and looked into the hall. She stepped out and glanced in each direction; no one was there. She fled back to the sanctuary of the room, slamming the door behind her, leaning on it, panting with dread.

For hours, Celia waited. She waited until even her hardheaded side had to admit he'd given her the freedom she no longer wanted. Outside the windows in the pitch of night, falling snow glowed around the lamplights bordering the street. She put on her coat and opened the door. She wasn't surprised at the emptiness of the hall this time, but she cried anyway. She wiped her face and stepped from the room. She shut the door, the small click loud as a hammer behind her—so final, so definite.

Celia walked along the hall on hesitant and unsteady feet. Then she started to run. She made it to the stairs, then all the way down to the main floor, secretly hoping he would be using the stairs as well, on his way back up to her. She didn't slow until she stumbled outside and into the white night. Snowflakes fell around her, in her hair, on her clothes. Her heart raced so fast she could scarcely breathe. She was alone and unbound, truly, for the first time in six days.

Six days that had changed her life forever. The snow squeaked under her feet, reinforcing her solitude. Sobs wrenched her chest, strangling her breath as she gulped frigid wintry air. "No, no, no." She started to run down the dark, deserted streets, trying to flee the solitude, trying to find him. How had she come to this? How had his misery become so entwined with hers? How had he brought her to life again? It was a dream, wasn't it? Did he really exist or had she imagined him? If she had, she didn't want to ask herself why.

Celia kept looking back, hoping he was following her. How could he be? He didn't know she'd gone. Yes, he did. She screamed out loud, "Damn you, damn you!" and stifled another sob, moaning instead, wishing beyond reason that he'd take her back, knowing with a deep hateful understanding that he wouldn't. The adventure had ended, and nothing remained but a bleak hole in her fully pounding, alive and sensitive heart.

Celia realized she'd found a main street. The usually bright street-lights shone dim in the now heavily falling snow. Eventually she made out that this street, too, was empty and that she stood in front of a police station. Why had he let her go? Why, when he knew she would have to tell them what she knew? She would have to give him away. Why?

And why did the thought of never knowing his name drive her to her knees weeping in desolation?

61

If he'd convinced her, she'd be gone when he returned. He waited until the night grew whiter with snowfall before he retraced his steps to the little inn. This had been the hardest day of his life, since . . . Even through all of the training, the hiding, and the years spent to get to this point, none of that had cost him what he now paid to leave her behind. He wanted to believe she'd still be there waiting for him. But he didn't. He decided to go back up to the room one last time. He would find it empty, he told himself. And then he would trace her, make sure she was safe. He didn't want her becoming a victim again. She'd had enough of that already, and so had he.

The room was empty, as he'd known it would be. He didn't stand there looking at the emptiness, he didn't go over to the bed—now cleaned of the broken glass and made up as if they'd never lain upon it together—to touch it, to somehow feel her one last time. Instead he closed the door and descended, the way he'd come, to the lobby. He paid for the damages and for another night, and left the lights and warmth of the hotel for the dark and familiar cold of the streets.

He knew she would eventually end up at the police station. He passed pubs and would duck in to see if any of them ran the news on their televisions. Nothing. No newscasts about her being found. She wasn't in any of the pubs either. He didn't bother trying to not think of her. He would have plenty of time for that later, once he knew she was safe.

He passed shadowed alleyways and side streets, peering down their lengths to make sure she wasn't in them looking for him. An hour passed before he found her. He stepped closer to the building beside him, to hide from her view, and watched as she fell to her knees in the snow. Then, her movements slow and labored, she pushed to her feet and stood there gazing at the front of York's main police station.

She looked small and forlorn as the snow whipped around her in gusts and wisps. Bare tree-skeletons marched along the walk she would have to take to the entrance. Her breath blew vapor out in small puffs that quickly disappeared. For the longest time, she didn't move. He ground his teeth against the urge to go to her, to reach out and touch her again, to claim her. He thought his resistance noble, but he wasn't fooling himself. He anchored his feet, clenched his hands in his pockets, and fought a hard battle that he didn't want to win, but knew he would.

She was the one good thing in his sorry existence. She was real and alive, the first beautiful thing he'd known since he'd started running, killing, and hiding. He would finish what he'd set out to do, but after that? He saw before him nothing but emptiness. She'd been right. Did the control he'd imposed upon himself for so long qualify as living? He knew it didn't, but the choice had been taken from him long ago.

Standing in the cold snow in the middle of winter, any enticing thought of her body on a hot, sandy beach forgotten, he watched the woman he loved, and he regretted not knowing her name.

She weaved as if ready to fall, and he refused the excruciating need to go to her, to hold her again, tell her how he still wanted her. She needed to stay strong on her course, and he couldn't help her with that. In the cold shadows of the night, sweat beaded on his forehead, a testimony to the effort it took to keep his feet securely in place. Rose called to him, reminded him. He had to finish what he'd started.

So the lovely woman who'd stolen his heart, and given it back to him, eventually took a small step onto the long, snow-littered walk leading to the police station entrance. He took a step back. She took a second step forward. His heart splintered into brittle shards when she turned around and searched everywhere for him, the harsh glare of a streetlight reflecting off her wet cheeks.

"I won't forget you, ever," she shouted, as if she'd read his mind. "I won't."

She straightened her shoulders and walked the rest of the way while he backed further into the shadows, disappearing into the darkness of night. His last vision of her was when she opened the door to the police station and took her life back into her own hands.

62

The team made it to the Leeds-Bradford airport. They found a van waiting for them and the driver informed Thain that it would take an hour to get to their final destination. Five minutes after leaving the airport, Rae's phone rang. Everyone stopped talking while she answered. Thain knew he wasn't the only one hoping for case-breaking news. She listened, her liquid brown eyes holding him to his seat. Flipping her phone shut, she said, "Celica Wight has been found."

Everyone started talking at once, but he shouted, "Is she alive?"

"Yes. She walked into the main police station in York. They've taken her to hospital."

Thain stared at his hands, holding files that he could no longer see. He asked, "Has she . . . ?"

"That's all they could tell me for the moment. She arrived barely an hour ago."

He shut his eyes for a second, and in the ensuing silence he opened them to find everyone looking at him as if waiting for an order, a command, something to tell them where to go from here. So he gave them one. "Listen, now that we know our kidnap victim is safely away from our suspect, we must intensify our search for him. Because if he's in his home territory, and is without Celia Wight to ground him, our job might be right next to impossible."

63

Earlier that evening, a tall, spare man had taken a room in a small, out-of-the-way bedsitting house. Now he undressed and lay upon the bed, determined to sleep. He needed to rest, to have a clear mind for the business to come. Now that the woman was gone, he was free to finish what he'd come here to do, and dawn would come soon enough.

But sleep didn't. He tossed on the creaky bed as if it were full of fleas. The room suffocated him until he donned his clothes and coat and went out to roam the streets.

He knew why he felt so restless. He wanted to hear what the news might report about her. She would tell them everything. He knew she had to. She'd have no defense against their need to know, or against her perceived dereliction of duty. She would feel pressured and guilty, which was normal.

Normal. What a word, and what did it mean anyway? Nothing about this situation was normal for him or her. He missed her. Half an hour gone since he'd left her at the police station, and already he missed her. He lifted his hand to his face and caught her lingering scent upon it. She was all over him, inside and out. How would he purge himself of her when she'd gotten so far, so thoroughly under his skin?

He shook his head and entered the small pub he'd just checked out, back, front, over, and around. It was as safe as anywhere right now.

"Celia Wight, the American novelist kidnapped in London six days ago, was found late this evening in York. The police are targeting that city in the manhunt now being stepped up for her kidnapper, who also seems to be the primary suspect in the brutal murder of York native Richard McLean in London last week."

He heard the newscast as he walked through the door, but all that registered was her name. Celia. Celia Wight. Her name was Celia. Then he realized that all the heads in the pub had turned toward him. All eyes stared at him. He glanced up to see a rough semblance of his face on the television, then a photograph from his school days, a profile photo a friend had taken right before that life had ended. It was enough.

As yelling erupted, he backed out the door, his face betraying nothing, and vanished into the maze of streets he knew so well.

They had his face. Now it would be harder. Not impossible but much, much more difficult. Rage tainted his view as he retraced his steps back to the bedsit. He'd have to be beyond careful if he was to succeed. She hadn't given him away. They'd found a photo of him. How? His parents would most likely have recognized him from the composite the police had somehow pieced together. He knew his parents had a copy of that old black-and-white profile photo. They must have seen a prior newscast and recognized him, even after all these years. His parents.

He decided to sleep elsewhere. He knew plenty of old buildings around the outskirts of York where he could find shelter from the snow. His steps pounded out a rhythm on the slick pavement as he walked. The rhythm drummed in his head, leaving him more alone than ever before. Without her—no, he pushed those thoughts aside and concentrated on the beat of his feet.

Their rhythm distracted him until he glanced up and recognized the street his feet had directed him to. Dringthorpe Road. A light shone in his parents' front room even at this late, or early, hour. He'd noticed over the years that at least one light always stayed on, as it had the night his life had been torn apart and he'd vanished from their lives. He wondered if his parents left it on for him, hoping that one day he'd come home. He wondered if they couldn't sleep for missing their son. Not for the first time, he wondered if they'd ever thought him guilty. He hadn't asked himself at the time, because his only thought had been to run, and to wreak havoc upon those who had killed Rose.

He resisted the urge to go and peek in the window, and this time his discipline hurt. For an instant, the young man he'd been ached with longing for the feel of his mother's arms around him and yearned to hear his father's strong voice reassuring him of his place in their hearts. He went around the back of the house to the familiar area behind his father's small garden shed. He checked the ground. Unchanged. They hadn't found his stash yet. Once they did, they'd know he wasn't dead. Maybe that would atone for his having left them in the first place. He had been so young, so naïve. He silently moved back to the lighted window and looked inside, all thought of resistance gone. He couldn't help this time but yield to at least part of his aching loneliness.

His parents sat in the living room watching television. He could see they were watching the news. His mother held knitting in her unmoving hands, giving her full concentration to whatever had captured their notice on the screen. His father perched on the edge of his favorite seat, engaged completely with the broadcast. In all the years the assassin had come to make his "deposits" in the ground behind the shed, he'd never—after the first time—looked through the windows of the house. When he came it was usually early morning, two or three a.m. as it was now, and his parents were always asleep. This time they were wide awake.

Fifteen years of ignoring the past had been obliterated because of a woman named Celia Wight. Though the boy in him yearned for something lost, the adult in him, the man he had become, knew that in his parents' hearts he had to be dead. Why, then, were they watching the news so carefully? He wanted to believe that they missed him. He wrenched himself back to the depressing reality of the present. What did it matter now? After he'd completed his mission, he'd think about the future. He climbed back over the fence and physically turned his back on Dringthorpe Road and the life he'd once lived, as he had so many times before.

If he wasn't careful, if he didn't keep his mind on the task at hand, he would have too much time to ponder the past—a past that now loomed over him as close as his future, and just as oblique. He didn't see his mother stand up, didn't see her move to the window he'd just left, didn't see her look outside, searching for someone who was no longer there.

64

Celia wanted to curl up and die. Stuck in the hospital in a horrible bed with cops hovering so near made her want to scream. Their presence drove her longing for him so deep she folded herself around the longing in her mind. Too much noise, too many lights and questions and people poking her, prodding her and trying to invade her body as he had never done. She wanted the silence of the last six days. She understood completely and undeniably now what he'd meant by silence being good for you. She'd never known it before. But she'd never known his kind of silence before, either.

She lay back and pretended to sleep. She wanted to forget where she was and what might come. She thought of him. She wondered where he was and what he was doing. Maybe he knew her name now. Ever since she'd entered the police station, her recovery and her name had been all over the news. Why hadn't he known it before? Hadn't he seen any other newscasts of her disappearance but the one she'd happened upon and he'd turned off? Didn't he watch television at all? Or read the papers? Maybe he'd known her name all along. It would be like him to keep a secret, an air of mystery, to be unreachable, unfathomable.

And yet he had told her about Rose. He had told her he was an assassin. Celia resisted the impulse to cry. She had seen him resist the storms raging inside of himself, seen the tense concentration of his body. If she cried now, here, the nurses or police would come and bother her, and she didn't want any more attention.

Rose. What a tragic, horrible way to die, especially after such joy. There was never more than one first time, and if Rose had been lucky enough to actually enjoy it, what a terrible twist of fate to then die by the hell of violation.

He'd been living with that story, with Rose's face and her screams inside him all this time, living with the knowledge of his own helplessness, his own violation—if living was the right word. Existing was more like it.

Celia wasn't a fool. She remembered those first horrific days after he'd taken her hostage, tied her up, and threatened her with those cold eyes and that steel blade. Now that she thought about it, he'd never said outright that he would kill her. But she remembered the day he'd cut her. He'd meant to kill her, but he couldn't follow through once he saw her blood.

She hadn't known at the time, but Celia knew now that she had Rose to thank for her life. It wasn't until later that Celia realized he couldn't kill her. Not because he didn't want to but because he couldn't. Not with Rose screaming and dying inside him forever. Celia's captor hadn't lied to her. His story was sadly and horribly true. She would bet her life he had never killed a woman. She thought he killed men because deep inside of him, deep inside the pain and unlivable truth he couldn't ignore, he had to kill those six boys. Did that mean he really was an assassin?

She sat bolt upright with that thought, but she quickly lay back against the pillows. She glanced at the door, afraid someone might have seen her. It was clear to her now. She couldn't relax because, knowing him the way she did, she had no doubt that at least some of those boys were dead. She was sure that if his story was true, what had happened to Rose and him was the reason he'd become an assassin. He'd have needed to hide, to practice, to learn how to kill those six young men without being discovered.

Her mind drifted back to the dark, empty, and snowy streets; to kneeling; and finally to standing in front of the police station. She had taken forever to make up her mind, had sensed him there and wanted to run to him. But he'd left her on purpose. He hadn't abandoned her. No, he'd done the reverse. He'd given her freedom back. He loved her and wanted to give her another chance at life. He'd set her free. He believed he'd traveled too far from the young man he'd once been, believed their worlds would not mesh.

Celia didn't want to admit he was right. But she had to. She couldn't live with a man who killed for a living, no matter how much she loved him. She might think she could, she might believe she was above society's conditioning right now, in the midst of confusion and longing, but she wasn't. Killing others for political or monetary gain was wrong. That fact, at least, was black and white, even if nothing else was, *if* he was an assassin as he claimed. But he'd been too careful about leaving a trail, too professional about everything he'd done, except kidnapping her. Yet even that he'd pulled off successfully. The only reason she was free was because he'd let her go.

So it was over. He'd gone. He would go on killing. She would go on living her safe and sheltered little life and write her safe little stories. Or would she? It all seemed meaningless now. Would he forgive her? Would he understand that she had to tell them about him? Of course he would. He'd known it from the moment he'd let her live.

Celia wanted the world to go away for a while. She wanted to curl up and hide. But there was nowhere to go. Wherever her captor was, she hoped it was quiet and dark. She hoped he was thinking of her.

65

A cacophony of voices talked over one another and shouted at them, cameras were shoved in their faces, and bright blinding lights lit up the entire front of York District Hospital as Thain forced his way through the jostling mass of journalists to the entrance. Clive followed and Rae struggled right behind him looking angry at the questions being thrown at them, at their delay in getting into the hospital. Thain knew better than anyone that the sudden appearance of Celia Wight was big news and a reprieve of sorts for them. He fumed at the delay but felt almost frantic with relief that she was finally safe. The question of whether or not her kidnapper was still in York wouldn't leave Thain alone, because he knew only one person might have the answer, and he didn't want to be the one to ask her.

He dreaded his meeting with Celia Wight. Most likely she would be damaged from this experience, especially considering her past. On the plane he'd acknowledged how much he wanted to help her to heal, to have a meaningful, normal life, if such a thing existed. He admitted that Rae had been right about him and his motives, but that didn't crimp his desire to help. Rae knew his obsession with Celia Wight had surpassed the one he had with the Wraith, and why. He no longer rationalized either one by linking the two and trying to make them one. Celia Wight was here, and the Wraith wasn't.

Since hearing of Celia Wight's safe return, he almost didn't care whether he found the man or not, or whether he could prove their suspect was the Wraith. All Thain seemed to care about now was her. And though he needed to talk to her, to glean what information she might have about her kidnapper, what he wanted to know, really, was if she was whole, or damaged beyond his help. How egotistical of him. Why did he think that he, of all people, could help her? He'd never been given the chance to help Agatha, but maybe with Celia he could prove his worth.

He pushed through his irrational emotions as roughly as he did the crowd, and they finally gained entry to the hospital. Once through the doors, Clive and Rae fell in behind him and let him lead the way. He concentrated on the three reports tucked under his arm, two of which he'd read on the flight up from London and one the police here in York had given him upon arrival. One report listed the names of the men who had been confirmed alive, while another listed those who were missing or known dead. The third reported what little the authorities had been able to get from Celia Wight, first when she'd stumbled into the York police station, and later at the hospital where they'd attempted to go over her with their usual thorough exam.

One of the medical team said that the exam itself had been an ordeal because Celia violently protested, screamed her head off and lost any semblance of control, insisting that contrary to the evidence she had not been attacked with a knife. She'd been so upset, the York police hadn't had a chance to show her Rae's composite photo or the profile photo the Kidnapping Squad had sent to them.

What he needed most, apart from meeting her face-to-face—*enough*, he thought. *Stay on track, Detective Sergeant.* What he needed most was for her to verify that they had a reliable likeness of the man. The store clerks they'd shown it to weren't decisive enough, not even with the black-and-white profile photo beside it. The profile photo was too old, or too young, depending on how one looked at it. Even the secretary said she thought it might be him but couldn't be sure. They'd had a confirmation-in-reverse from the bank robbers. None of them recognized the man in the photos. The seventh man was no longer thought of as one of the heist's crew. Better late than never, Thain supposed, to have a hunch confirmed. The one sure confirmation came from Duncan Elliott's parents, and yet that could be put under suspicion as well, if it ever went to a court case.

He decided that when he entered Celia's room he wouldn't pounce on her as the other police had, as the reporters soon would. He wanted to give her time, but knew he didn't have much to offer if they were to find Duncan Elliott, the Wraith, the kidnapper, or whatever anyone wanted to call him, before he killed again—because he would, at least once more. Thain knew it as if he were the Wraith himself.

He made an effort not to frown when he stepped into the lift with Rae and Clive. "You know that it's probably already too late to find Duncan Elliott."

They both stared at him. "What do you mean?" Clive asked.

"Without Celia Wight to give him clay feet, the man can morph through any net we erect to catch him, and with little or no exertion. If he's the Wraith, he's done it before, and we have evidence that even if he isn't the Wraith, there's nothing to stop him from doing it again . . ."

"Unless?" Rae asked.

"Unless Thain's theory is correct and we can find the sixth man-boy," Clive said and smiled.

"Right you are, Clive. Now who's the clever one?" He didn't tell them that his head was full of doubts, that his theory seemed so far-fetched that he already tasted a sour hint of defeat. Perhaps he'd become too used to defeat—when it came to the Wraith—to think there could be any other outcome.

He stood in the corridor outside Celia Wight's room, waiting, though for what he didn't know. Courage? He couldn't open the door. As much as he wanted to meet her face-to-face, he also did not want to. He felt like a teenager with a bad crush on the most popular girl in school. No way would she see him as anything but a cop trying to get something out of her. He wanted something all right, but not what she would think. Well, he had to do his job. Or did he? Couldn't he let Rae go in and ask these questions?

"No, I'm not going in there first. You have to do this, Thain. You've worked too hard to get here." Rae's mouth was set. "Go on, now. You're wasting time."

"Rae, I—"

She leaned toward him a little. "I know, Alban. I know. But do it anyway."

As he entered, the sudden lack of noise in Celia Wight's private room made him feel as if he'd stuffed cotton in his ears. A gentle pinging from the radiator as it attempted to heat the cool air was the only sound. Celia sat in the single bed, barely leaning back and stiff, her face tinted with an unhealthy blush. He couldn't believe she sat there, in the flesh, in color. He tried not to stare but couldn't stop. He saw a jagged scar on her bared neck and a bandage on her arm. Most of all he couldn't tear his gaze away from the distance in her now familiar eyes, which were astonishingly blue. He had stared so long at a black-and-white photo that he'd forgotten she had blue eyes. She said nothing when he walked in. The doctors all agreed she suffered from shock, and if he pushed her too hard, too fast, he could send her over the edge she already teetered upon.

If it were up to him, he would have taken a week to ask her these questions. He didn't have that much time. He had no time to coddle her, but he would. He had become too involved with her story, too aware of her sorrow in his core to ever hurt her even with questions. In fact, he wanted to protect her. Now he sounded like a sanctimonious prig. He cleared his throat, glanced at Rae standing beside him, and faced Celia again.

"Ms. Wight, I'm Detective Sergeant Alban Thain. This is DS Rae Bell. We are happy that you are safe. Your friends the Kings will be here soon. They've been very worried." Could he have sounded more stiff or robotic? Celia didn't register that she'd heard him.

"Ms. Wight, I know you need more time to assimilate what has happened to you, but I need to ask you some questions. Ms. Wight?"

She closed her eyes and sighed. "I know. About him."

"Yes, about him. Ms. Wight—"

"Celia," she said as if in a dream. "He didn't ask me my name."

He hesitated, but tried again. "Celia, do you know *his* name?"

She opened her eyes but still didn't look at either one of them. "He wouldn't tell me."

"Is he British?"

"He sounded British."

"I need you to try and remember everything you can about him, even the littlest things. We need to catch this man before he kills again."

She looked bewildered. "He didn't kill me."

"No, but he cut you."

"It was an accident."

"With a knife?"

"Yes. He stitched it up though I didn't want him to. It hurt." She made no sense, sounded like a little girl, and he reluctantly recalled the doctors' diagnosis. Yet he had to try again.

"Where was he taking you?"

"Here, I think," she said.

"To York?"

Celia nodded.

"Do you know why he came here? Is he looking for a way out of the country?"

"I don't know. I don't think so. Not yet. He was careful. Very clean."

"Celia, did he tell you why he kidnapped you?"

"Not in so many words. But I know why." Her face lost its passive blankness and sadness enveloped it in a familiar shadow. "I know why."

He glanced at Rae. She saw it too: Celia Wight's attitude toward her captor. His heart still beat, but slowly, with quiet anguish. He was writing down every word Celia uttered.

"Why did he kidnap you?" His voice was so soft he barely heard it himself. But Celia did. For the first time since they'd walked in the room, she looked directly at them.

"Because of Rose."

So their kidnapper and murder suspect was Duncan Elliott. He held his breath, afraid to break the quiet spell cast over the three of them. Rae wasn't breathing either. "Rose is . . . ?"

Celia looked at her bandaged arm, touched it with her other hand. "The only girl he ever loved. When he was young, when they were young, she was murdered and everyone thought he did it. But he didn't. He said there were six boys . . ."

Thain's hand paused over his notebook. *Six boys.* "Do you know when this took place, Celia?"

"Fifteen years ago."

"Did he say where this happened?"

"No. Yes. In a garden shed somewhere."

She was doing well, but he didn't want to shut her down. All he would ask her now was for confirmation on the photographs. "Celia, I need you to look at a photograph." Rae gave him the envelope holding the composite photo. He pulled it out and handed it to Celia. As she took it from him, he asked, "Do you recognize this man? Can you tell me if this is the man who abducted you?"

"Don't you know?" Celia looked puzzled that he didn't.

"This is a composite photo we've put together of who we think your abductor might be. We need your confirmation, to make sure."

He gave her face his full attention when she put her eyes on the photograph. He wanted to make sure she didn't lie to them. "What do you think?" He handed her the original blurry profile shot. "What about this one?"

Celia seemed mesmerized by the second image, seemed to forget their presence. He grimaced; he was right: Stockholm syndrome. The ordeal she'd gone through had been traumatic enough that she believed herself in love with her captor. He couldn't believe how fast that look on her face took his breath away, as if he'd been punched in the stomach. He had to put his personal feelings aside. With her, he wasn't sure he could. What was he thinking? This was going to be a problem, and not only for him. He imagined how the Kings would take this news, and hoped their friendship was strong enough to accept it instead of blaming her. He didn't blame her. He couldn't.

"It, it could be. I'm not sure . . ." Celia looked up at Rae. "This isn't very clear . . ."

He knew she thought it good enough. She'd recognized the man, though she wouldn't commit to it in words.

He glanced at Rae, questioned her silently, and she nodded. In spite of what Celia wanted them to believe, she had identified her kidnapper. The photo from Duncan Elliott's parents would clinch it, but when he reached for the composite photo, Celia let it slip from her fingers onto the bed. "Ms. Wight?" he said as he picked it up. "Are you all right?" Clearly she'd forgotten them. He saw it in her face. She was lost in her trauma.

"We should leave her for a bit," Rae said, her hand on his sleeve.

He nodded, frowning. He threw a parting glance at the forlorn woman in the bed and followed Rae from the room.

"You still need to show her the photo from his parents," Rae said out in the hospital corridor.

"I know, but like you said, she needs some time."

"She looks like she's been through bleeding hell."

He nodded, his eyes holding steadfastly to the envelope in his hand. "But she's a strong young woman. She's been through worse." He sighed and looked at Rae. "Time heals . . . and all that. You know."

"Do you really believe that?" Rae asked tilting her head to look up at him. He knew she alluded to his confessions—Agatha and his loss of her, and his estrangement from his brother over the assassination.

"Guess I have to, don't I?"

"I guess you do."

He tucked the envelope under his arm and shoved his hands in his pockets as he and Rae walked back to the office set aside for their incident room. During the questioning, Celia Wight's face had gone from sickly rose to pale white. Thain wished the old saying he'd given lip service to was true. He wanted to believe it, and not only for Celia Wight. Unfortunately, time hadn't eased any of his misery, and from the look of her, it had done nothing for Celia Wight either.

66

During a sleepless night spent walking the city of his birth, he'd gone over his plan until he was sick of it. The only change he foresaw was the need for awareness because of the photo. He could be recognized if he wasn't careful. He wore glasses again.

He knew where the last of the accursed six lived—the ringleader, the worst of them all, Pierce Ryan—because he'd spent months studying his prey's routine. Today he was a hunter, not an assassin, and carried the only tools he would need: his gloves, a roll of thick tape, and his knife. He would follow Ryan to his place of work at the Magistrates' Court. He would wait until Ryan left for his lunch break. Then he'd kidnap Ryan and make sure he understood the crime he was paying for, before cutting and then burying Pierce Ryan as he had the first four—alive. He would hear Ryan beg for mercy, hear his screams, until panic, terror, and the heavy, earthy rain of dirt stole his breath away.

Pierce Ryan usually lunched one street over from the courts at a pub where he was well known. He had a nice little life accessorized with a college degree, a wife, a kid, and a high-level position as a barrister. The hunter knew Ryan was happy and satisfied, living life according to his own terms. Too bad the bastard had deprived Rose of the same right. He wondered if Ryan ever thought about Rose and what he'd done to her. Wondered if he'd raped anyone else. The hunter didn't think of himself. Only of Rose.

Outside, amid the humid chill of morning, he waited, his collar turned up, his thoughts solemn, and he resisted the temptation to think of anything brighter, such as Celia. His thoughts returned to Pierce Ryan, who at that very moment left his abode for the last time, and set the final act in motion.

67

Thain's second visit to Celia Wight came a bare half hour after he'd finished the first one. She lay curled up on her side. The white of the sheets matched the hue of her skin.

"Ms. Wight. Are you awake?"

She didn't answer but sat up looking sullen and tired. Her fatigue found an echo deep in his bones. "I'm sorry to bother you again. You look completely knackered," he said.

"What do you need now, Detective?"

"For you to look at another photo. Ms. Wight, is this the man who kidnapped you?"

He placed the sharp, clear black-and-white photograph from the Elliotts into her hands. He watched her face as closely as he had the last time. Her pale face flushed; her surprised gasp gave him the last of the proof he needed to make an arrest.

Celia touched the photo, her fingers gentle upon it, as gentle as the look on her face.

"He's so young, and he's smiling," she said. "I saw him smile once, but it wasn't a real one like this." She gazed at the image in wonder and sadness. "You know, Detective, those boys stole this happiness from him, and from Rose." She dragged her eyes from the photo to him. He stopped breathing; she was looking right at him for the first time. "Where did you get this?" she asked. His pulse rate shot up with the effort to form an answer. He couldn't believe he was tongue-tied now.

"His parents," he began, getting his words back. "His parents saw the composite photograph on the news, the one that I showed you earlier? They brought this one to us. You've just confirmed beyond a doubt that your kidnapper is their long-lost son."

"He didn't think they would believe him."

"But they did. He left before they could stand up for him. They miss him, and they want to see him again. He was their only son."

"Oh, no."

He realized he'd leaned nearer, and he pulled back, not wanting to crowd or intimidate her.

"Where can we find him, Celia?" he asked her as softly, as gently as he could.

"I've already told you, I don't know. He didn't tell me anything about his plans. He only told me that bit about his past because I heard him having nightmares and calling Rose's name."

"And yet you became intimate with him?" He hated to ask her, really didn't want to hear her answer, though he already knew what she would say.

"Sort of. Yes, in a way. But he wouldn't let me into his thoughts or feelings." Celia stared at the photo, before she glanced up at him again. "What is his name?"

Thain backed away from her. He massaged his forehead and moved to stand by the window. He couldn't ignore that her heart beat in the same room as his own. She was much more real to him now, and her nearness destroyed every defense he'd thought to have against her, against his own wishes. He turned and looked at the woman he wanted to help through this trauma; the woman he hoped would one day allow him to be a friend. How could he hope to overcome what he saw in her eyes? He said, "His name is Duncan Elliott." Then he left.

68

Midday arrived and his prey finally left the courts. The hunter followed Pierce Ryan, who took a different route, one away from the pub where he normally lunched. In front of a two-story brick house Ryan stopped and rang the bell. A woman opened the door and let him in. It wasn't Ryan's house. It wasn't Ryan's wife.

Typical. This would mess up his timeline. He'd have to change strategy. Nothing new in that, only he wanted this over and done with. Celia's image badgered him, telling him he had no life. He wanted this last job done so Rose could finally sleep in peace, so he could move on. To what?

After patrolling all the exits and possible ways of escape that Ryan could use, the hunter stood outside and watched the house. He'd found two exits: a front and back door. He didn't think Ryan would use the back door unless given reason to.

He wouldn't give him a reason. The hunter wanted him alone. So he waited. Forty-five minutes went by before his prey came out, alone. But the hunter wouldn't act rashly. He knew the score. He knew Ryan's usual schedule; therefore, the relationship had to be new, in its first blush. The woman might watch from the window until her clandestine lover turned toward the street that housed the courts building. The hunter would have to take his prey, the leader of the pack, on his way home after work.

This time the hunter took a seat inside a small pizza restaurant right up from the Magistrates' Court, a seat with a full view of the building's front steps. He became a shadow no one paid attention to. He ordered coffee but wasn't hungry. He didn't let his mind wander. The hunt had begun. His attention remained focused on the goal.

69

The Kings arrived with open arms and worried smiles. Thain had sent word to them about Celia's recovery long before the press had hold of the news. He envied their special friendship with Celia, which made him think of the friends he'd left behind in Scotland, and his brother, and how long five years could suddenly feel. *Forget yourself, you lug,* he told himself. *You have a killer to catch. Concentrate.*

Since Eva and Philip King's arrival, Celia Wight wasn't cooperating as well with any of them as he'd hoped she would. She'd erected a wall even her friends, or maybe especially her friends, could not penetrate. She'd asked for time; stalling perhaps, hoping to help her kidnapper get away? The thought had crossed his mind more than once. He couldn't help but think of her reasons.

How could she believe she loved a man who kidnapped her, who had cut her after all she'd been through before? But victims of Stockholm didn't think rationally. Others must do their thinking for them until they can find help to get over it. Celia thought perhaps to stall them, and he guessed why, which spurred his decision—hard though the doctors would take it, hard though it would be for him to do. Time was their worst enemy when it came to her abductor, especially if he was, in fact, the Wraith. Thain and Rae entered Celia's room and approached the Kings, sitting like statues beside Celia's bed. Celia ignored them all.

"Mr. and Mrs. King, I need to talk with Ms. Wight, alone," he said.

"May I please stay?" Eva King said, trying to take Celia's hand in her own. Celia didn't respond.

He indicated that they should move toward the door. "May I speak with both of you first, in the corridor?"

"Well," Mrs. King said as she looked at Celia.

Philip King didn't argue. "Of course, Detective."

Clearly Mrs. King wasn't happy about leaving Celia alone. "Rae, would you mind staying with Ms. Wight for a moment?" Thain said. From the grateful expression on her face, he knew he'd read Mrs. King right.

"Of course not. Go ahead."

Once outside Celia's room, he went straight to the point. "I need information that she alone can give me. If you stay in the room, she won't talk." He and the Kings had already discussed Stockholm syndrome, and Eva looked distressed about it. Being a psychologist, she knew what lay ahead for her friend. "I don't like any of this," she said.

"Of course you don't. Who would? But you aren't going to help her, or the situation, with constant attention. Somewhere inside, she knows what's going on, but she doesn't understand it any more than you do. I know you are aware of this better than anyone."

"Of course I am. She thinks she loves that murderer."

"Most likely because she wanted to live, Mrs. King. Please, think of Celia right now. Only of her."

"What else, for God's sake, do you think I'm doing?"

"I think you're worried for your friend, and perhaps, not being able to help her right now, you're frustrated and missing the point."

"What are you not telling us?"

She was very quick. He sighed, knowing another test of his people skills was about to commence. "Mrs. King, you're a kind and devoted friend to Celia. If only you would listen to me as earnestly as you want to protect her, you would be of more help to her, and to me. I know you understand that right now Celia is traumatized. You also probably know that the most important thing you can do for her is to care for her unconditionally while I try to do my job and get this man in custody. Surely you must agree with that?"

Eva bowed her head. "Yes. I do. I only want to help her feel better."

"Why don't you find one of the counselors and talk to them while I talk to her?"

Eva bristled and Philip put his arm around her. "I don't need *therapy*," she said.

Thain was surprised. "You of all people can say that? Celia does, Mrs. King. As her best friend, why wouldn't you need it, too? What does it matter that you are a psychologist? This isn't going to go away overnight. She can't 'put it behind her' or 'get over it,' much less 'feel better' anytime soon. She's had a severe and traumatic shock, and whether you like it or not, she's changed. Maybe for the better, I don't know. But she'll never be the same."

Mr. King's glare changed. He accepted what Thain said. "Didn't I tell you, Eva, that I thought he was trustworthy? Detective Thain, we'll wait right out here. Do what you need to do."

Relieved, he said, "Thank you, sir." The Kings weren't ready to deal with the changes this experience had wrought in Celia. They certainly weren't ready to learn about her prior brush with death, or how mentally unbalanced she might be right now because of it. Celia would let them know of her past, if she so chose. He would not be the one to betray her confidence, especially because she didn't know he was aware of what had happened to her. He left the Kings huddled together in the garish light of the corridor.

Rae turned from the window when he re-entered Celia's quiet little room. He acknowledged her, set his lips, and went to stand next to the bed.

"Ms. Wight, I'm sorry to bother you again, but we need your help. I have to ask some more questions of you. I'm sure you know why."

Celia opened her eyes, which were glassy and red. The strain of her experience had left telltale signs of defeat but also determination. She sat up, reinforcing his initial impression of her strength. After what she'd endured, she had to be strong. But right now, he had to be stronger.

"What do you want to know?" The question was blunt and antagonistic, like the look she gave him.

"I need to know what he told you, where he took you, and, if you remember any weakness he might have had."

"Weakness? His past haunts him. I think he believed he'd forgotten it . . . like I did." She whispered at the end, but Thain heard what she said. He glanced at Rae and she nodded. She'd heard it too.

"I've given the information about Rose to those who can check on it." He didn't tell her they'd already known about Rose Etheridge. "Did he tell you anything else, anything at all?"

"No."

"Nothing?"

"No."

"Did he mention any of the six young men by name?"

"I told you, no."

"I'm going to read some names to you—"

"He never told me any names! Not even his own."

He put his hands up, palms facing her, hoping to placate her. "I heard you, I heard you." He pulled a chair over to her bed and sat so she could look down at him, not up. "Ms. Wight—"

"Celia."

"Celia, maybe he let something slip that you wouldn't recognize as being important. Please, we need you to listen."

Celia sniffed, but nodded without saying a word.

He held a short list of the men who were still alive and who were assumed to have known Elliott in school. One man had denied any knowledge of Elliott, but according to another schoolmate, this man and Elliott had fought once at school, right in front of everyone, over Rose Etheridge. He would wait to read his name until he knew for certain Celia was listening, that she would answer.

"Michael McNeil?"

Celia shook her head.

"Bernard Walters?"

He continued to read and she continued to shake her head at every name until, with four names left, he said the one he'd held back: "Pierce Ryan?"

Celia started to shake her head, then stopped, her face frozen. "What? Could you repeat the last one?"

"Pierce Ryan."

"I called him Ryan once or twice, because I didn't know what to call him."

"And?"

"And he told me never to call him Ryan. He hated me calling him that."

"Thank you, Ms. Wight." He glanced at Rae, who slipped out the door while he changed tactics. He didn't bother to finish the list. He'd been winging it on instinct ever since he'd been given the go-ahead; why stop now?

"Did he ever go to a bank with you?"

"No."

"So he had money on him all the time?"

"I suppose. I didn't pay attention. I was too busy thinking about how to get free without dying for it, and other things."

"When he cut you, you said it was an accident."

"He, he came back from shopping—"

"He would leave you alone?"

She nodded. "But he'd tape and gag me most of the time. One day he came back with the look of death on him. I knew he was going to kill me; his self-preservation had overridden whatever it was that had made him keep me in the first place. I didn't know, then, about his past, you see.

"He came at me, but I fought back. During the fight his knife slashed my arm by accident. I'll never forget the look on his face. He stared at the blood and stopped cold, like he'd seen a ghost. He dropped the knife, picked me up, and washed the cut. He said I needed stitches. I fought again. I didn't want him to touch it. But he tied me up and did the stitching himself. I blacked out. When I came to, I was on the bed in the dark, but I sensed him. He watched me as if he had the weight of the world on him. Toward the end it seemed he was tired of carrying it."

"Did this happen in a flat?"

"No. A hotel room."

"Do you remember the name of the hotel, or where it was?"

"I didn't know where we were most of the time. I knew London was big; I had no idea. I saw a sign once that said Mile End."

He had asked her this question before. He asked it again anyway. "Did he tell you anything else about himself?"

"No."

"Nothing about his work?"

Celia shook her head, but she looked up at him again, right in the eyes, hers watery-blue and full of grief. She tucked her lower lip under her teeth for an instant. A slight sob started as she took a breath. She didn't let her eyes leave his, and Thain began to melt.

"No," she said again, then, "Yes. Yes he did, at the end. He wanted to push me away. He said he killed people for a living, and I thought . . . at first I thought he was trying to make me afraid of him. But he wasn't, was he?" Her hands tightened into fists on the bed. "He wanted to kill those boys."

Thain couldn't move. Confirmation. He'd wanted it, but now that he had it, he didn't want it. He'd chased a man for ten years only to find out that the man had taken up those years because of a horrible twist of fate, two actually, or three. Rose Etheridge, Agatha, the assassination in Scotland. What a waste of time to think of such things. But they swirled in his brain, caught him off balance. He stood, couldn't think straight, paced, before he turned to her and rushed headlong into the next question: "Ms. Wight, do you believe you're in love with this man?" *Do I believe I'm in love with you? What about Rae?*

Clearly angry, she stared at him. "What kind of question is that?"

"Haven't the doctors asked you the same question?" Rashness took hold and made him a fool.

She cried out, "No, and how could it possibly make any difference?"

"I'm sorry," he said and sat next to her bed again, trying to calm down. "Ms. Wight, Celia, I, we must understand what you believe to be the truth."

"I've told you nothing but the truth. What are you talking about?"

"I've seen other women in your predicament, Ms. Wight. I've seen what's been done to their minds."

Her look spoke her contempt. "Kidnapper's syndrome or something like that. Am I right? That's what you think I have, isn't it?"

"Stockholm syndrome. The clinical definition is—"

"I don't need to know your *clinical* definition of anything. There was nothing *clinical* about what happened to me."

"Still—"

"You know nothing about me!"

"Do you love him?"

Celia stared at him and he didn't look away, as if it were a contest neither of them wanted to lose. Then she bowed her head and he expelled a breath he didn't know he'd been holding. What the hell was he doing? Yet he knew what he was doing, and that it was wrong. He'd promised not to push or hurt her or make her cry, and here he was doing all those things. He realized how much he wanted to climb this mountain, no matter how hard it turned out to be, to become her friend. He wasn't going to give up, like he had on Agatha, until he knew she would come away from this experience, this life-changing event, a more whole, more confident person. Listening to himself, he almost laughed—and almost cried. The image of his brother's face loomed in his mind.

She fiddled with the bedcovers. "I didn't, at first. I didn't know him. I was afraid of him. He was cold and harsh. Eventually I realized he made a point of keeping me afraid. He only directly threatened me in the beginning and that one last time."

"The doctors' reports state that you didn't have, mm . . . relations with him, but Ms. Wight, something happened to you in the past . . ."

She shook her head and steadfastly refused to look at him. "How dare you?" she whispered.

He backed off, thankful she'd responded and not demanded he leave the room. "I'm sorry. Please, I'm sorry, again. I shouldn't have asked you." What had he expected? He didn't know himself now, or why he had pushed, until more images, of his brother, of his parents flashed through his mind, this time more clearly. What had he done to his family? Why had he blamed them all this time, when he was the one at fault? He waited a little to give her, and himself, time to calm down. "Do you know where he's going?" he asked a bit more softly.

Crying now, she shook her head, and he berated his ineptitude with people. "Ms. Wight, truly, I apologize for upsetting you," he said, chagrined at his lack of tact.

"I didn't even know he was going to leave me," she said. Thain wanted nothing more than to take her hands in his and tell her everything would work out for her. He wished he hadn't caused her tears, wished he could wipe them away. But she wouldn't let that happen, not now. Instead he stood and handed her a tissue from a box on the table by her bed.

He sat back down. He couldn't abide her tears, didn't want to hurt her; he wanted to help her. He wanted to stop asking questions that were so hard for her to answer, but his time was running short. There remained one question left to ask. "Ms. Wight, *why did he let you go?*"

She stared at him blankly, as if reliving some other time. "I . . ."

A knock sounded on the door. "Blast it," he cursed under his breath. Hoping it wasn't the Kings, he opened the door. Rae stood there looking wary, like she knew something he wouldn't like. He glanced back at Celia. Her face had shuttered, telling him visiting hours were over. The intense moment had passed, and her revelation remained unrevealed. Rae's eyes met his, questioning him. He frowned, stepped into the corridor, and shut the door. "News?"

Her dark eyes brightened. "Pierce Ryan works at the Magistrates' Court on Clifford Street," she said. "I'd like to go if you're all right with that?"

He couldn't read the look in her eyes, but his heart reacted all the same. What a fool he was. "Why?"

"You know *he'll* be there. I want to see if I recognize him. I want to be in on this one, Alban."

Right up until that moment they'd kept a strict boundary between work and their personal lives. "Alban?" he said.

She didn't flinch or move. "I promise I'll be careful, *Thain.*"

"You can't promise he won't hurt you."

She grinned like a teenager. "Glad to know you care. May I go?"

He couldn't smile. He knew the caliber of man she might come up against. But he had no right to deny her. He said quietly, "I wish I could hug you right now." Then he pulled his shoulders back and said in a louder voice, as if anyone else could hear, "DS Bell, we'll need undercovers surrounding that building, and I want two more to escort Mr. Ryan here for questioning."

"Yes, *sir*," Rae said with a snarky smile.

"What? Did I say something funny?"

"No. I'm just wondering how long DI Carter will keep his elitist attitude with a more-than-likely new Detective Inspector threatening to assume his mantle of authority."

70

He watched the flow of people up and down the street. He watched those coming in and out of the restaurant, aware of each one and whether or not any posed a threat. No one did until the lunch crowd began to thin. A young Indian woman, perhaps in her late twenties, came in, and after placing an order chose a seat in his line of vision, blocking his direct view of the courts building steps. For the next fifteen minutes her attention was centered more on the view than on the novel lying open and unread on the table in front of her, and he realized he'd seen her before. At an Internet café a few days ago. She was a cop. If he remembered her, he didn't doubt she'd remember him. If he stayed, she'd soon notice him sitting alone behind her, if she hadn't already. He didn't need any unnecessary attention.

He stood and headed for the toilets. Once inside, he slowly reopened the door enough to see through the dining area and out the windows. He didn't want to leave the relative invisibility of the restaurant, but he knew he couldn't stay much longer. He'd have to find another place to keep watch—or would he? Just then, a large group of schoolchildren passed the restaurant, heading toward the courts building. He glanced at the empty serving counter, at the door: the woman and he were alone, for the moment. Pulling on his gloves he moved forward. As he neared the woman—the cop—he reached out and took her by the back of her neck. Her muscles tensed against his hold on her. He bent and whispered, "I have a knife an inch from your side. Step out the door and walk with me without a fight. I don't generally kill women, but today I might make an exception." She didn't move. He pressed the knife against her side. "Do you want to test me with your life?"

"No."

She stood, and his hand lessened its grip on her neck. She tensed again, but he was ready. He whipped her around to face him, keeping his eyes on the door and the still-empty serving counter. "What's your name?"

"Rae Bell."

He stared at her. She stared back, for an instant. "Detective Sergeant Rae Bell."

"Detective Bell, you have one last chance. No one can save you before I walk out of here. No one can stop what I'm about to do." *I've waited too long*, he thought.

"It's not too late," she said.

"You're right, it isn't. What's your decision?"

"I'll go with you."

The detective shrugged on her coat while he pushed her to the door. As soon as their feet hit the sidewalk, he casually matched their pace to that of the schoolchildren. He kept the two of them an easy three feet behind the group while noting the positions of the other cops blanketing the area. Such as the man who'd walked up to the bus stop and stood apparently reading the paper while a bus stopped and then continued on without his glancing at it. Perhaps the man knew the exact bus he awaited and didn't need to look, but why did he scan the entire street end to end before glancing back at his paper, and then start all over again?

And the man by the trash bin: how long did it take to empty a single bin? Dead ahead of the school group, two plainclothes policemen took the courts building steps two at a time and disappeared into the yawn of the large wooden doors. That's when he wondered what the police took him for. Could there be a better giveaway than entering in a pair? He shook his head and said, "If you know who I am and why I am here, why didn't you think I'd see this setup?"

"Are you really Duncan Elliott?"

The long-lost sound of his name spoken aloud sent a shiver along his spine. He ignored it. "Who I am doesn't matter anymore."

The cops had forced his hand, but he didn't care. He'd been in tricky spots before and knew if he chose to do so he'd get out of this one as well. He could also wait and strike another day. But he wasn't worried about getting away, yet. This was the day he'd planned for. He wouldn't give up now. Not this close to the end. Focused on the goal and how to pull off a spur-of-the-moment change in plan, he kept his hands steady and close to the policewoman. After all, providence was on his side, he thought, glancing at the bobbing heads of the school-children chatting away ahead of him. As soon as they passed the courts building, he would make his move.

But the group stopped and prepared to enter the building. He slowed his pace, took five seconds to think of sky-blue eyes and soft lips, and then forged ahead. He and the detective followed the children into the Magistrates' Court building. His time had come. His prey's had just run out.

71

elia had thought, when her parents died, when she was raped, and finally when she was abducted by a heartless stranger, that the fear and confusion she felt at each of those events was the worst she'd ever experienced. She guessed that at those points in her life it had been true. But it wasn't true any longer. Now, trapped in a nightmare, unable to move, in that heavy sluggish way that happens in dreams, especially when you want to run, she wanted nothing more than to escape.

Frustration clung to her like a chewing-gum-stuck-in-your-mouth dream, when you try to take the gum out of your mouth but it sticks to your teeth and the back of your throat and won't come loose. So debilitating, so frustrating. She wanted to flee from the sterile room where she was yet again held prisoner, until she saw Eva and Philip out in the hall and remembered her old life, the friends who had helped distract her from her past.

Celia got to her feet, ready to find her clothes. She'd been hiding in that bed too long. He, Duncan, was gone. He would vanish until another contract came up. Celia clamped her jaw shut as her chest tightened. How she would get him out of her heart she had no idea, but it was time to do something, anything, even if it was wrong. She glanced into the hallway at her agent, at her best friend, and watched as that detective walked up.

She resented how uncomfortable and defensive Detective Thain's presence made her feel, even as he treated her with respect and gentleness, most of the time. She didn't like to admit that it wasn't his words that forced her to question herself, it was his eyes—earthy brown, soft and somehow sad, somehow comforting. They asked her: if she did nothing, if she ignored the very beating of her heart and the stark fact that a life with any other man was out of the question, could she continue to live the rest of her life alone? Go on as before? It bothered her that although she had never, since the rape, cared whether or not she found love, she now tasted regret.

"Stop it, Celia," she said, fuming, as she tore her tiny hospital room apart. "Find your clothes." She couldn't find them. She jabbed the button to buzz the nurse over and over. "Where are my clothes? I don't want to be in this bed anymore," she demanded when the nurse answered the summons three minutes later.

"The police took them, Ms. Wight. I'll see what we can do for you."

Helpless as a baby. She couldn't even get dressed, because they held her prisoner. At least he . . . at least Duncan had let her wear clothes, had bought her new ones so she could stay clean. Celia moved to the window and gazed outside. The day looked as gray as it felt, and rain clouds threatened in the east. Duncan. Duncan Elliott. It was strange to think of him by his name. She wondered how long it had been since anyone had called him by it. It wasn't the name on the passport he'd carried.

It fit him, and she was glad he had a name that she liked. Not Ryan. She gazed out the window but thought of Duncan and his anger, his confusion, his frustration, his passion, and the look she'd last seen in his eyes before he left her. He'd been abrupt and cold, but she'd seen misery lurking beneath his now familiar wrath. She remembered the consuming love that he'd allowed her to feel, if only for a while. Celia clung to that love. She clung to the belief that it wasn't for nothing. That she was worth someone loving her that much. Was that what this was all about? 'If you truly love someone, then set them free' stuff? Was that what Duncan had believed?

A light knock on the door interrupted her thoughts. She turned as Detective Thain entered wearing a tentative smile.

"Ah, you're up."

"Yes." She glared at him, ignoring how the small smile changed his face for the better. A smile had changed Duncan's face too. "I've asked for some clothes."

The detective frowned. He seemed to do a lot of that. "We had some delivered last night. Didn't anyone tell you? They should be in here." He opened a built-in closet that she hadn't seen behind the bathroom door and pulled out a pair of jeans, a turtleneck sweater, an undershirt, panties, a bra, socks, and sneakers that resembled light hiking boots.

"Thought you'd prefer comfortable over fashionable?"

"Thank you." He'd thought right, and again she was disconcerted. Celia took the clothing from him and ducked into the bathroom to dress. When she came out she felt better, more in control of the jumble in her head. Meanwhile, Philip had come in, and he stood talking with Detective Thain.

"Better?" Thain turned to her, unobtrusively polite.

"Hello, Celia. Feeling any better?" Philip looked relieved to see her up and dressed.

"Yes. At least the clothes help me feel like a person again, not a prisoner. Had enough of that lately."

Detective Thain almost smiled, and Philip's attempt at one was a sad try.

"Glad to hear you have a sense of humor, Ms. Wight," the detective said.

"Celia."

He looked abashed. "Sorry. I keep forgetting your preference, Celia."

"So, you haven't heard any news?" she said.

Detective Thain hesitated. "We heard of a possible sighting last night in a pub. Everyone in the pub swore that a man matching the photograph came in, but as soon as he saw the news on the television over the bar, he left. Some of the patrons ran out after him but he'd disappeared. We sent a crew over, but of course they found no sign of him."

So Duncan had slipped safely into the darkness again. He could be on the continent by now. Celia's legs quivered and she sat before Philip could try and steady her. The wishful thought of him, Duncan, still being in Britain had helped somehow. With him gone, she felt alone in a profound deep-into-the-earth kind of way. Solitude. The anguish of utter loneliness as she'd never known it took her breath away. She would never fully recover from what he'd done to her. Duncan was imbedded in her truest self. He'd invaded her and left his spirit imprinted upon her core. She feared, and hoped, he would never completely go away.

uncan Elliott, with the detective beside him, slid easily into the Magistrates' Court building right behind the group of school-children, who were evidently on a field trip. The two undercovers had entered about five minutes ahead of the pack. He moved fast. While his arm was around the detective and the children were nearby, the police outside could do nothing to stop him. Duncan knew the layout of the building, knew where to find Ryan's office. No one stopped or questioned him as he made for it. He angled toward the door, but saw the secretary to his left. She said, "Sir, may I—"

"Stand up and walk over here to me. Do not make a sound or this young lady will die."

Stunned, the secretary did as he asked.

"Closer."

She took two steps closer. Duncan held the detective against him, her back to his front, his hand holding the ever-present knife now pricking one side of her long, vulnerable neck.

"Take the tape out of my pocket and tear off a strip. Bind her hands with it."

He flipped the detective around and the secretary did as she was instructed, though her hands shook. "Now go and stand by the door to Mr. Ryan's office. The detective will be safe if you do as I say once we are in the room. Do you understand?" he asked the secretary.

She nodded, speechless.

"I will kill everyone in that room if you don't."

"It's still not too late, Mr. Elliott—" Rae started.

"Detective, be happy you are not yet dead."

"Thain said you never kill women."

"It's your life. Do you want to risk whoever Thain is being wrong?"

"No, but—"

He sidled them up to the secretary's side. "Tape her mouth, and your own," he said to the secretary. Knives seemed to instill fear faster than guns when held against bare skin.

The secretary once again did as he demanded.

He kicked in the door to Pierce Ryan's office, giving the cops inside no time to move before he said, "Weapons on the floor, now," in case they had them. He pushed both women in front of him before he elbowed the door shut, noting that one cop stood to his right and the other in front of the desk, police badge held up toward Pierce Ryan. Good timing. Maybe Ryan hadn't yet been told his name.

"Weapons?" he said again. They pulled their weapons out very slowly and threw them on the floor. "Hands?" They held them up.

Ryan started to stand. Duncan Elliott said to the secretary, "Take the tape and secure them." He gestured toward the cops still standing with their empty hands in the air. Staring at Ryan he said, "You help her."

With no hint of recognition, Ryan responded with cool distain. "Why should I?"

"Her death is a foregone conclusion if you don't," he said, indicating the woman he held, his blade pinching the skin against her beating pulse.

"If you like."

Duncan Elliott didn't react to Ryan's apparent disinterest. When one of the cops started to protest, he applied pressure and the woman swallowed hard as a thin trickle of her blood began to seep.

Ryan held up his hands. "Wait. Enough," he said, shaking his head as if this were all a silly mistake. "I'll do as you ask, though I don't know what any of you are doing in my office. It's not like I keep a safe or any substantial sum of money here. This is a barrister's office, for God's sake."

The cop closest to Ryan started to answer.

"You, don't say a word," Duncan ordered; the cop shut his mouth but glared at him. "Lay on the floor," he motioned to the two cops. "Get the tape on them," he continued. The secretary and Ryan took the tape and secured the two cops' hands and feet. "Kick their guns into the corner over there." The secretary kicked the two guns into the corner farthest from the cops. "Now her." Duncan indicated the secretary as he moved toward one of the bound cops. The secretary lay on the floor as well and Ryan complied without a word, but his lips tightened. His hands fumbled a bit. "Tape everyone's mouths, and don't forget the detective's legs." Ryan did as ordered. Immediately after Ryan finished, Duncan forced the detective to the floor and slipped over to his quarry. He pressed his blade against Ryan's back, next to his right kidney. "Now it's your turn." He guided Ryan over to his chair behind the desk. "Sit." He bound Ryan to the chair and then checked Ryan's work on the police officers and the secretary. Once satisfied that no one could escape, he dragged each one to a different corner, separated, out of the way. Their judging and fearful eyes never wavered from him. He didn't care.

As he barricaded the door, Duncan didn't stop to think of how his plan had gone wrong. He knew every step he'd taken, and he knew why he had chosen this end to his tragic piece of theatre. After fifteen years, everything had come down to this moment, the final act. Once Pierce Ryan was dead, Rose would be free. He would be free. If the cost was his life then he would pay it. He would pay anything to be free. He paused and glared at his hostages. He had only one regret, but he couldn't—wouldn't—think of her now. The time had come to take final payment for two ruined lives.

73

Celia looked up as Eva came in and walked over to hug her. As she accepted Eva's embrace, she thought neither Eva nor Philip would understand the part of her that had feelings for Duncan. They couldn't understand, as yet, how he'd changed her—for the better, she thought. Glancing at Detective Thain, she caught a look in his eye that told her that perhaps he did.

His cell phone rang and broke the silent spell.

"Thain. Yes, what? He took her in with him? Yes, I'm on my way." Thain listened, his forehead creased as if he had to think fast, but carefully. Seconds ticked and the air thickened. "Clive, let me talk to him?" Not a full ten seconds passed before he said, "Sir, I respectfully disagree. I think she should come with me. Perhaps if he sees her . . . Yes, sir. Of course we can and will protect her." His eyes flicked to Celia, then to the floor.

"Thank you, sir." Thain closed his phone and looked at Celia, at Philip, then Eva; his face tense, serious, his dark eyes betraying alarm and excitement. "Duncan Elliott is holding five hostages, three of whom are cops, at the Magistrates' Court building on Clifford Street. I'm told it's about seven minutes from here by car."

"What? Who does he have?" Celia couldn't breathe while hope and fear fought inside her. Thain turned to her and her heart soared, knowing definitively what he would say next.

"Pierce Ryan. The captain of the York Police agrees with me. Ms. Wight, do you think you can draw Duncan Elliott out?"

"You can't make her go. You can't put her through seeing that man again," Eva protested, her arm circling Celia's shoulders.

"Eva—"

"Celia. It's too dangerous."

DS Thain interceded. "She might not have a choice, Mrs. King. According to Ms. Wight, Celia, I mean, Duncan Elliott may not kill women but he does kill men. An innocent man may die if she doesn't go."

"Innocent?" Celia's voice reflected disbelief as she gently pulled free of Eva's worried grasp.

"Right now, as far as we know he is innocent. And if we don't save him, we might never know the truth."

"Duncan told the truth."

"Ryan's testimony, if cross examined in court, could do a lot to get to the truth."

"I—" Celia started.

But Eva reached for her again, and her kind face showed that she was trying not to cry. "You think you're in love with him, Celia, but you're not. He's brainwashed you. I know about Stockholm—"

"Eva, that isn't why I have to go." Her friend's outburst had finalized Celia's decision. "I can't let those people die when I might be able to stop him." *And clear his name.* Celia took Eva's hands in hers. She held them tightly. "I must help. I'll be safe. The police won't let anything happen to me, or they wouldn't let me go, would they?"

It was as if Eva didn't hear her. "Have you thought he could take you away for good this time? Maybe he's thinks he's in love with *you* now."

Celia shivered. Duncan had fallen in love with her first. "With all those police around?" she said. "Eva, I can't hide from life anymore."

Philip, who stood behind his wife, gently pulled her into his arms, leaned over, and kissed Celia on her forehead. He smiled at her and said, "Do what you must. We will be here when you return."

Detective Thain stepped forward, and his words of understanding surprised Celia. "Mrs. King, remember how precious your friendship with Celia is, to you and to her. She needs your support in whatever decision she makes. This is a crucial time for her. She needs to trust her friends and also her belief in herself."

Eva turned from her husband and stood up straight. She looked at Celia with red eyes and a sniffing nose. "Of course I know all this. And you know I have your back. Right, Celia?"

Celia nodded. "Yes, of course." She hugged Eva and whispered, "You're my best ever friend." But Celia didn't need Eva's support like before. She was ready to live again and take on what she'd spent her existence avoiding.

74

The ticking of the clock on the wall was out of sync with the sound of Pierce Ryan's harsh and labored breathing. Ryan sat upright and stiff in his large padded chair, looking as if he was trying to act unconcerned. But his eyes had sharpened, like those of trapped prey staring at the hunter with no clear thought, only the instinct to escape.

The irony of Ryan's death happening here in a court building was not lost on Duncan. It didn't matter that Ryan wouldn't be lying out in the stony, cold field with the others. Though Ryan's death would be quicker than all but McLean's, before he died he would still experience the agony, shame, and humiliation he'd inflicted upon Rose. Ryan would still die knowing there was no hope for him, no one to save him, as had Rose. He would still die realizing he was the last of the six and that none of the others had escaped their fate. For himself, Duncan didn't care if the police officers and the secretary bore witness to what he'd confessed to Celia. But it would matter to his parents. In Ryan's private and well-appointed office of dark wood and lush carpet, Duncan, close enough to his prey to feel his heat, teased Ryan's raised chin with the point of his knife. He cut the tape on Ryan's arms. "Stand up and strip."

"What?"

"Strip. Clothes off."

Ryan leaned over in his chair and slowly untied his shoes. He kicked them off with disdain. "I don't know what you're thinking, but I've already said I have no money in this office."

Duncan smiled, but it was a grim one. Ryan still had no idea who he was. "Stand up," Duncan ordered. Ryan stood in front of him and began to undress. Soon the man stood in his underclothing, his skin maggoty-white with dark hair speckling his arms and legs. "Take it all off."

Ryan bent to slide off his undershorts, but instead, with a quick forward thrust, he bowled into Duncan, knocking him back into the wall. Upon impact Duncan lost his breath and his knife. A fierce ache radiated through his chest as he sucked air into his breathless lungs, fast. Ryan pummeled him with his fists, his face twisted in rage. "How dare you come in here and demand something for nothing! You sodding thieves are all the same."

While he was still trying to suck in air, Ryan's next punch came at him and Duncan feinted to one side. Ryan's fist smashed into the wall and he howled. Duncan took advantage and his hand struck out like a snake, grabbed Ryan's hair and pounded his face into the wall. Blood spattered as Ryan's nose broke against the hard plaster. Ryan's knees gave way even while he struggled to regain his footing. But Duncan threw him to the floor and taped his hands and feet to the stout legs of the monolithic desk. Then Duncan cut every last shred of clothing from Pierce Ryan's squirming body.

Ryan had proved he still had a mean streak, but Duncan had proved his training was better. Duncan's chest heaved until he regained his full breath. He checked the three cops and the secretary, and then peered out the large window behind Ryan's desk at the activity outside. He didn't want any more surprises before he finished this. It had to go down his way. The police had cleared all vehicles from the street in front of the courts building, and they were setting up barricades. He retrieved his knife from the floor and picked up the phone. He called the police. A bare minute passed before they patched him through to someone amongst the hive of cops in front of the building. A man answered and began to give his name, but Duncan interrupted.

"I don't care who you are," he said. "Just listen. I know you will try to use Special Forces. The barrister will be dead before they can throw one tear gas bomb, and your rescue attempt will be in vain. Think of your fellow coppers in here. Think of Pierce Ryan's secretary."

The policeman on the other end swore he wouldn't let the Special Forces in, but Duncan knew he lied. Duncan also knew what he had to do before they broke the window or breached the office door. He hung up the phone without another word. The policeman on the other end still babbled as the handset found the cradle.

Duncan checked the door again, and the window. No change so far. He yanked off one of his gloves, found a sheet of paper and wrote something down, found an envelope, shuffled the paper into it, and sealed it. He wrote a name on the envelope before slipping it into the inside breast pocket of his coat and pulling his glove back on. He knelt beside his victim close enough to smell the man's fear. He'd waited, planned, thought, dreamed of this moment for too long; he wouldn't let the cops take it from him. He finally allowed his blood-boiling rage its rightful place.

He pushed his face closer to Ryan's. "You don't have any backup this time, Ryan. They're all dead. It took five years for me to learn what I needed to know. Then I dissolved, became a ghost, a ghost that could kill. Did you realize the members of your gang had all vanished? I saved you for last, on the off chance that you might start fearing for your life. But of course you didn't. So I sent you the newspaper. Did you read it, the one that mentioned Richard McLean's brutal murder? I've castrated and buried four of your *mates*, alive, over the last ten years, carefully, to avoid official suspicions about their disappearances. McLean's death was notice that you were the last. You and me, Ryan. Fifteen years ago you took an innocent's life, and you stole mine."

Duncan watched, and grimaced as comprehension focused Pierce Ryan's mean eyes. "You . . . that's why the police asked if I knew you in school—"

"Yes."

"We all thought you were dead, Elliott."

"So it seems."

"So do your parents." Ryan actually sneered.

The evil man had been born with the compulsion to hurt. Duncan knew this, but the words sliced his heart as they never had when they'd been but mere thoughts in his head. Hearing them out loud cut through the myth he'd fooled himself with. The one telling him he didn't care. Celia had changed him in more ways than she would ever know.

But instead of cursing her as he once had, he realized she'd freed him to accept the destiny that had awaited him all along. He'd only postponed it to avenge Rose. He glanced at the naked man lying on the floor. Yes, he found that he actually and certainly *did* care. "Go ahead and dream of escape, Ryan. But there will be none for you. You gave no mercy in that shed fifteen years ago; I'll give you none here in your fancy office in the middle of York. Everyone will know what you did and how you now pay for those deeds. Your time has come."

"You deserved it, you piece of—"

"No!" Duncan yelled, his face heating, his blood roaring now. "No, I didn't! Neither did Rose! She didn't deserve what you did to her and neither did I. But *you* deserve *this*." Duncan's knife sliced down, cut in a deep jagged arc, and blood poured over Ryan's belly and legs, over his testicles, as his penis fell, left hanging by a thin strip of skin. "No one can save you now, you son of a bitch. I only wish you could live long enough to know what your life would be without your hideous cock."

Pierce Ryan had time to scream. Serenaded by Ryan's torture, Duncan threw a sharp glance at the trussed-up cops and the secretary. He didn't acknowledge the horror or the pity he saw in their eyes, especially the Indian woman's, before he moved to the window. He wasn't done yet. Ryan wasn't dead yet. Duncan needed more time. Across the street the police flitted back and forth, talked on radios, arranging themselves with bluster and tension, stuck as they were, waiting on him. He did a double take. What the hell?

Celia. Her small form, dark hair in familiar disarray, ran toward the Magistrates' Court building. A bobby ran after to catch her, but she ran faster. Another man caught her halfway across the street. He pulled her back into the mesh of cops. Duncan's eyes narrowed as he wondered who the man was, not only because Duncan recognized him as the cop he'd brushed by in the café a few days ago, but because he was now shouting at Celia with a look Duncan recognized. The emotion written on the cop's face, before he recovered himself, was familiar. Celia made Duncan feel the same way. Protection. He wanted to protect her. He watched as the cop retreated with her and pushed through to the phone by the police captain. Ryan's phone rang behind him. He ignored it. He stared at Celia, realizing that this was the first time he had gazed at her face and known her name. She looked worried, anxious to see him. "Celia." He said it out loud. The phone persisted. He couldn't see her anymore as the cops around her swallowed her up. He answered the phone. "Send her over."

"Duncan? Duncan Elliott?"

"Send her in."

"Send out the barrister first."

"If you know my name, you also know I won't do that."

"Then why should I send her in to you?"

"Because there are three cops and a secretary in here, all hoping I don't kill them as well."

"But you won't kill the women."

Duncan paused. Why did the cop think he wouldn't kill the women? What did he care why? "Do you really want to test that theory?" Duncan hung up.

He stooped again beside the naked and dying man. "I wanted you to suffer longer, but what is done is done. At least Rose will now be free." Pierce Ryan's screams reached higher as the blade bit across his inner thigh, severing the main artery. "You will now bleed out before anyone can save you. I relish your death, Pierce Ryan. I have waited long enough." Duncan stood and viewed the spectacle of his enemy's demise with no hint of compassion. He watched agony give way to terror, to madness, to hate in Ryan's eyes. The evil man spit on him, coughing, "All these years, Elliott, we got away with it. All these years everyone thought you were the murderer. Ha! You are nothing! Nothing, nothing!"

Duncan bent quickly and stabbed the cruel man in the cut that was already spewing blood from his pelvis. He left the knife there, his knife, in the mortal wound of his last mark. He had no more need of it. Quietly he said, "Not anymore."

The final deed was done. Now, perhaps Rose would, *could* rest. The mad light dimmed in the eyes of the man who had taken Rose's life and ruined his. Duncan didn't look away until there was nothing left but death. Then he glanced at the cops and the secretary bound up in the corners. They watched him, not terrified anymore, but wary.

"Tell them if you want to," he said. He stood, took off his bloodied gloves and threw them on the floor. "Tell them he knew why he had to die." He pushed to one side the cabinet he'd used as a barricade, opened the door, and left the office. He closed the door firmly behind him. Celia would not see the corpse. He would take his few precious minutes with her and make them last for the rest of his life—what was left of it.

75

*R*ae had better still be alive. She will be, because it's the Wraith in there *with her.* Thain's thoughts ran frantic lines in his head. His pulse accelerated as he watched Celia Wight run across the street toward the entrance of the building. He'd done what he could to talk her out of going in, but his words had been wasted breath, especially after Duncan Elliott called. Thain knew deep in his bones that he had actually talked to the Wraith, if only for five seconds. He also knew, after Elliott's demand, that his own cause to keep Celia safe was lost.

She'd assured him, "Duncan won't hurt me, Detective. If he were going to hurt me, he would have already."

"He wasn't trapped before. He wasn't in a corner."

"I don't think he's ever in a corner that isn't of his own choosing."

"The captain isn't convinced this is the way to bring him out."

"Can't *you* convince him? I want Duncan out of there as much as you do."

"This isn't a good idea."

"Detective Thain, what would you have me do?"

He stared at her, shielding his concern for her as best he could. "Come back, Celia Wight. Come back safely." She didn't smile, but she didn't frown either. She stared at him, right into his eyes, as her photo had a thousand times. He stood there, helpless in the face of her decision. This is how he'd felt all those years ago with Agatha, more than helpless, ashamed. He was fully aware that Rae was trapped in the clutches of a killer, that Celia was walking right into those very same clutches, and that he couldn't do a damned thing to save either one of them.

76

uncan watched from inside as Celia ran across the street and rushed through the wooden doors, one of which stood open. Her gaze cast around for him. He stepped from the shadows, still out of the sight line of any marksman's rifle that might be trained upon the foyer.

"Oh," she cried. Celia ran right into his arms. He caught her close and held her, grateful that he had been granted this last blissful moment. That he could *feel* such happiness. She clung to him and he smothered himself in her warmth, solid and real against him, and he inhaled her scent, his head next to hers. His lips found her neck, her face, her eyes, with longing, wanting so much more, knowing he would never have it.

"Celia."

"Say it again," she whispered.

"Celia."

"Duncan."

He pulled back to look at her. "My name sounds good in your voice."

"Yes."

He stared into her face; it shone with her joy in seeing him. This is what he would take with him. He would remember always the delight she felt in loving him. He didn't deserve it. He knew that. But it felt good anyway. His mouth found hers, kissed her long and deeply. He heard no screams, sensed no flashing horrific colors, no drums pounding in his head. He stopped long enough to whisper, "I love you" against her warm soft lips. It was all he could give her.

"Yes," she said, and she grabbed his hand. "Come with me, Duncan. Get the barrister and free the others. Come with me. Let them take you in. The detective out there, the one who brought me here, he wants to talk with you. He's says he's chased you for ten years, though no one believed him that you existed. He calls you the Wraith. You told me once that you were an assassin. Is it true, Duncan? Are you?"

The Wraith? How appropriate, when he'd referred to himself as a ghost. Duncan ignored the rest of her statement about the detective. He ignored her questions. He didn't care. But he had known she would ask him to give himself up. He'd counted on it. She wanted him to live no matter what.

"I'll come with you," he said. "We'll let them come and get the barrister and the others."

She looked behind him. "Where are they?"

"I taped them up in the barrister's office."

Her face cleared. "Oh. Well, they won't go far then."

"So speaks the voice of experience."

Celia smiled so brilliantly he faltered, almost thought he could really change what had to come next. "Come on. Lead me out of here. Lead me into the light."

Celia squeezed his hand and looked into his eyes, and they walked together toward the doors. He knew every eye would be on him and every rifle aimed at him the minute he left the building, so he kept Celia close in front of him as they pushed through the doors. His terms. It had to happen his way. He thought briefly of the envelope in the breast pocket of his coat as they began to descend the steps. He held Celia's hand. Halfway down he squeezed it, just once. She looked back at him, her face serious, but she smiled at him. Then she turned forward again.

That was the moment Duncan Elliott reached for the envelope.

77

"He's reaching!" someone shouted.

Celia heard something pop and zing by her ear, heard the thud and Duncan's grunt behind her as that something hit him. Duncan pushed her and she stumbled, almost fell down the steps. She screamed. In a nightmare she turned back to see another bullet, and another, slam into him, jerking his body with each hit as he fell back on the cold stone steps. She saw his mouth open, his eyes searching for hers as she scrambled back to him.

"No, no, no!" she cried over and over. She covered his body with her own, and the cascade of bullets stopped. When she heard running feet she turned to ward off the detective, screaming frantically, demanding he keep away. Sounds became muted; all she heard was Duncan's gasps for breath. She held him closer, crying, "It wasn't supposed to end this way."

"Yes . . . it was." Blood dribbled from the corner of his mouth. His tongue looked slick with it. "Celia." His hand fell from his coat and she saw a white envelope stained with blood. His blood.

"Why, Duncan, why?"

He labored for breath now, it rattled in his chest, next to hers. "The . . . letter. Read."

She took the envelope from his hand, which was already cold, already dying. She crushed the envelope to her as if it were her most prized possession. She tugged him closer, daring with a scathing look the detective and the officers encircling them. Duncan's hard rigid body softened against her. She sobbed. She couldn't help herself.

"Sh," he whispered in her ear. "Do you hear it?"

"W—what?"

"The silence."

"I love you, Duncan. Don't leave me."

"Never, Celia." He whispered as if he were already gone, already a memory.

She choked, couldn't get the words out. Her tongue felt thick. Her heart *hurt*. She didn't want to let him go. But she would. She had to. She knew what he wanted. Swallowing she said, "Go Duncan. Go to Rose."

"Rose . . ."

He was gone. Someone grabbed her from behind and pulled her away from him. Sudden jostling and police shouting reminded her of where she was. She struggled against whoever held her, and then someone else came and pulled her toward the far side of the street. She screamed Duncan's name over and over as black-clad bodies swarmed in like angry ants and hid his lifeless body from view.

78

Thain watched the scene unfold as if it were a movie that had been slowed to enhance its effect. Duncan Elliott and Celia Wight stepped from the huge double doors of the building. Where was Rae? Silently, he prayed she was unharmed.

Celia looked serious but determined. But it was Elliott he'd waited ten years to see, and the man's sharp eyes and the grim set to his mouth confirmed Thain's opinion that he was a coldhearted killer, no matter his painful past. How could a man make a living killing people for pay and still have a soul?

But when Elliott looked at Celia, his face transformed. The grim tightness disappeared, to be replaced by nothing other than love, which softened the harsh lines and made him completely human. Before Thain could acknowledge the depth of his surprise, Elliott reached his right hand up toward his breast pocket. Someone shouted, "He's reaching," and bullets began to fly.

The first bullet smacked into Elliott's chest as Celia stumbled forward, and Thain wondered if he was the only one who saw Elliott push her out of harm's way. Another bullet hit, and another. Screaming, Celia scrambled back to the fallen man. She covered him with her body and halted the downpour of death, but not before the steps beneath the assassin were stained red with his blood.

"Bugger it!" Thain launched across the street. He wanted to get to them before the others, and when he did he saw her, crazed and angry, frightened and possessive, crouching over Elliott like a mother tiger, screaming at them all not to come near. He wanted desperately to look away from the sheer vulnerability in her beseeching eyes, but he couldn't.

Thain called for an ambulance. Elliott was still alive; he handed something to Celia. Thain watched them hold onto each other as if they could be saved from what had already passed. He didn't look away as Elliott died, his head next to Celia's, his bloodied mouth whispering secrets only she could hear.

When the spirit in Elliott's body escaped, Thain reached down and pulled Celia off him and held her close. His heart thudded, deep and dark against her small body, which felt like an electric wire on fire, stiff and powerful in his arms, shocking him. He wished he could calm her, assure her all would be well. He knew it was too late for that. When two policewomen came to take Celia, who now struggled against him, he opened his arms and let her go.

On the steps, medics were trying to resuscitate Elliott. Three bullets had pierced the man's chest. Thain knew their efforts were futile, and he felt sick and hollow. His mind swirled, overwhelmed with the shock of all that had happened in such a short time. Elliott had escaped without answering Thain's questions. His daunting adversary existed no longer. Somehow, after all this time and effort, all he could think of was the waste of a life that had once been precious, and that was still precious to his parents and to Celia Wight.

He tore his thoughts from Duncan and Celia and they landed on Rae. He needed to find her alive and unhurt; he had to believe his knowledge of the Wraith still held true. He flew up the steps to find her.

Just as he passed through the open door, Celia's screams rang in his ears. She was fighting the policewomen, and he closed his eyes for a brief second, torn. Then a constable said, "Sir?"

"Yes? Have you found the office?"

"Yes, sir. And Pierce Ryan, well, he's tied to the desk, uh, naked. He's dead. He's a mess, sir."

"And the cops, the secretary?"

"Gagged and bound, sir, but he left them alive."

The relief that washed over him was so strong his eyes stung. He glanced back with regret at Celia, now being helped into a police car, before he followed the constable deeper into the Magistrates' Court building. He needed to run down the long halls to the office, but didn't. It wouldn't do for him to run in, grab Rae into his arms and kiss her, though that's exactly what he yearned to do. That would have to wait. But he did push the constable to a faster pace, and when the crime scene unfolded in front of him he looked for Rae before anything else. She stood to one side, a constable helping to free her from her bonds. Her eyes were wild and fierce, whether with fear or relief he couldn't tell. But when she nodded at Thain and pulled the vestiges of the tape from her wrists in a businesslike manner, as if she hadn't just witnessed a murder, a very gory murder, he understood her need to feel some sort of control.

Pierce Ryan had definitely paid for his deed. His body was even worse than McLean's had been. The proof that Elliott's story was true, the proof that Elliott was in fact the Wraith—even if Thain was the only one who knew it—was that Rae, the undercovers, and the secretary were still alive. Elliott hadn't killed any innocents.

"We heard everything, Thain," Rae said, coming to stand by him. This time it was his hand sneaking into hers, squeezing, making sure she was real and safe. She managed a small smile, a trembling one. Blast whoever saw what he did next. He put his arms around her slim waist and held her close. She stiffened, then relaxed and hugged him back. He gave her a slight squeeze before letting go. She grabbed his hand and held on, seemed to need his touch. She said, "Ryan confessed."

"Confessed to murdering Rose Etheridge?"

"Yes. He didn't deny Elliott's charges. He laughed at the fact that he and his mates had got away with it all these years. Even tried to rattle Elliott by taunting him with his parents thinking him dead. Where is he? Did you get him?"

"Yes. We did. He's dead."

Rae said, "I'm sorry. Now I'm glad we were witnesses to Ryan's confession."

Thain nodded. "Go and get looked at. I'll take over here if you like, DS Bell?"

"Yes. I'll prepare my report." She squeezed his hand and finally let go. "See you back at the station?"

"Yes." Thain, as he began to inspect the crime scene, realized he faced a new quest. Once all the witnesses were debriefed, once he had put together all the information he now had, he would clear Duncan Elliott of Rose Etheridge's murder. He wouldn't do it for Elliott. He would do it for Celia and Rose. He would try to give Celia closure in that way. He couldn't—and wouldn't—clear Elliott of the assassinations he'd carried out, but there was no way to verify him as the perpetrator anyway. Thain saw it as an ironic quirk of fate that though he'd found Duncan Elliott, once again he was left with only his belief in the Wraith.

Thinking of Elliott, Thain knew that before he could embark upon his next quest, he would have to find out about the envelope he had seen Elliott pass to Celia. After the crime scene inspection was done, Thain understood what had to come next.

79

Celia sat alone, wrapped in a blanket in a small room in the same police station where she'd come in out of the cold the night before. Was it only last night? She rocked a bit, back and forth, as if to generate warmth that she couldn't feel. As if the rocking somehow made time stand still, kept her mind from dwelling on what she couldn't bear to think about. She clutched the bloodstained envelope in her hand but couldn't look at it.

She closed her eyes and kept rocking, back and forth, back and forth. Slowly, ever so carefully, she stilled her body, opened her eyes, and let her mind focus on what she clutched in her hand. She took a long time to unfold the creased and battered envelope. She had never seen Duncan's handwriting. Her fingers passed over her name scrawled upon the surface, barely readable beneath his blood.

She turned the envelope over and slid her finger under the glued edge. She pulled the sheet of paper from within and started to read.

Dearest Celia,

You understand me better than I ever did myself. Maybe you are the one who can tell my parents the things I never could. The police should look for four bodies in the field between the race course and the Bustardthorpe allotments.

Please tell my parents I never stopped loving them. Let them know I kept watch over them. Tell Dad to check the ground behind his gardening shed. I always hoped he'd find it on his own. He should do what he thinks best with what lies buried there. Please, tell them I hope they can forgive me.

You, Celia, need no written words to know my heart.

Duncan

Celia stared at the letter while the paper turned warm between her fingers. To have so little when she wanted so much. But he'd always been a man of few words. She knew why, but she wished for more all the same.

She glanced up when Detective Thain came in. "You want to know what it says."

"When you're ready to tell me."

"He says you need to look in a field between the race course and the," she glanced at the paper again, "Bustardthorpe allotments for four bodies."

"Richard McLean, in London, was the fifth. Pierce Ryan makes the total six."

"He was the barrister?"

"Yes."

"Duncan told the truth."

"We haven't formally taken the witnesses' statements yet, but you should know that they all heard what transpired between Ryan and Elliott. After we've recorded their statements and the bodies have been exhumed, we'll know for sure."

"Too bad no one believed him fifteen years ago."

"He didn't give anyone much of a chance to. Everyone makes mistakes."

Celia closed her eyes and sighed. Only she knew exactly what had happened to Duncan Elliott that fateful night. Would she tell his story if it helped clear his name of Rose's murder? Would he want that part told, after all he'd done to keep it a secret? "If he'd let me go at the start of all this, you wouldn't have caught him. None of this would have happened."

"And Pierce Ryan would still be dead. We just wouldn't know why."

Celia opened her eyes and looked at the detective. He didn't look away. "I'm glad Ryan's dead," she said.

"Why?"

"Because I think he was probably the leader of the pack. I told you Duncan hated the name Ryan."

"Yes, you did. Still, it's up to the witnesses he left alive to confirm Elliott's accusations against Ryan."

Celia shook her head. "Duncan knew the truth. That's all that matters."

"For you, but not for me."

Celia pulled the blanket tighter around her. "I'll testify if I need to, to his innocence."

Thain paused. "I don't know what they'll do with this case now. My part in it is over."

"I told him about you. He didn't deny what you said about him; you found your mysterious assassin, the Wraith."

"I suppose. And I—well, you are alive."

"You should be happy."

"I should be."

Celia looked at him, surprised. "But you're not?"

Thain sighed and turned toward the door for a moment. He glanced back at her, and she pulled tighter the blanket over her shoulders. "Am I glad a killer is off the streets? Yes," he continued. "I'm not glad a vile crime turned an innocent into that killer."

Celia nodded, again growing a little less unwilling to think of the detective as a good guy. He didn't have to pester her for information; no, she now gave it to him as if she trusted him. She'd been aware almost since she'd first met him that he cared about *her*, and not only because she was a witness for him. He seemed to sense her havoc-wracked emotions and was able to say the right words at the right time, as he had with Eva and Philip.

Detective Thain shoved his hands in his pockets and continued, "Yet it happens every day, in every country. I guess it's a part of human nature."

Silence. She welcomed it, and yet it felt hollow, as if something were missing.

"Ms. Wight, Celia, I'm sorry but . . . You know I'll need the letter?" He was blunt yet apologetic about it, surprising her. She frowned and wanted him to leave.

"You have what you need, don't you? I told you what he wanted me to tell you. The rest is private, for me."

"It's evidence in a murder investigation?"

Bitter regret stung her, made her sarcastic. "I'll make you a copy."

"You can't mean to keep it?"

"Why not?" Now she was incensed. What right did he have to talk to her like that?

The detective's face became unreadable. He pulled his hands from his pockets, shook his head, and looked straight into her eyes. "Because—" He hesitated. "Because there are men out there," he swung his arm around as if encompassing the rest of the world while his glance fell to the floor, then lifted to meet hers again, "waiting to see if they have a chance with you." His brown eyes, clear and dark, pinned her to stillness; she couldn't move. "If you keep the letter, no one does." Detective Thain turned to leave, but he paused. With his back to her he said, "Elliott wanted you to live. It's why he pushed you away from him on the steps."

Celia stared at the door after Detective Thain left. Tears crept down her cheeks. She sniffed and finally broke down. She had no idea where to go from here. She hated thinking that the detective might be right about his view of her future. She sat there alone, holding the past in her hand, tightly, as if an army were trying to wrestle it from her.

Duncan had held on to his past until it killed him. Would she do the same? Become the nothing he had been? Who was she kidding? She was a shadow too, a ghost, a wraith, living on the edge of life, never jumping in—until he'd forced her to.

Celia sobbed, nursing the permanent wound Duncan's departure had left. But he himself, with that very departure, showed her the way.

Celia stood up, slipped the letter back into the envelope, and wiped her face, which didn't do any good, but she didn't care. She would grieve, she would mourn the loss of him, and, she would do what he'd asked of her.

Celia opened the door. Detective Thain, Eva, and Philip looked up as she stepped out of the room and into the hall. She looked the detective straight in the eye and handed him the envelope. Then she hugged the two people in her life who loved her, who wanted only for her to be happy. Maybe, in time, she would be able to. But not yet, not with her heart so raw and bleeding. Not until she fulfilled a promise. She turned to Detective Thain and said, "There is something I must do. Can you help me?"

80

EPILOGUE

Five days later, on Christmas day, Celia stood in front of the door to Duncan Elliott's childhood home, the house of his parents. She knew neither she nor they could move on without this visit.

She rang the bell and glanced over her shoulder at Alban Thain and Rae Bell, who stood by the police car waiting for her at the curb. They'd been rocks of strength for her the past week, shielding her from the press, setting her up in a hotel room, making sure one or the other was beside her during every interview with the police and press, even the US embassy people. And Thain had convinced Eva and Philip to sit on the sidelines for a while, until she had her feet under her again.

She heard a small click, and she turned around as the door swung open to reveal a tall man with thinning hair and a tired face. She searched to find in him a likeness to his son. "Mr. Elliott, my name—"

"I know your name, Ms. Wight. My wife and I have been waiting for you. Please, come in and tell us about our son."

An hour later, Celia stepped from the dark sorrow of the house into surprising and balmy sunshine. A lifetime had passed since she'd last seen such sunlight, and it was brighter than she remembered. Its golden warmth kissed her face and she smiled, wistfully, looking at the sparkling world the sun made with its rays raking the snow-covered ground. She lifted her arms and her face to the sky.

She turned round and round and round until she was dizzy in the white front yard of Duncan's parents' house, in their little neighborhood, simple and incredibly normal. The world had not changed. Everything was the same except her because Duncan Elliott had kidnapped her, had given her courage to face demons, and joy, and love. He'd been wrong: his love hadn't taken her down. Instead, in the end it had set her free.

Duncan was dead now. He'd left the misery of his life behind, but she knew he lived on in her, and in the boy he'd once been and who would never leave his parents' loving, grieving hearts.

In life, Duncan Elliott had been the wraith that Alban had named him. In death, he finally became real, solid again, a man. She wiped a tear from her face, felt its wetness upon her fingertips.

Celia looked at the sky, blue as his eyes, and whispered, "Thank you, Duncan." She, too, was now real.

Celia Wight surprised Thain, yet again, when she stepped from the Elliotts' residence, stood in the middle of their tiny snow-covered lawn, and turned in circles with her face raised to the blue sky, her arms uplifted as if in worship and joy. He could see tears sparkling on her cheeks.

Over the last week she'd given him hope, much sooner than he'd ever expected, that one day, maybe before too long, she would listen to his story and find him worthy of her friendship. He'd witnessed her strength, her vulnerability, and her ability to trust him, and in so doing found he'd begun to accept the way he'd handled Agatha's rejection, and the assassination; even the way he'd cut his brother to the quick when Ellis tried to tell him how proud he'd been of him.

Thain hoped that perhaps the new acceptance he'd found of his past transgressions could, in time, become forgiveness. He would forever regret that he couldn't help Agatha, but he no longer needed to blame his brother. Or miss his parents.

For now, he would wait and try to be a true friend to Celia, whose determination grew a little stronger each day. Rae was helping him learn that love and friendship meant more to him than being right. From these two extraordinary women he was fast learning patience, and the need to move on with his life. Glancing at Rae, who was smiling while Celia spun circles on the lawn, he realized that now was a good time for him to make his first step in that direction. He pulled out his phone, gently rubbed the screen's smooth surface, and then dialed a familiar number. "Hello, Ellis? Yes, it's Alban."

ABOUT THE AUTHOR

Lisa Buie-Collard has written three historical fiction novels. Her ghost story, Evangeline's Miracle was published in 2012. The Seventh Man is her fifth novel. She is currently writing her sixth. She participates in National Novel Writing Month, (NaNoWriMo.com) and will begin her seventh novel November 2014.

Originally from Florida, Lisa now lives in south Georgia with her husband. Their children have flown off to take on the world and find their way in it.

The Seventh Man was inspired by an article about the literally millions of CCTV cameras in the UK, two actors, one British and one Scottish, and her obsessing love of the UK in general. She hopes you enjoyed it.

Lisa supports her local women's shelter and efforts to promote awareness of violence against women and men alike, and its prevention.

Please feel free to contact her at **http://www.lisabuiecollard.com**. She would love to hear from you and urges her readers to leave reviews at **amazon.com** and **goodreads.com**.

COMING SOON

"Rain"

Every relationship has its secrets, but is this one too big? Annalyn and Jack meet in a Caribbean paradise and fall in love. After a whirlwind romance they decide to marry, but Annalyn discovers a dark and sinister lie that tears apart the life they've started.

Desperate to forget the agony of a past so well loved and so thoroughly destroyed, they each embark upon separate journeys to try and rebuild their shattered lives, loves and faiths.

But Annalyn and Jack can't build their futures or make peace with the past until the lie that tore them apart is put to rest.

Will facing the truth allow them to find the healing they each so desperately need, or will it only confirm that there are no second chances?